# THE RETURN

# THE RETURN

*Christ Has Died,*
*Christ Is Risen,*
*Christ Will Come Again*

## GAIL DAWSON MCNALLY

**CITIOFBOOKS, INC.**
3736 Eubank NE Suite A1
Albuquerque, NM 87111-3579
*www.citiofbooks.com*
Hotline:        1 (877) 389-2759
Fax:             1 (505) 930-7244

Ordering Information:

Quantity sales. Special discounts are available on quantity purchases by corporations, associations, and others. For details, contact the publisher at the address above.

Printed in the United States of America.

ISBN-13:        Softcover        978-1-962366-95-3
                eBook            978-1-962366-97-7
                Hardback         978-1-962366-96-0

Library of Congress Control Number: 2023923176

# Table of Contents


Prologue ...... 1

Part One – The Morning of The Return ...... 2

General Luís Antonio Gutiérrez ...... 3
Dawn of Hope ...... 23
Nina Shelky ...... 26
Panamá's Contadora Island ...... 32
Countess Caputo and the Cardinal ...... 37
Witness to a Miracle ...... 43
Father Jonathan Kennedy ...... 47
Denny Dennison, PhD ...... 50
The Descent ...... 54

Part Two – The Pope at Saint Peter's Cathedral ...... 60

His Holiness, Pope Damasus III – The Holy Father, Juan Carlos Gutiérrez ...... 61

Part Three – The Path to Hope ...... 72

Finding Paradise ...... 73
The New Disciples ...... 83

Part Four – Carrying Out TheMission ...... 91

The Negev Desert in Israel – The Evening before The Return ...... 92
Wings of Hope ...... 100
Flight Plan ...... 107
After the Descent ...... 112

Part Five – Reflections on a Grievous Matter ...... 118

Nina Shelky Writes of Contadora ...... 119
Election of the Pope – at the Conclave ...... 133
The Arguments – Rome ...... 144
General Luís Gutiérrez – Rome ...... 161
General Aaron Yakowitz – A Jew's Return ...... 178
Luís – Winning the Battle of Doubt ...... 182
The Undeniable Spirit of Eros ...... 191
Serina ...... 209
Father Jonathan Kennedy – A Lamb of God ...... 214
Jonathan's Cross ...... 227
Papal Affirmation ...... 234
Justification for Jonathan ...... 240
Jonathan and the Countess at the Vatican Museum ...... 254

Part Six – Doubt and Full Consent ..................................................... 261

The Child, Christian ................................................................ 262
Encountering Denny Dennison ............................................... 272
Funding for the Love of God and of His Servants ................... 280
A Young Eagle Prepares to Soar .............................................. 288
The Anatomy of Sin ............................................................... 294
The Cosmos Club in Northwest Washington DC .................... 296
Developing a Miracle Maker ................................................... 305
The Final Gathering of Holy Planners ................................... 316

Part Seven – Peace on Earth ............................................................ 322

Raising Christian ................................................................... 329
Onward Christian's Soldier .................................................... 341
Christian and Marcocito ........................................................ 346
Behold, the Angel of Death .................................................... 355
Appointment with Eternity .................................................... 362
Darkness ................................................................................ 370
Return to Eden ...................................................................... 374
Post Script ............................................................................. 389
Author's Note ........................................................................ 390
About the Author .................................................................. 393

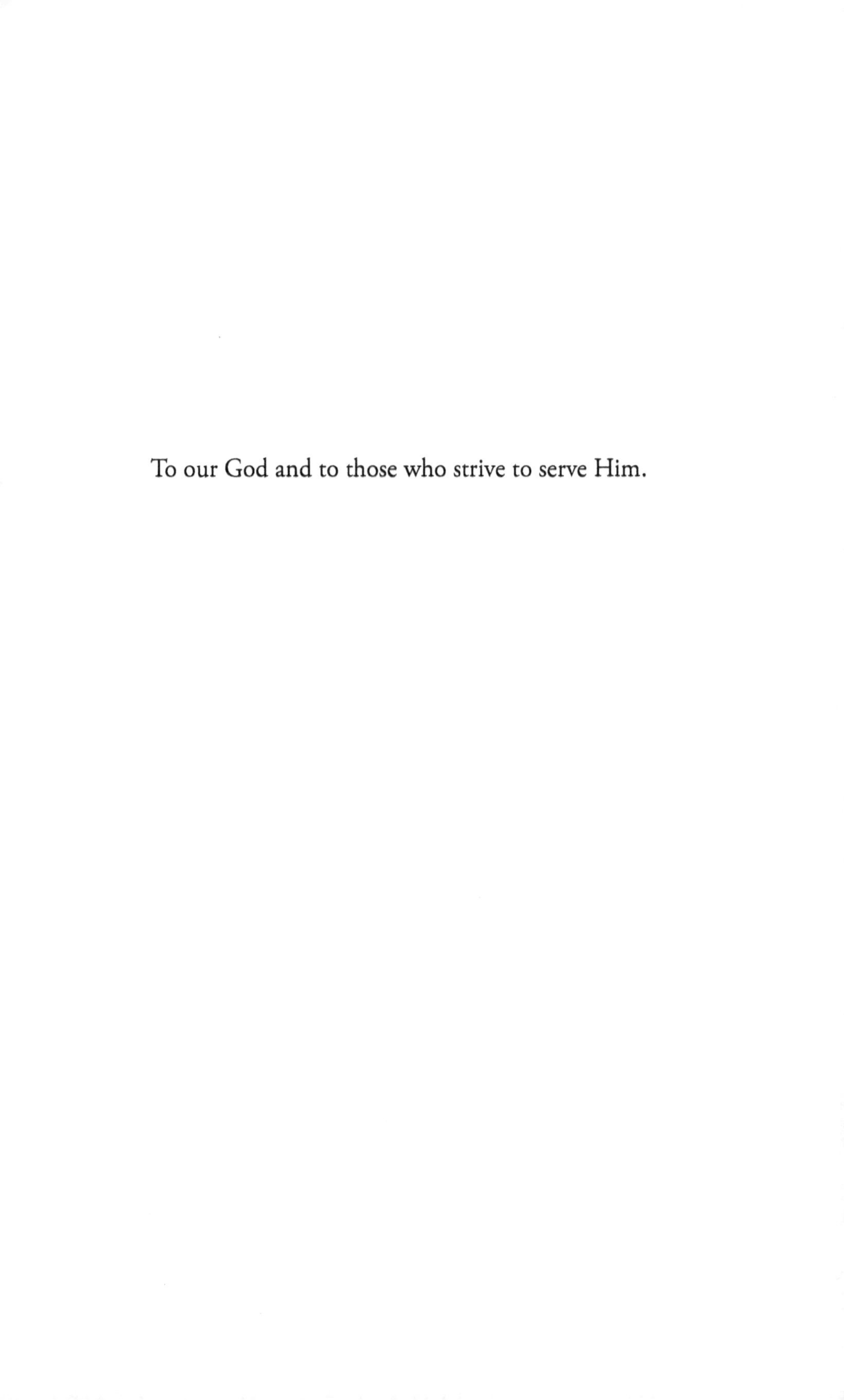

To our God and to those who strive to serve Him.

# THE PARTICIPANTS

**Christian** – The infant raised to carry out the mission of *The Return*

The Vatican and Rome

Cardinal Theodore "Teddy" **Arias** – A long-time resident of the Vatican in charge of finances

Countess Serina **Caputo de la Guardia** – A Colombian widow living in Rome

Cardinal Salvador **DeAngeles** – An elderly Italian cleric who is The Apostolic Penitentiary

Juan Carlos **Gutiérrez** – His Holiness Pope Damasus III, a Colombian and the first Latin American Pope

General Luís Antonio **Gutiérrez** – Brother of the Pope, head of the Colombian Armed Forces

Cardinal Diego **Hernandez** – Childhood friend of the Gutiérrez Family and Vatican Secretary of State

Father Jonathan **Kennedy** – An American, raised in Colombia, the son of the CIA Chief of Station in Bogotá, and a close aide to the Pope

Cardinal Adolfo **Romano** – The Pope's personal assistant, born in Colombia and a resident of Rome

### Panamá

Marcos **Rivera** – The Government legislator representing the Pearl Islands where *TheReturn* takes place

Mario **Rivera** – Marcos' father Marcocito **Rivera** – Marcos' son

**Jorge**, known as "Gordo," **Lucas**, and **Erik**, known as "Fulito," some of the Islanders who witness *The Return*

Teresa **Valdez** Rivera – Wife of Marcos Rivera

## Israel

Captain Alana **Dyan** – A young Israeli officer who teaches Israeli military tactics Brigadier General Avi **Noam** – The Israeli pilot who flies the mission of *The Return* General Aaron **Yakowitz** – Head of the Israeli Defense Forces and close associate of General Luís Gutiérrez

## Washington DC

Dr. Dennis "Denny" **Dennison** – An American Scientist
Nina **Shelky** – An American Journalist

Christ has died,

Christ is risen,

# Christ will come again.

# FACTS AND FICTION

*The Return* is a work of fiction, filled with fictitious characters. The descriptions of Panamá and the Pearl Islands are factual and accurate with one exception—Contadora Island where much of the story takes place is, in 2009, a developed resort island and not the primitive island described in the book—Gail Dawson McNally

**One of the 200+ Pearl Islands located 40 miles off the Pacific coast of Panamá**

# GALILEANS

They were still gazing up into the heavens when two men dressed in white stood beside them. 'Men of Galilee,' they said, 'why do you stand here and look up at the skies?' This Jesus who has been taken from you will return, just as you saw him go up into the heavens.

The Beginning of the Acts of the ApostlesActs1: 1 - 11

# Prologue



**CONTADORA ISLAND IN THE PEARL ARCHIPELAGO,
THIRTY-FIVE MILES OFF THE PACIFIC COAST OF PANAMÁ**

**April 2035**

The aging Colombian *niñera* named him Christian. Though her caring role was short-lived after Christian's illegitimate and unheralded birth in a small remote clinic in Colombia, her choice was prophetic. The name was considered visionary when relayed by the young Father Jonathan Kennedy to decision-makers within the Vatican.

Now, twenty years later, a vivid image in the dawn sky grew. The small audience of islanders watched Christian slowly descend toward their beach. As his flowing robes filled their view, the inhabitants below recognized him immediately as their Lord and Savior, Jesus Christ.

Upon seeing them, Christian's first thought was his satisfaction at being identified just as the remote planners had hoped. Those responsible—living and dead, witting and unwitting—had labored and schemed for this moment for over twenty years.

These were the first moments of the greatest deception ever attempted. The supreme Vatican gamble followed the labor of two decades, and the planned return of Christ to earth was to finally take place.

# PART ONE – THE MORNING OF THE RETURN

# General Luís Antonio Gutiérrez
**Saint Peter's – April 2035**

Colombian General Luís Antonio Gutiérrez sat quietly near the main altar of the long colonnaded nave of Saint Peter's cathedral. The eleven o'clock Holy Week mass was soon to be celebrated by his younger brother, His Holiness, Pope Damasus III, Juan Carlos Gutiérrez-the Pontiff, the Pope, the Vicar of Christ, and the spiritual leader of the Roman Catholic Church.

The critical hour was at hand. At the same moment that mass in Rome would end, the young man named Christian would descend to earth and appear to the witnesses below as our Lord and Savior, Jesus Christ.

The creators of *The Return* were on this day assembled at the magnificent cathedral in Rome. What was about to happen was unknown to two women present. They were, nevertheless, key to the project. Although duly reverent as they awaited the beginning of mass, the minds of those who knew alternated between their faithfulness as represented by the grandeur of Saint Peter's and their personal anguish over what was soon to occur. The Pope prepared for mass in a nearby room, confronting the greatest fear he had ever known. Despite his urge to do so, it was too late to call off the mission.

The plan had been in development for over two decades. Attention to detail and secrecy had been excruciating. The man to emerge from the sky this morning was exquisitely crafted to cleanse the world of its sins.

It was eleven fifteen on this sunny and crisp morning in Rome, and five fifteen on the tiny island of Contadora. General Luís Gutiérrez wiped his moist forehead repeatedly with a now damp handkerchief and frequently checked his watch.

Luís was acting in accordance with his personal agreement with God; forged, he believed, after he had been spared from death many times over the past two decades. Always a proud, erect and now graying man, Luís fervently believed in the righteousness of his actions. As the driving force for the project, his prayers for God's guidance over the last twenty years helped him see this mission through to its conclusion. And now, he nervously and eagerly awaited news that the descent had been flawless; such news could only presage a glorious result for the Universal Church and for mankind.

"Where has your foolish faith led you and your brother, the *Pope*?" Luís had been asked years ago, during a conversation with a captured high-level Colombian militant. "Why can't you accept that your God is dead, that the influence of his religion on world politics has only generated war and slaughter?"

"So, what do *you* believe?" Luís had asked, genuinely interested in the motivation of the enemy. The prisoner, defeated and fatigued, shrugged. "What does it matter? When you cross that threshold of death, if there is some grand deity-why should he think badly about my actions, my beliefs?" he said sharply, hitting his chest with a filthy palm, as he sat defiant in a small interrogation room. "Am I less lofty, less inspired to help my people, my country, than your corrupt, dictatorial demigods who covet the riches of nations and exploit the poor?"

Luís, himself tired from raids against guerrilla strongholds in remote areas of Colombia, looked deeply into the dark angry eyes and felt a bond of understanding. He wished he could release this poor devil. Instead the prisoner, one more of many, would languish in a crowded cell, be tried and, doubtless, executed. Now in Saint Peter's, Luís felt the familiar revulsion of so many painful memories.

Always a defender of The Catholic Faith, Luís endured an inner struggle to support the Church's worldwide efforts to maintain its role as shepherd to the faithful. Critics, with great frequency, gleefully predicted imminent collapse of the Church's dogma. "God's love of mankind is unconditional," an often repeated phrase in Catholic communities, rang hollow to increasing numbers throughout the Christian world. Like many insurgents in the past, the aggressive push by Islamic fundamentalists beginning in the latter part of the 20th Century had incorporated doctrines of Liberation Theology to proselytize the downtrodden and unfortunate. More than merely intimidating millions of Christians who bowed to appease these ruthless forces, the insurgents sought to convince the masses to take up arms against their leadership-to fight to correct perceived wrongs of centuries past. It was such an easy "sell" to the multitudes of the poor. Fear and ignorance of the radicals' motives caused cowering reactions to barbarous attacks.

Although dwindling in numbers, Christians continued to fall back upon their ingrained traditions of peace, love and forgiveness. Christian communities continued to pray, continued to believe that their faith and their Church would ultimately triumph. Tragedy and outrage spread, as civilization seemed to unravel under appalling acts of cruelty, all in the name of Islamic peace. As unrequited good intentions met with further attacks and prayers remained unanswered and caused a stalemate in any coherent response from the Church, her numbers continued to decline.

General Gutiérrez' anguish over the brutality he witnessed, particularly in Colombia, inspired him to lead the struggle that brought him to this magnificent cathedral this fine April morning. His world had endured a spiritual collapse long ago.

"Now, we're finally here," thought Gutiérrez, as he checked his watch again. He knew that notification would consist of a brief coded message from General Aaron Yakowitz from the remote staging area in Israel. The message would confirm or deny the descent of Christian on to the island. Luís tried to sit quietly in the noisy cathedral as the moments ticked away.

"Will you send troops?" inquired the US allied commander during the early stages of the war years in the Middle East, confident that the dedicated young General Gutiérrez would support the war efforts in the Middle East with at least a small contingent of the experienced Colombian troops under his command. By then Luís was fully invested in the mission of *The Return.* Leading the Vatican effort and immersed in the secret planning, he often fantasized the moment of the descent. It became difficult to focus on other matters, but his overt official position could not suffer, and he fought his preoccupation with the project. Colombia had enjoyed immense US military and anti-drug support over decades. Luís readily complied and sent troops to Iraq.

On the morning of their departure, Luís called the small cadre of highly trained soldiers to attention. General Gutiérrez addressed them. "I am confident that you will perform credibly, that the skills you possess in combat will only sharpen. Come home to your country with pride in yourselves and with new insight into the need to preserve peace and at the same time to understand the futility of hate. You will witness a good deal of it. Godspeed." As he embraced each, Luís felt the bond of love and pride for these men-they gave him hope and fortified his determination to lead Colombia into a future of peace. His secret life of dedication to the mission of *The Return* further confirmed the General's commitment to go well beyond the pains of Colombia and lead the world to a greater peace.

The great victory was, however, never realized. Early on, Luís lost several of his men in the Middle East conflicts. Their comprehensive training and abiding faith in God was no match for the Jihadists, for whom simple death of opponents was not sufficient, not adequate for the "infidels." Infliction of great pain through cruel torture seemed to delight fiendish minds. The tragedy of further loss only amplified the call from God in Luís's mind.

In subsequent conversation, Luís lamented to his brother, Juan Carlos, "the more peace and democracy are promoted, the more humane the treatment of our enemies, the more disastrous the results. Decency and compassion have proven counterproductive and useless. Our actions are viewed as cowardice-cowardice to be exploited. Damn it, Juan Carlos, can't you see the terrible outcome of these opposing forces? Our beloved Church will lose. Christianity will lose. Judaism will lose. All religions will lose-even the moderate Muslims will lose."

These words of frustration had poured from Luís years ago, during his early arguments with Juan Carlos Gutiérrez, then the Archbishop of Bogotá, Colombia.

Juan Carlos had listened to his infuriated brother with grief, realizing that world religious tolerance was fast deteriorating and acts of Christian tolerance ultimately fed the demise, contributed to, the downfall. *Is Luís right, will this precious faith of ours ultimately disappear,* wondered Juan Carlos. *Would God deny us this?*

As Luís presented more arguments, he sensed the sad and gradual acceptance by his holy brother of a stark future absent of Christianity. While groups of Islamic Fundamentalists continued to capture, torture, and murder faithful missionaries in many nations, an event took place that was to be the tipping point of Luís' intentions.

*"Habemos Papa!"* Luís heard the shout while standing in the center of the great plaza in front of Saint Peter's. "We have a Pope!" Luís unabashedly allowed the tears welling in his eyes to roll down his face, as he watched his brother, Juan Carlos, appear at the window above the crowd, smiling, waving and acknowledging the roar of acceptance. The massive assembly was acclaiming a new pontiff, the first Latin American pontiff. In his joy, Luís deemed the proclamation the heavenly sign he needed, as he envisioned the still bleak future ahead for the Church.

Indeed, the jubilation, the encompassing sense of values and human worth beinggiven yet another chance was short-lived, and the expected hope of Christian rebirth wasrapidly absorbed into the overriding modern world of faded ethics and ideals. Killingscontinued to spread throughout Europe and areas of North America. As the new Pope,Juan Carlos launched campaigns of verbal outrage and pleaded for the peace of Christfrom the Vatican to the pulpits of the world. As with his predecessors, these pleas provedfruitless. The numbers of the faithful people who remained unafraid and active continuedto decline. Luís saw it as God's influence, as God's urging to action, as he witnessed thediminishing courage of the Christian world.

"Where is your outrage, your defense of your own values?" the Vatican implored Muslim leaders. But most moderate Muslims continued their neutral positions, intimidated by the barbarous behavior of their depraved brethren. They, too, were targeted with brutality, as denial and blame fueled the growing chaos. As the world observed their helplessness, the scorn for their inaction diminished, and hope in Christianity further declined.

Soon after Juan Carlos' ascendancy, Luís had begun to sit in on strategic meetings with His Holiness. Present at these small gatherings were the Vatican Secretariat of State, Cardinal Diego Hernandez, and a handful of cardinals. Luís had been designated to provide high-level briefings on current world events and defense efforts. His research for the briefings convinced him more than ever that his concept for *The Return* was the path God called for. But before he could set forth his bold plan to the carefully selected group of participants he had in mind, he had to first convince and gain the approval of his beloved brother.

"What bright news have you for us this morning, General?" Luís looked into the lined face of Cardinal Salvador DeAngeles, the senior cardinal present and the Pope's Prefect of the Congregation for the Doctrine of the Faith. The tone of the Cardinal's question was sarcastic, in keeping with his normal gruff mood and his still-present unwillingness to accept political guidance from outside the Vatican.

Cardinal Salvador DeAngeles, one of the Pope's closest confidantes, spoke after Luís's dismal intelligence report, now relied upon to guide the Vatican's operational defense.

"My fellow brothers in Christ," DeAngeles shook his craggy head back and forth, "the media have planted seeds of doubt throughout the world. To what end? Is it a self- destructive power that makes them seem to want to hasten disaster?" He continued sadly, "Here within these walls of our Vatican, our strategies are thin . . . weak . . . hollow and ineffective against that confounded surging Islamic pressure. We are outraged at the teaching of hatred in Islamic schools and in incidents of children encouraged to watch and even participate in the executions of so-called 'enemies' of Islam. These demonic acts feed upon themselves.

"Forgive me, my colleagues." DeAngeles, usually stern, then appeared forlorn. "I am weary with defeat. I am profoundly saddened that none of us have the spiritual strength to deal with the obvious evil surrounding us. I am sickened by my own physical inability to stand up and fight. I am the watchdog of sin, and yet I am nothing . . . not a single beat in the hearts and minds of millions of misguided radicals."

Luís was encouraged by what seemed a small fissure in the gallant but ever weakening shield of Catholic defense. Luís remembered back to the day of a particularly brutal attack on innocent schoolchildren by fundamentalist extremists and the atmosphere of anger and frustration that pervaded the Vatican. He recalled Salvador DeAngeles fighting back tears of rage and empathized, even as he felt a familiar stab of guilt at knowing that the Cardinal's very rage needed to be encouraged, to become contagious, for the plan to find acceptance. There was little need however for Luis' grim tales to continue. The press and news media reported daily atrocities against the Church and Christian organizations worldwide. General Luís Gutiérrez placed his magnificent intentions in the hands of God. His efforts to portray the consummate Christian soldier were to soon succeed. He believed the careful plans in his mind would shortly be embraced by these holy men of peace.

Oblivious to the noise in the cathedral, Luís shuddered, recalling his duplicitous behavior in originally selling *The Return*. He shifted in the uncomfortable metal folding chair. With the momentous event now in motion and virtually unstoppable, Luís could not help but call to mind the events that led to this moment. Remembering the simple Jihadist mantra, "Death to all who disagree, even fellow Moslems," Luís reminded himself that Jihadists adhered to the ideology inspired by *their* God, who taught a moral essential—*Force world obedience to Islam; force it by any means necessary.*

Those within the Pope's immediate circle listened dolefully, as Luís relayed grisly tales of religious persecution. Waiting patiently for clues that these faithful shepherds of God were nearing the end of their reliance on *the golden rule,* Luís recalled the definitive words of papal friend and colleague, Diego Hernandez, the Vatican Secretariat of State.

"Where are the moderate teachings of scholars?" Diego cried out during one meeting focusing on the Israeli-Arab conflicts. "They've been dismissed. The hatred we witness daily for non-cooperative leaders is rampant. Israel remains targeted, as always, for extinction and is now coming within reach of annihilation. For these lunatics, death is king. Death is God. They are incapable of seeing through their mantle of blood. They are uninhibited by civilized restrictions and have cleverly used all perceived limitations imposed upon them by a reasonable world as an opportunity to appear victimized to the naïve-ourselves ncluded!" Diego's voice rose further. "Still," he shouted, "we cling to the theology of decency and human rights. In the eyes of God, it may be armor enough, but are we to believe that God wishes us to aid in the extinction of belief in his son, Christ Jesus?" As was the Catholic custom, Diego bowed his head quickly at the use of the name. Then lowering his tone, he angrily cried, "Why in Hell would He want us to accept that?"

At that time, over twenty years ago, Luís Gutiérrez, aware of the urgency of his plan and on the brink of success, still moved ahead with an unbearable patience. The project required years, and many days were consumed with worrying if there would be enough time. Luís had battled with the notion of failure and continuously forced it from his mind.

The years had passed; the work and planning were over. In a few moments, Cardinal Diego Hernandez would proceed with His Holiness, Juan Carlos, down the center aisle of Saint Peter's. All involved knew the calamitous outcome of a failed mission.

As always, Luís tried to block the memory of the decisive moment in which it was revealed to him that *The Return* had become the only path to the world's salvation. Unavoidably, his mind drifted to a long ago mass, also celebrated by his brother-then *Monsignor* Juan Carlos Gutiérrez. Luís had wept uncontrollably in the Colombian church during the funeral of their murdered sister and her husband, the Colombian presidential hopeful. The tragic events of twenty-five years ago churned in his mind, events which had brought him to this moment in Rome.

"Oh, it's beautiful," gushed his vivacious sister, as Luís attached the jeweled pin to the collar of her suit jacket. The pin, in the shape of a flag, was set with stones of the national colors-yellow diamonds, blue sapphires, and deep red rubies mounted in a gold disc and surrounded by a ring of Colombian emeralds. Tears of joy came to his sister's eyes as she embraced Luís. "I will treasure this forever, my dearest brother. Thank you."

"You will be Colombia's *new* treasure," replied Luís, letting her go and turning to clutch the shoulders of his brother-in-law in deep affection.

On a sun-filled morning in the ancient Colombian seaside city of Cartagena, the Gutiérrez family was buoyant as they participated in a massive political rally for Luís' brother-in-law. "We will bring peace to our long-troubled nation," the young candidate had pledged. "We have a detailed plan, an aggressive campaign to deal with the rebels, to attack the drug trafficking, and to use all our diplomacy and best efforts to work against the disturbing return of dictatorial leaders in our South American neighborhood." His rhetoric was familiar, but his forceful personality allowed more than a hint of promise. He assured the large crowd of war-weary compatriots that he would lead them in successful efforts against the endless cycle of death. "I will work tirelessly to end the failed ideals of Marxist and Communist infiltration, this blight that the nation has endured for decades. And I promise to fully confront the newest threat, the encroaching Islamic fundamentalists, who are even now the enemy of our enemies." Luís, standing on the raised platform with his family, noted the crowd's enthusiasm and smiled broadly.

Luís had vowed to help, and with military and Church backing, the candidacy had teeth. Both Luís and his brother-in-law had achieved some meaningful progress with the rebel factions for power-sharing through compromise and negotiations for greater political participation by all. Operating in the hinterlands for decades in their fight to overthrow Colombia's government, the ubiquitous armed rebels, also known as the *Fuerzas Armadas Revolucionarias de Colombia* (FARC), had plundered the Colombian people for decades. It had morphed from a Marxist rebellion supported by the Soviets into a drug-financed blight on Colombia's landscape.

But success had a price. Luís' work with other nations had rewarded him with praise from hopeful world leaders, even as success brought added threats of reprisal and death to the very allies he had nurtured within his country. Compromises were often shattered, and the wrath of the underworld zealots became horribly evident that day in Cartagena.

As the small group representing Colombia's new hope stood on the platform, they responded to the enthusiastic crowd and joked with each other. Meanwhile, assassins, using diversionary tactics, penetrated the secure area and brought a precipitous halt to the promising opportunity for national unity.

Prior to the rally, Luís had casually teased his sister about her prospective national and international role as the future First Lady of Colombia. "Ah, my handsome brother, I want you and Juan Carlos at our side always. We have strength together. You, the warrior; Juan Carlos, our man of God; and me. I will truly do my best to help Colombia and always make you proud of me." She had smiled lovingly at Luís. On the platform she enjoyed a final second of happiness, looking out over the adoring crowd.

Standing slightly behind in deference to the row of candidates facing the audience, Luís had briefly seen the reflection of the weapon. He had uttered a silent "no" as a staccato burst of gunfire miraculously grazed only his cheek and neck. Eight other military and federal dignitaries had suffered direct hits, some knocked off the raised platform by the bullets. Bodies dropped and lay still. Bullets pierced their foreheads, leaving small black holes in the skin and little blood. Bedlam broke out, as bodyguards aggressively wrenched Luís to the ground and shielded him from further gunfire.

During his time as a warrior, Luís had seen death frequently, but this was different. Freeing himself from his protectors, his face contorted with anger and pain as he saw shattered bone in the wounds. The stares of his beloved family caused him to doubt their lifelessness. For Luís, all reason was paralyzed and the now far-away gaze in his sister's blue eyes seemed to beg for justice.

As he knelt over the bodies, Luís remained in shock and denial, trying to convince himself they were only unconscious. "My sister, get up now, get up please." Blood from Luís' own superficial wounds dripped onto the light wool suit and seeped in between the crevices of the jeweled pin. Luís apologized to her, fighting off the heavy monster of truth, fending off the constriction he felt in his throat. Choking in agony, his military bearing and strength dissolved. He screamed from the torture of knowing, no longer seeing the chaos around him. Tears and blood mixed, forming small pools that gradually ran together on the pastel fabric. His hands dripped blood, now oozing from the large irregular hole in the back of his sister's head. Luís buried his face in her auburn hair, which still smelled of her shampoo and perfume and now with a growing pungency of blood. Somewhere in the crowd, he heard defiant shouting, *"Allaju Akbar."* (Allah is great!) Suddenly dumbstruck by this new reality, Luís collapsed on the pile of bodies, still begging his sister to get up in a rasping whisper.

In the panic that followed, the crowd near the shooter managed to wrestle an automatic weapon from him before knocking him onto the cobblestone street. By the time security guards arrived, the enraged crowd had repeatedly struck and kicked him. The assassin remained conscious, however, and was taken to a jail in a small rural town near Cartagena by several Colombian guards. Their orders were to leave him tied to a wooden chair in the small interrogation room, where he was in full view of other prisoners crowded into a nearby cell. Additional blows to his head and face by the guards were accompanied by the prisoners' taunts and terrifying suggestions of what was to come.

While General Luís Gutiérrez remained in seclusion, his regional commander, Colonel Jaime Santiago, willingly stepped in to avenge his Commanding General. A mid- level officer loyal beyond question to General Gutiérrez, Santiago waited in his nearby office in the jail. Santiago was angered at having his first free Sunday in two months interrupted but understood his duty. Wearing a neat khaki uniform, he listened to the guards' report, ignoring the sound of the blows being administered to the assassin in the adjacent room. Before dealing with the unpleasantness ahead, he visited a small washroom routinely used by the military personnel. He checked the gel in his hair, ensuring his carefully arranged style needed no attention, and then adjusted the small knot at the top of his black tie, staring at his pocked face in the grainy mirror above the sink. With any luck, he could finish this quickly and return to the pleasures promised by his adoring young wife. Walking into the interrogation room, he stood in front of the young murderer.

Colonel Santiago, unwilling to touch the prisoner, felt a few seconds of the empathy with which he was all too familiar. He had seen many like this-another young, vulnerable male with unspent hormones who longed for purpose in his irrelevant life among the poor of Colombia's youth. Like so many, he was inexplicably doomed to the cycle of poverty and violence. Jaime Santiago, underpaid but grateful to have avoided the life of the poor wretch in front of him, paced back and forth in the small room. He was eager to return home but loyal to duty. Duty meant carrying out the punishment and taking any blame in the unpleasantness ahead of him.

"So, let me guess," he said to the battered youth, "you were told that you would go on a great mission of death and destruction. Whoever convinced you to kill, to murder, your countrymen, *mi hijo,* was a pig! I can imagine his persuasiveness in convincing you that your undertaking would be greatly rewarded. Virgins, lots of 'em, in heaven, I suppose?"

Zealots within FARC and recently arrived Jihadists attempting full infiltration among the poor, assured young male *campesinos* riches for their impoverished families. "With the promise of Islam," they were told, "this wretched existence is short, and a life filled with Allah's blessings is beyond the wall of earthly being. The pain you may endure is short-your sacrifice brief-and paradise is forever." It was so easy to influence an impressionable youth who longed to hold a gun—to be somebody.

"Why don't you tell me who sent you to carry out this slaughter?" Colonel Santiago's tone was gentle, but the young man, in pain, remained defiant and spat on his interrogator's clean shirt. Santiago's reaction was immediate, and mixed with his anger was his realization that this would take longer than he first expected.

Roughly pulled up and handcuffed to a small metal pole in the center of the room, the killer's soiled cotton pants were pulled down to his ankles. His buttocks soon bled profusely from the biting leather strap deftly wielded by a low-ranking subordinate, who had little sympathy for a killer of the family of his idolized commander in chief. His mouth dry, his pain intensifying, the prisoner showed hints of caving in, as Jaime Santiago screamed demands for information;

but despite his splitting eardrums, the prisoner held out. The other terrified detainees, now quiet, watched fearfully from their dirty cell and listened to the prisoner's pathetic whimpers. They watched as the colonel picked up a rusted machete.

"You are a fool! Brave, but a fool," he mocked the insolent young man. "I will be anxious to learn how you find your paradise without your cock." Santiago calmly handed the machete to the waiting guard. Allah's promise faded quickly for the young man, as the jagged blade pressed into the dark curly public hair beneath his belly. With the cocaine and cheap rum now worn off, his head pounded and his bravado faded. He was soon easily convinced that with no manhood, the promised virgins in heaven would serve little purpose. With terror in his face and barely coherent, he blurted out names of accomplices and their locations. Uncuffing him, two guards dragged him from the room, his bloodied pants crumpled about his ankles and his penis shriveled into his scrotum. As he was pulled past the other prisoners, they became bolder and rebuked him for his betrayal and yelled *"hijo de puta"* (son of a whore) and other obscenities. Crying and gulping for air, he was tied to a wooden pole in the jail yard. In final disbelief and now silent horror, he watched as a grinning guard forced a pistol barrel into his mouth.

Colonel Santiago walked away grimly as the trigger was pulled and the bullet tore through the back of the assassin's neck and lodged in a nearby stucco wall. The other prisoners had moved from across their cell and crowded at the small window to watch the horror in the small courtyard. They recoiled in shock and revulsion, as bits of skull and flesh spewed through the window's iron bars.

By the time the commotion in the yard had died away, Santiago was already back in his office and had called a contingent of trusted soldiers into the cramped space located on the front side of the small building. "We must spend no more than three days rounding up the others," he told them. "You might offer small bribes to some of those already in the cell here to guide you to certain locations. I doubt after what they've witnessed they'll cause any trouble. However, shoot them if they try to escape. I will back you up whatever you must do."

Within the week, Colombian Special Forces had apprehended the remaining three guilty rebels. Discarded weapons were located, ballistics quickly analyzed, and credible witnesses from the assembly made accurate identifications of those captured.

Colonel Santiago was deeply devoted to the Gutiérrez family and knew he was going beyond his bounds in his actions but felt there was little rationale for a trial. He called several times to inquire about the health of General Luís Gutiérrez, his beloved commander-in-chief for whom he would walk through fire. He was unable to speak to Luís directly but was told of the General's complete trust in his decisions and his actions.

Not wanting to involve his own men any more than necessary, Colonel Santiago instructed them to tie the murderers alongside the rotting naked corpse slumped against the pole in the jailhouse yard. He then ordered the men to provide sufficient food and water to the remaining prisoners in the jail and to go home for two days. He would file a carefully worded report later that week and obviate any compromise of his men in the event of future investigations.

By the following morning, the three prisoners tied to the pole in the yard had repeatedly fouled their clothes and vomited from the putrid stench. They railed in fear and revulsion, as black vultures darted forward from their perches on the yard fence to peck at the decaying corpse. The inmates still in the cell shoved each other aside and watched from the small barred window in horror and fascination.

Colonel Santiago immersed a facecloth in cold water, added some of the shaving cologne his wife had given him for a past birthday, and covered his nose and mouth before approaching the prisoners. They begged for his mercy. He gently questioned them and promised to relieve their agony in exchange for further information. The men divulged more names and made frantic accusations against several Middle Eastern terrorist cells now in Colombia and neighboring countries. In their desperate hope for mercy, they revealed rebel camp locations and numbers and promised cooperation.

Colonel Santiago, knowing they would agree to anything if they could be freed from the vile corpse they were pressed against, felt revulsion at the sight in front of him but carefully recorded each name and location. Most were already known and included the infiltration by some known Islamic fanatics. But in his Catholic country, Colonel Santiago was now assaulted by a new fear. As he turned away and walked back into the building, he shuddered at the cry from one of the pathetic men—*"There is no God but Allah!"*

By noon, Colonel Jaime Santiago was somewhat satisfied with his progress but knew the months ahead would be difficult. He returned to his office and rinsed out the cloth. After adding more cologne he re-tied the cloth behind his head, covering his mouth and nose.

He opened the cell door in the main room and said to a prisoner, "Come my son, I have a job for you."

"No, no, no, Colonel, *por favor!*" The prisoner shook his head violently, believinghe was soon to be executed.

"Come now, or I will put this gun in *your* mouth." The prisoner soon had Colonel Santiago's pistol butt pressed to his temple, as he was escorted outside into the yard to within fifteen feet of the pole. The prisoner gagged and shook with fear.

"Here," said Santiago, putting a second pistol into the prisoner's hand and ordering him to shoot the foul humanity now wild-eyed at their fate. The prisoner hesitated and then hearing the release of the safety on the Colonel's gun, pointed the unfamiliar weapon unsteadily and shot three rounds into the hearts of the pitiful sagging bodies.

"Good shooting, you useless sack of *mierda.*" Colonel Santiago took the gun from the prisoner and ordered him to douse the pile with a small can of gasoline sitting nearby.

The Colonel tossed a lit match onto the first body and briefly watched the blaze. Fearful of his own rising nausea, he walked away, tidied up his office, and returned to his home in Cartagena.

Baptized and confirmed a Catholic as an infant, Jaime Santiago wondered at the premature and cruel death of the "good" that continued the cycle of evil. He was not sure justice had been served; but in this world of repeated savagery, he felt no remorse. He wiped his neck with the handkerchief and knew Señora Santiago would be happy to detect the lingering cologne when he arrived home.

General Gutiérrez had remained in his bed, numbed by grief and anguish until the morning of the funeral. On that day of mass and burial for his family, he felt anger at his brother's calm recitation of the many prayers for the dead. Juan Carlos' own suffering was cloaked in his profound faith in God, and he managed to make it through his eulogy, as Luís sat mute and dry-eyed with his sobbing family in the front pew.

"If we die with the Lord, we shall live with the Lord. If we endure with the Lord, we shall reign with the Lord." Luís heard the line and suppressed his utter contempt for the falseness of the words. Stifling the raging scream in his throat, he dutifully followed the family, as they approached the altar to receive Holy Communion from Juan Carlos. The two locked eyes, their hearts and souls bonding in love and loss. Monsignor Juan Carlos Gutiérrez succumbed to the excruciating longing he saw in the eyes of his brother. As he placed "the body of Christ" on Luís' tongue, he handed the communion chalice to the deacon and reached out to hold his brother in a close embrace.

During his career as a Colombian soldier, Luís had tried to gage the success of the battle. It was never enough to satisfy his ache for peace in his nation and the world. Now he felt his heart pull apart in longing, not for God's gifts, but simply for God. He railed against the warring actions in his life that stained his uniform with blood, created loathing in the hearts of the dead enemy's women, and caused tragic bewilderment on children's faces. Luís cursed the raw hatred of young teenagers. He knew their exploding hormonal energy and lack of experience would propel them into a short life of useless fighting.

Many times he had stood on a hillside, looking out at the carnage of another battle against the insurgents. For what? he thought. Most were so young and needed minimal propaganda to convince them to leave their families, their shacks and meager farms. They had only a slight understanding of the political ideology fed into their immature minds. But the sight of weapons soon to be placed into their hands created enough incentive to carry out ordered attacks. They saw only grand adventure and an opportunity to escape their monotonous lives.

Luís had witnessed this dozens of times. He envisioned world destruction by endless armies of ignorant youth and often questioned

God's rationale for the earthly presence of his pitiful creation. He remembered feeling doubt over agrarian reform programs his brother-in-law had wanted to implement among Colombia's poor. Luís lacked confidence that they would be sufficient to employ the children he met who, for centuries, had had little chance of a bright and successful future. He had seen too many failures.

Now as he embraced his brother, Juan Carlos, Luís whispered to him. "I want to go home," he pleaded. "Not to our house, but to a spiritual home, where there is love and peace. Why must we take so much life? Where is God, Juan Carlos?" he whispered, as he held his brother tightly and the communion wafer melted in his mouth. Luís felt nothing of the "peace of Christ" and ached for the childhood comfort he remembered when he believed, when he had faith.

Juan Carlos guided Luís back to the pew, where he kneeled helplessly in his sorrow. He felt not only personal loss but understood the suffering of the world's innocents, the hopeless youth throughout the world destined to become fodder for a storehouse of wretchedness that kept nations in constant chaos.

Luís looked up at the life-sized crucifix and recalled that part of the mass in which Juan Carlos recited the Memorial Proclamation before the Communion Rite—"Christ has died, Christ has risen, Christ will come again."

*Christ will come again, will come again, will come again. Christ will come again.* Luís repeated the words over and over in his mind, as the remainder of the communion host dissolved. An enveloping warmth from the words of promise surrounded him and a vision of the returning Christ crossed Luís' mind. He felt serenity—and something else. He felt a mounting *exhilaration!*

The mass ended and Luís exited the pew to touch the casket and feel the smooth wood under which his sister lay in death. As he walked with the slowly moving caskets from the altar to the rear of the church, his sister's joyous life and youthful beauty haunted him. The sense of devastation threatened again, and Luís battled the intrusion by quietly chanting—*will come again, will come again.*

Once at the cemetery, Luís no longer heard the incantations and braced himself as the caskets disappeared into their eternal graves. The future was now clear.

Sitting in Saint Peter's, General Luís Gutiérrez realized that this hour represented a triumph like no other. Over two decades ago, this highly acclaimed Colombian had convinced his brother and a select faction within the Vatican that the answer to endless violence in an indecent world was to allow Christ to return-as promised. "Allow" was difficult to translate, as Luís persuaded this small circle of confidants that man had acquired the technical ability to accomplish such a feat, but only through the grace of God. This patriotic and Godly man had persuaded himself and the others to go forward with a plan of hope, known among them simply as *The Return.*

During Luís' initial proposal to Juan Carlos, the promising Bishop had no inkling that he would become the first Latin American pope. Caught off-guard by his older brother, Juan Carlos stared at Luís in disbelief and wonderment. After attempting to comfort and counsel his brother on several occasions, Juan Carlos tried to avoid him. But Luís persisted, while attacks on Christianity and civilized society continued.

On this momentous occasion, Luís wore light-wool gray slacks and a navy blazer to blend into the crowd packing Saint Peter's. Dressed in civilian clothes, Luís avoided the attention his splendid uniform would have provoked. He had refused the special seating reserved for the Pope's family. Sitting alone, he felt a familiar "rush" of adrenalin, as he contemplated the future. *Today Christ will return to earth. Today will begin the unfolding of events that hold great promise for Earth's inhabitants.* Luís stared ahead, oblivious of the riches around him. He could think of nothing else, as he knelt on the stone floor of the cathedral and buried his face in his hands.

With the years of work completed, Luís wanted to be only a witness to what might unfold. The general ached to learn of the completion of the mission taking place thousands of miles away. He could envision the aircraft carrying Christian and checking his watch again, tried to imagine its current location over the Pacific Ocean. Luís would take no credit for the successful outcome of *The Return* and prayed he might even be spared the blame—at least on Earth.

In full regalia, Luís had joined the Pontifical Swiss Guard for breakfast earlier that morning, an event leading to the May observance of the Guards' anniversary. As the highest ranking military officer in Colombia, he had been asked by His Holiness to address the new members as part of their swearing-in. Luís deemed Juan Carlos' request a final gesture of his love and full confidence, despite the uncertainty to come.

Luís had often conversed with the young men of the Swiss Guard. *Would they lay down their life for the Pontiff? Would their resolve be tested and found wanting in this tiny magical kingdom?* Untried and unknowing, he wondered if these blue-eyed descendants of Helvetia, so renowned for their fighting prowess centuries ago, could stomach the sight of atrocities and brutality that Luís had repeatedly witnessed during his career.

Addressing them, he began: "Gentlemen, today marks a milestone for you and your institution. At this anniversary-now past the five-hundred-year mark-you will be tested as never before in a world fraught with strife. You can draw inspiration and strength from the faithful legions before you. You cannot know when your trial may come. But, you must be ready."

Standing in his military uniform at a podium in the guard barracks, Luís looked out at the young faces, shrouded by medieval Spanish helmets brightly plumed in red, complemented by their blue and orange puffed-sleeved uniforms. White-gloved hands held halberds, weapons from the 15th and 16th Centuries that combined a battleaxe and pike on a long handle. The professional soldier in Luís wondered how well-trained these young recruits were in the use of such barbaric bludgeons and if they would be effective in protecting the Pope.

"I have always been inspired by the life of Irishman Edmund Burke, a British statesman, a respected political thinker and writer. Like you, he accepted challenge, and as you *will,* he committed errors. Burke said, 'My failings are defects in my virtue, not an impurity in those virtues. The virtues are worth the striving-the defects can be worked out.'" Luís paused, hoping the truth of these words penetrated the young minds.

Looking at the rapt faces of the guards, Luís had been sorely tempted to confide in them what he hoped would occur this day. He knew they would remain ignorant of *The Return* until the islanders revealed it. *How would that happen? How long would it take?* Luís wondered for the hundredth time. "Sadly," Luís had refocused, "today is no different from yesterday, from last year, from last century. The necessity for struggle against injustice and suffering remains. The need to protect the Holy Father remains. You carry a unique responsibility in a world of inexplicable hatred for our faith; hatred or indifference-the public ranting of an ignorant mass, or the silent emptiness of a godless society." Luís gripped the sides of the podium. "An ignorant mass perhaps, but a creation of God, a creation that deserves our efforts to promote spiritual freedom and love of humankind."

Luís became overwhelmed with emotion. "Do not overlook the thoughtless destruction of the material and spiritual riches represented by this small empire. Defending and promoting the faith simultaneously is a daunting task, gentlemen. But as Edmund Burke wisely advised, 'All that is necessary for evil to triumph is that good men do nothing.' You are good men. You must continuously reaffirm the values embodied in our traditions. You will face trying circumstances. *Always* do your best."

Luís finished his remarks, saluted the group, and left the podium. Applauded and praised by Guard commanders, he struggled to remain patient throughout the ceremony. With polite excuses, he returned to his room to change for the mass. Once showered and dressed, he sat at a small desk in his room, reviewing every detail of the plan until it was time to leave for Saint Peter's. He felt a profound loneliness.

# Dawn of Hope
**Contadora Island – April 2035**

Before the vision could be presented this morning, careful research had established that most believers—and many who professed not to believe—imagined Christ would return to earth directly from heaven. Thousands of descriptions and images of Jesus had been studied. The planners were convinced that most envision Christ as a Caucasian of average height, with shades and textures of brown hair, hazel eyes, and a slender masculine body. Despite bodies of work depicting Christ as having blonde, red or black hair and as having Negroid or Asian features, the planners concluded that superficial differences in appearance would be insignificant to the drama of the spectacle. All agreed Christian should appear as a credible and pleasing combination of the products and fantasies of artists who had shaped the imaginations of millions over the centuries.

As the news of *The Return* would spread throughout the world, it was anticipated that descriptions by the few who witnessed Christian's descent and lived in his presence on earth would lead to new artistic renderings. This was indeed very desirable.

It is a predictably clear, dry-season dawn over the tiny Pacific island off the coast of Panamá. Descending gently, Christian can identify the surrounding islands. As he gets closer, many of the figures below—known only from his study of photographs—now became recognizable. He is fully recovered from the force of his abrupt ejection from far above. Protective lenses leave his eyes unaffected by the surrounding artificial light and airborne debris. Years of research and experimentation to conquer the hindrances presented by gravity and to maintain Christian's physical safety had been daunting. Extreme frustration with repeated failures often threatened success, and the secrecy required forced the key participants to come up with elaborate cover stories. Through the endless rehearsals possible unforeseen events were created and tested. Christian, faced with practice errors, rapidly developed conditioned responses, and as the weeks leading up to the mission wound down, all marveled at his ability to so easily accommodate the challenges. Those closest had to conceal their affection for the young man and keep secret their inward admiration of the beauty of Christian's inner and outer appearance.

As Christian descends, a shining aura surrounds him, while behind him the sun inches upward, presaging another sunny and cloudless day on the island. All on the beach can now clearly see a bright figure coming toward them in the limited light of dawn.

Christian knows the need to elicit shock but feels sadness over the fear he causes. All the routine chatter of a people going about their daily lives has been silenced. Only the gentle waves ignore the drama in the sky. The stillness breaks with a clearly audible flapping, like laundry in the breeze, as Christian comes closer. The sound of the billowing fabric is the only comfort to those below because of its familiarity in an otherwise mystifying scenario. The islanders remain motionless as they behold the descent.

Men watch from primitive fishing boats bobbing offshore. Others on the beach have been preparing nets. Children, at play in the sand, stop and stare in wonder. Several stand on a dirt road leading down to the beach from their hilltop dwellings. At the top of the hill, one man dressed in a white shirt and slacks stands motionless with a tight grip on his morning mug of coffee, poised just below his mouth.

The lives and habits of the islanders have been carefully catalogued—births and deaths have been closely monitored. The numbers and locations of those below were well known. The transfixed group is exactly what Christian expects to see, and he longs to be among them.

Some islanders mutter, *"Dios Mio."* (My God.) *"Dios, nos ayuda."* (God, help us.) One young girl simply says to her companion, *"Es Jesus!"* (It's Jesus!)

At this hour, the fishermen in their boats are normally watching for the schools of silvery fish in the dark water approaching their baited nets and often darting away to escape. But now their nets are neglected and spread loose on the surface. The men stand and strain to balance themselves in the movement of the boats, eyes glued to the vision above. For a brief moment, they consider jumping overboard and swimming to safety, but where?

The pre-dawn atmosphere had been disrupted earlier by a booming crack and distant rumble, reminding those below of thunder. The piercing sound was caused by high-altitude maneuvers that split the sound barrier as the unseen aircraft slowed to deliver Christian and was briefly unsettling for those who heard it.

Awakening some, the islanders would have anticipated such rumblings later in the year, when loud thunder preceded the rainy season's drenching *aquacerras,* common from May to December. During those months one could watch the dark masses cross the sky, hear their rumbling, breathe in their distinct smell, and anticipate the driving rain to come. The forewarning normally allowed enough time to take shelter to wait out the short deluge. Laden with moisture from warm Caribbean waters, the clouds would release fat droplets, causing a downpour onto the mountainous backbone of the isthmus. As the storms journey fifty miles across Panamá to the Pacific, the rains become a rippling gray- blue curtain.

But it is almost Easter, the time of "the dry season"—*el Invierno,* the winter, with its sunny days and balmy breezes—that commenced shortly before Christmas.

This dawn, like the thousands of dawns of centuries past, promises a full day of sun. Weather-wise, it is a perfect morning for Christ to return.

# Nina Shelky
**Saint Peter's – April 2035**

"*Ciao,* Bernardo," Nina told her colleague and veteran editor in the Vatican Press Office. She once had helped him to obtain interviews at Saint Patrick's in New York.

"I'm in Rome for a few days, taking a break, and I'm feeling spiritually needy. Any chance you might be able to score me a ticket to the mass at Saint Peter's tomorrow morning? I'll even buy you lunch," she said enticingly.

"Ah, Nina, *bella. Come stai tu?*" replied Bernardo enthusiastically. "Of course, of course. Where are you? I'll meet you for lunch, bring you the pass, and we can catch up on the world. It's a big Holy Week mass tomorrow. You'll get the full show," he said a little irreverently. Bernardo happily made the arrangements. Giddy with excitement, he greatly admired Nina as only a Roman can. He loved to be seen with beautiful women, and with Nina he could flirt and act flamboyantly— perhaps a little outrageously—knowing full well there was not a prayer for successful seduction. It was always obvious to him that her heart was elsewhere.

"Please, drop me here at this corner," Nina directed her cab driver the next morning. She was still several blocks from Saint Peter's but wanted to avoid traffic and take in the fine April morning. She paid the driver and walked toward the cathedral from the *Via della Conciliazione* (the Way of Reconciliation) and entered the massive square in front of the basilica surrounded by great stone hemicycles. Tall and slender with a confident stride that drew attention to her well-coiffed blond hair and excellent fashion sense, Nina was stunning in a dark blue suit with a complementary striped cape, soft black leather boots and gloves. She ignored the stares, as she marveled at the portico formed by the massive Bernini columns and thrilled at the sight of Saint Peter's entry in front of her.

As her eyes were drawn to the top of the enclosure of the cathedral, she recalled Bernardo's humorous instruction, "Remember, Nina, those larger-than-life sculptures guarding the railing of the portico are saints. We are told not to look them in the eye if you feel any sin. They stand up there as admonishers to all the faithful, human and sinful, below. How can they can look at you and believe you have no sin?" he teased her.

The twelve apostles, reportedly holding the instruments of their own deaths, exhibit their martyrdom from the top of the cathedral. Massive statues of Peter and Paul stand at the sides of the first set of stairs leading to the entrance. "Check out Peter's big toe, it has been rubbed smooth over the centuries by the fingers of passing tourists," Bernardo said. "I don't think Saint Peter would mind, since if the story is true, he lost his feet when his charred body was taken down after his inverted crucifixion." Nina shuddered and felt astonished by the sacrifices of those who gave their lives for the survival and growth of the Catholic faith.

Giving Saint Peter's toe a respectful touch, Nina walked up the steps to the cathedral and looked back at the plaza. Many groups of people from all corners of the world were making their way toward the entrance.

"*Buon Giorno*, good day, Miss. Welcome to Saint Peter's." A short elderly usher with a thick Italian accent and a keen eye for women of all nationalities recognized the well-dressed and attractive blonde to be an American, and he liked to show off his English.

"*Buon Giorno, Signore, grazie,*" Nina replied, returning the linguistic courtesy and offering a charming smile.

"*Pleeze, pleeze* allow me escort you to a good *seet* near the altar," he said with a flourish and a dramatic gesture of his hands. As he gave Nina a thick program, he proffered his arm with a questioning smile.

She nodded graciously, took his arm, and was escorted to a seat on the aisle near the front of the nave.

A Washington journalist in her 50's, Nina Shelky suffered from misplaced devotion. Her Catholicism had gone astray many years ago. Despite the "fallen away" status, which she blamed on her hectic schedule, vacationing in Rome allowed a more relaxed agenda and, thanks to Bernardo, the opportunity to attend the invitational mass. In the large crowd, she was grateful for the escort to her seat. Aware of her fortunate location so close to the front, Nina knew she would have an excellent view of the Pope and his entourage as they made their way down the center aisle. Recognizing the Church's worldwide struggle to stay afloat, Nina experienced a deep reassurance and renewed attachment in being part of the celebration of today's mass.

Nina was an unwitting participant in *The Return,* her presence among the momentous gathering on this particular morning purely coincidental. Nina had never met General Luís Gutiérrez, his brother Pope Juan Carlos Gutiérrez, or the others involved in *The Return* present at this mass. With no knowledge of the Vatican's decision to choose Contadora Island off Panamá's coast as the site of *The Return*, Nina nevertheless knew the island intimately.

An assignment that took Nina to Panamá in 2000 included Contadora, a forgotten resort that during the 1970's had served as one of the Panamá Canal Treaty negotiations sites. Seeking a few quiet days to finish her report about Panamá's progress since it had assumed full control of the canal, Nina lingered. Once on the island, the tropical breezes and crystal clear waters altered her focus. She fell deeply in love, both with the island and with one of its inhabitants, Marcos Rivera.

Nina's later writing about the island was to have a definitive impact on a great Vatican gamble. In the throes of passion two decades earlier, her article had been a byproduct of her ardent and unexpected obsession with Marcos. Her writing, with its sensuous and captivating style, caused the island, a small speck on a great ocean to be chosen. A Cardinal, a prince of the Church whom she would soon observe in the mass processional, had read her article long ago. In doing so, he realized immediately that the search for the location of *The Return* was over.

And, with no knowledge that in just an hour or so Marcos and the other islanders would witness the descent of a man they would believe to be Jesus Christ onto her beloved Contadora, Nina sat quietly as Marcos' image emerged from the caverns of her memory. Faced with the grandeur of Saint Peter's, she tried to shake the intruding memories. But even with all its beauty, Saint Peter's was the result of the creations of others—not a match for the memory of her island lover. Nor was it even close to what Marcos would soon experience thousands of miles away. Nina couldn't know that at this moment and distance, even after years of separation, Marcos reciprocated with reminiscences of Nina foremost in his mind, while standing on a hill above his beach, unaware of the sight he was about to behold.

Waiting for the mass to begin, Nina tried to concentrate on the art all around her. Every inch was painted, gilded, sculpted, or tiled with elaborate mosaics. Her eyes could not focus long on a single object but finally rested on one of the plump cherubs that posed in their marble prisons against the lower interior of the transept. They appeared loving and diminutive in these massive surroundings, even though they were over six feet high. There was so much within these walls that even years of study would be insufficient to absorb the beauty.

Emotionally moved to be in the Vatican and to hear the Pope say Mass, Nina nevertheless felt alone and ached to share these moments; to have a hand to hold, a shoulder to rest on, a companion who would feel the same inner spirituality. Her thoughts again returned to Marcos, vivid in her memory despite an absence of more than twenty years.

Never very devout and critical of religious programming that seemed superficial and often phony, Nina wondered why the yearning for spirituality sometimes disguised itself in noxious humor or in the mocking of those who embraced Christ. Now Nina recognized the void in her core, a sense of personal loss. The ache for Marcos, a longing that never quite left caused a spiritual and physical barrenness. Remembering their discussions about religion as intimate, refreshing and simple, Nina embraced Marcos' logic. She had argued over the anxiety aroused by the maddening obscurities of faith and the untold suffering allowed by a supposedly "loving" God. She had ridiculed religious rules and thought them arbitrary—edicts that Roman Catholics were expected to embrace, or at least accept, without question.

"Have faith, Nina. Just believe," Marcos had often gently instructed her.

Observing the crowd, Nina noted the piety of many, and she silently joined in the collective prayer for a reversal of the Church's precipitous slide throughout the world's consciousness. Here at Saint Peter's, the greatest cathedral ever known, Nina found it difficult to grasp the growing persecution of the faithful and the dwindling numbers of the Church's followers.

Nina recalled Bernardo, a self described "good Catholic," reminding her. "Nina, we all struggle with our faith. Certainly, it was *man*, not magic, who composed the great writings of the Jewish law and subsequent Christian testaments." He had shrugged and pursed his lips. "Divinely inspired? Perhaps, but what does that mean? There were many gods long before the Old Testament. Why did *they* disappear?"

Nina had acknowledged Bernardo's reasoning, and at the time felt her own doubts resurface. But now, experiencing this magnificent tribute to the one God, she struggled to feel spiritual conviction. In this unsurpassed structure with its many popes buried in the catacombs, the bones of Saint Peter himself beneath the great altar, she let go of her doubts. In this splendor it all felt right. Authority seemed resolved, and closeness to God felt authentic. She flipped through the thick mass program and read the words of The Acclamation—"Let us proclaim the mystery of faith. Christ has died, Christ is risen, Christ will come again."

"Would He?" She wondered, skeptical of the promise of faith.

Now twenty years after the inception of *The Return*, the inhabitants of the tiny blue-green island were about to begin their daily task of collecting its bounty from the surrounding sea. But the emphasis on the ordinary—food, clothing and shelter—would soon be overshadowed by the extraordinary. They were to encounter a miracle.

As the time approached for His Holiness to appear, Nina was among thousands of fidgeting faithful. "I wonder how many of us are left," Nina mused. Turning to the front of her program, she perused a description of the cathedral in several languages: *With no permanent pews, Saint Peter's was constructed in the era of building the great Basilicas.*

*The massive edifices were built for purposes besides celebrating mass and without a place to sit, were designed to accommodate great crowds which were required to stand for the duration of any event. Providing heat was not a consideration for early Roman buildings. Any discomfort from the cold was overcome by body heat and considered insignificant in the mild winter climate of Rome. Summer heat was a different matter, but the massive stone chilled during the winter months and cooled the interiors of buildings for part of the summer.*

Bernardo told Nina that several popes had died from the oppressive heat, creating a dire need for relief. The construction of Castel Gandolfo, a summer retreat, was completed in the cooler hills away from the city. Among the thirteen other buildings with extraterritorial privilege outside the Vatican proper, Castel Gandolfo was a papal favorite.

Mass would soon begin. Nina prayed for her own peace and for that of a decaying society and for a halt to the progressive erosion of the Catholic faith. Her thoughts were interrupted by the commotion at the rear of the cathedral that signaled the entrance of His Holiness, Damasus III, the Colombian Pope, Juan Carlos Gutiérrez.

# Panama's Contadora Island
## The Pearl Archipelago - April 2035

Panamá's Contadora Island, a busy resort in the nineteen seventies and eighties, had declined thereafter and was almost forgotten after full implementation of the Panamá Canal treaties on December 31, 1999. By then, after twenty five years of treaty "transition," the eleventh-hour political choreography to reverse the inevitable, to continue Panamá's love-hate partnership with the United States was over.

Panamá, created in 1903 by the United States, overcame Colombian resistance to its new foreign control and allowed the unencumbered construction of the Panamá Canal. In a few strokes of the pen, gambling its future under the protection of the United States of America, Panamá stepped on to the world stage. In the relatively short span of one hundred years, the small nation enjoyed a position of wonder and envy by its world neighbors. Its dazzling showcase for world shipping, the Panamá Canal, was deemed the Eighth Wonder of the World and changed the nature of global commerce.

The immaculate US Canal Zone had thousands of neat houses sitting in rows on manicured lawns. Administrative buildings, golf courses, club houses with restaurants and shops, swimming pools, the finest American schools, and, with the onset of World War II, strategic military bases dotted the landscape on either side of the 50-mile long waterway. Although the treaty implementation was a gradual process begun in 1978, the 8,000-plus buildings; the vast infrastructure and technical achievements; and the engineering marvel, the Panamá Canal, all ultimately fell under the status of the "*ex-* Canal Zone." After the treaty, formerly pristine Canal Zone town sites filled with neat homes painted only white, rapidly morphed into new communities reflecting a more brassy tone and the bright colors typical of Panama City suburbs.

With little property zoning, deserted US military bases were developed into attractive gated communities or into garish neighborhoods blaring tinny salsa music from open windows, while rows of wet laundry hung on lines between houses and trees drying in the Panamanian sun. As the city spread in reaction to its newfound status as full owner of a world class enterprise, its suburbs grew in the mixed pattern common to all cities.

Downtown Panamá City, clogged with traffic and mushrooming high rises and bound by the canal to the west, had no room to move south without tumbling into the ocean and so sprawled eastward along the Pacific coast.

Panamá maintained an enviable position. What had been a tiny nation under the protection of the great Goliath to the north, Panamá was suddenly thrust into the arena of the world economy, joining the competition among larger, richer nations. Despite its small size, the country had a unique blessing of a choice geographical position. Along with its inheritance of the "path between the seas," Panamá also received a new world respect and admiration.

From the earliest days of Spanish colonialism, this extremely colorful chunk of real estate became a crossroads for commerce. The Inca gold also attracted an array of players who came to fulfill various roles—charlatans, dictators, revolutionaries, celebrities, businessmen, drug dealers, and political asylum seekers. In the 1800's, the American "49-ers" paid exorbitant fees to cross the isthmus on foot, by mule or rail in their rush to get to California for the promised riches of gold. They were a diverse people. They were young, old, healthy and sick. They had varying agendas—both nefarious and honest. All were adventurous, and many, unable to complete the trip, got as far as Panamá and stayed. Collectively they forged a nation.

In the early days of Panamanian independence, the ever-present underworld of greed and exploitation spawned an economy with little governance. Others struggled for a toehold of lasting national integrity, often relying upon American largesse. For the United States, patience and generosity paid off in creating the circumstances for the most magnificent engineering and construction project ever undertaken. The Panamá Canal, completed in 1914, fulfilled the dreams of many who, over the centuries, imagined a shipping crossroad that would defy the small land barrier. The narrow strip of land that is Panamá was deemed trivial as an obstacle to the coveted sea lanes of the mighty oceans. Carving out the waterway was, however, an enormous challenge that ultimately provided a new order in the world's global commerce. Panamá was buttressed by a century-long American presence, a colonialism that blended with a mixed populace of Europeans, Americans, West Indians, Chinese, and native *Mestizos*. The fabric that became Panamá was steeped in many cultures and traditions.

When, at the end of the 20th Century, the curtain lowered on the vassal-state stage and the US left, the new country was flush with a heady independence. Freed of its militant and repressive dictator, General Manuel "Tony" Noriega, and padded by secret bank accounts, Panamá surged forward. Beyond the new and capable administration and ten-mile swath of the former Canal Zone, development soared. While real estate development burgeoned along Panamá's Pacific coast, the islands lying forty miles off the coast faded from public consciousness and renewed their beauty in relative isolation.

Contadora, a small speck among the 200 plus islands that make up the Pearl Archipelago, quietly regressed to an earlier time.

"Good fishing, Mario?" asked the woman hanging just-washed clothes in the sun.

"Ahhhh, always good fishing now," replied Mario. The aging father of Marcos Rivera walked slowly back up the hill. He did not mind the renewed isolation of his island.

Tourism money had dried up during the 90's, but Mario had spent all his life on the islands and had seen visitors come and go. He was an integral part of the chain of azure and green paradise known as the *Archipelago de Las Perlas*, the Pearl Archipelago.

As a guide during the years of tourism, Mario often took visitors out on the hotel's boat and told stories. "The name, 'Islands of Pearls,' is accurate enough," he explained. "In pre-Colombian times—that's before you were born," he teased the young women, "the Pearl Islands were ruled by Indian kings, and their subjects dove for pearls for ornaments and trade. Some world-class pearls were found in these waters. Back then, that kind of news aroused the greed of the *Conquistador*s, who, not content with looting pre-Colombian gold and silver from native tribes, found a new treasure beneath these crystal waters—pink, baroque, cream and white pearls."

By then Mario would have his audiences intrigued. "Not only the Spanish, but for several centuries, these islands hid an infamous lot of pirates, who looted the Spanish settlements and galleons and plied their trade from bases hidden in these islands." Mario had flown on the small Otter planes that served the islands and was intrigued by his own story. "Isn't it amazing how a world, not yet in flight, named these islands? When you leave, your small plane will not fly high enough; but in a high altitude plane, you would see these islands as a string, forty-miles long of lush green pearls set in an azure sea."

Mario never tired thinking about this or the circumstances that brought his forefathers to these white beaches.

As the 21$^{st}$ Century began and the political dust settled on the mainland, the islanders along with a handful of employees who chose to stay despite the loss of work, reverted to a more primitive state in an astoundingly short period. Aside from the remaining houses and the now somewhat rundown hotel, Contadora looked much as it did when seafarers found it long ago. Native vegetation replaced landscaping which was no match for the forces of nature.

This became evident during the wet season's profuse growth. Aided by voracious termites that conquered even cement structures and changed man-made edifices into nourishment and into their enormous dun-colored nests around depleted branches, plants and animals flourished and reclaimed the land the termites helped to clear. Fish, shrimp and the clawless lobsters, the *longostos*, re-populated the warm surrounding waters, all to Mario Rivera's delight.

Mario lived on Contadora before, during, and after the wave of tourism. Always agile, Mario's seven decades were evident only in deep lines etched from the outer corners of his eyes when he smiled or squinted against the island sun. The lines made him appear wise and unafraid, which he was after being exposed to all of recent history and yet enjoying a life unimagined by most of the world.

On this April morning in 2035, life on the small island would change forever.

# Countess Caputo and the Cardinal
## Saint Peter's – April 2035

Sitting across the aisle from Nina in Saint Peter's was the Countess Serina Caputo de la Guardia, heiress to a centuries-old Italian family fortune. Although her knowledge of the actual events of *The Return* was vague, Serina Caputo was intimately involved.

The countess had simply paid for the mission in exchange for personal salvation and  perhaps more immediately, the forbidden love of the Vatican's Secretariat of State, Cardinal Diego Hernandez. Despite the vagueness of her investment, he money was a spiritual offering, a gracious gift to a morally impoverished world. At this juncture, ne ther of them equated moral impoverishment with the morality of their own behavior.

On this morning, Serina Caputo, long ago widowed, wore a simple black suit and silk scarf and sat near the front of the church. Her trust in her beloved Church was fragile, and no reward for her significant investment was evident. Blessedly unaware of her critical role in the grandest scheme for peace ever conceived, Serina did not know that events would unfold thousands of miles away just as the rituals of the mass for peace were taking place this morning. Her thoughts traveled back to a day long ago in Milano.

Twenty years earlier, the Pope's childhood companion, seminary classmate, and dearest friend, Cardinal Diego Hernandez, waited for Serina at a kiosk in a Milano plaza.

They were to meet there for lunch, and Serina had only an inkling of Diego's motives.

She had been as oblivious back then of the lengthy and agonizing secret debates over the plan for *The Return* as she was this eventful morning in Saint Peter's. Serina was also ignorant of Cardinal Hernandez' two daunting tasks—locating the site of *The Return* and finding the financing. In a seemingly miraculous combination of events, Cardinal Hernandez resolved both issues that day. While avoiding addressing his inner ethical struggle, a providential distraction would spare him from confrontation.

Waiting for the Countess, Diego had picked up a travel magazine in which he found an article about a small Pacific island off the coast of Panamá. Close to civilization yet isolated and sparsely inhabited, the island of Contadora struck Diego as ideally suited for staging *The Return*. He became fascinated with its obvious geographical advantages but also noted a passion in the unknown author's vivid description. He would have to see for himself, of course. Cardinal Hernandez did not know of Nina Shelky or her *affaire d'amour* but believed the evocative article was more than a routine tourist advisory. At the same time the burden of finding the perfect location was lifting, he was disturbed by his inability to deny its pleasurable effect on him.

The second issue—the enormous sum of money required—still troubled him. He had struggled in his battle between denial and approval of *The Return*. Now in full agreement with the small Vatican group committed to saving their Church, Cardinal Hernandez needed to persuade the Countess to pay for the mission without actually revealing the plan to her.

On that sunny morning in Milano, Serina window shopped the elegant boutiques in the glass-enclosed mall on the grand piazza. As she walked, she ignored the magnificent Duomo to her left and scanned the plaza looking for Diego. She quickly spotted him at the far side of the cathedral, leaning against a kiosk, reading a journal.

This morning Cardinal Hernandez dressed in civilian clothes—a light cashmere sports jacket over a sweater and slacks. Even wearing his black suit and white clerical collar, women weakened in their unspoken resolve to avoid "men of the cloth." Diego was accustomed to female attention and had learned to ignore the not-so-subtle stares and approaches. With Serina, however, his conscience remained conflicted, and his feelings, decidedly less-than-holy, persisted. Diego held on to his sacred beliefs but was aware that after so much time, desire would not loosen its grip on him. Today Diego would open the Countess' purse strings and cement the project's financial backing—the coins of grand hope—to reverse the mortal threat to the Church. The matter of his soul, the betrayal of his vows . . . he could not foresee.

Before meeting Diego, Serina had taken stock of herself. Acknowledging her weakness, she vowed to suppress her raging emotions. Yes, she wanted to give for her salvation and for the good of the Church, but her determination to be financially generous yet scrupulous in her personal conduct was daunting. Lofty goals were inseparable from intense desire. Serina barely hesitated in parting with her money, even without knowledge for its use. She never contemplated a risk to the Church's integrity or her soul. On that day, obedience to the teaching of the holy Catholic Church wilted in the intensity of longing and fulfillment. The consuming need, presented on an airy mantle, disguised any imperfection of souls. While they stood on the plaza and the world within the Duomo of Milano progressed, the plaza birds gathered about their feet, hoping for food and their own survival. While the world of schoolchildren, vendors, and tourists played out their roles this afternoon as on any other afternoon over the last 500 years, persistence of the human ache of the flesh was, for Diego and Serina, the only focus.

Serina knew that her acts that day, both temporal and spiritual, might not have been pleasing to God. She knew that she should have paid heed to the flaws in Diego's vague explanation for the use of her wealth. In giving to the Church without question, however, was it possible that the reality of their sin might not exist? If the mission was for God, would He not forgive? Serina knew her reasoning was probably unfounded, but she had been comforted by the thought, and after twenty years remained comforted. Today in Saint Peter's, the stunning countess was at peace, enriched by life's purpose. She felt closer to a heavenly reward and marveled at the depth of her love for Cardinal Diego Hernandez.

On this day in the splendid aura of Saint Peter's, both Nina Shelky and Countess Serina Caputo watched His Eminence, Cardinal Diego Hernandez, proceed with His Holiness, Juan Carlos Gutiérrez, Pope Damasus III, down the aisle of the great cathedral. When the Countess' driver had delivered her to a VIP drop-off point at the side of Saint Peter's, members of the Swiss Guard and the Vatican household greeted her and escorted her into the cathedral. While stepping out of her car, she noticed an attractive blonde woman walking toward the basilica, neither of them aware of the role of the other. Wearing a lace *mantilla* over her pulled back and coiled hair, Serina looked radiant, as she opened the mass program and focused on the Liturgy of the Word. She relished the blend of age-old Jewish tales of the Old Testament with the letters handed down by messengers of Christ as a fitting Judeo-Christian compromise. Later, she respectfully stood up in her pew as the gospel was read.

Like many thousands, Serina held fast to the truth of the gospels, those accepted renditions of the teachings of Christ attributed to four story tellers—Matthew, Mark, Luke, and John. The accounts varied, but incidents in Christ's life were the common thread woven throughout the four missives. Serina wondered if the first account attributed to the tax collector, Mathew, had been read by the second author before he and others later created similar accounts. Did a stenographic capability exist to record the reputed direct quotes by Jesus to relatively obscure persons?

She knew that no one had proof of who wrote the gospels and who embellished the fragments of writing over the centuries. The recognized and accepted names were handed down and referenced as the Disciples of Christ. The actual writing was attributed to unknown scribes and groups of monks laboring through the centuries. Versions referred to as apocryphal were deemed unacceptable by leaders of later burgeoning religious movements and were relegated to the vast quantity of writings that didn't quite make it into the current day bibles and missiles.

The gospel of Saint Peter described a looming ten-foot-high resurrected Christ. In her studies, Serina had found this retelling of Christ's life attributed to Saint Peter both appealing and humorous. She wondered about the integrity of the process which vetted the merits of the authors. Clearly, mortal men, considered divinely inspired, made these decisions. The periods during which the gospels were written are not well-established, but it is known that the teachings of Christ were interpreted and recorded years after his death. *Knowledge about the life of Jesus is extremely limited,* Serina thought, *but no limits exist on the quantity of words and edits and interpretations.*

With the mass in progress, Serina's thoughts were interrupted by the Holy Father's voice, now delivering his homily. Those who knew Juan Carlos detected a slight weakness in his delivery. *How much time could he devote to a review of messages to the faithful? Who decides what messages are to be delivered here and abroad and from the Pope's window to the throngs in Saint Peter's Square during his Wednesday appearances?*

The Pope scanned the crowd for a long time before he spoke. "It is a great joy for me to be with you around this Altar of Sacrifice. We recall that, as the Second Vatican Council reminds us, the Eucharist is 'the source and the summit' of all the preaching of the Gospel. In the Eucharist, we praise the Holy Trinity for the blessings of the past. We celebrate Christ's presence with us now; and we are strengthened to fulfill our own role in the saving mission of the Church. Let us join our hearts and voices this day in prayer for the entire Church, for her clergy, for all her laity and, in a special way, for the sick and suffering. May the Word of God continue to bear fruit and flourish in all the land."

The homily was the prelude to commemoration of the crucifixion of Christ, an instruction to repentance. Serina listened to the cherished words, unaware that Juan Carlos Gutiérrez, her friend and her Pope, was at this moment, experiencing extreme fear and guilt as he suffered the inner conflict over what would soon happen on a little island far away. He was also in great physical pain.

Rising, the congregation recited the *Credo,* also known as the Profession of Faith. The prayer is part of the *credendum,* those beliefs that form the basis of the Catholic faith. General Intercessions were then recited—prayers for the sick and the dead, for personal *petitions* in the mind of each attendee, and for the survival of faith throughout the world. *It is a lot to ask,* thought Serina. *And so little is answered.*

From her close proximity, Serina noted Juan Carlo's stooped posture and ashen face. The Pope, even though spared the actions and detail of the years of planning for *The Return*, was suffering a weight of dread over what was to come. He could not begin to unravel the complexities of the project nor did he know the roles of others present at this mass. All would soon cross a common threshold together.

# WITNESS TO A MIRACLE
## Contadora Island – April 2035

While mass was in progress in Saint Peter's in Rome, all but a few on the Island of Contadora slept.

"Come, Marcocito," Mario whispered in the darkness, rousing the child from his hammock. "If you don't hurry, I'll beat you to the ledge and catch the first fish. It'll be a big one, I know," he teased the young boy, who was already rubbing the sleep from his eyes.

As dawn crept across the sky, Mario and his grandson Marcocito walked to the beach on the island's northeast side. Early morning fishing was their daily ritual, and actually catching fish was almost incidental. Beyond the pleasure of receiving admiring smiles and compliments from the women as they carried the fresh fish up the hill, above all, grandfather and grandson cherished the time together. They rarely missed a single morning, only the very few occasions when Marcocito flew to Panamá City with his father, Marcos. As the islands' legislative representative in Panamá's unicameral legislature, Marcos tried to make the trips educational and fun for Marcocito. Though infrequent and always a disappointment to Mario, Marcos believed the occasional exposure to the nation's government was instructive for his young son.

"And, my little *hombre,*" continued Mario tugging the brim of Marcocito's ball cap, "we will visit Theresa today. I know how much you miss her, and she misses you as well." With his simple faith, Mario believed that Marcocito's mother, dead at a far too early age, watched over them from the rock niche, where five years ago they had placed her ashes and surrounded the area with protecting cacti and bougainvillea.

Both would be vibrant and colorful against the otherwise dry landscape. Even though Marcocito suffered frequent bouts of melancholy over the loss of his mother, the love and affection he received from his father, grandfather, and their extended family was abundant.

As the son of the beloved elder Mario, Marcos was well-respected. During the last election, turnout was impressive, with voters arriving by small boat caravans from other islands. They cast their ballots into a cardboard box carried to the island and placed on a folding table in the now shabby hotel lobby. Voting was diligently watched over by a member of the national voting commission from Panamá City.

Few islanders filled out annual tax forms. Exercising their franchise by casting their votes, the bureaucracy of the mainland was not something they took seriously. The reverse was also true—with little revenue coming in from scant populations, the government did not pay much attention to the islands. Life continued in its primitive way, as it had before the years of tourism.

Still, Marcos treated his elected office with a genuine effort to represent his people with dignity and effectiveness.

Upon awakening this morning, the aging Mario had heard an unusual far-away thunderclap. It aroused his curiosity, but unsupported by any corroborating weather signals, the prospect of fishing with his grandson soon overcame any concern. Moving down the worn road, Mario and Marcocito began exchanging observations about the morning weather and the condition of the seas. Mario, unfettered by the mental complications of a highly-educated mind, imparted the basic knowledge and wisdom of his years to his grandson. Mario realized, as he had with Marcos, that the child would need formal training later on. For now, they exchanged jokes about who would catch what that morning.

They wore rubber flip-flops to protect their feet against the heat of the road and sand. "Real" shoes were reserved for trips to the mainland. The thick soles of the rubber thongs protected the bottoms of their feet from small burrowed stingrays that stab painfully when disturbed. On the rocks, the thongs protected them from sharp edges and allowed easier navigation over the bumpy rounded shells of native snails that laid tiny white eggs in thousands of small craters in the rocks. Created over centuries, the indentations ranged in size from a nickel to a saucer.

Meanwhile, Marcos stood at the top of the hill as he did every morning, holding a mug of *café con leche,* rich coffee laced heavily with milk, prepared by one of the women. Relishing the brief time of quiet thought, Marcos had acquired an ability to make out the activity on the dark beach below. He knew the islanders well, and he was familiar with their distinctive silhouettes, as they went about their respective chores. When there was sufficient light, Marcos would walk the short distance over the eroding island roads to his small office near the hotel to complete legislative reports before catching the noon flight to the mainland. The early mornings were relished for their quiet and their magical ability to lift his melancholy and offer comfort.

In the hint of the promised sunrise ahead, Marcos barely discerned the fishing boats arriving at the cove from the small nearby island of *Granito de Oro* (Little Grain of Gold). Each morning crews from the small cluster of primitive houses on the hill above their beach, *Playa Manta* (Beach of the Manta Ray), walked down the hill to join the small fleet. Marcos could hear the slap of the water against the brightly painted hulls and the usual banter through the still air.

With the onset of Holy Week, all government offices and schools shut down in the small Catholic country. But on this morning, Marcos planned to take the late morning flight to the mainland for a legislative luncheon at the Presidential Palace before the holiday recess. He relished the calm moments with the islanders and wished he didn't have to leave.

"*Oye, muchachos,* hurry up. The *longostos* don't have watches," the heavy leader, Gordo, playfully shouted to the stragglers coming down to meet the boats. "*Vamos! Rapido!*" Marcos smiled at the interruption, as he heard Gordo's strong deep voice urge his men to row away from the cove. The tide was now coming in and getting out of the area near the beach into deeper water took extra strength from the oars.

Marcos smiled contentedly at the activity, lifting his mug to his lips and focusing on the sight of his father and his son now pulling back their poles to cast their lines from the jutting jetty that projected from the left side of the beach to form the graceful cove.

As Marcos' eyes scanned the horizon, he was struck by the appearance of an unfamiliar bright dot in the sky. Marcos' mind fought to deny the presence of a growing speck of light, upsetting the dawn's tranquility. As the object grew larger, Marcos' puzzlement was replaced by astonishment and then a growing fear. He stood paralyzed, trying to make sense of the panorama before his eyes.

Mario and Marcocito had crossed the cool sand of the beach and were already at the end of the rock jetty. At low tide a flat ledge approximately five feet in width became exposed, creating a path to the end where in the early morning fish fed off tiny creatures clinging to the ancient boulders in deeper water. The ledge allowed Mario and Marcocito the leverage they needed to cast their poles into the sea. Later in the day, the ledge would disappear beneath the eighteen-foot Pacific tide, and waves would slap onto the rock surface and against the wall of rock that rose up behind them to the level land above. Their hooks were baited and as Mario adjusted his rod and the line of his reel in preparation for casting, he felt his grandson's small hand abruptly dig into the skin at his waist. Fearing the child had lost his balance, Mario reacted by grabbing Marcocito's upper arm. There was no resistance, and the look on the boy's upturned face was wide- eyed with awe. Mario saw where Marcocito looked and blinked to adjust his focus—a figure dressed in billowing white fabric, surrounded by light, was descending slowly from the sky toward them.

Unable to move, Marcos remained on the hill some 300 yards away. The light of the dawn had increased only slightly, but and Marcos could now make out the dark shadows of more islands in the distance, the still-gray horizon at the end of the glassy sea, and the terrified, crouching figures of those he loved shielding their faces from the approaching vision in the sky.

# FATHER JONATHAN KENNEDY
## Saint Peter's – April 2035

Father Jonathan Kennedy, now forty-five, stood at the back of the altar in his usual position as one of the Pope's assistants. The candles and incense, as well as the crowd, seemed oppressive this morning at Saint Peter's. He felt faint and out of breath, as he tried to rid his mind of the events occurring elsewhere in the world.

A devoted servant of His Holiness, Father Kennedy had shouldered colossal responsibilities that covered the twenty years of the mission. By the end of this mass, his work would be finished. Having stewarded *The Return* to this climactic day, Jonathan Kennedy had felt little peace over the last two decades. Delicate negotiations with the Central Intelligence Agency had been conducted in extraordinary secrecy and resulted in a contract critical to the hopes of world peace. The few involved tried to erase the blatant contradiction presented by this contract, a contract negotiated with the Israelis. In exchange for massive aid and military assistance, a small cabal within the Israeli defense forces had agreed to plan and transport Christian, masquerading as Jesus, to the designated drop area on Contadora Island. It was so absurd that the two agents involved at the CIA wondered if it were actually a cover for another project.

Christian the infant, Christian the child, and then Christian the valiant young soldier of Christ, whom Jonathan loved with his heart and soul, had been Father Kennedy's primary and most compelling responsibility. Having been tasked to find, educate, and train Christian—the incomparable child who had agreed to risk his life to try and save the Church and Christianity—had given Jonathan unimaginable joy. Having to eventually entrust him to the Israelis was agony. He now begged God for Christian's safety.

As for the daunting task of the mission itself, Jonathan's simple explanation of thechallenge of *The Return* had intrigued the renowned American scientist, Dr. Dennis Dennison, over a lunch in Washington two long decades ago. Known as "Denny," the well-known playboy and atheist had agreed to undertake the scientific research to realize the technical means to bring about *The Return*.

Distracted by his thoughts, Father Kennedy had not observed the Pope's weakened stance. He looked up as the choir began the familiar opening phrase, "Gloria to God in the highest and peace to his people on earth " *The Gloria. How many times have I repeated "The Gloria," and how many times by the millions of the faithful has it been recited worldwide?* As Father Kennedy retreated to his natural affinity for math, he tried to calculate such an absurd number in a futile effort to divert his mind from images of Christian. *Had the millions of repetitions of praise by young and old in hundreds of tongues over the centuries pleased God and maintained a tranquil civilization? Apparently not, as the current wrenching turmoil in the world would attest. What more is needed? More of the same? That's not realistic,* he thought. *But the mission, this unprecedented, outrageous gamble of a mission, would it please Him?*

Jonathan was unaware that Nina Shelky had recognized him, as she scanned the crowded altar after the procession. It took Nina only a few moments to recall where they had met. Their encounter had been long ago, and Father Kennedy had never read her passionate article about the tiny island, so influential in determining where Christian was soon to descend.

Struck by Jonathan's haggard appearance, Nina wondered about this American who evidently had been selected to serve His Holiness. She thought back to their meeting at a scientific conference in San Francisco, where the famed Dr. Denny Dennison spoke of amazing technical advances that would allow meteorological and atmospheric manipulation. She was there to report on the conference and had wondered at that time about the reason for the young priest to attend.

Nina recalled how her journalistic curiosity made her seek him out prior to the formal dinner held in the adjacent ballroom.

"Are you trying to convert this crowd, Father?" she had quipped after an initial conversation at the evening cocktail reception.

"That would be an achievement, wouldn't it? Do you think they're all wondering the same thing?" he joked back. "Actually, the Vatican endorses most science, and similar to your job, they want to keep up with all changes of significance. As a personal matter, I must confess," he went on, "that I have an interest in space and space travel. After all, one day I may need a ride to heaven." He smiled broadly, as he saw his humor throw her off a bit.

In reality, Father Kennedy had attended the conference years before to observe and better understand Dr. Denny Dennison before approaching him. After the sessions of the day, Jonathan was giddy at the prospects Dr. Dennison represented. He hoped his light bantering with the young blonde journalist would keep her from taking him seriously. At that long ago event, Jonathan had managed to conceal his inner turmoil. This morning the fear in Jonathan's mind for the safety of Christian many miles away could be seen in his troubled face. When the congregation stood to hear the gospel, he looked up and with alarm noted the weakened appearance of the Pope, only feet away.

Nina pondered Father Kennedy's connections to Rome and his obvious closeness to the Pope, Juan Carlos Gutiérrez. She filed it in the back of her mind to investigate later and turned her attention back to the altar.

# Denny Dennison, PhD
## Saint Peter's – April 2035

In her observation of the gathering in the cathedral, Nina Shelky caught sight of another familiar figure, a huge man with thick white hair standing near the rear of the cathedral. Even though it was crowded and difficult to see between the masses of people, Nina recognized him as Dr. Denny Dennison. She wondered at his presence here. It seemed unusual in light of her meeting both Denny and Father Kennedy in San Francisco years before. She briefly considered any ongoing friendship between the two when the altar bells started ringing during the Liturgy of the Eucharist. Nina turned her attention back to the great altar.

The large man was indeed Dr. Denny Dennison, although this morning the jovial scientist Nina remembered looked tired and sad. Years before, having given the affirmative nod to Father Jonathan Kennedy and accepting the challenge of *The Return*, an acceptance he came to believe was mysteriously "meant to be," the American scientist had reached far beyond the confines of his field of Geo-engineering in order to meet the unprecedented technical challenges of his assignment.

At the moment, Denny was sweating profusely, his usual cocky self assurance was gone, and he appeared agitated among the crowds continuing to enter Saint Peter's. Through the rows of people, Nina briefly saw Denny's trembling hands wiping his face again and again with a handkerchief. *Hardly the bigger-than-life braggart I met in San Francisco,* she thought. *Why is he here?* Nina wondered, since the famous Dr. Dennison was reputed to be not only a Washington playboy, but a confirmed atheist. Nina didn't know that at this moment, Denny was oblivious to everyone. As the seconds ticked by and the mission was imminent, he was filled with apprehension and fear of God. Far greater than the disgrace of failure might well be the sin of success!

In earlier years, Denny had never allowed time or space for God. Sin was simply a throwback to the myths of his childhood. Despite what felt like a sharp prod to his conscience now and then, he stuck with a simple axiom—that inserting God into any equation would be admitting that a scientific explanation was impossible. In his Geo-engineering career, no one had convinced Dr. Dennison that tsunamis or earthquakes occurred because God was angry. For scientists such as he, this line of thinking was an absurdity that led down blind alleys.

"Float a human down to a small island?" Denny recalled the amusement he initially felt in his first meeting with the young Father Jonathan Kennedy. *What was my exact moment of conviction, my acceptance of Jonathan's Kennedy's challenge? The challenge? To float* <u>*what*</u> *human down to what small island in the Pacific? And why? Why did I agree?* Thinking back Denny recalled that he had agreed quickly—too quickly—to what would prove to take over his life. He knew this immediately and yet was unable to deny the dare, the test of his ability. Trying to understand the magnificent motive while seeking to solve the technical barriers, he soon faced the first hints of personal conflict. The obscure crevices in Denny's mind, where the total denial of God was housed, were filling with new possibilities. He confronted the contradictory risks of incurring sin versus performing a wondrous accomplishment for mankind. *Still,* thought Denny, *if I deny God, doesn't that obviate any judgment? Sin is its own executioner,"* Denny recalled reading somewhere.

On that day long ago, Jonathan had unknowingly bored a tiny hole into the armor of Denny's defense against the existence of God. The very concept of sin, an idea routinely dismissed over the years, grew as the project progressed. Denny's realization of his profound responsibility also grew with the defeat of each obstacle to success. He soon found himself thanking God and, in time, came to wonder at *any reason for science* if there were no God.

Over the years, Denny kept his growing conversion to the faith a secret. But as the time grew closer, he confessed all to Jonathan

Kennedy. Kennedy, delighted and in awe of the blessing of conversion, treated Denny's new found faith as one more approving sign from God. For Denny today, judgment by man of his scientific capability no longer mattered. It was only God's judgment he feared.

When Denny watched the Pope progress down the center aisle of Saint Peter's, he felt deep respect and affection for this Church and for its efforts on behalf of a broken humanity. He never met the Pontiff, Juan Carlos Gutiérrez. The security issue was too complicated. Denny didn't know until later that he had been identified to His Holiness by Father Kennedy. As the entourage moved down the long aisle, Juan Carlos briefly sought out Denny. As their eyes met, the Pope made an almost imperceptible nod in Denny's direction, as he bestowed a private blessing on him. Denny looked into the face of the Pope and felt awe at the sight of this great humanitarian, this brave shepherd to the world, who refused to accept the outrage against his own and against the rest of the world.

Denny took a deep breath and shrugged his huge shoulders as the mass began. He was no longer of two minds and accepted that the probabilities in nature were not always responsible for the human experience. *God could indeed stage a miracle,* he thought, *now, will He allow it?* Father Kennedy had reluctantly contacted Denny in Israel earlier in the week, where he was monitoring the final days before the mission, to direct him to come to Rome for the mass. To preserve security, it was deemed wiser for Denny to make his way from Israel the day before.

Bitterly disappointed at not being with Christian before takeoff, Denny knew his work was finished, and he acquiesced.

The powerful bond between the scientist and the courageous Christian had developed over their years of work together. With great love for Christian and his remarkable fearlessness, Denny demanded ever greater competence of himself to ensure the safety of the noble youth and that of the Israelis entrusted with Christian's life.

Denny longed to be with them in the desert at this moment of launch. He had vainly searched for credible ways to fit on the mission aircraft, to guide all to a safe and successful conclusion. In the end, the Vatican leaders convinced him of what he already knew—it was impossible for him to go. Physically, his enormous bulk would not fit into the aircraft. He did however, fit into the cavernous Saint Peter's.

As morning passed in Rome, the sun had yet to rise on Contadora Island. On that remote tropical island nine thousand miles away, the inhabitants sleeping in warm Pacific breezes under a thick blanket of fading stars would forever remain unaware that Denny Dennison's extraordinary undertaking had enabled a solitary aircraft to swiftly approach their quiet home and deliver Christian into their midst. For all the grand intentions surrounding the flight and for all its magnificent technical achievements, the aircraft's mission was simply to give the gift of hope that would renew God within the hearts of men.

# THE DESCENT
## April 2035

Christian's rapidly disintegrating devices to safeguard his hearing were no longer needed. They loosened and fell away. He left the temperature-regulated bubble that provided superb life support during ejection into the stratosphere and subsequent descent down to the gradually warming, oxygen-rich, lower atmospheric levels. Shielded from near-space conditions at the drop altitude, Christian experienced no discomfort. Through the early stages of his descent, successively larger drogue chutes had deployed in a critically timed sequence to slow the protective bubble. With the anticipated prevailing trade winds, this ensured a precise approach toward the targeted beach.

Insofar as was humanly possible, the means of Christian's descent into the sea off Contadora's shore were well-concealed. The equipment required for support during his final descent had been constructed largely of transparent materials and treated to ensure rapid dissolution upon contact with the warm tropical water. The whole operation was designed to be well hidden from the inevitable future inquiries about the legitimacy of *The Return*.

Now released from the elaborate technical confinement, Christian became aware of the soft repetitive noise of the billowing fabric wound around his torso. The fabric closely matched the hand-woven linen of over two thousand years ago. The chance of anyone's retrieving the material was very slim, but even if recovered and identified, the fabric would continue to decompose. It was highly unlikely that clues that might betray the mission's true origin would be revealed.

The research and engineering for Christian's descent, perfected over the years by Dr. Denny Dennison, resulted in the visual impression now taking place—a wondrous, credible, and enchanting sight to the audience below.

Deeply gratified at the apparent success of these first moments, Christian wished that Denny were present to witness the flawless execution of the descent. In the overarching concern for Christian's safety, meticulous attention to detail had been key during his rigorous training. Reacting with ever-greater triumphs after even the smallest flaw in performance during the years of rehearsal, Christian believed that Denny could somehow "sense" this perfected finale. The bond between the young "imposter" and the scientist had become so strong that prying them apart 48 hours before the mission had been emotionally wrenching.

"I pray God lets me look upon your face again, my son," said Denny embracing Christian for the last time.

"We will see each other again soon," Christian replied. He felt no certainty of this but refused to show his own fear and wanted to leave no doubt in the scientist's mind.

In the first moment of recovery from the constraints of the ejection and descent, Christian silently thanked Denny's genius and focused on the scene below him. The serenity of the low tide quelled Christian's anxiety. Miniature breakers, creating rhythmic sounds, interrupted the stillness of the shallow water. Christian knew this peaceful low- tide melody would later change dramatically to a boisterous symphony of crashing waves, hurling themselves forward to rearrange the shoreline. The schedule of the operation included Christian's arrival at this precise moment, when tide and prevailing winds determined by the eternal forces of the natural world would be in favorable sequence. Nothing save the hand of God would alter nature's exquisite timing. The heavenly order continued.

Although a large section of the beach awaiting Christian's arrival remained smooth and undisturbed after the previous high tide, footprints were visible from the fishermen's dawn trek from their small houses down the hill and across the beach to the sea. They had waded out to their boats from nearby islands. A few women hurried after them to deliver forgotten lunches for the long day ahead. Small children took advantage of the freedom provided by the lack of supervision and played in the sand. They would be tasked with suitable chores later in the morning. Older ones busied themselves repairing nets. Two young girls tended to laundry in the shallow water that was now rising and inching toward shore again. All preferred to get chores done before the sun rose high in the sky, when they napped during the hot afternoons.

As Christian viewed the scene below, he knew the surface of the beach would soon be chaotic—covered with footprints created by the frenzy of activity surrounding his entrance. He also knew that the beach had no ability to record the event. The sea was master in this matter, and over the next six hours, progressively mounting waves would again assault the white sand. The tide would reach further up the beach to cover footprints, re-position shells, cover and uncover rocks and coral, hurl branches to shore and then recede once more, leaving a renewed surface. This tide, just as the millions before it, continued the everlasting cleansing of the shores of earth twice daily—and today would erase all visible or traceable evidence of Christian's arrival.

Ever closer, Christian could hear the faint sound of crabs scuttling along the rocks and the fainter noises of tiny sea creatures sucking in life and burping out minuscule bubbles, while clinging to existence and waiting for salty water to cover them again.

"God's gift," thought Christian, marveling at their unique knowledge of the ebb and flow of the tides—their cue to be born, to eat, mate, and die. He could see the small schools of fish near the jetty-like formation of rock that formed the cove of the beach. There was no turbulence, and clear water swells bumped against the rocks tranquilly, gently carrying the brightly colored tropical species.

The people and their faces gradually came into focus. Christian scanned the small crowd staring at him, transfigured in wonder. His life to date, the totality of his being was designed for this assignment for God. The years of rigorous training, his doubts and ultimate acceptance of this unheralded mission now engulfed him. Christian—masquerading as Jesus Christ and having survived the precarious journey—realized that the fullness of his purpose would now be tested.

The thought remained, as he dropped into the warm sea at the end of the natural jetty fifty yards from the beach.

Breaking through the softly rising swell making its way toward shore, Christian felt the sandy bottom and was reassured by its stability, as he deliberately made his way through the surf that reached just below his chest. He felt the gentle tug of the waves encouraging him in the direction of the beach.

The artificial trappings of this amazing descent were all but gone. Undetectable restraints on Christian's shoulders and waist had submerged with him, quickly disengaged, and were totally absorbed by the still, dark seawater. The restraints rapidly disintegrated beneath the white fabric while the fabric itself slowly melted into the water's surface. Those who witnessed Christian's re-emergence were too engrossed in the miraculous sight to note the technical wonders simultaneously taking place. All systems had worked flawlessly.

Within seconds, Christian was almost naked, clad only in a white linen loincloth. He quickly readjusted it about his legs, genitals and waist. Christian, needing a moment's respite, sought the large rock he knew would be there for him to rest his arms upon, reached up to grasp its smooth edge, and laid his palms and face on the warm flat surface. The rest of Christian's body was soothed by the gentle pulse of the sea. He felt relief and his spirit soared with the flush of first success.

Behind the large rock, an uneven wall rose another five feet to a wide ledge where a man and a child stood frozen. They held fishing rods and stared down at him. Christian knew who they were and expected them, as they had been there every morning since Marcocito had grown old enough to navigate the jetty with his grandfather. The child's eyes were wide with astonishment. The two involuntarily yanked their poles up and were poised to back away from the edge, to press into the false security of the rock face that continued upward behind them. They did not understand what they were witnessing but knew that something momentous was taking place.

Despite his limited primary education, Mario had little difficulty reconciling images of Jesus Christ left by priests visiting his village school with the wonder he now observed. He wasn't well acquainted with scripture and mass attendance had been infrequent, since priestly visits to serve a declining population at the resort had decreased over the past decade. But Mario knew the basic story of the New Testament. He and the rest of those watching from the beach and the hill behind them perceived that this man, who had descended from the sky, *must* be the Savior!

*"Jesus,"* Mario uttered weakly, distressed but instinctively knowing this figure to be Jesus. Christian had but a fleeting second to take in the glorious sound of this single word. It was enough.

*"Jesus?"* Mario said it again tentatively, and then, in unbridled acceptance, cried out. *"Jesus, Jesus!"*

The perception of "Jesus" by this islander signaled the culmination of a decades long journey. It was the ultimate objective of those who had conceived the event years before—those who had expended millions to pull it off, had remained loyal to their vows of secrecy, and had destroyed lives—perhaps even their own souls—on the gamble to restore God's grace to a troubled earth.

"Have you come to take us, *Jesus?*" Mario's own question mystified him.

"No, my son." Christian, reassured by the recognition and acceptance he heard in Mario's voice, replied softly. "There is much to accomplish and you must help me."

"Are you God? Are you *Jesus?*" asked Marcocito, overcoming the numbness of his initial terror and feeling braver after hearing the first words exchanged by his grandfather and this man.

"I come to you from above," replied Christian, as he turned his tanned face to Marcocito and regarded him with a gentle expression. "I have been sent here as He Who is yet to Come. I will be with you for only a little while."

Mario and Marcocito nodded, even though they did not comprehend his meaning.

They simply did not know what to do next.

Christian, fully anticipating their confusion, smiled and with convincing authority said, "Come, help me to shore." Letting go of the edge of the rock, he steadied himself and moved slowly, parallel to the jetty. With the incoming tide, he held his arms out of the water with his chest slightly forward, his chin and face turned upward. In a gesture that was borne in his soul, Christian clasped his hands together in sudden realization of his reality and gave thanks to those who had made his safe landing possible. He felt overwhelmed by the meaning of this first contact. Looking at this humble representation of mankind on the beach and on the road and the hill beyond, the reality of the mission and the significance of shepherding this small flock filled Christian with great joy.

# PART TWO – THE POPE AT SAINT PETER'S CATHEDRAL

## The Morning of The Return

# His Holiness, Pope Damasus III – The Holy Father, Juan Carlos Gutiérrez
## April 2035

His Holiness, the successor of Peter, was the one upon whose shoulders blame could be easily placed. Juan Carlos Gutiérrez had, at the onset of his papacy, been the longed-for agent of spiritual change. Many now thought him to have been beloved, but ineffectual, in a broken world. For those who remained skeptical over the validity of the amazing event on Contadora Island, Pope Damasus III would be linked to the small historical group that, through the centuries, considered possible candidates for the title of the "anti-Christ." But, on this critical morning, the Pontiff Juan Carlos Gutiérrez was also a mortal man experiencing personal agony.

Juan Carlos would soon celebrate a papal mass. Despite the possibility of catastrophe destroying *The Return*, as pope he had no direct influence in the detailed planning. He was protected as much as possible by the others, and outside the mental anguish that had become a constant companion, he carried on his duties, with little change to his day-to-day life. Juan Carlos stayed the course in Catholic teaching and Canonical law but with increasing distress, watched his world change around him.

Canon Law was never a best seller. Dry and tedious in its rules for the Catholic Church, Canon Law held little interest for the masses, causing uninformed criticism of doctrine and dogma by many.

As Pope, Juan Carlos refused to acquiesce to the ever-present din of opposition for the Church's traditional policies. He carried on the policies of his predecessors. Although they were labeled as archaic and lacking compassion, he remained loyal to the historic dictums of Canon Law, even with his own soul on the precipice of disaster.

The Pope, as the "Universal Church's" ruler, has sovereign and absolute power— not by elective right, but by *divine right* ordained by God as per the Canon Law. Papal conclaves convene only to designate a new Pope. The electing Cardinals constituting the conclave have no other powers. It is impossible for them to make a mistake while guided through the selection of a new Pope by the Holy Spirit.

But in the agony of consenting to *The Return*, Pope Juan Carlos had contravened every law, historical ecclesiastic dissertation, and his own encyclicals, as well as of those before him. Still, he clung to the hope of eternal mercy and forgiveness.

Other than in small pockets of a now-savage world, Juan Carlos' search to rekindle the Faith had been dismal. In accepting *The Return,* Juan Carlos had accepted an incomparable risk. Long ago he chose to take the chance that *might* pull an insane world back to a higher level of worldly conduct. *Would chaos diminish when the world learned of the event? Could the new Word rescue the weak and the 'fallen away' and cause them to reaffirm the basic values of humankind? Would those now empty of faith return to God?* This good and holy man, this Pope Damasus III, was convinced that he *must* try. When all had been set into motion twenty years ago, Juan Carlos accepted that his commitment to humankind depended entirely upon the success of *The Return*.

"Come, my children," the Pontiff spoke to the entourage that stood in respectful silence, waiting with him for the cue to process to the altar. "Let us go in the grace and forgiveness of God." He cut his pre-mass prayer short and moved into place.

Entering Saint Peter's basilica, there was the usual noisy scuffle by those vying for a position that would allow a glimpse of the Holy Father. Worshippers stood on their chairs, forbidden camera lights illuminated the magnificent sanctuary, and the already uneven rows of chairs slid across the marble floor to become even more disorderly. It was obvious why Saint Peter's used cheap chairs. Civilized behavior deteriorated as tourists clamored for a clear shot of His Holiness and temporarily lost any sense of reverence for the Pontiff.

Juan Carlos Gutiérrez had had many blessings in his life—he was the first Latino pope, His Holiness Pope Damasus III, the Bishop of Rome, and the Vicar of Christ. But now he was a thoroughly troubled man, as he made his way down the center aisle of Saint Peter's, resplendent in his cloak and vestments. He and his entourage entered from a secure and guarded elevator on the right side of the nave near Michelangelo's heart- wrenching sculpture of *La Pietà*. Mary now held her dead son behind bulletproof glass to protect further destructive acts by deranged humans who, Christians are taught, are created in the image and likeness of God.

Juan Carlos proceeded slowly toward the altar, escorted by cardinals, priests, and altar servers. Some acolytes held ornate candlesticks. Other solemn-faced attendants carefully grasped censers of incense by a chain in their left hands. The column moved together through the open corridor, created and protected by the Swiss Guards, brilliant in their medieval ceremonial uniforms. Most worshipers were able to see the Pope's aristocratic and handsome features clearly, but all too briefly.

As he gently smiled and blessed the throngs, Pope Damasus' mind was far away. He thought of his Colombian homeland, bringing to mind difficult relationships with the diverse Latin American governments in their never-ending struggle against drugs, insurgencies, crime, corruption and killings. *Always the endless killings,* Juan Carlos shuddered.

Violent opposition groups were forever in armed conflict in a complex world of nations. As one leader would emerge and mature, he would often present as a Gandhi-like leader, concerned with poverty and hopelessness. He would become the new hope. After induction into office, he would soon be drawn into the quagmire of bureaucracy, lost in the very corruption he had campaigned against. As he moved up the political ladder—and after subjugation by money and influence— the path of peace would disappear. The promised change did not take place; disillusionment followed; and a jaded electorate turned its back on the legitimate political process as the ranks of the insurgency swelled once again. The pattern went on.

Juan Carlos glanced around at the overwhelming magnificence of Saint Peter's. *What, oh Lord Jesus, humble carpenter, son of an even humbler carpenter, would you say in reaction to the wealth of this tiny, exquisite city, isolated and serene in a chaotic world? What would you say to me about the priceless surroundings along this short journey to your altar?* He raised his eyes and looked about the cathedral. He had learned to tune out the crowd and to allow the artist in himself to take over, if only briefly. Juan Carlos could never resist the celebrated genius surrounding him—the rich works of painters, carvers, weavers, and sculptors—all created to "glorify God." *In truth, it is nothing but 'merchandise,'* he thought, *deemed worthy enough to grace these spaces.*

He looked about as though seeing it for the first time. His eyes rested on the alabaster window above the chair of Saint Peter. The window, surrounded by golden clouds and angels flying between rays of light, was divided into twelve sections to honor the Apostles who carried the words of the Gospel throughout the world. Juan Carlos knew the scene represented the unchanging gospel of the Holy Spirit, portrayed as a dove in the center of the window, flying along the span of the centuries to accompany and guide its Church. The sight of the chair of Peter, symbolizing continuity of the doctrine and promising infallibility, now stabbed at Juan Carlos' heart. *Will our Beloved Church triumph over the inherent sin in the event to take place, as it has done so over heresies throughout the centuries? Am I not sponsoring a false glorification of God, that which is taking place far away as I walk this path?* The Pope continued down the long aisle, immersed in his dismal thoughts and barely aware of the unruly audience.

By the time the Pope reached the end of the aisle, he felt a familiar dizziness. The structure of the apse was second nature, and he managed to cover the uncertainty of his footing, as his tall frame ascended the marble steps. He regained his balance and pressed his palms against the linens on top of the altar. Singling out faces in the crowd, Juan Carlos tried to clear his mind but could not ignore increasing pain in his shoulder and arms. *Fatigue,* he told himself. *When Easter is completed, when the mission is a quiet fact or a colossal failure, I will retreat for a few days—Castel Gondolfo perhaps, or home to Colombia.* His thoughts trailed off as fatigue and discomfort increased.

Thousands of dilapidated metal chairs scraped on the marble floor. Juan Carlos grimaced in pain but carried on, aware of the eyes upon him—children, young men, women, families, the old and infirm—all had their hopes fastened upon him. His appearance stood in contrast to photos of the past when he moved among humanity with vitality and confidently delivered his unswerving moral message. *Now,* he thought, looking at their concerned faces, *I have no more messages. I can only send Christ back to you and pray that he will be successful where I have failed.*

Cardinal Diego Hernandez, the Pope's Secretary of State, watched uneasily from the side of the altar. Having noticed the anxiety in His Holiness earlier at breakfast, Diego knew that Juan Carlos was preoccupied. He showed it. They all had endured it, of course. Conversation had been stilted for days, as Diego and Father Kennedy avoided further discussion with the Pope about *The Return.* The three had looked at each other with deep intensity prior to proceeding down the aisle. Diego detected, or thought he did, that Juan Carlos had changed his mind and wanted to abort the mission. But the players here and across the oceans knew cancellation was no longer an option. Diego silently prayed. *Oh God, our Father, help us.*

The Pope, the Cardinal, the General, and the priest, all recounted the risks being taken and the realities that brought them to this moment—a world turbulence largely caused by multitudes who fiercely resisted all attempts to instill peace. Century after weary century, resistance had mounted and become more and more destructive as complex western technology was expropriated for evil purposes. Juan Carlos had accepted the reality of the appalling human condition in its blind rush toward disaster and was convinced to act. The gamble of *The Return* had to be right! Since the planners' first tentative meetings, little had changed within nations. Indeed, fear and hatred had grown. The hope and promise of the new millennium had been washed away in blood. In the twenty years it took to select, raise, educate, and train Christian to become the returning savior, none of man's efforts at diplomacy or conflict had resulted in lasting peace anywhere.

As Pope, Juan Carlos had long tried to overcome the pretext that *in the name of God,* young Jews and Arabs continued to slaughter one another; that *in the name of God,* African and Arab tribes wiped each other out with excruciating cruelty; and that *in the name of God,* Islamic extremists cut off thousands of human heads and raped, tortured, and stoned women simply because they tried to be women.

Who were these fanatics, clinging to dusty countries of savage wilderness? Rather than work toward progress, they would destroy, ruin the very land and life they longed for and yet professed to hate. *Peace meant surrender and death, so peace was not an option.* The rhetoric of co-existence was lost on a people who believed that, without a *true* Messiah, there was no way to peace on earth. *Peace on Earth* was now a meaningless concept, revived annually by increasingly fewer Christians celebrating the birth of Jesus Christ.

*God, my God, which side holds your favor today?* Diego Hernandez had heard his pope agonize. *Was it ever possible to have peace instead of war in the name of God? How could the site of the origin and the intent of great religions have inspired such monstrous deeds throughout the Christian, Jewish and Muslim lands?* Cardinal Hernandez recalled squeezing his eyes shut and shuddering at the same conflicts renewed over the centuries. *Nothing has changed. Nothing ever really changes, and now my 'Papa' Juan Carlos, the latest in a long line of popes has been as unsuccessful as those before him. Oh God,* Diego said to himself, *will we be forgiven for our well-intended action? Will it solve anything? Father, show us the way.*

"In the name of the Father, and of the Son, and of the Holy Spirit," Pope Damasus began, his voice strong as mass commenced, and he performed the familiar sign of the cross. Thousands replied, "Amen." The Pope, his arms stretched to embrace the crowds, reawakened the pain. "The grace of our Lord Jesus Christ and the love of God and the fellowship of the Holy Spirit be with you all." And they replied, "And also with you." Progressing through the Penitential Rite, asking mercy and forgiveness for sins, Juan Carlos realized that this would be his final petition for forgiveness for what was to come. A choir began to sing "Glory to God in the highest and peace to His people on earth." Then, shortly after his homily, Juan Carlos began the Liturgy of the

Eucharist, that part of mass in which the preparation of bread and wine is completed. The entire congregation sang the Preface Acclamation "Holy, Holy, Holy "

As the mass approached the Acclamation, Juan Carlos struggled with distractions—haunting images in a mind that for so long had been filled with spirituality and love for his God and for mankind. Now, the Pope felt helpless. Uninvited memories filled his mind, as the images of infants and toddlers with bulging bellies, skeletal bodies of men, and the hanging dried breasts of women darted in front of his lids. "Your Lord is kind and merciful," he had told lifeless sunken eyes throughout Africa.

Juan Carlos had pondered the power of "lust." The human sex drive was a gift from God that drove pitiful creatures in Somalia, Liberia, Ethiopia and other countries during an African tour. *How could they physically 'want' one another,* wondered Juan Carlos, noting their emaciated frames, their rotted teeth, and their eyes covered with flies? *Did they love?* The human coupling was an unstoppable urge, like hunger. But lust was the only urge they could fulfill. The rest only a desperate struggle for survival.

"And *your* God—your heavenly Father above—is always with you to bring you comfort," he had said to the thousands of open mouths, hoping for a credible kernel of spiritual food as much as for the real thing.

He thought of the empty gaunt faces in Africa. The Pope saw no God there, but he ministered to them in fear and reverted to the pre-Vatican II philosophy that offered only a promise of heaven to the poor. *What else was there to say?*

"Take heart, my brothers and sisters, for the rewards of heaven are great. Your heavenly Father will not abandon you. Keep your faith and share it with each other," he admonished, as their initial curiosity over his presence among them faded into stony indifference at his hollow words in a world of words.

During his last trip to America, he was briefed on the alarming trend of *no* religious affiliation; to the closing of catholic schools, to the diminishing numbers of priests and the vanishing orders of the catholic 'sisterhood' of women. Reaching out to AIDS victims in hospital wards, the pope saw the watery eyes of men, women, and children losing their life's essence. They watched him cynically, searching for some message of hope, some forgiveness, some understanding which was not there. Dying men, many whose loins ached for only another male, did not understand his message. Loathing *this* world of intolerance and ignorance, Juan Carlos blessed those for whom judgment was passed before birth and sins paid for by the very act of living and wasting in a slow death. *Is there a chance of heaven for these people? Is this abomination just a joke, a misunderstanding—whose joke—whose misunderstanding?*

*Why must the rampant sexual deviations of the world be thrust at my holy office? My Church's constant, adamant denouncements of homosexuality force recognition of my own struggle with sexual desire. How detached can I be? Where is the mercy for me, a mere mortal driven by global circumstance to ever more and more sexual conversation, sexual speculation, sexual behavior—without fulfillment? What about me, Lord? Are there no issues more important?*

Instinctively jerking himself back to reality, Pope Damasus III looked up at the expectant worshipers and voiced clearly, "Let us proclaim the mystery of faith." The audience reverently responded, "Christ has died, Christ has risen, Christ will come again."

Looking out over the crowd, the Pope thought about the proclamation, repeated so often. *Christ has died, Christ has risen, and Christ will come again Do they believe*

*it? Who said it first? Christ himself? What body, laboring over the question of what to include in the 'ordinary' of the Mass, determined that the faithful required such constant reinforcement—like a child learning his multiplication tables—in order to make Christ stick?*

His Holiness pondered the reaction if this congregation knew that very soon a new *Jesus* would actually arrive! This worried Pope felt a small surge of pleasure, as he visualized one final time the exuberant image of a great success. Although riddled with doubt and guilt over the years, he had allowed himself the occasional release of expressing this fantasy in several paintings now resting in the studio in his apartment.

The relief was short-lived. In the next instant, His Holiness, Pope Damasus, felt a shooting pain across his shoulders and down his arms. The suddenness of the massive attack allowed only brief time for denial. Clutching at the altar of Saint Peter's for the lasttime, Juan Carlos struggled to stay upright but acknowledged the pull of death as he was unable to stop the buckling of his legs and the loss of feeling in his hands. Cardinal Hernandez bolted over the altar and caught him as he sagged. A muffled cry rippled through the crowd. Some rose in alarm, while others fell to their knees and crossed themselves. The Swiss Guards, their awkward halberds useless to strike this invisible foe, could do little but form a line of defense at the base of the altar

In Diego's embrace, Juan Carlos watched a fading world. A blurry vision of Michelangelo's "Creation" on the Sistine Chapel ceiling came into view. He saw Michelangelo's faith and his grasp of the human body—the image and likeness of God. He loved and envied the passion that allowed Michelangelo to elucidate God in a painting. As his vision faded, he had one last hope for the glorious success of *The Return*. Diego held him as he uttered, "Why today of all days? God forgive us, Diego." Juan Carlos' body slumped heavily as his life force left his body.

Only seconds earlier, with tears welling once again, Nina Shelky had averted her watery eyes from the Pope and the altar. She raised them to Bernini's 17th Century bronze *Baldacchino,* an ornamental canopy atop spiral columns rising from the main papal altar. It was high above Juan Carlo's body but still far beneath Michelangelo's basilica dome.

The sudden unspeakable intrusion of gasps of horror and cries of despair filling the cathedral broke into Nina's reverie, causing her to shut her eyes to force them away. She instinctively crouched in defense and then cautiously peered between the weaving bodies in front of her, as the congregants tried to grasp the circumstances.

The commotion in front of the altar was chaotic. Figures rushed toward the collapsed pontiff. Unable to stop the call of destiny, Juan Carlos' body now lay atop the confession of Saint Peter, where the body of the Prince of Apostles reposed deep beneath the glittering marble surface of the altar.

Luís bolted forward from the end of the first row to aid his brother. The guards parted for him, and during the short sprint, Luís felt both love and loss while the fear of his brother's demise oddly enhanced his certainty of success of the event now taking place far away. So attuned to his brother's thinking, Luís had sensed Juan Carlos' doubt just moments before. The Pope's collapse was his final acquiescence—a final gift to his brother. Juan Carlos would now watch over the realization of their venture. Luís was certain. Calm, as he envisioned God's mercy in His judgment on His servant, Pope Damasus III, Luís reverted to childhood beliefs—that his beloved brother already had his place in eternity and was witnessing events from afar.

His cassock slightly impeding his speed across the altar to his stricken Pope, Father Jonathan Kennedy tried to cope with the reality. *Is my pope dead? He can't be dead!* Jonathan felt the stab in his soul, as the past twenty years rushed across his mind, and at the same instant, begged for success of the mission that would vindicate his Pontiff's faith in all of them. He exchanged a knowing glance with General Luís Gutiérrez. *Knowing what?* Jonathan asked of no one, detecting Luís' emotional mix of sadness and triumph. *Where was Christian at this moment?*

Cardinal Hernandez knelt at the head of his Pope. He saw the now-distant gaze of the Holy Father. The Pontiff was gone, his gaze now peaceful. Diego had often watched his friend in thought and always believed that Juan Carlos was able to penetrate the invisible wall at the edge of the universe. He felt that now, as he witnessed Juan Carlos pass through into eternity. *And see what?* Diego wondered, *Approval for The Return from God the Father?*

Diego looked back a few pews, into the face of an older and now more beautiful Countess Serina Caputo de la Guardia—Serina, whose bank accounts had been offered up to finance *The Return*. Her eyes brimming with tears at the agony she knew her beloved Cardinal was experiencing, Serina saw something else on his face and knew they were both already contemplating the uncertain future.

Juan Carlos Gutiérrez lay in death on the elaborate altar, high above the bones of Saint Peter, as thousands wept and prayed, confused as to what they should do next. At the same moment, on the other side of the world, Christian was slowly descending near a small island where on the beach below, a meager band of untouched and unaware humanity awaited him.

In her later notes, Nina Shelky contemplated the sudden death of Juan Carlos Gutierrez. She wondered if the Pope, this Damasus III, had been asked, would he have changed the circumstances of his death? She also noted in her jottings, *Did the Holy Father implore God on my behalf before he died? As he died? When he died? I feel forced to beg the seemingly childish question. What if there was nothing?*

# PART THREE – THE PATH TO HOPE

# FINDING PARADISE
## Contadora Island - April 2001

Marcos Rivera's most impressive trait was his relative height in comparison to other islanders. He stood over six feet tall. His straight black hair, neatly combed back from his face settled at the nape of his neck. His eyes held a hint of a lighter shade, a distant genetic trait, in a strong face with a well-defined mouth and narrow nose. Prepared for his travel to the mainland this morning, Marcos wore gray slacks and the typical casual dress shirt of Panamá; the cotton *guayabera*. With long-sleeves, elegantly embroidered white *guayaberas* were perfectly acceptable at the best parties. The tropical heat made them ideal when worn outside trousers. Men were relieved when *Guayabera* was designated as the preferred dress on printed invitations. Occasionally Marcos wore a coat and tie but only for official events in the *Presidencia*. Otherwise, constituents thought starched and ironed *guayabera* to be quite proper for their island legislator.

Growing up, Marcos often acted as spokesperson on behalf of the island people; an intergenerational gift from his father, who had cultivated the friendship of visiting dignitaries and businessmen over the years. Mario never pushed, but using his gentle charisma, managed to get his son into first-rate mainland schools. With his own natural ambition and drive, Marcos netted a scholarship for studies in political science and agriculture at the University of Virginia. The result was a highly-educated young man who missed his islands, and with hopes of contributing to their wellbeing, returned home after graduation. Marcos felt dedication to these specks of nature tossed across the Pacific Ocean and to their sparse primitive societies. Armed with and education and much to Mario's pride, Marcos applied his brain and his physical labor to various construction and development projects. He stood out and was soon elected to represent his small island constituency of a few thousand souls spread over several of the two hundred or so islands.

Marcos' comprehensive efforts toward island improvements were popular. With respect for his demonstrated effectiveness in lobbying, party officials granted him concessions for the islands—clinics, electrical plants, wells and desalinization plants, agricultural assistance in crop transfer and livestock, and the increased purchase of seafood by mainland restaurants. All were initiated because of his political acumen.

Leaders within the political parties urged Marcos to strive for a Ministry position. Some saw the government concessions to the islands as reasonable and as generating potential favors in return Fully aware of the political game, most of Marcos' requests were granted.

The regenerative effect upon the lagging economies of the islands reflected favorably upon Marcos. Within the traditional give and take of politics, he assisted his mainland associates whenever possible. Now in relative isolation, the islands' lack of greedy demands allowed Marcos to remain neutral and to avoid, as much as possible, the inevitable heated debates so prevalent in the chambers of the Legislative Palace.

Today on this quiet dawn, Marcos Rivera, now holding the title of *Ministro,* observed his father and son on the beach below, happy to enjoy the sight before starting his workday. The memories of twenty-five years ago soon worked their way to the front of his mind—the scent of her, the sound of her voice, her laughter.

"*Permiso,* sorry to bother you again, *Senor* Marcos, I"

Marcos looked up from his paper and held his hand up with a knowing smile.

"Again? Who is it this time?" the young legislator queried the even younger messenger, who brought requests from the public affairs office for interviews about the islands.

"It's a lady reporter." He shrugged his shoulders. "She wants to talk about the treaty."

"Doesn't she know the treaty has already taken place?" asked Marcos, seated in his office and now mildly exasperated but still smiling at the young messenger.

"I don't know, but I think so. She's *muy bonita, Honorable Diputado* Rivera," he said, addressing the young legislator formally in hopes of avoiding his annoyance.

"Okay, okay, *gracias, chico*," said Marcos kindly, taking the request from the young boy. He would adjust his schedule to be on the island the following day when the reporter arrived by plane.

Waiting for Nina Shelky's plane, Marcos leaned against the wooden railing at the base of the staircase leading up to the island's small terminal. He watched the Canadian Twin Otter touch down on Contadora's undersized runway. Marcos had learned to fly the planes at an early age and at twenty-five often wished he could do so more often.

Marcos was the youngest member ever to be elected to the Legislature. As the chosen leader on the islands, he recognized the public relations value of a good story to both Panamá and to the journalists bent on prizing out another tale about Contadora's role in the negotiations that brought about the Panamá Canal Treaties. The treaties, formally signed in 1978, gradually reverted the historic and vital waterway to full Panamanian control, assumed at the end of the 20th Century.

Marcos had conducted many such interviews and was unenthusiastic about another, but he always complied. He had work to finish, but it would have to wait. He watched the familiar sight of the approaching plane lifting and gliding in the soft crosswinds toward the end of the runway before it gently touched down. The plane taxied for a short distance and stopped a few yards from where Marcos stood. With engines shut down, the door opened, and the small staircase was rolled over and secured. The few passengers emerged.

At the sight of the slender woman alighting from the plane, Marcos felt an unexpected rush—a physical jolt. As she descended the steps, her blond hair blowing in the morning breeze, Nina Shelky was beyond beautiful to Marcos.

For her part, Nina felt captivated by the enchanting view of the small distant islands from the air just moments after takeoff from Panamá City. She thrilled at the sight of paradisiacal beaches. Her imagination conjured Eden, and she wondered if there existed a place in which somebody finds perfect happiness. She had noticed only a few people on the beaches as they circled Contadora Island and approached the runway from the south. Touching down on the somewhat neglected runway on the stretch of high ground above the beach, Nina could see a man leaning against a railing at the side of the runway. As the plane came to a stop, she continued staring at him, even as she released her seat buckle. There seemed to be no other person to meet her, and she was startled at his broad smile as she descended the few steps from the plane.

"*Senorita* Shelky?" Marcos queried hopefully, approaching Nina. He felt disturbed and flustered at the sight of her. As they met and shook hands, Nina also struggled with words.

"It's very kind of you to receive me, *Senor Diputado* Rivera," she said, experiencing a mild shock of awareness at her reaction to this man. Marcos bowed slightly, already engulfed in the inexplicable magic of this woman.

The attraction traveled back and forth on an unseen path between them. The mysterious fire of human desire was instantaneous, as this man and the island merged into a sweet oneness for Nina. The next phase would soon follow. A heavy curtain of desire would drape itself around her, and she would reach through it repeatedly to draw Marcos into her body and into her mind. Marcos and Nina soon gave up most of their individuality as they lost themselves in one another. Much later they tried unsuccessfully to define the immediate engulfing magnetism.

They talked during the short ride in Marcos' open car to the small house Nina had rented for her visit. Discussing the islands' past and pointing out various plants and birds, Nina had difficulty concentrating on anything but the strong bronze profile next to her. Showing her over the property, which sat on a small hill above a white beach, Marcos hesitated. "*Senorita* Shelky, I have some papers to clear, but could we continue this evening? Would you have supper with me?

The house is stocked with good wine and cheese. I'll bring a fish that will have just jumped out of the sea," he smiled shyly, "and *ceviche* and fresh fruit."

Nina looked into his face and briefly considered the outcome. Marcos was irresistible, and Nina's sense of propriety had all but collapsed. "Thank you, I would enjoy that very much." She watched him drive away and entered the small house to unpack. After showering she explored the kitchen and found it well appointed and stocked.

Not much later, Marcos reappeared. They sat on the wide veranda and with the intoxicating sounds of waves below, Nina managed to take some notes over wine and *ceviche*, fish marinated with lime and onion served in small pastry cups. They continued to talk while fresh snapper was broiled over the outside grill with the setting sun and the darkening view of the ocean and the islands beyond. Marcos picked a lemon from a tree in the front yard while Nina prepared a salad from greens and tomatoes that Marcos had brought along. Squeezing wedges of the lemon over the fish, Nina savored the simple fresh food and the man seated across from her.

Later, taking a blanket from his car and toting small splits of cold champagne, Marcos led Nina down a cement staircase that curved against large ancient rocks and onto the beach. Lit by a full moon, Nina saw magic in the silvery light illuminating the small particles of silica in the sand, as Marcos talked about the islands with more than his usual affection. Exposing his belief that he was part of the sand and the ocean—that he felt as "one" with these islands—Marcos spoke earnestly, trying to convey to Nina his passion for belonging here. Seductive but shy glances were shared, and in the seconds following the disappearance of a shooting star, conversation halted, and they reached for one another. He found her lips, and as her lack of control very briefly crossed Nina's mind, the outcome no longer mattered.

Sun-drenched days followed, with walks across the island's beaches and child- like play in the clear waters. As they explored each other, Nina saw this new world through the eyes, mind, and body of Marcos Rivera. The mystery of fulfillment during ecstatic late nights left them dazed, even as conversation expanded. In the basic give and take, generosity by each was dominant. They couldn't give enough to each other, and they ignored their strikingly different existences. Brushing aside the private thoughts of an unworkable future, their days were blissful.

In lovemaking with Marcos, Nina experienced a small exquisite death, placing within her the promise of a more perfect world. She reveled in happiness, felt exhilarated, and told Marcos that her unrestrained love and, yes, her lust for him, were the greatest gifts she had ever known.

Nina's feelings poured from her pen, and as Marcos left her to complete his own work, her formal report was pulled together on her laptop. Handwritten notes and prose and the magnetism of this island were written on clean sheets at the side of her computer.

They were to be later merged and edited for a separate piece. These words felt in such depth seemed somehow inspired by heaven above, an added tender description of the islands she had not anticipated. For now they were private.

Since early treaty negotiations had taken place on Contadora Island during the 1970s, Nina had wanted to capture the setting in her report. In her pre-trip research, she learned that the retired US Ambassador, Ellsworth Bunker, a career diplomat, headed the first US negotiating team.

The team had stayed in rented homes on Contadora and conducted discussions walking along its pristine beaches. Nina noted this in her report:

*"Being part of the team for the Panamá Canal Treaties was about as good as it gets in the world of diplomatic negotiations. Here, Diplomacy does not demand stuffy clothing and formal settings. Wading in clear warm waters and walking along soft sandy shores must have provided a most harmonious venue for the give and take of treaty discussions. A small hilltop building, which served as the island's theater and church, was occasionally used for the sake of propriety—an image for the official meetings attended by the press. At these meetings, shirts and shoes were expected. At other times, accepted dress was shorts or a bathing suit, sunglasses and sun block. Sandals were optional "*

Nina Shelky didn't finish her official assignment until she returned to Washington. Flying back to Contadora whenever she could, she added to her unofficial writings about the Garden of Eden she had discovered. While in Washington the words spilled out, commanding her attention, and taking her back again and again. When it was finally pulled together, the resulting piece was sent to Nina's friend Bernardo Carpenello, a news colleague in Rome.

Recognizing Nina's sensuous tone in the article, Bernardo sent it on to a small Italian publisher who labored trying to sell a small selection of Italian magazines. The young Italian set the English article aside, and in the abundance of material in his small office, it was ignored for some time. When he eventually picked it up, pleased with himself for his command of English, he read and then read again. Very much a romantic, the young editor was captivated and set about translating Nina's rapt description and inserted the article into a travel journal. In the process, attribution was lost, and in time Bernardo forgot about it.

Unaware of the translation, Nina had no knowledge that the Vatican Cardinal Diego Hernandez had read her passionate dissertation, nor did the very *Latin* Italian who published the *anonymous* piece have any notion of its power in the subsequent assessments and scrutiny of Contadora Island. Leading Diego and later Luís and Jonathan to its shore, the choice of Contadora was thus a providential piece of the puzzle of a great Vatican gamble.

Marcos was not mentioned by name in either of Nina's writings, but he remained within her. As the years went on and she was promoted to positions of greater responsibility, she would often hold the unique blue-green stones she kept on her desk and by her bedside. She easily recalled where she had picked up each one from the beaches of Contadora. They helped her relive the beauty she and Marcos had shared.

After reading Nina's article on the plaza in Milano, Cardinal Diego Hernandez contemplated the unknown author. *Under what circumstances had it been written?* He never resolved his question, and queries to the publisher were unsuccessful. In his mind, Diego chose to believe the discovery of the island a gift of almost divine guidance. The vivid descriptions of Contadora, of the isolation, the climate, and the characteristics of the inhabitants beckoned him. Once the island was quietly investigated, it was apparent that it was the perfect place to stage *The Return*. Unable to acknowledge the unknown author's role, the Cardinal believed that if *The Return* succeeded in changing a world so jaded and renewed the sense of Christ's presence in even small segments of humanity, he or she would be eternally rewarded for the enchanting description of the island.

The impassioned relationship between Marcos and Nina lasted intermittently over several years. Nina traveled back and forth from her Washington news job, encased in her desire and in time, hating the gradual intrusion of reality that chipped away at the edges of their differing lives. They knew that at this stage of their lives, commitment would end in failure. Although Nina's mind tried to shut out any thought of the relationship's not working, she knew her deep obsession for this man blocked out logic. In time slivers of common sense made their way into her mind. Timing was decisive, and their timing was off. After the final departure the physical longing remained. *Their time,* wondered Nina, *could it be postponed?*

Marcos remained deeply in love with Nina and for years shunned any suggestions of matrimony. Now in his 40's, and at the urging of his father, Marcos entered into marriage with his childhood friend and companion, Teresa Valdez. A skilled lover, a lesson learned and a title earned in the folds and curves of Nina's body, Marcos was tender with his wife but uninspired. His gentleness was calming to Teresa, and at an advanced age for childbearing in the islands, she gave birth to their son Marcocito.

While their lives were devoted to their child, Marcos fought his memories and resisted the ever-present temptation to reach out to Nina. Even with the added physical appeal from the appearance of silver in his thick hair, Marco's stark good looks never aroused Teresa's jealousy. She knew a little about the blonde American journalist and was fully aware that Nina Shelky swam through Marco's dreams. Often observing her husband on the beach, Teresa knew that his gaze at the blue-green sea held memories unknown to her. While Teresa was not an educated woman, she understood that the presence of another woman in Marcos' mind might be distracting but it kept him faithful to his island family. Marcos expanded their hilltop home to provide rooms for Marcocito and Mario with a wide veranda to incorporate a commanding view of Playa Manta below.

If Teresa wished for more, she kept such wishes locked in her heart. She maintained a cheerful attitude and enjoyed the importance of her status among the islanders.

Shortly after the birth of Marcocito, Teresa became ill with a seasonal flu from a simple exchange of words with a store clerk, who handled Teresa's purchases during a rare trip to Panamá City. The determined and lethal virus had danced off the moist chubby hands of a sick child onto those of the clerk. Needing her job, the clerk ignored her own symptoms and carried on despite aches and fever. She transferred her illness to the innocent and unknowing woman from the islands.

A few days later back at her home, Teresa tried to convince herself that the fever and chills she had developed would pass. She alleviated her discomfort with cool cloths against her head and cups of strong lemongrass tea. She drank mixtures of honey and vinegar and hot soup. Her fever grew, and despite her protests Marcos brought a doctor in from the mainland, who urged a transfer to a city hospital. But an adamant Teresa scoffed at his concern and begged Marcos to let her remain on the island. Teresa hoped her natural resistance and her island remedies would see her through, but within a day sensed that she was probably incapable of fighting the viral enemy within her.

She was correct. Her lungs filled rapidly with fluid and a day later Teresa Rivera died in an afternoon sleep at the age of 40, while Marcos was catching his plane from the mainland. Mario, on a pearl-diving trip to islands south of Contadora, was unaware of Teresa's illness and death. Her son, Marcocito was at her bedside with his aunt, Teresa's sister, and even in his childhood recognized that he was losing his mother.

Through the months that followed, Mario and Marcos struggled with their grief with a child to comfort them. Sharing the loss, they fell into a pattern of one or the other shouldering the pain. Each helped to lessen the burden of sadness for the other. Teresa's island family rallied and helped raise Marcocito, who seemed wise for his young years. Time moved on.

On this Holy Week dawn, Marcos, now 55, stood on the hill above the beach of Playa Manta. He treasured the sight of the people he loved and inwardly accepted that he would never be over Nina. He was happy in this small kingdom of islands that were his responsibility; b t her long absence detracted from what had long ago been paradise for him.

In the next instant, Marcos was confronted with the growing speck of light in the yet-dark dawn sky. He knew he should shout at his father and small son to alert them, to warn them, but did nothing. Nina swirled in his thoughts along with the struggle to determine his next move. He tried to deny what he soon recognized as a human form gently floating down from the sky and could feel his father and son's fear.

Once again, his thoughts reached out to Nina. *Is it Christ? It can't be Jesus Christ. It is Christ!"* Marcos felt he was speaking to Nina. She remained in his mind and heart even as his hands came together in desperate prayer. In seconds, Marcos sensed his soul react with understanding and acceptance of the sight before him. He visualized eternity and his place in it.

Marcos knew then that whatever was to happen on this morning, it would change everything—not just within the boundaries of Contadora Island but well beyond. The urge to act, to respond to the inborn instinct to protect his father and son was unnecessary—Marcos realized that whatever was to come, there was nothing to fear.

*Playa Manta, this small speck of white beach on an island occupying so little space on this battered planet, will now hold great meaning. It will become a name of significance for Christians and non-Christians, greater than Lourdes, Medjigore, Fatima, or Guadeloupe. It will be studied, researched, combed, and picked over by later generations seeking its secrets. As those involved in The Return pass to eternity, the depth of the mystery will be left to the doubters, who will not believe that good can prevail. The small island will become a beacon of hope and curiosity as it nourishes the spiritually starved.*

*Nina Shelky Washington DCJanuary 2036*

# THE NEW DISCIPLES
## Contadora Island - April 2035

Christian, viewed as Jesus, had his initial contact with Mario Rivera and his grandson, Marcocito. With great apprehension, the two now made their way back along the rock ledge. Mario was unable to take his eyes off the figure wading to shore, but Marcocito turned back briefly to look at the spot where they first saw "Jesus" descend. He looked for the glint of sunlight upon metal, which he thought he saw for an instant, but the bright light and the unbelievable sight were all-consuming. Whatever produced that momentary flash had disappeared. Mario and Marcocito picked their way along the ledge, above but now parallel to the wading Christian. Keeping pace with each other, the three arrive on the beach simultaneously

Along with Mario, Marcos, and Marcocito, only a few dozen others observed the spectacle. On the opposite side of the cove from where Mario and Marcocito stood, six men fishing in two small boats from the nearby island of *Granito de Oro* were positioned some two hundred meters off Contadora Island's Manta Beach. At the same time, Pleto Guevara and Jorge Westerlan, the *Cuna* Indian bartender and the Jamaican cook at the sparsely populated hotel located further east at the next beach, were just entering the hotel kitchen to pull off their usual early morning breakfast raid before their work day began. They observed Christian's descent over *Playa Manta* from the kitchen windows. Dumbfounded, they wordlessly dashed from the kitchen onto the edge of the hill in time to watch the final moments and to see the figure slip into the water. They scrambled down the incline and ran along the shoreline. The few guests at the hotel remained asleep.

Pleto and Jorge would tend to them later without revealing Christian's presence. The small numbers of humanity that would interact with Christian recognized immediately that despite their ignorance, they had been *chosen.* They would remain quiet until they knew why.

From the first fishing boat off Playa Manta, the leader of the fishing flotilla, Jorge Emilio Flores, watched the descent. Without hesitation, he softly called out *"Jesus"* at the sight of the heavenly figure floating down just several hundred feet away. With all attention directed skyward, the two primitive boats momentarily bobbed and heaved, bumping into one another. Jorge remained transfixed as he felt inadequate. Intimately familiar with the waters and known for springing into action at any incident, Jorge's common sense told him he was powerless to do more than witness the event.

Jorge's fleet consisted of four fifteen-foot dugouts made from strong island trees with cross benches at bow and stern. Only two were in the water this morning. The third and fourth sprang leaks the day before and were under repair on the beach by their usual crews.

These hardy fishermen spend their days at sea. Their boats are unique. A center crosspiece has a hole under which sits a small iron pail on a block of wood, positioned at the bottom. The pail is refilled daily with wood chips or charcoal for a small fire. A grid of construction wire serves as a grill to cook meat or fish and pots of rice and beans are carried aboard and heated on the fire for the mid-day meal at sea. Jorge eats a lot of rice and beans and his size has earned him the nickname of "Gordo," which has stuck since childhood. It means "fat," but over time has become an endearment and holds no slight.

Ever the entrepreneur, Gordo has an informal agreement with a restaurant in Panamá City for his catch. The agreement, secured only by a handshake, was the result of a chance meeting in the waters off *Granito de Oro* Island. On a fishing outing with friends from the mainland, the restaurateur's boat developed engine trouble, and as they watched the land disappear over the horizon, Gordo appeared in his boat to rescue the now desperate city dwellers, adrift at sea with a dead engine and a radio with a drained battery.

Several bottles of the local beer *Cerveza Panamá* and discussions about fishing followed Gordo's repairs, and they parted in friendship with a verbal contract. Protecting his waters, Gordo's catch improved over the years. With far fewer tourist anglers, the catch was abundant and of consistently good quality. The restaurant had an enviable reputation. Gordo knew the habits of red snapper, bull-nosed dolphin, bonita, wahoo, corvina and the delectable *langostas*, the Pacific variety of clawless lobster. Shrimp were only netted for island consumption, as large fleets of "shrimpers" operated in deeper waters with commercial nets. They were territorial, and Gordo avoided confrontation. His crews fished with nets, poles, and straw basket-like traps woven in various sizes, depending on the prey.

Being a member of Gordo's group was a blessing. Jobs were scarce, and if Gordo found favor in you and you worked hard, your family ate well and shared in the profits.

On this morning, Gordo's fishing crew, Fulito Sanchez and Lucas Perez, unwitting of the new role they would soon play, were hopeful of a bountiful catch. Fulito was the outcome of a brief romance between his island mother and a Scandinavian crewman from a sailing vessel and his physical attributes included pale blue-gray eyes and bleached hair against a deep olive complexion. "Fulito" was yet another nickname, this time for "Erik," which his mother believed was the name of the blue-eyed and blonde Scandinavian who had fathered him. "Fulito" translated as "little Blondie" was handsome, with this compelling physical combination. He adored his mother and never pressed her for details of his father, who long departed was unaware of Fulito's existence.

Fulito and Lucas Perez had been close since childhood. Lucas believed Fulito held some kind of magic, because he looked different from everyone else on their small island. As they grew up, they roamed the uninhabited islands together, and at age fifteen began to take their small boats further into the unexplored southwestern islands of the archipelago. With the boat's small engine they couldn't venture far, but on uninhabited islands they found elongated oysters that produced irregular pearls and rare shells. The pearls were not of a commercial quality, yet were sought-after by tourists during the 1970s and '80s as souvenirs of *Islas de Las Perlas*.

Both Fulito and Lucas had worked at the hotel as waiters and bartenders and enjoyed the attentions of Canadian and European women tourists, who had no qualms over brief holiday affairs with attractive islanders. Many young women reasoned that the concept of sin took a vacation when *they* were on vacation.

Fulito and Lucas made a striking pair. With their complementary coloring and unconscious sensuality, the twosome enjoyed abundant attention from women tourists. They were just teenagers when they began to use their "natural talents" to fill their pockets. With their monetary gains, they built concrete houses for their mothers and sisters. They gave Gordo fishing equipment and bought cigarettes, Panamá Rum, and *Seco*, the clear and potent byproduct of the sugar-making process.

When political machinations on the mainland fouled tourism, a return to isolation and a subsistence existence on the island became a reality. Fulito and Lucas resumed their ancestral fishing vocation while waiting for tourists to return. Now almost thirty years later, they were still waiting—until this morning.

In the second boat, Marcelo Ruiz and Javier Marquez, younger apprentices for Gordo's team, monitored the drop of the sturdy straw basket traps into the water. A skill taught by their mothers in childhood, the traps resemble fat-bottomed jugs that taper into a long thin neck at the top. The woven traps, loosely tied at the wider bottom for access to the catch, become pliable through soaking. The thin neck at the top of the trap is turned inward, forming a smooth tube-like entrance into the cylinder where bait is placed. Shrimp, crabs and the larger langoustines, enter and remain snared by the roughened edges of the inverted reeds inside the neck of the cylinder.

When the traps are later pulled in by twine tied around the center, the bottom is opened, and the catch is transferred to buckets. These remarkable basket traps work well, but the twine to hold them is always maintained carefully in the corrosive salt water. Despite the water's clarity, which allows the men to see approximately twelve feet down, and despite being strong swimmers, they disliked making unnecessary dives to retrieve lost traps.

Marcelo and Javier were in their late teens. Both were born after the islands' commercial decline. They knew only their current, slow-paced and uneventful existence. Few remnants of the wild days remain, and the raucous tales told by Fulito and Lucas sometimes shattered their youthful innocence. The islands now seem fixed in a bygone time, a time when pirates used them as hiding places in earlier centuries. Marcelo and Javier are skeptical of most of the tales, but they love to hear the stories and are a satisfying and wide-eyed audience for Fulito and Lucas. They never saw the boom of construction and development of tiny Contadora. A generation has passed since those halcyon days, when the world courted the tiny island. They have scant knowledge of that era, but their own miraculous era is now at hand.

Along with the construction and tourism, much of the historic Panamá Canal treaties were negotiated on Contadora Island during the 1970s. With the death in 1981 of the strongman dictator and frequent visitor to the island General Omar Torrijos, Panamá lost its luster. Since the island provided General Torrijos a pleasant drinking hole and one more locale for the womanizing dictator's dalliances, he had been generous in providing for its infrastructure. In the power struggle that followed, subsequent leadership ignored the iron-fisted dictator's legacy. Manuel Noriega had taken himself very seriously.

Plagued with a pocked face, small stature, and reputedly unremarkable manhood, he applied a harsh approach and established a reputation for corruption, convenient disposal of his enemies and ballooning drug trafficking. The glory of Contadora and of the nation soon faded.

With Noriega's fall after the 1989 "Just Cause" US invasion, attention focused on the mainland as the implementation of the treaties took precedence. It was a quiet transition, and the valor of the thousands who dug the "big ditch" along with the memory of American forces that operated the wondrous canal and presided over the spotless swath of the Panamá Canal Zone gradually dimmed.

The Pearl Islands returned to a quieter time.

Now, in the faint light of dawn, Marcelo and Javier, ever mindful of their livelihood, hold on to the lines of their traps, even as they freeze in fear at the sight in front of them.

On the beach are more future apostles—Rene Sanchez, Fulito's younger brother, and Raul and Tomas Campos, two teenage nephews of Gordo's who lost their father to illness and were charged with the support of their mother. All apprentices to the small fishing group, this morning busy themselves jostling and joking with one another as they repair holes in the nets. Acting as young men everywhere, and having some limited exposure to films, video games and other electronics during their rare trips to Panamá City, work was not always taken seriously.

But the sight in the dawn sky now fills them with fascination. As Christian grows nearer, however, fear of the unknown grips them. This is no video game. They have nowhere to go. They stand up, clutching the cords of the nets, moving closer together, trembling and expecting disaster. But they do not run away. Nobody does.

Physical purity did not last for long throughout the islands. Innocence was short- lived and normally did not make it through childhood in this primitive environment. Yet, a virginal adoration of this descending man would emanate from Marisol and Ana Velasquez, sisters aged twelve and fifteen, who that morning were carrying out their weekly laundry chores. Poised in the shallow water, they had begun to scour and beat clothes against the rough rocks exposed by the low tide.

Earlier, they had placed the soiled clothes into sheets and tied up the corners. Like their mother and grandmothers before them, Marisol and Ana carried the bundles on their heads with perfect balance, even when walking down the steep hill. Once at the beach, they allowed the clothes to spread out in the shallow water at the left side of the cove where large rocks subdued the tidal currents. Other than losing an occasional sock or headscarf, they could keep track of the colorful wash. Their load consisted of coarse cotton fringed shirts and T-shirts emblazoned with local beer logos and acquired during infrequent trips to the mainland or left behind by visitors. They washed *montuna* skirts, tiers of bright colored cotton with a bottom ruffle worn with simple peasant blouses. These were church and party attire. Jeans and printed stretch pants were now a coveted part of a girl's wardrobe.

Clean clothing was a common island ethic. Despite their poverty, which they didn't recognize as such, certain standards survived the centuries. A fastidious and mostly self-sufficient people, after an initial scouring, Marisol and Ana would pile the wet clothes on their heads once again and walk to the stream of *aqua dulce*, the fresh water that trickled over rocks from a small stream near the beach. The flow was now in the dry season and it took longer to rinse the clothes. The girls were always anxious to get chores done before the heat of the day.

Marisol was first to see the sight above. "Ana, Ana, look! Oh Ana, what is it?" Marisol cries fearfully aware that her little sister might be in danger. Close to Ana, she holds a sheet against them in a protective gesture, while the family wardrobe floats and spreads apart in the water. Their youngest sister, Maria, age 7, and their little brother Antonio, 5, play on the beach as usual, oblivious of their elder siblings' activities until this moment. They hear Anna's first cry. She wants to shout a warning but cannot take her eyes off the figure in the dawn sky.

On the hill above, several women fall to their knees in fear for their families on the beach. Watching and waiting they cannot know their future role, cannot begin to conceive of the celebrity status soon to be theirs. At this instant they have no understanding of their historical mission for good—their destiny.

Most of the other fifty or so inhabitants have slept through Christian's descent.

Interruptions of dreams were brief as sleepy heads turned on their pillows and rested in hammocks. Not yet ready to begin a new day of earthly existence, these islanders slept innocently, unaware that a miraculous event was occurring. The small population would know soon enough however, and despite the few actually witnessing Christian's descent, all would soon feel the disruption to their lives. A disruption calculated to re-humanize and re-Christianize a cynical world, a wrongdoing world.

The tide, the time, the climatic conditions, all had been painstakingly researched for the descent, and the planner's accurately anticipated the actions of the new disciples.

These unlikely individuals, ignorant in their innocence, were to become apostles. Only they would bear witness to the wondrous marvel floating out of the still pre-dawn sky.

They would see this flesh-and-bones man as their "Jesus," and as yet unknowing, they would experience ridicule and close scrutiny as his new disciples. They were the perfect exclusive group, witnessing a colossal wonder. Self-doubt about what they witnessed would be overcome by mutual reassurance. Their story would be told over and over again, and the world would change for the better. At least, that was the goal.

While darkness ebbs on Contadora Island, the morning sun in Rome on this crisp April day is high overhead. At Saint Peter's, participants in the final mass of the Pope witness their pontiff slump to the marble floor of the cathedral's great altar. To some crying in the cathedral will come the scripture warning, *no one knows when his hour will come.* Still the dying Pope occupies only a small niche in their hearts, as they plead to God for their *own* Salvation. Sad and scared, the "Papa" is leaving them, all of them. Those blessed with unquestionable faith, assumed that Pope Damasus would go instantly into paradise, and they prayed for his intercession. Many others doubted the promise of eternal life. Such was the state of the world.

# PART FOUR – CARRYING OUT THE MISSION

# THE NEGEV DESERT IN ISRAEL – THE EVENING BEFORE THE RETURN
## April 2035

On a remote airbase in Israel's Negev Desert some 12 hours before the Pope's final mass in Rome, a small group of highly-trained personnel checked and rechecked their equipment and instruments.

The pilot, Israeli Air Force Brigadier General Avi Noam, now retired from active duty, had been selected years earlier to fly this mission. Dedicated to his country and to the Israeli Air Force, Avi was a true warrior, honed by years of intense combat. Later, time itself became a new enemy as Avi struggled with personal demons. Unable to leave the memories of the terror of war behind, his exhilarating successes in combat missions of earlier wars were overshadowed by what many Jews considered a botched effort and a lack of Israeli resolve in southern Lebanon in 2006. Later fighting never resulted in total victory and frustration within the military ranks was widespread. Plagued by depression, Avi mourned what he considered the loss of his nation's pride and steadfastness. Long ago successes were diluted and lost their meaning.

When presented with his new mission, a mission that promised the prospect of potential world change, Avi reacted with stark disbelief. As he carefully examined General Yakowitz' face, looking for some humor and finding none, he gradually absorbed the incredible information and what was being asked of him.

Even with doubts clouding his mind, Avi trusted Aaron Yakowitz and soon felt alive, filled with renewal. Working through the details of mission planning, he first examined its feasibility. Here he was on unfamiliar ground, as the mission forced what was essentially a regional air force to reach out thousands of miles away and operate without the usual "close-in" logistical support. *Could it be done safely and effectively at such a distance?* he wondered. *Will the world buy this?* Avi had weeks of nagging doubts about the mission's acceptance by the world at large. As he continuously pondered *The Return*, reservations about his role slowly declined. Plunging into the challenges and marveling at the technical accomplishments of Denny Dennison, Avi was won over. The global implications would be known and pondered when the time was right. He concentrated on the tasks ahead and poured his unrestrained energy into assuring success.

He was a fighter pilot, after all, and not a diplomat.

All the thinking had been long ago, and the hour was now upon them. With little knowledge of the others involved, his contacts throughout had been restricted to Aaron Yakowitz, General Gutiérrez, Dr. Denny Dennison, and, of course, Christian—the "star of the show," as Avi envisioned him. Like the rest he had grown to love this courageous young man. Joking remarks during their rigorous training together only slightly camouflaged Avi's fear for Christian's fate. Although he teased Christian and suggested to him that he should remember that Jesus was, in fact, a Jew, his own traditional beliefs ultimately relied on the hope that Christian now represented. For Avi, the only focus now was for success and for lasting peace. Being part of this "long shot" possibility was more fulfilling than any assignment he could imagine.

In the pre-mission silence, Avi sips a cup of strong coffee with Aaron Yakowitz.

Christian has just left them, commenting as he departed, "Have more, General Noam. Unlike those who surrounded Christ in his last hours, filled with this brew, you could not possibly fall asleep on me." Avi laughed, appreciating Christian's efforts to diffuse the tension. All the care and confidence couldn't accurately predict when either of them would next walk on firm ground.

Christian slept in a narrow bed in a small room nearby. A kneeler has been positioned against the wall, and a small wooden crucifix hung above it. Before getting into the bed and falling asleep, Christian knelt and moved his fingers lightly over the crucifix, passed to him as a child by Jonathan Kennedy from Pope Juan Carlos. Losing himself briefly in Christ's physical suffering on the cross, he thought about the agonizing pain of nails piercing one's hands and feet. *What would I do faced with such torture?*

Christian shuddered. His own burden at this moment was staggering. *I cannot back out now.* Opportunities to abort the path that had been chosen for him were rarely considered.

He understood that the time for doubt was long since past. The mission would soon be underway.

Cared for and comfortable through the years, Christian often pondered the great mystery that was Jesus Christ. *To hang on a cross— alone—Christ's complete faith in his heavenly Father was singular, a faith without precedence. But then He was God, the Son.*

Deeply comforted in his steadfast faith, Christian believed he had the reassurance of Christ and the forgiving love of God; and so the young re-creation drifted off to sleep alone, buoyed by his faith and confidence in the science that promised safe and smooth deliverance for his mission.

Twenty-year old Christian is parentless, but not fatherless, having been raised by men of the Church to play the grandest role in history. Bordering on perfection, physically and mentally—his superb ability in and under the water, in strength and endurance is a result of his daily routine. He spent hours in a pool strengthening his swimming strokes and technique. At different beaches Christian embraced the challenge of the waves by bodysurfing, snorkeling, and scuba diving. While doing so, he learned to appreciate the ocean's beauty, strength and abundance of life. In awe of God's creations, the physical adjunct to Christian's mental preparation offered balance to his life and to the journey to come.

Christian's physical conditioning included the completion of rigorous Navy Seal and flight operations courses that sharpened him to optimum capability. The facility with which he accomplished his training astounded his instructors. Although highly impressed, they were carefully relieved of all memory of the mission preparation through methods of distraction, hypnosis, and drugs. Denny had intensively researched the phenomena experienced by heart surgery patients and others in traumatic situations in which the subjects had no recollection of their operations or their ordeal. In time, he devised a successful combination. Although the process was unrewarding and sad for those who had developed deep affection for Christian and had so admirably contributed to his success, the essential need for secrecy justified the actions.

Those responsible in the Vatican knew that Christian must be a corporeal and spiritual phenomenon. By all indications they believed that they had accomplished their goal of creating a splendid human exemplar, one with great compassion.

The cardinals involved, who could only observe indirectly, watched Christian's physical and intellectual development, periodically learning of progress that was key to the success of the plan. Even Cardinals DeAngeles, Romano, and Arias, now well into their 80's and realizing the limitations on their own mortal existence, had reveled in the progress relayed to them.

They prayed to live long enough to see it through, while knowing the improbability. All of them experienced brief and irresistible temptations to view Christian as superior to the original. The shame and guilt over such pride and arrogance sent these good men into frequent confessions with one another.

These small lapses were understandable, perhaps, and symbolic of their intense pride in their protégé. They hoped that their self-satisfaction was not so much conceit as proof of what God had allowed them to do.

When Christian awakened, a little time remained to meditate before beginning his final mission check. The painstaking preparations to produce the stunning effects of the descent were only one aspect of the plan. The second and just as essential was Christian's ministry to follow. It would be short, only thirty days—thirty days to instill the glory of faith in a handful of humanity and to instill within the new messengers a burning desire to spread the news of the return of Christ to their island.

Promulgation to the world would begin with Christian's spectacular descent from the sky onto a small, little-known island. The great unknown—the risk—was how Christian's presence would touch a scornful world, a world in which untold millions throughout histo y had died defending often unconvincing causes for an array of deities.

The book of Revelation, foretelling a thousand-year period of peace following the Second Coming of Jesus Christ, generated many imagined scenarios over what kind of peace it would be—a degraded world without human life or a sub-human life without the conflicts and differences that have accounted for so much agony in the progress of mankind?

*Is that the only environment that would allow such a peace?* The cardinals debated in their onfessions. *What about God's creation, man? Was he a total failure? A mistake that should be scrapped and begun again? How could that be?* The very unknown was the linchpin that encouraged, yet terrified, the planners. The time in Israel is eight forty-five in the evening. The duration of the mission is nine hours, with the descent to commence at five forty-five the next morning, local time.

In Rome, the hour is eleven forty-five in the morning, within minutes of the completion of the ten o'clock high mass in Saint Peter's.

Christian looked at the small clock on his bedside table in the sparse room. Earlier he had reluctantly swallowed the pill they gave him, but his sleep was fitful, as he was helpless to block his anxiety over the tasks ahead. All the encouragement, the training, the testing on religious dogma, languages, philosophy, the simple culture of the islanders he was to encounter, the physical preparation, the trial runs on remote Israeli beaches and in the skies over the Mediterranean, and the constant psychological grounding were tested by the solitude that engulfed Christian during these final hours. He ached in an odd way and wondered if he wished for a woman's arms or the comfort and tender embrace from a mother he had never known.

He felt perspiration seep through the thin cotton fabric of his pajamas, as he tried to pray and contemplate the agony of Jesus long ago.

Fighting the mongering wolf of temptation, a temptation to allow the heady air of self-importance to mingle with the terror of the unknown, caused bile to rise in his throat. He performed the breathing exercises taught to him and recited, *Saint Michael the Archangel, defend us in battle.*

Trying to block the foe—his own doubt—Christian considered the unknowns. *Will I fail?*

*Will I wake up in Hell? Will I contribute to a better world? Oh God, why have you never answered?* He imagined himself breaking out into the cool night and simply running; disappearing as though he had never existed. General Yakowitz had anticipated the possibility of a last-minute bid for escape. Guards who believe Christian to be a minor political prisoner would prevent any such occurrence. They remain posted at his door.

Although Christian had exercised frequently in nearby facilities, the small room he now occupies has no window to provide any time reference. The hours tick away on a small clock set to Panamá time during the prior week, helping to ease the adjustment of Christian's mental and physical shift to the time zone of his destination.

The time at hand, Aaron Yakowitz awakens Christian. Left alone for the final moments, Christ an prepares to bathe and concentrates on scrubbing his body in the rush of hot water and smell of the strong soap he has grown accustomed to over these last weeks. Returning to his room dressed in a simple robe, he awaits those who will outfit him for the flight.

The most difficult moments are the final goodbyes. Christian walks out on to the tarmac, aware that the details are already dimming in the minds of most of those who cared for him and prepared him for this flight. They will forget him within twenty-four hours. This extreme requirement causes Christian loneliness, and he will soon have a long and dangerous journey during which only a handful remain who are aware of his existence.

Christian embraces each of them, staring at their faces in the darkness, committing them to memory. Ready for takeoff, Avi waits for Christian to board. When he does, the ground crews finish their tasks and are dismissed. The only one who remains  to watch the take-off is General Aaron Yakowitz, Commander of the Israeli Defense Forces and now a co-conspirator in the search for the goodness of God. For Christian, the absence of Denny Dennison is particularly distressing. Being called back to Rome—an understandable imperative—had caused the normally happy-go-lucky scientist and his pupil, his charge, *his Christian*, great dismay.

Thousands of miles away, dressing to attend the mass in Saint Peter's, Denny is barely able to stand the anticipation and knows his patience will be tested as he awaits news of the journey soon to take place. To overcome anxiety, Denny imagines he is there with Christian, intent over the details as he guides him through the procedures for the final time. Before his departure, they had promised each other to recite their check-off list as a prayer and silent communication. It is a soothing exercise for both.

His unique experiences over the last few years have defined Denny's present worldview. Yes, once "acceptance" had wormed its way in, he had been filled with eagerness for the challenge and the intrigue he was taking on. He is still surprised at what he describes as *a bombardment of faith. Luck, pure luck,* he thought, but knew his dedication to the purity of the goals of *The Return* and to Christian's safety and success drove him. He knew his pledge to this project was pure, an honorable act. As he finishes dressing and leaves his lodging, he calls upon the courage born of his newfound faith to help him over the disappointment of separation from Christian at this key moment.

Denny approaches the steps near the sculpture of Saint Peter, oblivious of Nina Shelky, who is taking in the scenery of the plaza while walking toward the same steps.

Thinking of Christian, Denny is also unaware of Countess Serina Caputo emerging from her car nearby, and he has no knowledge that it was the Countess's great wealth that had allowed him the freedom to pursue every technical challenge presented by *The Return*.

Denny, Nina, and Serina, unmindful of each other, proceed to the entrance of the great basilica. Their connection to one another is imprecise, but they will soon share in the same wondrous plan.

"*Shalom*, Avi. Go with God."

Earlier on the tarmac in Israel, General Aaron Yakowitz had given a final salute to General Avi Noam, who returned it from the cockpit. There was no co-pilot.

# WINGS OF HOPE
## April 2035

Avi used the long hours of practice runs to think. As the aircraft to carry Christian added more and more technical equipment, Avi first took flights across the oceans with simulated equipment. Denny told him to think like a great lover, perfecting every move and touch to achieve an ecstasy, a oneness with his airplane and with the maneuvers.

"Success, my boy, will be sweet," joked Denny. "A sensual climax like never before known." Denny believed some good-natured repartee dispelled the tension. He often grappled with his own fear, and the bantering allowed him to hold down the anxiety.

Initial flights were designed to test outside detection and to train Avi to personally confront any challenge or inquiry from those not connected to the mission. He held the rank of Major when his role began some years ago, and now, as a still-youthful General, Avi uses his flights to think about Israel's cycles of violence and failed attempts at peace. Having taken part in the senseless slaughter among the nations of the Middle East, Avi submitted to the clutches of progressive despair—a spiraling vertigo that tore away his confidence. At the bottom of hopelessness, he sought solace in alcohol and comfort in the arms of unknown but willing women trying to purge their own devils. Avi yearned for peace, a quiet peace to quell the noise within his soul.

The ultimate realization of Hell occurred long ago on a gray drizzly morning when Avi woke up naked in a cheap hotel near the Mediterranean beach resort of Netanya. His money and watch were gone. His knuckles, stiff and painful, were covered in dried blood.

Trying to flex his hands, Avi struggled to recall events of the previous night through the pounding in his temples, but his memory was blank. His head pulsing with pain, he managed to get dressed and maneuvered himself down filthy steps to a desk manned by an elderly clerk, an old veteran who, blessedly, felt his pain and placed a old black telephone on the counter.

"Is there someone you can call?" he inquired kindly, sensing a certain distinction in Avi and realizing that along with his stripped dignity, the man in front of him was penniless.

"*Shalom,*" muttered Avi, grateful for the small kindness of the old man and of the prostitute who had at least left his now dead cell phone, and his wallet, minus the cash and credit cards, on the bedside table. Ashamed, he fingered his military ID card as he called a member of his unit. When they came for him, he found relief among these men he loved and with whom he had fought. Their loyalty was true, and his comrades offered soothing words as they gave him a calming sedative and cold water. Avi woke up hours later in the base hospital, fearful of escalating self-destruction. He agreed to treatments for the depression that haunted him.

Word got around quickly. Having been transferred to a quiet clinic for rehabilitation, Avi recovered. Within a few months, he was visited by his commanding general Aaron Yakowitz, who was well aware of the young Colonel's reputation for skillful daredevil flying. Putting his well-known charisma to work, the general talked at length, revealing much of his own career and early life. Somewhat confused by flattered by the general's sincere interest in him, Avi looked forward to successive visits, feeling a growing bond with Aaron Yakowitz. On a sunny afternoon when Aaron invited Avi to lunch at a club near the rehabilitation facility, the much-recovered young pilot was unprepared for the conversation that ensued.

"Colonel Noam," Aaron had addressed him with formality, but a formality filled with warmth, "my visits with you have been rewarding to me personally. It is possible that you may suspect ulterior motives. You would be quite right, although I assure you of my deep confidence in your ability and my great respect for what you have managed in your own repair of yourself." General Yakowitz looked away and then directly at Avi. "I pray you have not been offended at my need to get to know every detail of your life and your capability, as I would like to propose a mission for your consideration." General Yakowitz continued, mindful of Avi's guarded reaction. "The mission will be top secret, will take years of planning, and the execution will involve daring—a danger beyond our comprehension—but most of all, it will offer *great hope*."

Inwardly bristling at any possibility of participating in yet another outburst of retaliatory killing, Avi was unimpressed. But General Yakowitz knew that the formerly brash and highly competent Israeli pilot was a perfect choice for the mission, and ignoring the barely perceptible discomfort in Avi's body language, suggested that Colonel Noam think upon his own future and accept without reservation the assignment Aaron had in mind for him.

During their parting, Avi was moved by General Yakowitz' passion, as he reemphasized the *prospect of hope—a project that promised the absence of death and destruction.* Avi noted an unmistakable honesty in the pleading for his service.

Two days later, Avi called the number Aaron Yakowitz had given him and agreed to meet in another café nearby. Although not in uniform, General Yakowitz laid out the plan for *The Return* with a crisp military approach. Unlike most military briefings, however, there were no charts or documents. Sitting in disbelief, a pale Avi only grasped that for now, he was not allowed to think; that there were no strategy papers he could slip into a briefcase to study later, and that he could only listen. Fighting the urge to argue a betrayal of the Jewish faith, Avi grasped the significance of disclosure, which Aaron had cautioned him about at the start of the conversation. Disclosure would indeed be catastrophic. General Yakowitz' look provided Avi a flash of warning, wordlessly informing him of the prospect of his elimination should any leak occur.

Avi Noam began to speak, but Aaron Yakowitz already read his mind. "Both of us, and very few others, are aware of the unthinkable consequences of any word of this getting out. I want only your pledge, Colonel Noam. Once I have that and the assurance of your courage to go forward, I will arrange to have you transferred to advanced training facilities. Over the next few years, if God so wishes, we will prepare to carry out the mission."

Avi looked away from Aaron Yakowitz and thought of the commitment he had made on the mountain of Masada so long ago. He thought of the wretched dark abyss, which he had occupied only a short time ago. He thought of the love and confidence which had gone so far to rescue him. This miracle of hope was now being offered to him—*yes, a miracle,* Avi thought. Whether the miracle was manmade wasn't important now. All his speculation prior to this meeting over what the General wanted of him could not prepare him for this, but he soon saw a noble future for himself and a new approach to hope for Israel and for his fellow man.

Looking back at his commanding officer, Avi felt a smile cross his face. "*Shalom,* my dear brother. I am at your service."

"*Shalom,*" replied Aaron Yakowitz softly.

Avi rapidly regained his health and optimism. He began a vigorous training program and then took long endurance flights and conducted advanced maneuvers. Even though he was somewhat of a loner, he was later selected for the rank of Brigadier General and assigned by General Yakowitz to a vague department of *special projects.*

Increasingly grateful for his rehabilitation and his role in this great undertaking, Avi then met several times with Luís Gutiérrez.

Luís and Aaron Yakowitz gradually entrusted Colonel Noam with the deeper purposes of the mission.

The concept of heaven and Hell had not shaped Avi's life as much as his abhorrence of ritualistic suicide and mass murder in the name of religion. Having witnessed repeated attempts to eradicate Judaism, Avi easily aligned his thoughts with a Christianity now enduring similar hatred. Bedeviled by frustration and stalemated by stubborn enemies, General Avi Noam felt no further doubts once he was made aware of the existence of Christian.

Even before their first meeting some years later, he felt admiration for this young savior and for his role in the great holy gamble for peace.

Finally meeting Christian, Avi completely understood the hope Christian represented.

General Avi Noam and Father Jonathan Kennedy never met. There was "no need to know," a phrase common in intelligence circles and a condition that Father Kennedy, the son of a high level intelligence officer, understood. Throughout the exacting and tedious rehearsals and the continuing drilling of faith and doctrine into Christian's mind, Father Kennedy relayed details of their progress to His Holiness and to General Luís Gutiérrez via Cardinal Hernandez.

As the final year unfolded, the small handful of players approached the culmination of their years of work. General Luís Gutiérrez spent the majority of his time in Israel overseeing the project with Aaron Yakowitz. Cardinal Hernandez and Father Kennedy made several trips to the islands to discreetly observe the population around the beach and to confirm their daily habits. The routines of the islanders proved to be predictably consistent, rather like playing the same song over and over or repeating the same prayer again and again. The two clerics, representatives of the Holy Father, traveled in secret until they arrived "home" to their national flocks in nearby Colombia. For these trips, they flew on commercial flights dressed as sports fishermen.

From the air, they were able to observe the undeveloped border area with Colombia at the southeast end of the Isthmus of Panamá. Known as the Darien, it was often used by FARC rebels to escape the Colombian militia. The Pan-American Highway remained uncompleted in this area, ostensibly due to the residual fear of Colombian cattle bringing hoof-and-mouth disease into Panamá, but perhaps more importantly to prevent further infiltration by FARC. Both Cardinal Hernandez and Father Kennedy marveled at the dichotomy of purpose between the FARC rebels and their own.

Flight time from the capital, Bogotá was just an hour to Panamá City. Once there, Luís arranged fo the short trip to the island by private launch. It was an exhausting travel schedule.

After Jonathan's initial contact years before with the CIA in Washington, the agency's involvement was minimal.

The strong urge by the few knowledgeable colleagues of Jonathan Kennedy's father to direct events was blunted by a gut feeling to remain remote, always a wise decision by the agency in covert matters. Procedures for making contact were in place, should Jonathan require assistance. Otherwise, hope for a peaceful outcome was the only wish. The two officers involved from the inception of the project retired, but remained assigned to Father Jonathan Kennedy under a special arrangement. Father Kennedy in turn monitored Dr. Denny Dennison.

The bond between Denny and Jonathan Kennedy had deepened since their first meetings in Washington. Exchanging news of technical progress and the marvel of Christian's development, they avoided the enormity of the deception in their communications. Still, both recognized the mix of fear of failure and, at the same time, apprehension about success. Faith in God was not so much discussed as simply felt between them.

To lighten difficult moments, Denny often joked about *ne plus ultra*. The term meant "no more beyond—the highest point capable of being attained," and he first used it on Jonathan when he had a particularly discouraging day. After breaking through this and the barriers they had known to follow, Denny and Jonathan fell into a comfortable relationship and learned to joke as much as possible.

"How's it going, Denny?" inquired Jonathan, as he divided his time among his tasks. These included monitoring Denny's progress, island research and habits of its occupants, the rearing and education of Christian, and the limited liaison with the CIA.

"I've hit *ne plus ultra* once again," Denny teased Jonathan. "I just need you to talk to God about global conditions that night, so our boy doesn't tumble through space like some out-of-control cosmic chunk."

Wrestling with his science-versus-religion conflicts, Dr. Dennison plunged into the work of *The Return* and told himself that whatever the outcome, he had been blessed with a phenomenal assignment. Still, as he experimented with aspects of the mission he fought off moments of sharp concern, particularly regarding Christian's physical safety during the descent.

"You know, my dear Father Kennedy, Christian is the finest physical specimen I have ever seen, but he is still simply human. Tell me something," said Denny, as he poured over calculations on a yellow-lined pad with a stubby pencil. "Now that we have the DNA thing pretty well nailed down, it's difficult to understand supernatural goofs like the breaking of DNA that cause horrific diseases. Telling me that 'God works in mysterious ways' seems a bit lacking, don't you agree?" Denny gave the priest an exaggeratedly perplexed look and smiled. "Still, I have come around to thinking that if God allows us to crack DNA, there is no telling in this ugly world how He may view our plan to put *Him* back on the map. If I were He, I'd be fairly pleased with thee and me. After all, we're doing the best we can."

Jonathan knew he needed to stop bristling every time Denny tried to lift his mood with a mocking tone about God. Still, he felt his stomach churn with doubt. He had long ago learned to enjoy Denny, while holding onto his priestly integrity; but it was often difficult, as some days his guilt was overbearing. Here they were—the scientist and the priest—indulging in childish arguments while contesting each other's viewpoints. During occasions of doubt, Jonathan would seek a quiet dark place outside of Washington or Rome, and on clear nights he would scan the heavens and feel his being reinvigorated.

# FLIGHT PLAN
## April 2035

The journey from the Negev Desert to Contadora Island off the coast of Panamá would cross ten time zones in nine hours. Numerous routes to the drop zone had been investigated. In the end, weather and national airspace regulations dictated the route. Christian and General Avi Noam would climb in a northward direction from a high- security Israeli airbase in the Negev Dessert. Rising rapidly to the stratosphere, the aircraft would reach approximately 50,000 feet within minutes and attain supersonic speed. At this point over northern Israel, the aircraft would turn west, cross the Mediterranean Sea—staying clear of all land masses—and head out into the Atlantic.

Leveling off at fifty thousand feet and undetectable to an observer below, it would draw normal attention from ground controllers. The Israeli Defense Force radar identification code, established for irregular training missions early on, precluded alarms by air control facilities on the ground. Just west of the Azores, an Israeli tanker would perform air-to-air refueling. The tanker crew would be told that refueling was part of a training exercise and they would loiter afterwards to repeat the procedure on *The Return* trip.

Avi would proceed over the Atlantic and cross the Isthmus of Panamá westward to the Pacific, passing over the two hundred or so mostly uninhabited islets that make up the Pearl archipelago at a point seventy miles southwest of Panamá City. As determined by the prevailing winds, the aircraft's speed would gradually be pulled back upon reaching a precise longitude/latitude. By then Avi would have reversed direction to head toward the soon-to-be rising sun and would approach the eastern horizon of the archipelago with further reduced velocity.

That would be the critical moment—*the* moment. Denny Dennison had worked for years to overcome the physical obstacles to Christian's descent from the aircraft in a manner that would convince witnesses below of the coming of a heavenly figure. Traveling back and forth to Israel on extended trips, Denny developed strong professional relationships with a small number of Israeli scientists keen on air-control technology, and with General Aaron Yakowitz, who made all avenues available for the affable and talented scientist. In giving themselves over to *The Return*, Denny Dennison and Aaron Yakowitz were soon bound in their astonishing conversions. In quiet discussions, Jewish faith and atheistic logic gave in to the new promise of their choices. For his friends and colleagues, Denny successfully manufactured a variety of cover stories that included hints of a controversial secret love affair abroad.

With months of rehearsal and testing now completed, the final briefing took place a few hours prior to the mission. Denny's absence was felt. As General Noam gave final instructions to the small ground crew, Aaron Yakowitz sat quietly with a cup of dark coffee in the back of a nearby room, observing through one-way glass and wishing for the presence of the brash and ever-amusing Doctor Dennison. Aaron would have liked to have Denny's reassuring presence with him. He felt the pain of internal conflict the dedicated scientist must be enduring in Rome, struggling to clear his mind and preparing himself for the papal mass at Saint Peter's.

The others in the briefing audience had been through this drill many times and had not been informed that this was the finale. The single CIA representative and two Israelis from the Israeli Defense Intelligence Agency handpicked by General Yakowitz would monitor the operation from highly secret vantage points, created for the drop in Washington and Negev.

Avi had learned it all in exquisite detail and could easily envision the chronology of events to take place. As had been endlessly practiced, drogue chutes would ease the capsule to twenty thousand and then ten thousand feet before they dropped away one by one. When positioned, the deployment of the transparent parachute canopy would trigger temporary illumination to create highly dramatic rays of almost blinding light. Through years of development and repeated testing, Denny Dennison had managed to produce an illusion that, in its briefness, created a memorable impression of a miraculous event. At one thousand feet over the beach, the fabric around Christian's body would appear as billowing robes. He would be viewed with arms outstretched and slightly down. The last undetectable parachute would fall away when he hit the shallow clear water off the small rock protrusion, where Mario and Marcocito were to eventually stand awestruck.

During the grueling training, possible detection of the fall-away capsule and breakdown of any remaining equipment was considered. Perfecting every phase, it was ultimately deemed a slight risk, mitigated by a propellant that would deflect it from Christian and out of sight. Once in the seawater, the large amount of fabric would float briefly, sink, and dissolve rapidly; leaving Christian dressed only in a swath of linen made from carefully woven cloth using archaic techniques. It had been calculated that the frontal display of the descending figure and the overpowering shock of the scene would rule out any immediate speculation on the *how* of the scene for the simple peasant audience. This miraculous *coming* would appear completely credible to the unsuspecting viewers on the white beach below.

The grandeur of the event would be completed by the utterance of one of the children on the beach, "*Es Jesucristo!*" (It is Jesus Christ!) Although this hoped-for response would be unknown to the men who labored to make it happen, Avi imagined these words being spoken and instantly believed and embraced by the others. Such a culmination would be the perfect climax to Christian's journey and set the stage for the new beginning. Avi Noam imagined hearing the child's exclamation and smiled as he thought of Denny's reaction. Denny, Avi knew, would weep with joy. It meant mission success for the technical effort. The vastly more difficult effort ahead would depend upon one person—Christian.

Several thousand miles away from Rome, General Noam is at the controls of the mission-modified long-range reconnaissance aircraft.

The flight is going exactly according to plan. Avi, although confident, knows that aborting is always an option, but cannot contemplate any such failure.

After refueling from the tanker, the flight across the Atlantic proceeds uneventfully. Everything is now in order. Years of work and planning are about to be fulfilled. At the appropriate moment near the objective, General Noam instructs Christian to exchange his fixed oxygen breathing system for a small portable bottle and crawl back into the capsule in the rear of the aircraft. As Christian closes the airtight hatch, he and General Noam exchange final looks and salute each other. They both wonder if they will meet again, but both doubt it. Shielded from view, Christian removes his light temporary flight suit and maneuvers himself into the complex attire and apparatus designed by Denny for his descent.

As dawn approaches, Avi is high over the Pearl Islands Archipelago. He can faintly see the now-familiar tiny islands, surrounded by their halos of white beaches. He cannot yet make out the light and dark shadows of reefs and rock formations but from practice runs knows their locations beneath the crystal blue-green waters.

Inside the capsule, Avi signals to Christian, soon to be "the Savior returned," that the moment for release has arrived. The capsule drops away from the plane's belly and begins a rapid fall to forty thousand feet, where the first system of chutes engages, reducing the speed of its plunge. At twenty thousand feet, an additional chute breaks free slowing the capsule down even more. Reaching ten thousand feet, a barometric signal tells Christian he will be free of the capsule in ten seconds. The final translucent chute unfolds and fills with air as Christian gently falls through the atmosphere. Shielded against the chill by a breakaway wrap, it is now safe to breathe ambient air, and Christian feels the warmth trapped in the billowing fabric flow over his body. He proceeds in a lazy fall toward the small beach on the Pacific Island. Christ is coming again.

Far above the island, Avi watches the capsule carrying Christian disappear below him. Denny did not exaggerate the sensation. Although he cannot watch the actual landing, the moment is dizzying and wonderful. Making a wide turn, Avi heads eastward and soars through the early morning sky. He knows this will be his final flight and feels contentment in the beauty and freedom of the skies and the certainty that a supreme being is with him.

# After the Descent
**April 2035**

Mario reacts first, while the child, Marcocito, remains motionless at the sight of this man dropping out of the sky and now walking slowly toward them through chest- high water. Recalling vividly the blinding brightness and billowing white cloth of only a moment or two ago, Mario notes that it is gone. The man he had seen falling from the sky in robes ballooning around him is now naked from the waist up and clothed in white cloth about his waist and groin. How had the rest disappeared?

Feeling the child's apprehension, Christian remains quiet as he slowly makes his way. He looks from Mario to Marcocito, with his intense and commanding gaze finally resting on Mario, who knows some sort of action, some movement, is now required. Unable to speak further, Mario realizes the need to get ashore and points to the ledge, moving his fingers in a beckoning motion toward the beach. Christian takes Mario's direction willingly and makes his way through the shallow water with his hand on the rock outcropping, until it is no longer necessary to use it to steady himself.

The two fishing boats move in cautiously toward the beach but with greater speed, so that they pass the man at a distance. They do not start the small engines at the back of the boats but use oars instead, heeding an unstated condition for silence. They do not attempt to row near him, and without a word spoken, each knows that he is witnessing an unparalleled event—the arrival of *Jesus*. Overcoming a desire to flee rather than confront this unbelievable situation any further, they do not take their eyes off this vision, even while coasting to shore and beaching the boats.

Despite their preoccupation with the man in the water, that act is still performed with care. They rarely come ashore at this beach, and knowing that the tide is coming in, they are careful to ensure their boats' safety. At first they stand nearby to them, ensuring an avenue of escape in the event danger presents itself. They watch as Mario, one hundred yards away, walks toward the beach along the rock shelf at the same pace as *Jesus* in the water below.

Marcocito follows but stops several times, pushing against the hard wall of rock with his left hand and holding the pole in his right. His eyes remain riveted on the powerful figure, and he bites into his lower lip, a normally harmless habit. This time, emotion causes him to bite hard and he punctures his lip, tasting blood but feeling little pain. He wishes the ledge were much longer, as did Mario. They are trying to anticipate what might happen as they step off the last part of the rocky path on to the beach and the man steps out of the water.

Awaiting their reaction, Christian moves carefully. He steps ashore, his cloth dripping and clinging to his tan body. He knows their first impression of the sight of his descent and departure from the ocean is critical to the task ahead.

When fully out of the water, Christian turns and looks out over the sea and toward the sky. Momentarily disregarding the frightened and anticipatory eyes upon him, Christian is overcome by the relief and amazement at what has just occurred. After years of preparation, he has actually arrived at his destiny and appeared before this small group. But for the moment, he forgets them. He raises his arms and clenches his hands with his head up in gratitude to God, his Father, for having brought him through a most incredible journey. This heartfelt gesture causes even greater wonder among the islanders.

Wanting to preserve and extend the magnitude of these first moments, Christian looks tenderly at each member of the small group. He recognizes most from the last eighteen months of remote monitoring. Several newcomers who witnessed the descent from a greater distance are cautiously approaching the beach from the hillside. This had been anticipated by the planners and was an omen of their future success in spreading a message of peace to a world far beyond the boundaries of this island. This island had escaped the chaotic horror and demise of what was considered the "advanced" societies of the outside world, and these simple people, spared civilization's destructiveness, are to be the new disciples.

The impact of Christian's visual image seems to be well set. The islanders are completely fascinated. Minutes ago, this man was floating down toward them in a swell of white robes and blinding light, and now he is standing on their beach. How could this be? Who else could he be but Jesus? Gordo and Lucas and several others fall to their knees in full realization of what they are witnessing.

But now the beginning of a critical conversation is at hand. Even though man had begun speaking thousands of years before the birth of Christ, Christian and all the planners had often contemplated the thought processes among these islanders versus that of learned people in universities and within all religions. There is no library here. Although the islanders can read and write, and Christian is aware of their basic education, he does not know the extent of their intelligence. The gamble was that his presence would over time create a faith that would be proselytized through the simplicity of their innocence.

In and of itself, this was a strange contradiction. For without the advanced technical and philosophical understanding and the decades of planning that *could only be put into action through man's ability to communicate*, this moment would have never been realized. Still, a more worldly location replete with sophisticated knowledge and cynicism would have thwarted any hope of success. Placing this grand illusion in an advanced society would have exposed it to merciless dissection and politicization, rendering it useless.

Marisol and her sister, still in a state of fear and wonderment, manage to gather in their laundry from the shallow water. They did not pay attention to what they were doing and simply piled the dripping clothes, on top of a rock. A blouse and skirt fall back into the water, lazily drifting in and out with the waves. The girls retrieve them and pile them up again, never taking their eyes off "Jesus." Finally able to move, Marisol, with her sister in hand, wades to shore to the spot where Christian stands with Mario and Marcocito. Everyone waits.

Trying to maintain some control, Gordo urges those behind him to stay close. Like a platoon leader sneaking up on the enemy, he glances back to make sure they are close behind him, instinctively feeling that they would be in less danger if they presented themselves as a single mass of humanity. No one anticipates immediate physical danger, as Christian stands on the shore with nothing in his hands or on his person. However, no one can fully anticipate the impact or begin to understand the meaning of this miracle in their midst.

"Do not be afraid. I come in peace." Christian's voice is clear, deep, and soft.

Glancing at each other and trying to make sense of the moment, the unassuming group experiences fleeting seconds of considering him some *loco,* a crazed intruder on their beach; but the vision of his descent is too vivid and fresh. They struggle with the impossible, and yet, here it is before them.

Marcos Rivera, having managed to overcome his initial shock, hurries down the road and is now on the beach next to his father and son. His leadership role in these islands seems insignificant at this moment, as he tries to get a mental grip on his place in this event. In the uncomplicated minds of these creatures of God, Jesus Christ is standing on their beach. He has come to their island. Although their understanding of the future is vague, some of them recognize that a great new purpose to their lives is spreading out before them.

For long moments, the islanders look intently at the stranger. Christian's body is superb. Deeply tanned and invigorated by calculated exposure to sun and sea over the years to acclimatize him to a tropical climate, he brushes his burnished hair, which just reaches his shoulders, away from his face. He has a short beard and briefly wonders if the islanders will accept without question the details of his appearance. Cautiously, they move closer. Finally Marcocito hands his fishing pole to his grandfather and bravely extends his small hand to Christian. Christian gently takes it, grateful for this small gesture and at the same time feeling overcome by the enormity of his task. Christianlooks into Marcocito's eyes and sees in them the child's trust—and something more.

Months after *The Return*, Nina Shelky wrote in her notes—*I remember these gentle lambs of God. They existed in a world of blind faith. They had no understanding of the intricacies of theology and lived day-to-day, with only a dim concept of eternity. A rudimentary religious education and word of mouth had taught them the fundamental tenets of the exi tence of God and the Holy Trinity, as practiced and accepted in their Catholic country.*

For the islanders, insight into their purpose on earth remains unclear. The small group standing on the beach and those observing from the hill and along the short road experience an emergence from obscurity. Life, until now, has blissfully followed the primitive paths of their ancestors.

Not sure what to do next, they collectively move closer, concerned that this being before them might disappear as quickly as he appeared. Without knowing why he has come here to their island, but realizing it must be for an extraordinary purpose, they do not want to lose him. Marcos, desperately hoping to find the right words finally speaks.

"We are poor, and we do not know you. How could we know you?" Marcos, holding a master's degree, felt the ignorance of them all. "Why would you come here to us?" he blurts almost angrily, trying to disguise his fear as well as his inadequacy. Then, in a softer tone, he asks, "You have chosen us for some reason. We want to know you, but we are powerless. Please help us to understand why you are here. If you will stay with us, we can accommodate you."

"Yes," Christian replies gently, glad of the opening of dialogue. "I will be here for only a short while. I will help you to understand, and I will be here long enough for you to develop courage in your faith. A faith that you have been selected to spread beyond this sea, just as before."

Like so much of the world, these islanders have only a meager understanding of their own existence. Now Christian can easily identify with their ache to know. The image of how his new apostles thought he should look, how he should act—this image presented to them now was all they knew, and it was familiar. They knew nothing of Mohammed or Buddha or Luther but now see a recognizable incarnation of their imagination. Christian recalls Saint Augustine's words on faith—"You would not be searching for me if you had not found me."

Children crowd around Christian as the group leads him up the dirt trail to their tiny village of simple concrete houses and bohios, huts covered with watertight palm fronds. Two of the women produce clean shorts and a T-shirt with some simple leather sandals. One stares meaningfully at Mario, as she gives the clothing to Christian. Mario picks up on her signal and shows Christian to a private area. He reemerges in minutes, and soon breakfast materializes. Christian sits at a wooden table and hungrily devours fruit and eggs and toasted bread, washed down with sweet dark coffee. The islanders stare in fascination as Marcos tries to instill some normalcy by sipping coffee with Christian. Marcos is briefly aware that he will miss his plane to the mainland and that his work in the *Asemblea* in Panamá City today will not occur. *My plans for today, my plans from this day forward?* He wonders how the still unbelievable events of today will change them all.

When he finishes eating, Christian looks at them. "Thank you. Your lives will take on a new meaning as of today, and you will have much to do in the future, but the Holy Spirit will help you. You will succeed because, I can easily say to you, *you* are the image and likeness of God, our Father."

# Part Five – Reflections on a Grievous Matter

# Nina Shelky Writes of Contadora
## April 2001

American journalist Nina Shelky walked out of Tocumen International Airport on the outskirts of Panamá City. The heat was intense—Nina felt as though an oven door had been left open. Nina's assignment was to assess the record of this small nation in its first year of ownership and operation of the Panamá Canal. In the searing heat, she better appreciated the grueling task of canal construction and the decades-long job leading up to full treaty implementation at the turn of the 20th Century.

Wearing lightweight slacks and a cotton blouse during the April "dry" season, Nina had been traveling through Central America for a week to research background for her piece in *The Washington Times*. The memory of the chilly winter in Washington had faded. She loved the initial blanket of heat she felt as she exited the terminal but sensed that this climate was far different from the relative coolness of San José and Guatemala City. This continuing tropical heat was going to take some  getting used to. Within minutes, Nina felt her blond hair sticking to the back of her neck, and she tasted salty perspiration above her lip. Not forgetting the Washington snow she had left days ago, she welcomed the arrival of a small air-conditioned van.

The venue and the challenge of reporting from Central America was a welcome change after monotonous hearings on Capitol Hill. Listening to seemingly endless political harangues, Nina often wondered how government functioned at all. It seemed little was accomplished amidst the dreary bickering—each side accusing the other of wrongdoing.

In Panamá, too, politics were a high priority. In fact, it was the national stimulant.

But in contrast to the US political scene, the debate over decades had been conducted by a myriad of small parties with hazy lines of demarcation. Coalitions were formed as elections drew nearer. Under a "quotient" system designed to spread representation, ambitious *politicos* who were frontrunners of splinter parties were still reasonably certain to be rewarded with a ministry or seat in the legislative assembly.

Nina's assignment—to provide the Panamanian perspective on the issue of Central American unification—was presenting her with an educational exercise on *nacionalismo*. In her notes over the next several days, she wrote:

*"Within each small country in Central America, resistance to merger exists at all levels. There is a fierce unwillingness to go much beyond trade agreements. Historically, Central America's geography has been volatile. Panamá, once considered to be part of "South" America, became a province of Colombia in 1831, when that nation, along with Ecuador and Venezuela, gained their independence. Panamá remained a province of the Republic of Colombia until 1903, when—with backing from the United States in exchange for allowing them to build the Panamá Canal—it became independent.*

*Additionally, there was a nation of Central America in the early 19th Century, consisting of the present-day countries of Guatemala, Honduras, El Salvador, Nicaragua, Costa Rica (which included a region which is nowadays part of Panamá), and a portion of the modern Mexican state of Chiapas. This was sometimes known as the United Provinces of Central America or the Federal Republic of Central America. Even though politically one nation, Central America existed as a loose confederation, resulting from a government downfall in Mexico, which had been in control of these quasi-states at the time—1822. The confederation lasted sixteen years but was fraught with old disputes and conflicting political theories. At the time, "Nationalism" was called "Separatism." However, by any name the political and cultural differences in the small republics ended hopes of a single, unified nation.*

*Panamá, with its graceful stretch reaching out to two continents, was born blissfully naïve and lucky. Blessed by events and by its unique geographical position, this northwest province of Colombia took on world recognition, as opportunity beckoned and a railroad materialized with the irresistible lure of California gold in the 1800's. Courted by many, it wasn't until 1914 that the dream of a "path between the seas" was finally realized by the United States and the SS Ancon steamed through the locks and lakes as the first 'official' transit of the completed wonder, the Panamá Canal. The little nation, despite its early objection to the demarcation of the US Canal Zone spreading roughly five miles on either side of the waterway, became the crown jewel of the region and basked in its newfound role as the "crossroads of the world."*

*This slender isthmus has extraordinary pride—and for good reason. Panamá's self-confident nationalism, resulting from successfully equating itself with the United States during the lengthy canal treaties process in the 1970s, had created a sense of importance over and above its small size and population. And why not? Panamá has something unique—a canal that is now completely Panamá's, a canal that carries an enormous share of the world's commerce; a canal that provides extraordinary global leverage for a nation the size of New Jersey.*

Unification with the rest of Central America? Certainly not." Nina learned.

Over several days, Nina interviewed officials within the government and within the *Autoridad del Canal de Panamá* (Panamá Canal Authority), known as the ACP. As much as she tried to engender some optimism on unification of the Central America she had visited, it seemed it would never happen. Nationalism, always strong throughout Latin America, had become a confusing ideal, as nations became embroiled in conflict after conflict and the nationalistic lines became blurred. Islamic fascism had crept into otherwise leftist regimes. Loyalties fell away as fundamentalists created ever-wider intra-country divisions. Indications of Islamic inroads into the higher echelons of governments had become real and disturbing. At the time of her visit, Nina felt little impact of this revolutionary process, but as years passed, she watched the erosion of democracies in the region.

Throughout her educational travels in 2001, Nina tried to remain objective. She was largely successful, until she happened upon the small island of Contadora, off the Pacific coast of Panamá. There, she would encounter a new world in which she would forget the ongoing power struggles and the looming homicidal plots of the free world's enemies. Nina would blend into the fabric of God's earthly creation, and on its white beaches, Nina would drown in the joyfulness of simply being a woman. Soon she would encounter passion. She met Marcos.

As Nina recorded her findings before dusk one evening, her jottings did not seem to convey what she had intended. She felt distanced from her assignment, but the writing itself felt strangely pleasurable and sensuous. She had to repeatedly force herself to refocus. The effort was tedious as she tried to put a new spin on this repetitive tale of small-country intrigue. Nonetheless, even a discouraging report was necessary. It was what she was being paid to do. Nina turned her attention to addressing the role of the island in the original treaty negotiations, during the last quarter of the 20th Century. As Nina watched the tide, she compared the insistent waves on the white beaches to the persistence of the undercurrent of sexuality, each crashing wave obliterating any remaining resistance.

Now midnight in her small rented cottage, she sat on the top step of the staircase leading to the beach. The moon was full and lit up the sand so that the scene below seemed like silvery daylight. Nin watched Marcos' muscular male figure walking below. At the sight of him, she immediately became aware, once again, of her fever of distraction since her arrival on this island. She felt the grip of desire and shamelessly anticipated the next hours as Marcos started up the staircase.

Trying to describe the island itself through a haze of passion, Nina found that her words pictured the island's attributes in terms quite different from her normal reporting. She felt she had little control, and so she let the words flow. During those magical days, the lure of the extreme tides was exceedingly captivating, far more so than endless politicking. But the on-going mystery of the satisfaction of physical desire was, for Nina, overwhelming.

Marcos' knowledge and description of the tides was, in Nina's sensuous state, highly arousing. She had difficulty concentrating on his explanations when they stood at the water's edge the previous afternoon. Marcos spoke of the waves' creation by winds and currents, as the swells of blue, green and gray water roiled across the vast ocean surfaces.

"Quite like us," he explained, standing close behind her with his hands and arms around her body in the warm shallow water on the quiet empty beach. "The moon and the earth are magnets. The strong lure of the moon causes the oceans to reach out in its direction."

Marcos moved back and bent down to draw a basic diagram in the sand. "When the sun and moon are aligned, gravitational forces cause beautiful, very high and very low 'spring' tides. When they move away from alignment, the gravitational forces tend to cancel one another. Then, my beautiful Nina, tides are not as dramatic. They are called 'neap tides.'"

Nina leaned against him, unable to allow space between them. Marcos continued caressing her shoulder, "Our moon moves around the earth, and together, they travel around the sun, giving us a combined gravitational force. It causes the oceans to rise and fall, and since the earth rotates as well, two tides occur daily." Marcos stood up. "We revolve along with it all, Nina. I am often frustrated with my inability to identify who God is, but when I think about creation, it all leads back to Him. When I was at school, I recall a discussion that debated whether all this," Marcos swung his arm out into the air, "started with 'something' or started with 'nothing.' If it's nothing, doesn't that suggest then that the whole universe started in a non-material certainty—is that God?" Marcos looked into Nina's eyes questioningly. Nina was moved by Marcos' deep thoughts.

In observation of him and his splendid physique, her consideration for his intellect was only lighthearted. Now the attraction took on another layer. Nina was not very religious after adulthood yet now felt an added gift from the man who stood before her. As she recalled her own non-existent search for God, she grasped that this affair might well provide far more than physical satisfaction.

Marcos smiled at Nina's inquisitive look and said, "Tonight I will show you a full moon that is close to us. It will create a very high tide known as the 'perigee' tide. For now," he whispered pulling her close to him, "for now, it will wait. I would like to show you a very private little niche of nature, a small cave. I would like to make love to you there." He picked up the thick beach towel, kissed her, and led her down the beach.

They soon reached a solid expanse of flat gray-green rock. The surface was smooth and resembled a floor of large square sections. It was dry and warm, exposed to the sun after the first wash of the day from the earlier high tide. It led to a small cave, which offered a roof and a cool interior. The floor was covered with powdery white sand that, while trapped, was cleansed with each tide.

Marcos spread the towel and sat down. He reached for Nina's hand and she sat down beside him. He knelt in front of her, placed his hands on her bare thighs, and pressed his lips against her knees. His strong touch and the sight of his thick hair made Nina clutch the back of his head and then his shoulders and strong forearms. Looking at this sight of Marcos, Nina realized the pleasure was hers alone. He could not see nor could he realize the effect it had on her.

Marcos reached up, tugged at the straps of her swimsuit and moved his face to her breasts, clean and salty from the ocean. She pulled upward, away from the thin fabric. Pulling the straps off her shoulders, he moved his mouth over her nipples, retreating to the tips to gently tease them between his teeth. He would later remind her of their hardness, staring at her over drinks with the tip of a swizzle stick between his lips.

Marcos raised his head and searched her face, as he removed her suit and then his own. The pressure of his body caused her to spasm, as he reached beneath her and lifted her toward him. She was aware that her legs had slid about him.

*Don't think anymore,* she told herself, as they joined together. It was joyous. She pressed her fingers into his back and pulled the hair at the base of his neck as she lost control and heard the throaty sound of her own cries coming from somewhere deep inside and filling the emptiness of the cave. Tears flooded Nina's eyes as the waves of sweet spasms subsided. Marcos moved off to her side, and she nestled against his chest in blissful weakness.

They dozed briefly, but then Nina sat up, feeling a small chill. *Guilt?* Perhaps the child-like guilt of knowing it was a beautiful day outside this cave. *What are you doing indoors?* She could hear her Mother chiding on summer afternoons. She looked down at Marcos, resting peacefully. His skin was dark and invited her touch. She held her tanned arm next to his and was again startled at the difference. She considered how much this contributed to her fervor. Would she feel less sinful were his skin lily white and not "bronze," "burnished," "varnished," or "caramel?" She smiled to herself, realizing that her tussle with words, the habit of descriptions and definition never left her. However, she reasoned, no words could adequately describe what she had just experienced. *Why him? Why me?* Nina thought. *This act of love, what decides its selection process? That remains forever mysterious."*

The wonder at her attraction to him caused Nina to think upon this bodily act required for procreation. *And that act, the physical merging of two beings is the truest pleasure of the body. For the rest of life, the body is a container for the mind. The body eats, sleeps, and moves to satisfy and transport the mind. These moments are to be cherished.*

New desire began to build as she watched him and only then heard the call of the ocean. She got up and stepped naked out of the cave into the sunlight. The tide had been low when they arrived and now oblivious to their passion, had begun its journey to shore.

A small pool from the previous high tide remained in the rock formation directly in front of her. She eased herself into the shallow clear water, and her mind told her she had never felt better. She was falling in love. Lingering in this joy, Nina fought the intrusion that eventually worked its way into her mind, telling her of the absurdity of such an emotion by a white city girl.

After a few moments, she stood up on the flat rock to dry off. She looked out at the incoming tide and realized that like the tide, nothing could stop this liquid feeling of desire within her. Thinking back on Marcos' speculations about God, Nina believed only a loving and giving God could give or take such ecstasy.

Marcos came up behind her. He pressed against her, and she felt dizzy with wanting as her knees buckled. He turned her toward him, lifted and carried her back to the still warm thick beach towel.

Walking the beach early the next morning, Nina's euphoria remained within her.

They had cooked fish late in the evening, drank wine, and slept in bliss. Her lips were swollen and she felt giddy from Marcos' lovemaking. Slight discomfort deep within her was an odd added pleasure, as the mild pain reminded her over and over again of her happiness. They had been given an extraordinary gift. By whom? she questioned, as she found herself in a moment in which the world's secrets—this time, this place, this man—were hers. She recalled Marcos' explanations from the previous day. The tide was at its ebb, and Nina marveled at broad white expanse of exposed beach. The Atlantic Ocean was modest, with six feet of normal tide. It was beautiful when calm, yes, but weather could cause the Atlantic to rage out of control. Here, the power of the Pacific was quieter. *Well-named,* she thought, looking out across the great expanse of quiet ocean. *La Pacifica,* she said to herself. It sounded like it looked. In the morning sun, Nina stared at the receding water, changing her focus from the whole impression and instead noting the detail of walls and floors of exposed rocks, coral, and sea life.

After enjoying the warm water, she Nina slept on the soft sand beneath a colorful umbrella and awoke as sound seeped in amidst her dreams. Nina's attention to her journal was weak, no match for the persistence of the sea's sounds. They fractured her concentration, commanding attention. The small waves broke on the beach and nature's music soothed the senses.

Nina's jottings reflected the pleasure of the previous day and night with Marcos. She tried to describe the complexity of her vulnerability, her sense of safety, and the trust required in the give and take of fulfillment through ecstasy. *The gift of orgasm is multi-faceted—a recess from worldly pressure, a sense of intense well being, of oneness, of being encased in light and yes, even holiness. Could anything equal this gift? Is itartificially enhanced here in this paradise?* Nina picked up her journal and noted the thought in the margin. She would describe the experience of human joining later but rightnow only wanted to feel it. She wondered if the tides played a role in her unrestrained behavior. Thinking more about the islands, Nina resumed writing.

*The Pearl Island Archipelago starts roughly thirty-five miles southwest from the Panamá mainland and continues into the Pacific for about seventy-five miles. The islandsseem an afterthought of God, the artist eager for added detail with his brush of tropical colors. The little islands are dotted across the blue-green Pacific waters in a string-like pattern. Closer exploration of the shorelines divulges an ancient connective tissue. The cliff walls of these islands, jutting up from the beach, expose gray-green and uneven- layered surfaces. They resemble thick torn fabric, and it is apparent that if the right edge from a neighboring island were located, they would fit perfectly together.*

*The soft ripples of the ebbing tide grow quieter in ever-smaller laps of waves. New orchestrations begin. Cicadas tune up and will shortly drown out other sounds with their eerie music.*

Nina scanned the bare trees, leaning over the rocky cliffs toward the sea, trying to locate one.

*Tropical cicadas are formidable-looking creatures, sometimes four inches in length. With transparent chromatic wings, they resemble huge, lumbering flies. Islanders pick these harmless creatures off a tree and stroke them in child-like wonder until the cicada grows impatient and escapes to a tree to continue its haunting mating call. At nature's beckoning, cicadas emerge from their long hibernation and cling to trees and bushes to dry. Males, equipped with magical legs that produce shrill music to lurefemales, join thousands in an ear-splitting chorus, and add to the dry season drama, a drama that is short-lived. Mating, completed in less than two weeks, brings an end to the compelling music.*

*Birds pick off the exhausted and dying masses, and the musicians disappear. Tiny eggs are left behind. They hatch, and larvae burrow back into the earth to ensure next season's song. New soil, created by tens of thousands of skeletons shed early on to enrichthe earth remind one God's rhythm—dust to dust?* Nina wondered, feeling that her state of mind urged Godly attribution.

*Another contributor to the drama is the tropical termite. Residing in massive nestsof dried mud molded about thick branches, the termites are charged with the cleanup of dead and dried wood. In their search for food, the inhabitants of hard nests find structures constructed by man an easy challenge. Their subtle strategy is often unnoticed and if left unchecked, these islands would return to their natural state as the termites tidy up man's follies, by slowly consuming his dwellings.*

Nina stopped and watched the silent movement of an iguana on the long branch of a tree, precariously rooted in the sharply angled rocks of the cliff walls. The iguana blended itself with the color of the branch and repositioned himself for greater sun exposure, allowing his reptilian body to absorb oxygen. Blending in and remaining motionless was necessary for the iguana's survival, and Nina had noted them in a brilliant green disguise among the bright tropical cactus and, like this one, as dull as dry wood. *What else but a gift from God?* The motionless iguana kept a sharp eye on Nina, as she resumed her writing.

*Animals and insects are but one force here. The thick plant life stages its own offensive, with massive incursions onto manicured lawns no longer tended by man. Winds, rain, and tides are yet another force in the concert of the tropical environment.*

Nina turned to pages she had written earlier. As she read what she had learned from Marcos about the tides, she felt the memory of his holding her against his body and she shivered in pleasure. Marcos' descriptions of so much about the islands created a new concept of God, a God so different from the fearful images from her childhood.

*The positions of moon and earth during March and April are the visible outcome of a precise heavenly nudge. Extremes in the tide occur annually for short durations during the dry season near the time of Easter. The pace is leisurely but steady. Progress toward the extremes can be measured by the ever-growing width of beach at low tide and the unrelenting encroachment up the beach onto the cliff walls at high tide.*

*The Pacific tides, eighteen-foot marvels, "clean the pool" twice a day.* Nina smiled at this description heard from Marcos. *The tidal action, depleting and swelling the ocean surface around the islands, occurs roughly every twelve hours. It would be a God- given clock for humanity, were it not for its poor accuracy. The annual period is correct, but a daily variation held in check by a moon on its own schedule, make the high and low tides slightly later with each succession. Was this an "error," or did the architect* deliberately provide varying low tide light and low tide darkness for all his creatures?

The tides do more than toll a daily chime. The noise of thousands of tiny feet andclaws, shell-like legs, microscopic suction cups, and swaying antennae add melody to thelow tide's newborn waves. Tidal pools form in thousands of ancient depressions amongthe rocks. These vary in size, from as small as a dot to the size of saucers and platters.Each supports its own life, as deposits of tiny snail eggs develop and await their moment.

When the tidal pull reverses, the small waves grow—slapping to expand and regain the uncovered sea bottom and beach. The incoming tide rears abundant waves in rapid succession. They break and crash further up the beach until they hurl themselves against dusty walls of rock or meander into small coves above the sand line and disappear into dry crevices.

The tides possess a feminine orderliness with their need to scrub clean and to re- arrange the decor, by the continuously swirling sand. During this cycle, a low-hanging branch growing from the rock walls will touch the beach. The next month it will be two feet off the beach, as the sand is sent elsewhere by the tides. Who benefits? Who suffers?

When the moon dares closer to its host, its magnetic effects are dramatic. Low tide during Holy Week results, as the submissive sea retreats to an appointment far away,where it bulges out onto the other side of the earth. Rocks and shore, coral and creatures of a different world are bared and naked. They appear so vulnerable. The earth, a seemingly feckless parent, abandons responsibility, and the sea cavorts elsewhere. Then, as in an apology, it returns home once again.

At its extreme ebb, the ocean floor reveals sea urchins "walking" slowly on long slender black spines. Anemones, with their tubular tops stuck to shells, wait patiently for the waters to return. Sand dollars with a center pattern termed the Holy Trinity lie on the wet sand. Small transparent creatures, resembling clear tubes, move themselves along byengorging their bodies with sand and then squeezing it out, leaving behind wet ribbons. Univalve oysters, rough with whorls of shell growth, suction themselves against the rockswith fierce tenacity. The short exposure allows thousands of creatures needing sun and air to stimulate reproduction. Was some oversight by a careless Creator "fixed" with these extreme tides?

In her official article, Nina wrote of Panamá's progress since the turnover of the canal to Panamá at the end of 1999. The official act of turnover had been completed a day earlier on December 30th to mitigate potential trouble. Anticipation had been building during the final weeks prior to the conclusion of a treaty that had been slow-cooking since 1978.

Keeping some semblance of her journalistic obligations, Nina emailed her laptop report to her office in Washington with a brief note about taking some R&R "in country." As a freelancer, she no longer wanted to open the computer in this environment. Instead, writing on the island by hand in a clean journal was an intensely personal experience.

Early the following morning, after Marcos left her limp in her bed to fly to Panamá, Nina lay quietly for a short while and then, energized, sought the sight of the beach and sea below the house. She cut up a papaya, scraped away the tiny black seeds and squeezed half a lime over the fruit. With a pot of coffee brewed and toast with guava jam on her tray, Nina settled down on the porch to enjoy her breakfast and wrote again:

*CONTADORA ISLAND – April 2001*

*I sit overlooking a white beach, a speck upon a pearl in a string of pearls scattered in the warm Pacific Ocean. Named by pirates, these early visitors had no aerial view. I did, and the name is most fitting. The pirates may have dubbed them "The Pearl Islands" to announce the abundance of pearls found in these waters. However, the islands stretch in a long line, like a carelessly flung necklace. It is decidedly more idealistic to believe in men who had a romantic streak. No one knows if the early seamen were poets or simply mercenary thieves defining these tiny islets.*

*None of the islands, save the largest, El Rey, used during World War II by the Americans as a Pacific landing strip, is even a mile square. Contadora, my enchanted island, blessed with a dozen powder-white beaches, was part of a purchase by forward- thinking visionaries in the 1960s. Of the dozen islands purchased, Contadora was the most beautiful, the most sensuous, the most desirable.*

*In the 1970s the island drew international attention as homes, hotels, shops, utility plants, lakes, and small worker villages were constructed. Imported plants, birds and animals replaced wild boars brought to the island prior to development. An attraction for visiting hunters, the boars were evicted, as homebuilders sought a more glamorous atmosphere.*

*Those who fished and snorkeled and explored these islands during the pre-development years were never disappointed. The environment was Eden and held countless species of fish. Brightly striped snakes wriggled along the underbrush, trying toremain unnoticed. Fat iguanas, with their talent for assuming background color, native toads and frogs, spiders, termites and numerous insects existed on the island for centuries.*

*Natives, whose brush with tourism was, gratefully, not long enough to dispel theirlove of privacy and solitude, felt a "homecoming," as commercial activity decreased in the 1990s.*

*It is late March, the ebb of the Dry Season. Palms and aloe plants, the croton, andvarious squat and long-stemmed cacti, are unique in their ability to extract the last moisture deep within the ground and thrive. Bougainvillea flourishes, flaunting its purpleand pink beauty, boasting of its resistance to long days of burning sun. They are true adaptors.*

*The remaining plant life lies in wait until the first rains. The dry bare trees and branches have a simple stark beauty against the blue skies. Their bleakness induces a gentle lethargy across the island. Still, they hold a secret promise and wait patiently for what is to come. With the first rain, islanders actually watch the greening of their land within hours. It is the rainy season's toast to its own arrival, a rebirth of all living things.Yesterday, my friend showed me La Playa Manta, the beach below a hilltop where he lives. A dirt road winds down to the beach, an exquisite expanse of powder white sand within natural rock jetties that form a perfect cove. He tells me the beach was named for its protective arms of rock which resemble the mouth of the manta ray. When the cove is rich with fish, mantas feed and play here. Seeming to embrace the fish they feed upon, thegentle giants frolic in the warm surf and occasionally leap out of the water, causing an enormous splash when their huge bodies slap against the surface of the sea. Walking out on the flat edge of the rock "arm," one is struck with the suitability of the name.*

Nina remained on Contadora for ten days and returned home. She was in an odd agony after several weeks in Washington. The ache of separation from Marcos was unbearable, and she returned again and again in her thoughts, always adding to the pages of her journal:

*I find that I once again believe in love, believe in God, and cherish this chance to witness the rebirth of life brought to these islands by the sweetness of heavy rains. I too am reborn, as I open myself to the power of my beloved's embrace, to the inviting open- mouth cove of Playa Manta. Lying in the sun, I want the rock arms to close in on me, to hold me captive as a witness to the floral profusion on the hills above. After days of life-giving rains, the inhabitants of the triple-canopy rain forest begin their struggle for survival in an unrelenting climb to the sun. In this tangled war, the trees with thick sturdy trunks would seem the victors. Still, like camp followers, with no other means of making it through battle, vines cling with root tentacles to the soaring branches of the larger trees. With persistence, they often smother their hosts in a profusion of growth.*

*I climb with them as they seek the sun's magic—the magic that is this paradise and its people—its very special people.*

Nina held on to her notes. They represented only a small portion of her life, but doubtless, the most important, the most memorable and cherished. Even in her weakest moments, however, she maintained a grasp on the future, an understanding of the certain collapse of a permanence whose time had not yet come. Despite Marcos' dismay, he sadly agreed on the reality of a life without each other, at least for now. *Later*, thought Nina, baffled by her own decision, *Later.*

Recovery was difficult and slow. Nina took on more demanding assignments and attained status and recognition in Washington. She convinced herself that Eden was only postponed—the crystal waters, the seduction of the tides, the magic of shooting stars on moonless nights, and Marcos. It had a strength that would never totally release her.

In time, Nina organized her notes into an article and sent it off via a colleague in Rome. By the time it was read in Milano by Cardinal Diego Hernandez, the Vatican Secretary of State, years had passed. The island's pull had, however, remained.

# Election of the Pope – at the Conclave
**Saint Peter's Square - April 2010**

General Luís Antonio Gutiérrez stood on the great plaza near the center obelisk in front of Saint Peter's. The day was overcast and chilly, but the crowd did not seem to mind, as they awaited the wisps of white smoke from the Sistine Chapel heralding the selection of a new Pope.

Luís, unable to control his emotions of joy and at the same time fear of the future, stared at Juan Carlos, as he appeared at the window above the plaza of Saint Peter's, his face wet with tears, his mind already envisioning a future world. Luís knew that if his brother, Juan Carlos, was not elected to the papacy, his own passionate obsession to conquer galloping world evil would never come to pass. He believed that reversing a world so damaged by hatred and terror would not, could not, be brought back to decency by anyone else. To bring about colossal change required not only the combination of Luís's military position and the papacy of his brother as pope, but an inner circle of trusted players already identified. The key participant, other than the yet-to-be-identified rescuer and the yet-to-be-created savior, was the *new* pope-to-be; and that *had to be Juan Carlos Gutiérrez.*

Realizing that he would be placing his brother in an unprecedented position and knowing that Juan Carlos would need to be protected and distanced as much as possible from details, Luís nevertheless knew the plot could not advance without the occurrence of this moment, without his beloved brother's consenting to the project's going forward. The moment brought with it an end to the days and nights of agonizing soul searching that tormented Luís and always resulted in the same conclusion. The moment delivered, for Luís, his conclusion that God had created these favorable circumstances for him. He was certain of it. He had somehow foreseen that Juan Carlos would be elected as the pope, and the final pieces of his dream would now fall into place.

Although Luís had secretly created the blueprint for *The Return* over a period of years and kept coded notes in a small safe in his home, the details were locked in his mind. He would gradually reveal them to those who were to be part of this mission. Some he already knew he could count on, especially Cardinal Diego Hernandez. A childhood friend from a middle class family, Diego was a loyal confidant of Juan Carlos. With Diego's later appointment by Juan Carlos to the position of Vatican Secretariat of State—the job almost a given—Diego would be key to the plan.

Diego's allegiance to the Gutiérrez family was unquestioned. The three of them—Luís, Juan Carlos, and Diego—had been close since childhood when all served as altar boys. Later, Diego's political and business ambitions changed. Despite heartbreak while still a student over the loss of his first and only love, Colombian socialite Serina de la Guardia, the voice of God persisted. The Gutiérrez brothers knew of Diego's painful indecision and supported their friend in the tug-of-war for his heart and soul. Juan Carlos had always wondered at Diego's final shift from the physical to the spiritual. He attributed his prayers to the answer for Diego's dedication, as they both moved through the Church hierarchy.

From a wealthy Colombian family that was part of the ruling class that included the Gutiérrez family, Serina had anticipated a future life with Diego. Both struggled with his fidelity to God, and, at last, Serina accepted that she could not compete with the Almighty for Diego's love. God was a formidable competitor for any woman, and Serina's own Catholic upbringing forced her to release Diego graciously. But in her private frustrated sadness, she cursed God and the influence of Juan Carlos Gutiérrez. Luís would have happily stepped in to replace Diego, but Serina's loss for a long time to come was an obstacle for advances by any man. "We're all victims of God's power," she told Luís, as she struggled with her young grief.

As Diego answered the beckoning of God, the tear in his heart remained painful. Forgoing Serina had been brought about by Diego's dedication to prayer. He prayed diligently and kept his focus on Christ, as he followed Juan Carlos into the priesthood. Support from the Gutiérrez family and impressive efforts benefiting Colombia's poor influenced the decision-makers in Rome and created a path of promotion for both Juan Carlos and Diego. As time passed, Luís was well aware that Diego's plunge into ever more responsible positions within the Catholic Church disguised the lingering void in his heart.

Giving up on his hope of separating Serina from her brittle relationship with God, a frustrated Luís resumed a life of womanizing that often kept Father Diego Hernandez overtime in the confessional. Called upon to provide Luís penitential absolution, Diego recognized his failed efforts to reform Luís's morals. "I'm a failure at saving your soul, Luís, and there are moments when I wish I could ignore that I am bound by secrecy. Maybe Juan Carlos could knock some sense into you."

"Keep trying, dear Father Hernandez, don't give up on me!" Despite the less- than-holy bantering, Diego Hernandez sincerely believed that Luís was an extraordinary Christian soldier and was often perplexed by his own acquiescence to Luís's seductive points of view during any quarrel. Diego smiled to himself, as Luís was most convincing, usually over the moral legitimacy of a conquest.

As the obsession for *The Return* consumed him, Luís noticed a change in himself—a decreased appetite for pursuing women. Even though Serina de la Guardia remained an attraction, she was soon removed from both his and Diego's lives. Luís, sometimes believing himself to be clairvoyant, felt certain that in the complexities of life, Diego Hernandez would one day be immersed in a far deeper relationship with both the Church of Rome and with Serina de la Guardia. Luís did not reveal his premonition to the then-young priest *Father* Hernandez, later to be called His Eminence, *Cardinal* Diego Hernandez.

After the horrific and senseless murders of Luís and Juan Carlos' sister and her husband, Luís depended on his brother and Diego for strength and for priestly comfort and reassurance of a merciful God. The long period of haunting nightmares caused a crippling seclusion and months passed before Luís resumed command of his country's military. Time allowed him to push through the grief, a time well used to not only study the burning rage of enemies but to deeply contemplate his plan for restoring reason and good.

In his studies of human conflict, Luís' advanced his knowledge of the tribulations in Latin America and the radical Islamic culture, mired in antagonism for the West, hating its Judeo-Christian reconciliation, and unable to overcome its dearth of tolerance. Factional hatred and the inability to overcome a prolonged non-productive state appalled Luís. Added to this inner rage, Luís felt guilt and empathy over the plight of the poor suppressed Catholic majority throughout Latin America. Divisiveness within nations created pain for the masses in Latin America, as attempts to overthrow governments reversed fragile gains.

While progress in Latin America lagged, the nations of radical Muslims believed that the only acceptable outcome in their countries was a restoration of their ancient world power. With limitless wealth in their great lakes of black gold, leadership suppressed any efforts by the deprived masses toward progress. The medieval religious power controlling the multitudes discarded the notion of separation of church and state. Adherents to Mohammed had no intention of rendering anything to Cesar, especially if Cesar could be characterized as a westerner—just another infidel. Their determination to vanquish western culture threatened the very continuity of Christianity. Luís could feel its demise—the religion based on the life and teachings and examples of Jesus Christ. Apathy and relinquished strength caused Luís visions of doom for the people of not only the Judeo-Christian world but indeed of *all* the world's religions.

To restore faith in the Holy Trinity and his Christian God, Luís was willing to risk his soul. He believed that by bringing Christ back to earth in a humble setting, the hopes of God-fearing people in other lands would, in time, be renewed. *The Return* would bringa halt to the destruction of civilization fed by hatred. The plan could renew belief in the Savior, Jesus Christ. *Would the heavenly seat of judgment find cause to rejoice?* Luís felt it could not be otherwise.

By the time of Juan Carlos' elevation to Bishop of Colombia, the plan for *The Return* was developed in Luís's mind, and the campaign to convince Juan Carlos and Diego to move beyond reliance on the disappointing power of prayer went into effect. He discussed with them the anomaly of witnessing a Christian church full of the faithful, while the world's mosques filled with those whose invocations to Allah included a resolve by many to eliminate the infidels.

*To whom were they all praying? To the same God? In the throes of battle, whose prayers were heard? Whose were answered?* Luís, aware of his own powers of persuasion, thought ceaselessly about the presentation of the logic to convince the inner circle that would carry out *The Return.*

For Luís, the human calculations required were extensive. Vaults needed to be unlocked for the project's financial blood. Without fiscal patronage, the plan could not be launched. Aware of Serina Caputo's vast wealth, left to her by her husband, Luís also knew her weaknesses—a soul mired in sin; the origin of that sin being Cardinal Diego Hernandez. Although Luís's brief pursuit of Serina after the death of her husband was futile because of her devotion to Diego Hernandez, he knew her trust was essential to preempt any loss of her interest in the Vatican. As events played out, he need not have worried.

His thoughts interrupted by the noisy crowd around him, Luís stood among the throngs of the f ithful, the devout, and the curious. Luís was not concerned about the thieves that also worked the crowd. The thieves were possibly atheists—but no guarantee.

With no remorse over removing wallets and purses from a righteous crowd, the saintliness of the potential victims did not cloud the professional judgment of these skilled robbers. Despite his impatience, Luís enjoyed the human spectacle all around him while he waited.

These moments in Saint Peter's square fueled the Church and were the crowning glory of organized religion. This was the apostolic succession, the pinnacle of Catholicism, and the grand rebirth of hope for thousands of Christian churches created since the time of Christ. Only weeks ago Luís stood here, as the death bells rang through the air over the square, bells that were heard beyond the Tiber River into Rome itself. He recalled the words and traditions when a Pontiff dies.

"Dear Brothers and Sisters, our beloved Pope has returned to his Father's home." The Vatican spokesman had intoned the words. His announcement, made after the ritualistic tapping on the dead pontiff's head three times with a silver hammer, an ancient process conducted to ensure that a pope would not be buried alive, was proclaimed along with the mournful bronze bells. The bells performed a twofold role. They conveyed the sorrowful news but also delivered solace, allowing the sting of death to serenely fade away and prepare the faithful to joyfully receive a *new* pope.

When the conclave assembled, the people waited, as they had for centuries, for the spiral of white smoke that would appear from the back of the Sistine Chapel, heralding the successful selection of the new pope. Even the pickpockets in the square would pause in their work to observe the smoke changing, as chemicals altered the color of the smoke from the secret ballots burning in the stove. At the moment of the decisive ballot, smoke magically changed from black to white. The wisps of pallid smoke from the smoldering ballots announced that God had guided those gathered in the sealed room of the Sistine Chapel to a conclusion. A new pope had been chosen.

Their work completed, the attending cardinals were released from their self- imposed imprisonment. They donned their four-cornered red *biretta* hats, satisfied that the hat's significance—a Cardinal's commitment to spread and defend the faith, even if it meant spilling his blood—had been carried out.

Days earlier, Luís had accompanied his brother and Diego back to Rome from Colombia for the conclave. After the deceased Pope's magnificent funeral, the brothers departed Rome and spent a few days at home in Bogotá before starting a three-day tour of the country. Luís had orchestrated the trip by military jet, first north to Medellin and Bucaramanga then on to the northern coastal cities of Santa Marta and Barranquilla. The beach city of Cartagena had been avoided, as Luís could still not look down upon the site of his family's assassinations.

They visited Cali, the land of flowers and often foul play, and traveled east to Buenaventura.

Everywhere they were met with crowds of well wishers, and Juan Cardinal Gutiérrez asked the rich and the drug lords, as well as the humble and poor, for their prayers for the upcoming election. It was an emotional trip for the brothers and for all the family, as awareness encompassed them. Juan Carlos was a top contender to ascend to the throne of Saint Peter. The entire country was jubilant in anticipation.

Even the long-time enemy of General Luís Gutiérrez, the contentious FARC, paused in its warring. Driven by poverty and furious hormones, the young Turks of revolutionary groups, with weapons in their inexperienced hands, wielded as much power as they could ever expect in their usually short lives. Nurtured by the insatiable habits of drug users and mostly ignorant of why they fought, they attacked, kidnapped and murdered, spreading fear throughout Colombia.

However, this week their own *nacionalismo* surfaced, as they followed the news about the probable election of their fellow countryman. They contemplated their futures and some overcame the excitement of their fledging careers in terrorism and death, inherently realizing that having a Colombian pope would create an enormous responsibility for this land of conflict. Some would opt out of their violent lives to strive for peace, and many would be killed for their audacious thinking.

Although Luís had been lobbying on behalf of his brother for years, the pace accelerated after the death of the Pontiff. He intensified his marketing of Juan Carlos to Cardinals from around the world. All who would play a role in the gathering in Rome for the holy election had been vigorously lobbied. Luís spent time with elderly Cardinals, who, according to policy, could no longer vote if they had attained the age of eighty. But as elder statesmen, they were influential. Without marking a ballot, their preference often appeared in the vote of a younger protégé.

And so the continuity of experience, coalitions, politics, general haranguing, and soothing words echoed through the Sistine Chapel. It was a remarkable campaign. The press followed it diligently, as did the voting Cardinals, many of whom were meeting each other for the first time. Although secrecy was maintained to avoid overt politicking, the usual spies spent hours watching television coverage, testing the waters, and reporting to someone who would, in turn, report to the voting Cardinals. By the time the conclave began and the righteous voters were secluded, Cardinal Juan Carlos Gutiérrez was world known, and it was reputed that he was a shoo-in.

As General of the Colombian Armed Forces, Luís demonstrated unstinting valor in his efforts to rid his nation of the infamy it bore in the long war against insurgencies. These battles, the result of the never-ending push of coca and marijuana plants throughout vast plains of the Colombian landscape, rich with fertile soil, grew Luís's courage and his reputation. Finally overcoming his desire for revenge over the assassinations of his sister and his brother-in-law, Luís replaced the negative energy with his drive to move Juan Carlos to his destiny as the leader of the souls of the Christian world; while he, Luís, moved toward his destiny of saving that world.

The journey to become Vicar of Christ, the Holy Father, Pope, Bishop of Rome, and assorted other titles was attributed to roughly five percent apostleship and ninety-five percent politics.

During the centuries, less-than-holy shenanigans by powerful Italian families propelled popes into the Holy See. Juan Carlos noted the power struggles within the Vatican, even as he and Luís watched newer democracies in Latin America, forged from war-weary factions during the 1980s, slide and crumble.

"Does history ever take a new turn, Luís?" lamented Juan Carlos, reading reports of disenchanted countries forming new coalitions, exploiting increasingly valuable oil, tin, copper, and lithium in dangerous moves, nationalizing their industries, and alienating international friendships. "They drift ever leftward and further away from their Christian roots. I am distraught with my inability to lead us back to God. I imagine this planet *Godless* and wonder what the centuries of faith will have meant if we face a world without Him."

"I know your doubts remain, Juan Carlos. Thousands of years of effort and vying for power are part of the planetary landscape. But we *must* continue to exercise our diplomatic and military talents, as those before us did. We have yet to conclude a workable arrangement among the warring factions in our Colombia or in the world. As for the love of God, the work to peacefully lure those in grief for their lost souls is our only chance!"

As they watched the great population exodus from all over the world, they were more aware of the Latin American dash to the United States and debated the effects of large numbers scrambling to find a way onto the golden streets of America. While those who made it vied for jobs and resources outside their home country, millions more remained trapped in poverty.

"The fabric of permanent Catholicism among our Latino brothers has unraveled, and new spiritual avenues are sought by this innocent populace bombarded with technology and new choices." Now Juan Carlos succumbed to despair.

After the election, Luís noted an increasing guilt in his brother. "Juan Carlos, we have work to do, and the to-be-expected push and pull through the tiers of the Vatican hierarchy are behind you. Even feeling some sin of pride, try, for God's sake, to give in, and for a little while, enjoy the trappings of this magnificent state!"

As Pope Damasus III, Juan Carlos smiled weakly at his brother and surrendered to the joy of his office. He walked with Luís through the passageways of his fortified citadel. Although he had done so on numerous occasions, Juan Carlos had never taken it for granted. Its history was rich, turbulent, and grand. The *modern* city of Rome continued to function over the human bones and architectural skeletons of *ancient* Rome.

Over the centuries the pastoral and political autonomy of the Vatican had been lost and found again and again. Juan Carlos recalled the end of the reigns of the French popes in 1378, when Urban VI fled to Avignon after his defeat by troops loyal to the Roman pope. And so began the Western Schism, when the Roman Church, challenged by an anti-pope in France, was recognized by some regularly-ordained bishops. Still the effort outside of Rome was unsuccessful in regaining moral authority.

Juan Carlos was grateful for the ancient guidance given at The Council of Constance ending that schism. Pope Martin V had accepted the doctrinal supremacy of the Council and the reaffirmation of moral leadership of the Bishop of Rome over all other bishops—the mission bestowed by Christ Himself on Saint Peter. *Will what I do grant mercy from God? Did the popes of the schism draw mercy?*

As Juan Carlos strolled through the grove of lemon trees in his *Citta de Vaticano* on a balmy evening, he pulled a leaf from a low branch. Rubbing it between his fingers, he lost himself in the scent. Gazing at the brilliant yellow fruit, it seemed truly miraculous that life was fed to the leaves and the lemons through thin but sturdy veins of life.

He closed his eyes and considered his boundaries—Saint Peter's Square, the Vatican walls, and the Palace walls of the Holy See. He thought back to his inauguration.

Prideful but irresistible feelings surfaced as he remembered the dream-like events.

"Come, Holy Father, it is time to go." Juan Carlos heard the choir chanting, invoking the help of saints. He made the slow walk, passing through the drawn scarlet drapes hanging from the logia with the tapestry depicting Christ telling the apostles to be *fishers of men.* From this porch entrance to the basilica, the new pope, His Holiness, Pope Damasus III, stepped into the glaring light of a brilliant Italian morning. The sight of hundreds of thousands of well-wishers in the great plaza made him tremble.

He proceeded with the *pallium* stole, embroidered with red crosses to represent the five wounds of Christ, draped over his shoulders. The *pallium* represented the weight of the lamb, a reference to the burden of papal responsibility.

*Simon, son of John, do you love me? Tend my sheep, feed my sheep. Amen. When you were younger you dressed as you wished and went where you wished. But when you are older you will stretch out your arms and someone else will dress you and lead you where you do not want to go. Follow me.*

Juan Carlos heard the words as he sat and felt the arms of the ornate white and gold-gilt chair under him. He tried to put the words out of his mind. *Follow me, followme.*

The ring of the Fisherman was now on *his* finger. The ring of the Fisherman, Saint Peter, cruelly crucified upside down at the circus of Nero so near the Vatican, was now on his finger.

Juan Carlos wondered what Saint Peter wore at his fiery crucifixion, shuddering at the thought that Saint Peter was set ablaze and was later cut away, leaving only his feet. Suddenly, the gold miter with the white skullcap beneath it felt heavy on his head, as did his dark gold robes around his body. He turned to the Cardinals of the electorate, who were seated nearby wearing their pale gold robes and varying caps. All eyes were upon him. Swiss guards in gold and scarlet stockings and knickers, large silver helmets with red plumes, and starched white collars held their spears, appearing ready to defend their pope to the death.

In the reserved section, Countess Serina Caputo sat, struggling to make sense of the opulence, as she compared it to the simple scene depicted in the tapestry of Jesus instructing the apostles by the river Jordan.

Nina Shelky stood nearby in an enclosed area reserved for the press. Not wanting to miss any detail, Nina resisted taking notes but later wrote: *The new Pope is an aristocrat. It was easy to recognize that as I studied his face and that of his brother, General Luís Gutiérrez. The Church of Christ for the Pope is the entirety of Christianity, with its millions of men of every race, nation, and culture. I once read that the "Church that flowed from the lanced heart of Christ" was immutable andso often stilted in its progress. I wonder how this Pope will deal with the seemingly insurmountable obstacles in this terror-ridden world. Even with the full armor of God, will Pope Damasus III be able to stand against the wiles of the devil? As he enters this Basilica to the sound of trumpets, will his subjects feel he possesses a superhuman greatness? If not"*

# THE ARGUMENTS – ROME
## April 2010

They left His Holiness walking in silence back through the long ornate corridors to the apartment occupied by Cardinal Salvador DeAngeles. As the Vatican's elder statesman, the Cardinal maintained his position as Prefect of the Congregation for the Doctrine of the Faith. He rang for tea and then poured brandy while they waited. The six men settled into the old and comfortable overstuffed leather chairs that the elderly Cardinal had scattered about the room for lengthy meetings. Since his aging frame could no longer tolerate straight-backed wooden desk chairs, he always provided some comfort for visitors, even those burdened with great sin that desperately sought his counsel.

Cardinal DeAngeles loosened his collar from the fleshy folds of his neck. Now eighty-three and with most of his clerical life having been spent in research and writing drafts and speeches for various popes, the Cardinal oversaw and advised numerous authors on Vatican publications. As the accepted "last word" on right and wrong, it was feared he would reject out-of-hand the preposterous idea of returning Christ to earth. But he would be needed if the plan were to work.

Cardinal DeAngeles had witnessed more earthly moral decline than most. Having endured decades of seemingly hopeless attempts to ward off ever-present demons through ecclesiastical instruction, he had developed gnawing doubts about his contributions to the good of the faith. His speeches written for delivery by the pope supplied words of steadfast loyalty to the teachings of Jesus Christ, never sidestepping the challenges posed by fundamentalist Islamic terror, with its threats of annihilation to Jews and Christians alike. Cardinal DeAngeles drafted messages to the world that focused on the implausibility of Islam's inclusion in the free realm of pluralistic societies, pointing out its internal conflicts and slaughter, which repeatedly contradicted its own teachings. He battled the distortions heaped upon ignorant populations by extremists. His heavy hands penned words that were voiced by weary popes trying to find the vocabulary of reason.

DeAngeles sought without success to find proponents of decency within the ranks of Islamic clerics, credible representatives who might wholeheartedly participate in constructive conversations with representatives of Christ's Church. For him, the pen had sadly never proved mightier than the sword. His efforts only brought this initially dedicated and robust lieutenant of the pope to the point of exhaustion.

During a critical earlier conversation with His Holiness when the concept of *The Return* was revealed to him, the Cardinal initially felt himself mentally paralyzed, but then somehow *released*. Juan Carlos had held the Cardinal by his broad shoulders and tearfully uttered, "My dear friend, Salvador, I need to confess to you a bold idea of thought, of sin perhaps; an idea so immense that once you have heard it, you will realize that it counters all that you have believed and taught forever. We may be doomed for even letting it pass between us. Will you listen to me with an open mind and an open heart? You don't have to, of course," Juan Carlos then said quietly, "but even if you cannot embrace this scheme, I have a great need for your understanding and forgiveness."

Salvador recalled the tremble of Juan Carlo's hand and searched the Pontiff's eyes, trying to detect some sign of evil that might infect his own soul; but he saw only pain and uncertainty. Feeling a dangerous curiosity about the information to come, Salvador hesitated and then said, "My child *and my mentor*, Juan Carlos, you have entrusted me with much over the years—yes, even well before you became my Pope. I too have witnessed the unending horrors that have attacked our Church and its solemn dogma from many angles, but I have witnessed only your steadfast faith. Whatever it is that troubles you, if you wish, Holiness, unburden yourself." He waited.

Within a few moments of their conversation, Cardinal DeAngeles collapsed upon his bed with his eyes closed, trying to understand the Pope's vision and courage . . . or his folly.

As the raging danger and evil marched ever closer, Salvador DeAngeles, was surprised and almost amused at himself for never having even considered the possibility of Christ's return. Upon hearing and ultimately accepting the plan for *The Return,* he wondered, *was this, grievous as it may be, the answer to the increasing danger to the Church?*

Reviewing his life, it seemed now to have been rather empty. *Oh yes, there were words—millions of words, all trying to impart the message of our faith as it was handed down to us. The message is not clear in any one gospel, and there are many gospels. But our gospels—Mathew, Mark, Luke and John—were selected by Constantine and the Council of Nicocea as the Truth. "We are the way." We won that contest early on,* DeAngeles thought. *We chose the New Testament biblical writings— the acceptable gospels—all the governance and law. The mountains of works deemed "unacceptable" languish in libraries, universities and caves, for all I know. We excluded the gifts of many in our grab for the power of Christ's favor. If what we've concluded is the flawless truth, if it has always been right, why must we keep justifying it? Why do we endlessly battle the omnipresent propaganda of evil, the mindless desire for wrongdoing?*

Cardinal DeAngeles' soul-searching had been diligent, but it was over. Now he sat comfortably and contentedly; as he contemplated the discussions ahead with the others, who, he realized, had undergone the same excruciating process and had somehow *still* opted to participate. He said a prayer to the Holy Spirit for guidance.

Cardinal Adolfo Romano scanned the room through thick glasses and seated himself in what he thought was the least desirable chair. Adolfo Romano disliked having anybody see him in a state of what he considered human frailty and rigidly maintained his composure. As the Pope's somewhat stuffy personal aide, Romano often appeared bird-like in his short and irregular movements and sudden stops and starts. He had an unhealthy looking pale complexion and rheumy blue eyes, which he frequently dabbed with a folded handkerchief. Self-effacing and lacking humor, Romano was considered boring by many in the Papal staff.

Juan Carlos, however, had recognized Romano's value years ago in Colombia, in the coastal city of Barranquilla. As a rookie priest and Italian-born Colombian, Adolfo Romano had single-handedly talked Colombian guerillas out of a hostage standoff in the city's Justice Department. With simple reason and by guaranteeing them safe passage, he saved their lives and those of officials held hostage. His outward meekness masked his loyalty and his courage.

Pope Juan Carlos knew the need for the project's absolute secrecy. Romano more than met this requirement—Adolfo could manage secrecy. But in addition, His Holiness was always impressed at Cardinal Romano's ability to ferret out information and yet shield the Pope from unwanted "listeners." It would be both foolish and difficult to exclude him. His constant proximity to Juan Carlos and his unusual talents were vital.

Adolfo Romano would shoulder a good deal of the Pope's burden. He would dedicate his life to it, and when it was completed, he would spend retirement with his few remaining family members in Tuscany.

Following the group into the room, Father Jonathan Kennedy resisted sitting down, hoping that standing by the door would signal that he expected a brief meeting.

This would dismiss the madness and give him relief from the relentless clang in his ears and the oppressive weight on his mind. He wondered what he was doing here and what they wanted of him. Feeling vulnerable and uncomfortable after his initial meeting with His Holiness, and as the others seemed to ignore him, he closed his eyes, embracing precious seconds of denial that he was even present. Kennedy doubted that this monstrous notion of bringing Christ back to earth would actually be embraced by these august officers of his Church. *My Church*, he lamented in his mind. *This can't be my Church. I'm dreaming.*

A fearless lion of a man, Cardinal DeAngeles then boomed out from across the room. "Sit down, Jonathan. Sit down. We'll be a while." Father Kennedy obeyed.

Cardinal DeAngeles yanked at his collar with a massive finger and tried to begin.

In a decidedly awkward manner, he blurted out, "I know it's absurd. We may be in the throes of committing the most colossal mortal sin ever conceived by man." Reverting to childhood teachings, he tried to grasp a word for the enormity of the plan they were about to discuss. He felt his mature wisdom disappear. "It's like we've thrown off and discarded the very essence of our belief, like shedding snakes. Have we become instant nihilists, banishing our faith to the realm of personal opinion?" Despite past days of agonizing contemplation, clarity was elusive once again. DeAngeles succumbed to twiddling his massive thumbs in inarticulate helplessness, searching for the words to go on.

"My dear DeAngeles," interrupted Cardinal Romano, recognizing the cerebral paralysis affecting his old colleague. They all focused on Romano, surprised at his taking the initiative. His always-strict composure remained while he quietly spoke. "It is beyond sin, beyond sacrilege, beyond blasphemy." He looked around. "Is it borne of *hubris*, or . . . ." He rigidly held his knees in an effort not to display emotion or fidget and continued. "Or are we entertaining the possibility of doing something simply for the sake of civilization? If you think of civility," he chuckled dryly, "not one of us is really civilized."

"What's that supposed to mean?" Cardinal DeAngeles asked, now drumming his fingers against his abdomen. Though grateful to have given up the floor, he now felt chagrined and slightly ashamed of himself, wary of some implied offense.

"Ah, some attain a degree of civility, but it is rote. Look at this table," Romano gestured toward the small table, holding the brandy and glasses. "Were this table not here with its carved legs and inlaid surface, were this crystal decanter, full of man's creation— this wonderful brandy, which we sip from civilized-looking containers and hope to enjoy more of . . ." he groped for some small humor. "If they were to cease to be, we would quickly revert to the cunning of animals and adjust to the absence of these civilities. The mentally and physically fittest of us would outwit and outmaneuver the others."

Cardinal DeAngeles regained control of the discourse, "I might fight for the remaining brandy," he said, folding his hands on his chest and smiling, "while Cardinal Arias over there would kill for the last of Sister Agnes's fudge brownies." Cardinal DeAngeles had found his voice again, and Cardinal Teodoro Arias, difficult to amuse, remained quiet and smiled mirthlessly at him from across the room.

Laughing at his small joke, Cardinal DeAngeles pulled himself up and approached the decanter of brandy. With a flourish, he poured himself another drink. "You bring up an interesting point, Cardinal Romano. Civility, as we have tried to establish it, has been the classic example of an exercise in futility." Holding up his glass, he continued. "Our more natural and ungracious state is evident. I just now demonstrated it in my observation that the decanter level lowers. In my greed I needed to 'get mine,'" he said, raising the glass to his lips and swallowing deeply. "I further demonstrate this futility in my ill kempt desk, my animal-like snoring, which, according to most of you, resembles a primal scream, my disheveled appearance upon awakening, gastric imbalance, and rotting breath. No wonder that long ago I chose not to reveal my incivility to women. Thank God, I am allowed to flop about these elegant surroundings, where I am cocooned in the trappings of civility, and able to fool the outside world. I thank God for accepting me, brute that I am." He let himself sink back into the chair. "Granted, many struggle to lift the curse of poverty, but most of the world ignores it and lets the poor wallow in hopelessness in untidy dwellings, eating what the rich discard, and wearing filthy clothes forced on their backs in the name of 'decency.'"

Cardinal Diego Hernandez, silent up to now, knew his friend was skirting the issue. He waited for an opening and began to speak. "With your kind permission, Cardinal DeAngeles, can we direct our thoughts to the subject at hand?" Diego felt his tension renew but plunged ahead. "Bringing Christ back," he felt an instant of revulsion at the phrase, "or *someone who is perceived by others to be Christ,* seems spiritually impossible, unthinkable. But is it physically possible? Its intrigue, its astounding possibilities have consumed me. Yes, I admit my desire to take on this challenge, as I have allowed myself to accept its righteousness of purpose. I have tried to break it into pieces, and I am reminded of secondary school journalism. Who will this Jesus be?

What will be his mission? Where will he go? Who will see him? It is easy to rationalize the 'why,' but the 'how' is still beyond us and forces us into the arena of high technology, an area that could prove a great threat to the Church. That terrifies me almost as much as my current fears for my place in eternity."

Diego looked at the group, sympathizing with their distress, as they faced the reality of the conversation, dealing with their own nerve, their own righteousness. Diego wryly added, "All of us may meet that destiny sooner than desired and going through with this outrageous plan ought certainly to redefine anyone's expectation of eternity."

"Well," interjected Cardinal DeAngeles, "I'd love to hear yours one day, but at this strange moment, we are contemplating the *granddaddy* of *all fantasies*." He leaned his bulk forward and in a serious tone continued, "This may be defined as a disastrous misadventure in the 'playing God' arena, but it has, nonetheless, challenged our intellect and logic, as well as our ethics. I'll grant you my extreme poverty of technical knowledge, but I believe I know what I don't know. That is, I believe the technical challenge is doable now, or will be, as we approach the actual mission. I even agree with Cardinal Hernandez as to its need, and I scare myself saying that." He looked puzzled. "There's a certain contradiction here—at its conception, the world was blissfully naïve.

Early man accepted various gods that filled his needs and satisfied his understanding. With the birth, crucifixion, and resurrection of Our Lord, we have clung to the True Faith. For many more hundreds of years, we've remained ingenuous enough to unquestionably grant credibility to the mountains of teaching asserting that *Christ Will Come Again!* The only thing we've accepted that *we don't know* is the timing."

"Ah, but the 20th Century," he stared at the brown liquid in the small brandy snifter between his hands. "The 20th Century and now this moment in time have got to be as phenomenal as the one in which man first stood up. Technological leaps that make it appear as though our brains finally went into gear. Isn't it fantastic that flight—a skill that mankind coveted since he first saw a flying creature—once conquered in the early 1900s was common within decades. Rockets were being hurled into space, making the unheard of, the impossible, *almost* commonplace. The world population experiences rapid assimilation of technology. If that persists—and I haven't a clue why it won't—it could wreak havoc on the Church. It could ultimately deny the very existence of Christ as God. Yet," he sighed, "technology is now the very tool we require to bring Him back."

Cardinal DeAngeles walked to a large globe on an ornate three-footed pedestal and began to turn it slowly. "You know, I have always loved these globes," he mused out loud, as though to completely change the subject. Yet, the others knew he was simply stalling, while he prepared another thought, orbiting it in his mind as his fingers lightly turned the shiny sphere. He traced a line north from Mongolia across the Bearing Sea through Alaska and beyond the Hudson Bay to the southern tip of Greenland. He continued his imaginary trip over the Atlantic. Touching the British Isles, he crossed the Channel and continued down through France. He hesitated at Paris, resisting the temptation to dwell on his early years and pressed further southeast to Italy and Rome. His mind diverted as he recalled making that journey to Rome as a young priest. Now, nearing the end of his clerical career, he wondered what destiny a different life would have brought him. "I see myself as a dot, standing in this room on this spot on this globe. But I am in familiar surroundings, and I have a comforting sense of where I am." Continuing his mental meandering, he picked another potential digital route, delighting in his imaginary travel, reluctant to return to the conversation at hand.

"Terror has always been with us, hasn't it?" He didn't look up. "Since the beginning of the 21st Century, accelerated world terror attacks have generated a yearning, a resurgence of a deep yearning for the reassurance of Christ's promise. This reassurance is sorely needed in a world of aging men and women, trying to spiritually ready themselves for death, while society derides and mocks Christian spirituality. What a strange dichotomy that the failure in societal values and the presence of madmen who hope to destroy the world has, incidentally, pretty much been pulled off with the help of modern technology."

Cardinal DeAngeles had questioned whether a non-judgmental return of Christ— not the eschatological breaking-in of the ultimate Kingdom of God—would defeat the contempt hurled at him and others in a deteriorating Catholic society. "What kind of proof would this planet's cynical population demand in order to believe? Never before have we had such an educated Catholic citizenry. I wonder," he said mostly to himself, "who is left, who is reconciled to the moral and ethical teachings of the Church?" His voice trembled slightly, as he spread his hands about the basketball-sized globe and looked at his small audience with a bright face. "Or would the sheer desire *to believe in such an occurrence* be *so* widespread and impassioned as to soften the hearts of the hardest among us?"

Diego interrupted. "Recall the ninety-four Synods, Your Eminence? Pope John Paul refused to budge on recurring issues. Should it be otherwise? What percentage of Catholics truly wishes an iota of change in the Church's cherished dogma and law? Should she *ever* yield to the noisy clattering of the few to overturn doctrine based on faith? What has caused his Holiness, Juan Carlos, so adamant in his own devotion to Church laws, to now toy with a thought so overwhelmingly uncharacteristic?" They all looked at one another, suddenly acutely aware of the immensity and perceived blasphemy of the entire conversation.

General Luís Gutiérrez, who had held back in deference to the Cardinals, now felt that the moment for him to speak was at hand. He stood up from his leather chair and asked quietly, "Do you recall the speech Ronald Reagan gave for Barry Goldwater back in 1964? Reagan said, 'If some among you fear taking a stand because you are afraid of reprisals from customers, clients, or even government, recognize that you are just feeding the crocodile, hoping he'll eat you last.'" He squinted at them and smiled, trying to lighten the mood, to lift the increasingly heavy burden the strange dialogue was placing on them. Luís quietly begged for a collective approval and did not want to appear as his brother's instigator.

"So, my dear Princes of this beloved Church," Luís went on, "God may forgive us for attempting to recreate Him in this manner, because we are doing it for Him and for the common good. But I doubt He'd ever forgive us for giving in. We're not depleting the religious account. It seems that humankind, that's us, has been created as an anthropological disaster, but would God trade us in for a wiser version? Our faults are evident. Will He condemn us for trying to overcome them?" Luís looked at the small august group with a sense of guilt, knowing he was at the brink of persuading them to share in his corruption.

Feeling the authoritative need to relieve the General, Cardinal DeAngeles, spoke up, "Remember, gentlemen, that the human mind is a subtle machine. It spends, if not as much time, certainly devoted time, to the concealment of truth as to its discovery. In these instances, the target of the mind is its very self. Although it may be said that the greatest self-deception is among perpetrators of violent crimes, certainly the push-pull tug-of-war over the existence of God, the trinity, the virgin birth, the resurrection, etc., etc., runs a close second." He looked into his brandy. "I venture to say the very notion of 'faith' pleads for constant fortification." He took another sip. "Unlike the repulsive indifference of the criminal or the terrorist, however, faith struggles within itself for its own disloyalty. By our choice of vocation, we preach theological virtue and boast of our total belief in God and a trusting acceptance of His being and His will. Well gentlemen," he let out a long sigh, "let he who is without a little doubt now and then be the first to step into heaven. I envy him."

Cardinal DeAngeles, now enjoying the confidence the brandy provided rolled on. "Is it our mission to exact or demand fidelity on theology alone?" He shook his head. "We have, after all, no proof, not a lot of logic, no material evidence. We chose a tough profession, gentlemen. But then," he chuckled, "I'm awfully glad I'm with the fellow who initiated this profession. I can hardly imagine the brain teasing in the heads of our protestant brothers. While correctly pointing out the unfortunate tendencies and consequences of medieval theocratic government, they have split themselves into smaller and smaller entities—quarreling and dividing Christ into ever-tinier segments with each generation that has a new idea of what or who He is. We, gentlemen, may be misguided and damned to Hell forever for trying to bring Him back, but I like truly believing that God will show us mercy for knowing *Who* we're trying to return. And all Christians will agree, I hope."

The others gazed on him silently, with empathy, with respect for his contorted logic that so mirrored their own. Luís could feel the glow of hope reaching through the dread of the encroaching Godless world he continuously witnessed militarily. Although after so much time he was amazed by it, Luís reasoned these holy men knew more than he thought. He realized they understood the threat to the Church, to all of Christianity, far more than he did. Like a true salesman, he knew the moment had come to simply shut up, at least for now.

During this complex discussion, Father Jonathan Kennedy sat in the back of the room, had listened and said nothing. It was the first time he wished he were old. *Old* allowed suppressed doubts to surface and air without fear of hierarchical recrimination or accusations. He found himself admiring these troubled human beings, these men with the same spiritual frailties as his own. Jonathan envied Cardinal DeAngeles. He would be dead and gone before the project was executed. Jonathan felt it allowed Salvador DeAngeles a greater freedom to express himself.

After seconds of silence, another voice was heard from across the room. "When would this be done, where would it be done, and how much would it cost?" The deep, serious voice was from Teodoro Cardinal "Teddy" Arias. The small group turned to the rough face, whose deep lines hid none of life's sufferings. Cardinal Arias, tasked with keeping track of the Vatican's vast financial holdings, had moved past theory and now wanted answers.

Although Church leaders throughout the world historically petitioned their congregations for the funds to operate the Holy See, few knew the intricacies of papal finances. Cardinal Arias was master of the mystery that always shrouded the fiscal arrangements of the Catholic Church.

With no obvious sources of wealth, he had managed to guide dioceses in their payments of millions in expenses, without having to divulge amounts or origins of funds. Thieves, drunks, drug addicts, and most embarrassing to the Church, pedophiles, had caused Cardinal Teodoro Arias—affectionately ca led "Teddy, the Bag Man" behind his back—to soften the sharp edge he presented publicly. He felt personal anguish and disgust for the fiscal disgraces, which had confronted him over the years, but possessed the skills to enable the Church to avoid financial disaster. An original member of the Vatican's Latin American faction, Cardinal Arias was an economist and financial wizard. With this reputation, "Teddy" had been entrusted early on with Vatican financial control and had served several papal reigns.

Although Cardinal Arias rarely spoke of his inner feelings about the prevailing religious dogma that justified rules prescribed for the faithful, approaching him with the concept of *The Return* was a delicate moment for the Pope. When he met with Arias in a private session, the Pope recited his distress over terrorism, starvation, disease and poverty throughout the world, and Arias wondered what it would cost to fix it.

"I wonder," the Pope spoke, looking deep into the eyes of his old friend during their earlier conversation, "if Christ were actually to return to our troubled planet, what would happen? Would he save us? Sometimes I think that only such a cataclysmic event would focus the world's attention to the colossal damage we, as God's people, are inflicting upon ourselves and our political, social, and ecclesiastic environments. My lifetime of preaching and studying has convinced me that Christ's promised return to earth may be our last best hope to rescue its peoples."

Juan Carlos had looked at Cardinal Arias, trying to gage his response to this last statement. Cardinal Arias returned his gaze passively, not revealing his thoughts. "If one accepts the truth of what I have just said, should we then wait passively for His return? Are we, the leadership of Christianity, willing to wait like lambs in a flock surrounded by wolves for the deliverance promised by our Lord Jesus Christ? Will the times permit such passivity? I think not. We believe in Christ's coming again, of course, but our inability to predict its timing obliges us to take a more active hand or . . . or to accept that we will succumb to the pack and that our destruction will be at their hands. Would that not mean that they were right all along?" His Holiness heard the desperation in his own voice as he searched Teddy Arias' face for doubt but saw only a slightly quizzical expression. "So far, so good," Juan Carlos thought before going on, "God help me."

"Suppose, just suppose that we could make it *appear* that Christ had returned to us, to light the way to our salvation and not to our demise by the wolves of this world. If there is any chance we could succeed, is it not our obligation, our *duty,* to at least *try*? Would it not be a sin to allow the slow agonizing death of this great institution?"

Teddy Arias sat quietly for a moment. When Juan Carlos had called him in for their private meeting, Cardinal Arias had feared another Church scandal but instead found he was taking part in the most astounding conversation he had ever had. His orderly and analytical mind struggled, trying to absorb this extraordinary discussion. Juan Carlos did not hesitate before posing the question, "Hypothetically, my friend, *if* we were to attempt this unorthodox plan, how would *you* approach such an idea . . . financially?"

At the end of the Pope's question, Teddy Arias felt calm. In an instant his mind had made the leap across the chasm that held dangerous questions of ethics, morality, and sin to the safety of statements, ledgers, and calculators. This was something he could deal with—numbers.

They were his life preserver, and he grabbed on. There was no confusion. Numbers never lie. His mind began to work, calculations blazing across his mind's eye.

Juan Carlos realized that he had found the key to his friend's consent and waited for him to speak.

"Holy Father," Teddy said, "we can spend and collect and spend with little danger of wiping out the piggybank. I realize the confidentiality required, but when there is a plan of action, I will be ready to prepare a financial plan and a positive response regarding the amount of money required to conduct such a venture." Cardinal Arias took Juan Carlos' hands and said without smiling, "You are visionary. You may be wrong, but you are courageous. My moral remorse, if I have any, has not yet confronted me. If it does, I will deal with it."

The two men looked at each other. Teddy Arias, normally void of emotion, embraced his Pope and turned to leave the room.

Being frequently tasked with confronting the amazing lengths to which human weakness stretched discipline within the clergy, and determining a course of action to pay for its mistakes was commonplace for Cardinal Arias. Here in Cardinal DeAngeles' quarters, the conversation with Juan Carlos seemed long ago, and despite his initial shock, Cardinal Teddy Arias had mentally pushed aside any notion of a "mistake." The challenge of the funding now intrigued him, and he approached it like a puzzle to be solved.

Cardinal Arias looked at this small group of good and holy men over the always- cloudy lenses that sat near the front of his nose. He spent endless moments removing them, wiping them, and returning them to the bridge of his nose. They would slide once again to his protruding cheekbones, where trapped moisture caused a constant haze. Despite this annoyance, he knew his figures intimately. The Church had vast holdings in stocks and real estate, liquid and otherwise. Teddy Arias took a decidedly secular pleasure in developing market strategies to create sizeable profits on an almost daily basis. The funding for this undertaking . . . was it there? Arias would have to know more.

Years of managing investments had caused Cardinal Arias to presume more than a custodial position. He considered the Vatican wealth as though it were his own. "His" bank, once a dungeon, was tucked away in a medieval tower. With no branches, no MBA bankers to foul the waters and only a handful of employees, Archbishop Teodoro Arias closed down as much outside scrutiny as possible. He had counted the beans for a long time and wanted no repeat of financial scandals and collapses such as those experienced in the 1970s, when the *Banco Ambrosia* in Milano sold shares to the Vatican and lost over a billion dollars in a series of international gambles. No, Teddy Arias disliked any unnecessary revelation about *his* money.

Noting the look of concentration on the group's faces, Cardinal Arias continued. "Gentlemen, before you even try to answer my questions regarding this, shall we say, mysterious approach to our beloved Church's precarious state," he quipped, "have your minds not already been cluttered with innumerable would-be miracles just as this project proposes? So many 'miracles' flood our gracious walls, begging for recognition, acclaim, and validation. How much thought have we given to substantiation of this ludicrous plan? Have you judged the risk? What damage control factors can be incorporated, if fraud is suspected?" He poked his finger in the air. "And, I tell you fraud will indeed be trumpeted by the Church's enemies and, perhaps, proven. How do you expect us to wriggle out of this if deceit is traced to us and we are dubbed the world's greatest quacks? Have you considered the consequences for our beloved Church? Is it worth it to destroy centuries of faith?" Arias pondered his feelings of renewed doubt as he listened to these conversations and confronted his own fear.

There was silence as they all evaluated his remarks. Father Kennedy felt great relief as he clung to the possibility that Cardinal Arias' words would void the whole plan, and life could go on as before.

Cardinal DeAngeles finally heaved a sigh and broke the silence. "Well, well, well, dear Teddy, you have dared to touch on the unforgivable . . . *failure*. Obviously, we need the fewest, finest brains available. By the sheer ability of those brains, we must also provide for failure. Once examined for even a remote possibility, doesn't it seem reasonable that a scapegoat must also be identified?"

The group looked to Cardinal DeAngeles for an answer to his own question; and while addressing their inquiry, he casually smiled through closed lips and said, "I was thinking of the Israelis. You'll recall that the Jews invented the word 'scapegoat?' The Bible tells us that on the Jewish Day of Atonement, a goat is symbolically filled with the sins of the community by the high priest, who then sends the animal into the wilderness. The scapegoat is an unfortunate creature. It wanders in blissful apathy, appearing well groomed and giving the impression it finds life rather enjoyable. Unfortunately for the scapegoat, the sins grow heavy, and he becomes a beast of burden."

Cardinal DeAngeles looked over at Teddy Arias. "Please, Cardinal, whether or not you agree to this plan, you're being here assures your complicity. With your immense financial talent, I hope you might apply that ability to the, shall we say, 'unusual' bookkeeping that may be required. The Israelis may indeed be a scapegoat for us, but they will be an expensive one, don't you think?"

Cardinal Arias brightened somewhat. "Undoubtedly; however, an offer put in the context of the greater good of The Jewish State could be highly attractive to them. Possibly, we might well be able to help alleviate their strained defense budget."

DeAngeles grinned, "I'm sure the entire free world, what's left of it, would welcome a little help in that area."

"Are we at a point, gentlemen, where we can address the first of the five Ws— when?" asked Cardinal Hernandez. "For the sake of argument, I believe the event should take place at or close to Easter. There's a certain historical resonance to Easter, and even though it may be too obvious, it has an identifying quality. Time-wise, I believe it is acceptable to stick with the original dating."

"Yes, yes, of course—Easter," replied Cardinal DeAngeles. "But which Easter?

And where?"

"The Pope has suggested an infant, raised for this very purpose." Father Kennedy looked around at them, now unhappily assuming his appointed role. "He would make this return to earth in his late teens or early twenties. He would make only a 'visit.'"

They all looked up and stared at the younger priest, who had been inconspicuous in the background and had not uttered a word until that moment. The thought of an infant raised for this purpose caused them all to examine their own mortality and realize that if this event took place, most of the participants would not be around to witness it. They would participate in planning but would be dead before its execution. They wondered if they would witness it from above, hopefully from the heaven they all yearned for, sitting at the side of the God to whom they had devoted their lives. Even as they wondered, they felt conflicted, frightened in their sometimes-lagging conviction that such a place existed. This handful of men also knew that if the critical secrecy were maintained—a difficult task—they would take the knowledge of this event to their graves. If one of them were to reveal it, the fate of the others would be damnable beyond imagination, and certainly beyond any forgiveness of an angry God, the Father.

Cardinal Hernandez broke the silence. "I envision a remote area with only a small number of witnesses. The power of a crowd seems initially appealing; but the future impact of a group which is minimal, of varying ages, and composed of both men and women is what I envision—a small remote society, one that is not well-educated but sheltered and able to accept through the lens of their simple faith the presence of a savior—a savior bringing the message of God. I see it as the best possible way to penetrate this jaded world. Whoever these people may be, they may walk into Hell, but they will be armed with a legend."

"You speak, Diego, as though you have already thought of such a place."

"I haven't, but I see it in my mind and know that it must exist. I will find it, if that's what you want me to do."

Cardinal Teddy Arias extended his open hand toward Diego. "Yes, I agree that you should seek out the location, your Eminence. I also must propose that you first find adequate funding. I have my doubts about this focus on the Vatican itself. It cannot be connected with this project. Should we encounter any difficulties, I can set aside funds to ameliorate them, but it appears that this will require an almost limitless revenue stream. There must be firewalls in place to protect the Vatican, to protect His Holiness. It is difficult to place a monetary price on this undertaking," he looked thoughtful. "Perhaps you have already thought of alternative funding from private sources?"

Cardinal Hernandez felt his heart beat a little faster, as the fond image of the Countess Serina Caputo formed. *She has the money,* he thought to himself. *Would she support a project that she would have little or no knowledge of—a project that would have such devastating consequences if it were exposed, or if it were a failure?* He tried to block out the thought that he and Serina would perhaps not live long enough to see the results.

Diego shuddered at his unspoken love for Serina. He wondered again about the significance of his often-contemplated corruption in the eyes of God versus the monumental task ahead. He reasoned that God was well aware of his weaknesses—his love of Serina and his commitment to this mission.

He stood up from his chair and walked over to the decanter of brandy. "I think, gentlemen, that I may be able to secure the funding." He poured one last drink, tipped his head and swallowed deeply. As Diego walked toward the door, he was frightened but smiled confidently, and hoping to part on an upbeat note, said to Cardinal DeAngeles, "If I can fill the coffers, will you promise to fill the decanter before I return?"

# General Luís Gutiérrez – Rome
**April 2011**

General Luís Antonio Gutiérrez was in heaven, or at least believed he would be if death struck at that instant.

This moment was glorious. He was in Rome, in the Vatican, in Saint Peter's. His brother Juan Carlos was the Pope, and he, Commander in Chief of the Armed Forces of Colombia, was about to be knighted, inducted into the coveted Equestrian Order of the Knights of the Holy Sepulchre.

"Welcome, Gentlemen." The young priest who choreographed such events solemnly greeted the candidates gathered at the statue of Saint Peter in front of the cathedral. He smiled at them pompously and with an overbearing authority, walked ahead of the group, who glanced at each other with amused smiles. "We will now proceed under Bernini's colonnade to the Bronze Door of the Apostolic Palace. There you will be saluted by the Swiss Guard as we enter the reception room." The young priest spoke with an exaggerated accent that, although affected, added elegance to the event. Luís soon forgot about him and allowed himself to sink into an irresistible feeling of self- importance, of being one of the chosen for this ostentatious ceremony. He reveled in the splendor of his surroundings. He was a commanding sight in his full uniform, as he mingled with members of the honored group and joined several conversations.

"We are in jeopardy of losing this great institution as we know it," Luís overheard one say to several others. "Losing what?" asked Luís introducing himself. All deferred, knowing that the impressive-looking

Colombian General was family to His Holiness. "Losing our Church, losing world clout," replied the man, visibly frustrated at the apparent naïveté of the question. "Our Catholic schools are rapidly disappearing, attendance at mass is low, and the Islamic radicals harass Christians and attack missionaries the world over. The Muslim minority in many nations is not only growing but using their numbers to intimidate."

"And what do you make of all of this, sir?" asked Luís politely, looking for added confirmation of what he already knew.

"I see it and read about it throughout the United States. Here in Europe, the millions of slaughtered Jews of World War II have now been replaced with many more millions of Muslims. How do we absorb them and their basic aversion to tolerating Christianity, their perception that church and state are one? We are all witnesses to the goal of Muslim cleric rule, and I'm worried that our Christianity is being systematically shoved aside." He looked at Luís directly. "I am thrilled to be here, to be inducted into this order by His Holiness, your brother, and I wish I had greater confidence in my own ability to help reverse the trend of decline."

Another man chimed in, "I'm afraid I agree with you; and my concerns also stretch to the alarming rise of atheism. Oddly, it seems to have grown as a backlash to Islamic terror—an added and maybe unexpected plus for the perpetrators of 9/11 and other terrorist acts, which have become so pervasive. It is difficult to determine our true role and why God seems not to acknowledge that the technical and scientific advances of the developed world may eventually hand the terrorists the weapons they need to destroy us."

*That will soon be tested*, thought Luís.

"Our beliefs may not matter much by then." The man looked grim. "I am here today to further pledge my commitment to Christ. I wish He would give us those signs of encouragement he gave to the prophets of old," he smiled mirthlessly.

Luís looked about this elite group, who had earned favor within the Church and been selected for membership within the ancient, chivalric order. They were intensely Catholic people and recognized for their generosity and spiritual and religious pursuits. Being haunted by *The Return* and its details and dangers, Luís was bothered by an underlying sense of futility brought on by the ceremony. He fervently wished the mission of the Equestrian Order of the Knights of the Holy Sepulchre *could* be realized and *could* return the Catholic Church to its unwavering center of a world devoted to Christ.

"Regrettably," another American commented, "the ideals that spawned the Crusades in the Middle Ages are now beyond modern understanding. A campaign like that in contemporary times involving state-of-the-art and possibly nuclear weapons would mean staggering death counts. Besides, none of us are up to it, not like the guys from the old days. We're donning the same white robes with the crimson cross, but we'll not bear the arms they took up after the conquest of the Holy City."

"Still," the first man replied. "Look at us! We bear a heritage bestowed upon us by the Papal Secretariat of State. Wearing the Cross of the Five Wounds of Our Lord, the Cross of Godfrey, and the Cross of Jerusalem is our privileged right. I hope I wear this cross with dignity and humility. I wish I could fill the world with the Cross!" He spoke with sadness.

Noting the dejection in his voice reinforced Luís's convictions. He would have enjoyed the reaction of this group to the plans for *The Return*. They might well affirm the precarious path the planners had chosen. Dangerous yes, but *The Return* held wondrous possibilities.

Once settled into their seats and the homily of the mass at hand, Luís listened to the words of his brother, the Pope, and hearing those words, envisioned a time long ago.

"The first Crusade, a miraculous event," began His Holiness, "was forged by the faith implanted in the minds of Christian men, who, being insulated, had little need or desire to look beyond their own environment. Their surroundings—their parish churches—were their world. Few ventured farther than the next village. Almost no one knew the vast areas across the mountains or even beyond the next valley."

Juan Carlos knew the words he now spoke were simply ceremonial. No one would rise again to such a need. "But there was faith," he continued, "a faith so strong, fanned by the Word of The Lord and fostered by itinerant preachers that fixed a clear vision and an urgent desire to free the Holy Sepulchre of Jerusalem from the grip of the infidel.

"One thousand years ago, Pope Urban II exhorted the Catholic faithful to rectify this outrage to Christianity. The vehemently Christian believers were so inflamed by Urban's words that they left their fields, their mills, and their families and dedicated their lives to march into the Holy Land. They ventured onto the highways and byways and across mountains and deserts to reclaim the venerated symbols of their Lord, Jesus Christ, and pray upon His empty tomb. The True Faith was to be restored to the land of Jesus through a living, practicing, sustaining, and viable Christian congregation."

Juan Carlos knew that none of them, including himself, had the strength to truly confront the danger, to raise a sword, to seek out the elusive enemy of his Church. His eyes rested briefly on Luís, and his mind fought against the reality of *The Return*. *Dear God, was there no other way?*

"It was in Clermont in 1095 that Pope Urban uttered the great battle cry—*DeusLo Vult.*—God Wills It. It remains today our singular motto. From this came the Order of The Holy Sepulchre of Jerusalem that you accept today, approved by Pope Pascal II in 1113 and established to lead the militant Christian assault against the Muslims. The Order remains a symbolic reminder of the endless quest for Christ, and indeed, vigilance is more necessary today than ever. No other such society or organization of the Church so profoundly reminds us of our sacred duty."

Luís, stirred by the faith of the crusaders, had always stressed mass attendance by his troops and their families throughout Colombia. As General of the Armed Forces, he continually provided security, honor guards, and transportation for the hierarchy of the Colombian Church. He often traveled with the clergy to villages to deliver food and other needs to the people, and he had been highly recommended to the Vatican for membership in this prestigious Order. It was convenient, of course, that His Holiness, Pope Damasus III was his brother, the first Latin American pope.

Despite the bloody history, the reality in the late 1900s was that Jerusalem welcomed the Christians back. Arriving, often with lagging faith, thousands renewed their spiritual passion by visiting the attractions in The Land of the Bible. The *Via Dolorosa* filled daily with "religious tourists," tracing the fourteen "stations of the cross." The "stations," depicted in every Catholic Church, represented the stages of Christ's agony and death and were walked every year in the old walled city of Jerusalem by throngs who reverently shared the burden of moving a large wooden cross through the winding stone-paved passageways of the Christian Quarter. It became the object of pilgrimages, and many pilgrims underwent transforming experiences, creating a new relationship with *their* Christ.

During the frequent religious festivities, Jerusalem's cash registers rang merrily, even among the most fervent disciples of the great religions. Exceptional ecumenism existed within the shops of the old walled city. Confronted with the opportunity of separating dollars and shekels from tourists in a passionately righteous state of mind, all theological disputes were put aside.

"Come in, come in." Muslims cheerfully lured Christians into their shops full of church vestments, carvings, icons, and crosses. Arab street vendors hawked rosary beads in one hand and an array of headscarves in the other. Stock included worry beads, Christmas ornaments, crucifixes, and replicas of the Holy Family, as well as camels and donkeys carved from native olive wood. "Cash was King," and everyone got along.

In one sense, the Order of the Holy Sepulchre had accomplished its mission. In fact, by the 20th Century a host of Christian religions occupied the Church of the Holy Sepulchre, and each had their niche. Some were grander than others, but the Greek Orthodox Church had precedence and their distinctive glass lanterns hung in profusion near what is considered the actual tomb of Jesus Christ. Their much-coveted control began as a reward bestowed by the 12th Century Arab leader and victor of the Crusades, Saladin, for their support in opposing the Romans and overturning earlier victories by their opponents.

Inside the rambling structure that is the Church of the Holy Sepulchre, Muslims have for generations sold candles to devout Catholics just outside the entry and exits of the celebrated tomb. For the Muslim proprietors of the tomb and the small dome on a nearby hill from where, it is said, Christ ascended into heaven, no sense of hypocrisy existed. The atmosphere of spirituality for Holy Land visitors had for centuries permeated sacred remains, and Christian visitors, for the most part, overlooked the ecclesiastical compromises. Most remained oblivious to the political realities of the sacred dwellings—that it is not possible to view these places without being shepherded by Muslim merchants is lost on most. For others, trying to retain an aura of holiness, trafficking Christian icons proved difficult. Some Catholics, expecting to be greeted by a member of the Catholic clergy—maybe even Saint Peter himself—were left with a sense of being exploited. It was difficult to reconcile the historical decisions, the need for income to maintain these holy places, and the annoying and seemingly unavoidable presence of non-Christians.

Tourists in Jerusalem, often hot and tired and uncomfortable in the maize-like jumble that was the walled city, often wished the docents of the Church of the Holy Sepulchre would hurry it along. "Ownership of the church," it was explained, "came about in an unholy series of events. Bickering over certain areas still persists, as only recently, Monks from the Ethiopian Orthodox Church and others from the Coptic Church of Egypt required hospitalization, resulting from clashes over control of the church's rooftop."

"Was that when soldiers in the courtyard needed to pull them apart?" a young woman asked.

"Yes," the docent replied, grateful for the question. "Soldiers, armed with M16 rifles monitored a standoff between a Coptic, who had dragged a chair to the rooftop courtyard for some fresh air, and the Ethiopian Orthodox Monks, who claim it as their "territory." It was quite an unexpected sideshow.

Few visitors realize that an 1852 document allowed six different denominations rights over various sections of the church.

The rooftop feud has yet to be settled, and none of those six denominations has acquired rights to the front entrance either." The guide happily noted some renewed interest in his spiel. "That piece of real estate and, I might add, the great responsibility that goes with it was given to two Muslim families by Saladin himself." The docent asked the small group, "Who knows who opens and closes these massive doors?"

"More Muslims?" a young man shrugged.

"Correct!" the docent beamed. "Two Muslim families, the Joudeh and the Nuseibeh share the daily ceremony. The Joudeh deliver the key each morning to the Nuseibeh, who then unlock the door, and after locking the church each night, return it to the Joudeh.

The increasing intimidation of and prohibitions to visiting Christians had all but closed off the church. Catholics having to buy candles from Muslims was perhaps insignificant and even profitable to a few, but such affronts were outrageous to many and represented a further erosion of the sacred surroundings.

General Gutiérrez, sitting in Saint Peter's, felt one of his frequent moments of mental overload. With mass well underway, the adult General Gutiérrez tried desperately to hang onto his holy state of mind and fought the urge to revert to thoughts of his younger days. It was a recurring temptation to release the responsibility he had taken on and to think back . . . back to the roughhousing and bawdy teasing at the strict but progressive Jesuit Academy in Panamá City, where both he and his younger brother, Juan Carlos, attended school. A few years older, Luís always protected Juan Carlos. Their father was in Panamá frequently on business, and the short flight from Bogotá offered safety from the strife and kidnappings in Colombia and presented opportunities for happy reunions for the family.

Luís later married within the Colombian upper class, but duty pulled him away from his high society wife too often. Both succumbed to outside temptations, and his marriage dissolved without the birth of children. Although Luís enjoyed a good deal of female companionship, he often kidded his disappointed family that no woman would put up with him.

While Luís entered military service, Juan Carlos responded to God's call and began his priestly duties at a small Colombian village. The church was poor. It offered little chance of income from a Sunday collection, and young Father Gutiérrez, for some years, depended on the largesse of his loving family in Bogotá.

The brothers flourished and advanced. Luís moved up through the ranks, and by the time he became Lieutenant Colonel Gutiérrez, he had commanded numerous campaigns against the insidious leftist insurgencies throughout Colombia. After attending the Staff and General Officer Course at the military School of the Americas, he returned to the school as a visiting professor.

It was during this assignment he met Aaron David Yakowitz, a mid-career Lieutenant Colonel in the Israeli Air Force. At the time both Luís and Aaron, preoccupied with settling internal disputes and fighting wars in Colombia and Israel, paid less attention to the *laissez-faire* attitude in Europe and the United States concerning growing Islamic assertiveness fueled by petrodollars. The weakened West deferred to encroaching Muslim populations taking advantage of free speech and civil liberties. Terrorist factions launched destructive operations throughout the world.

Dressed in attire reflecting their different cultures, the two young warriors struggled through the personal events that shaped their views of life as they matured and fought for their nations. Witnessing tragedy in both families, Luís and Aaron sought to understand each other's challenges. There was comfort in sharing the confusing obstacles to peace in their respective countries. Their friendship grew while they worked together at international military classes. They debated global terrorism and attended each other's military convocations, as promotions occurred and responsibilities increased.

When Luís felt his epiphany descend upon him after the family funerals, his anticipation of the potential effects of *The Return* rose, and it became difficult to contain.

He forced himself to move cautiously. Once the key figures were convinced to go forward and Cardinal Salvador DeAngeles suggested Israel as a key participant, Luís again felt the guiding hand of God and knew General Aaron David Yakowitz would play one of the most important roles in the project.

The necessary pieces were coming together.

Israel – 2015

Luís flew from Rome to Tel Aviv on El Al in civilian clothes. He had spoken by a special phone encrypted for secure communication with General Aaron David Yakowitz, Commander of the Israeli Defense

Forces. Their conversation had been warm and friendly but concise. As a matter of military courtesy, Aaron offered to send an Israeli military escort to pick Luís up at the airport.

"You are most gracious, as always. I'm probably developing paranoia, but I think it's wiser if I simply meet you at the agreed location." Luís' refusal was understandable, and the Israeli General immediately complied, knowing the need for security. Unable to resist, however, he asked, "So, how will I know who you are? Mustache? Shaved head? Baggy tweeds?" They laughed. "You'll doubtless be dressed like one of the great prophets."

Their rendezvous was to be at a small hotel just off the main square in Netanya, a resort town less than forty kilometers north on the coast near the Lebanon border. It was March, and the hotel would be sparsely populated, thus offering privacy as well as relaxation. They planned to spend their time mapping out the strategy for the Israeli role in *The Return.*

"Welcome aboard, sir," said the attractive El Al stewardess, impressed with the good-looking man entering the 747. At Tel Aviv, Luís had presented a US passport in the name of Professor Ramón Ordaval.

Luís's previous trips to Israel had frequently been on behalf of Juan Carlos. Over decades diplomatic efforts by Vatican emissaries to allow a free flow of Papal representatives into the Holy Land had begun to eat away at Jewish resistance. But with the increased violence, Juan Carlos never visited. Others in the Vatican had entered Israel using false documents to avoid muddying negotiations. Many of the Vatican clergy had a longing to touch, kiss, and pray at the sites that represented the foundation of their belief. There was a yearning to walk where Christ walked, of homesickness for a land never visited, a need for fulfillment.

The same existed for Israel's Jews traveling to Rome. Many held underlying compulsions to seek a greater relationship and understanding with their Jewish brother, Jesus Christ. It remained a complex issue, as most Jews still resented the ancient Christian accusation of "deicide"— *the killing of our Lord.* Most also rejected the "Jews for Jesus" society that had built up over time and was viewed as the consummate guilt trip.

General Yakowitz had succumbed to Luís's persuasive arguments some time ago.

He empathized with Luís's personal anger. But the chaotic state of the world had caused them both to feel the threat of losing unquestioning adherence to the Judeo-Christian lawsof God. Radical Islamists, gaining in their pursuit of Israel's eradication, had created a new environment. With Israel's elimination, Christianity, today's secondary target, would become the new mark.

The two generals shared the conviction that military retaliation meant certain world destruction. It was in the best interest of the globe to find a new path. A Godly solution could ean hope.

*Yes,* thought Aaron over and over, *Luís's arguments are sound—the collapse of faith would mean the end of civilization in Europe. Islamization would occur.* Aware that the very word *Islam* meant "submission," Aaron was forced to accept that millions of Europeans and, indeed, the free world, were *still unwilling* to acknowledge that they were already in the process of submitting.

General Yakowitz' temple pulsed as he contemplated the tasks ahead. *Would this seemingly insane plan work?*

The commitment had germinated ten years earlier, when Lieutenant Colonels Aaron David Yakowitz and Luís Gutiérrez served together in Bogotá. They were conducting a joint command as part of an exercise in which a small crack team of Israelis instructed a handpicked group of Colombian militias in anti-terrorism tactics.

Luís, delighted to see Aaron again, took the handsome young Israeli to a mass for the military, celebrated by his brother Juan Carlos, by then Colombia's Archbishop. The two soldiers were a striking sight. Luís's thick black hair, aristocratic features, and fair skin contrasted with and complemented Aaron's sandy curls, angled nose, and bronze complexion. After a family dinner, they managed to break away to a club in Bogotá for late night drinking, socializing with women, and, as always, in-depth conversation in which they explored their different backgrounds.

During their military, religious, and political conversations, Luís enjoyed and appreciated the fascinating tales Aaron told of Israeli history and war. They compared stories of the ceaseless conflicts with Colombia's insurgents and with Israel's contentious enemies. The warring in Colombia was now well beyond small groups of leftist idealists operating out of remote mountain retreats. With Soviet support long-gone and Chinese support lagging, they had developed into heavily financed operators of illegal drug trafficking. The traffickers used insurgent armies to protect their growing fields and to build and defend runways for their drug-laden aircraft. Though insurgent leaders gave lip service to the idealistic dream of a utopia-to-come by overthrowing the corrupt government; the kidnapping "business" and participation in the lucrative drug market were the only real game for them.

At subsequent reunions, Luís carefully prepared his close friend by continuing to talk around his main issue. Sympathetic to Luís's plight, Aaron reminded Luís that his own country's pride and dedication to Zionism was also its greatest threat, as was all conflict in the name of God.

"We are, in Latin America, overwhelmingly Catholic and unencumbered by religious strife at the moment," Luís commented. "Still, we *have* experienced zealotry in some Islamic incursions. We have religious tolerance, but in truth, it has never been tested. The entire hemisphere needs to strive for the peace of Christ to enter all of humankind."

Colonel Yakowitz calmly listened to his friend speak of his Savior and then replied. "Do you remember our study of Princeton's Barnard Lewis? He gave us insight into the decline of Islamic domination? For a millennium Mohammed was "the man," and Europe feared the demise of Christendom. Moslems had conquered Syria, Palestine, Egypt and North Africa—all old Christian lands—and were even spreading into the Balkans, Sicily, Spain, Portugal, and parts of France." Colonel Yakowitz lifted his glass, "you know what saved Christianity? Not Charles Martel at the battle of Tours but the turn of the economic tide. Although exploration of the New World was ridiculed and criticized for a time, access to trade with tropical lands not blocked by the Arabs brought great wealth to Christianity and reinvigorated the European economy. The surge of trade happily allowed Britain, France, The Netherlands and Russia to roll back the Islamic incursions. For this great lesson I give you . . . you may buy the drinks!"

"Still," Luís interjected, "the Muslims, as the conquered party, fought the acceptance of the 'new order.' They didn't take the defeat graciously."

Aaron sighed loudly, "I doubt they ever will."

"And to think we all basically believe in the same 'God, the Father,'" Luís said with some bitterness. "But Aaron, you must know deep down that Judaism needs more than miracles to gain world power. Conversion to Christianity might well be advantageous." Luís smiled at his friend provocatively.

Aaron knew he was being baited and replied, "Of course we believe that everything your Christ did is truly inspiring and promotes the basic concept of good versus evil. Surely though, my good friend, a man of your intelligence cannot deny the obvious." Aaron looked at Luís and spoke deliberately. "The Messiah is to bring peace on earth, and to date there is no peace on earth. I could certainly go along with logistical and generational delays from your 'guy,' but really my good friend, over 2,000 years?"

Luís reluctantly let a smile form. "Ah, dear Aaron, be patient. In your faith 2,000 years is nothing." Privately, in his fight to defend his faith and his nation and despite years of Catholic training, Luís was appalled at his inability to fight Jewish logic.

"This is true, Luís," Aaron conceded, "but let me shift to my theory that Jesus may have meant that 'peace on earth' would occur when you were lying in it." They both laughed. "I act on the premise that the presence of Israel and her people represents the true existence of God, period."

Aaron tried to cover some of his underlying fear about the rise of anti-Semitism in Europe. He was well aware that it had long-existed among native Europeans, due in part to their great envy for people with a competitive and fighting spirit. Contemporary anti-

Semitism for native Europeans had in some ways become similar to anti-Americanism.

"It is sadly apparent, Aaron," said Luís, "that so many people previously unwilling to resist evil now detest those of us who, unwilling to submit, remain prepared to fight. Accepting submission shows their increasing fear for their own lives, and somehow they perceive an aggressive Israel to be the root of their fear." Luís shook his head.

"As Catholic and Jew," Aaron added, "we have witnessed growing hatred for Israel and the Americas. Do you think it's a coincidence that Colombia and Israel are two nations so preoccupied with their craving for a relationship with God?"

As the years passed and Aaron rose through the ranks to become General Yakowitz, the New York accent he had acquired during his early years in Manhattan schools diminished. He had moved to Israel with his parents when he was 13, after his father had completed fifteen years with The United Israel Appeal, coaxing millions of dollars from the pockets of American Jews in New York and up and down the East Coast.

Upon arrival in Israel, Aaron was welcomed "home" to an elite kibbutz. Later, as a young well-educated Jew with a moderated accent and connections, he easily found employment marketing the Israeli aircraft industry.

Attending the finest schools Israel had to offer meant Aaron spent much of his time in Tel Aviv. Although he thought Tel Aviv to be a rather ugly city plagued by horrific incidents of terrorism, he enjoyed the nightlife, meeting women, and swimming in the warm Mediterranean Sea. When he entered the obligatory military service, Aaron was thrilled to have found his calling and dedicated his life to the defense of his nation.

He trained with the Israeli Defense Forces' (IDF) elite Armored Corps and took his oath of allegiance on the famed hilltop at Masada, never looking back. His career took off.

After Aaron met Luís at the National War College at Fort McNair in Washington DC some years later, they would diligently study strategy and history during the day and  later devote themselves to late evening "social studies," amazed at how easy it was to gain rapid intimacy with American women. They deemed the city "blessed" with an abundance of sexy, ambitious women who were searching for straight ambitious men.

Seduction was easy, and they enjoyed bantering about the women they had met. The laughter and bragging was never confused, however, with their serious discussions about military tactics and, inevitably, politics and religion.

As time passed, the two men formed the tight coalition that would allow Luís's plan for *The Return* to gradually include a new key participant, General Aaron Yakowitz.

Soon after Aaron and Luís assumed full command of their nations' military forces, Juan Carlos Gutiérrez was elected to the highest position in the Catholic Church and became His Holiness Pope Damasus III. Luís marveled at how the pieces had coalesced. The moment was at hand, and Luís prayed that a God who loved them all would guide his proposition to Aaron David Yakowitz.

"It's tough to pinpoint blame," commented Aaron one quiet night at the Officers Club. Luís, on edge about the conversation to come, had suggested a quiet corner of the sparsely populated room. Both men were in civilian attire and pleasantly relaxed after a day of intense classroom exchanges. The blueprint for *The Return* was now a Vatican reality, but in order to bring it about, Luís needed the commitment by Israel. "We are victims," continued Aaron, "of the classic breakdown of a nation . . . a divisive culture within a single state, ethnic lines that stretch far back into history, and uneven and unequal demographics."

"But you have good and able government, Aaron," said Luís, sipping his scotch.

"It governs a remarkable country surrounded by unremarkable countries ruled by radical Islamists who, forgive me, want to 'kick your ass' and who covet the land you have madefertile. But your *good* government always strives to serve its basic obligation, to 'serve and defend its people.'"

"True," said Aaron nodding, "but tell me, in the final analysis, does your Christ, who came from our land, make any difference?"

"I wonder, Aaron," Luís continued tentatively, "had the Jews followed *this* Jew, Jesus Christ, would our combined numbers have been sufficient to overturn the threat so pervasive today? Is it possible, as has been suggested, that Christianity . . . specifically Catholicism . . . is simply the continuation, the fulfillment, if you will, of Judaism?"

"That's an interesting thought and certainly nothing new. As you well know, both Jews and Catholics have been converting back and forth for quite some time for a variety of reasons—economic, political, and social."

"Yes, of course," Luís replied. "But Aaron, surely you acknowledge that the early Christians were Jews? During the time of Christ, did the Jews not profess the reality of one God? Did this belief not mature into the Catholic Church? Was Christ—a Jew—not the Son of God as well? Does Jewish rejection of Jesus Christ, their own son, equate to a Jewish rejection of God?"

"Look, Luís, as I said long ago, the true Messiah was to bring peace on earth. That has not happened, my friend. We have no peace on earth. Are you suggesting that because the Jews did not accept Christ, the absence of peace is our fault?" Aaron felt a small spark of anger that almost immediately subsided. He looked at Luís questioningly. "I often think that only a world disaster will put it all to rest and allow for a new start."

Luís detected his opening. He felt the deep secret words rise up through his throat and slip off his tongue. "What if we could bring him back, Aaron? What if we could stretch our God-given human capabilities and bring Christ back to earth to give all our people a new start? His renewed presence on earth could strengthen us with the zeal to counter some of the excesses of wicked men. It would take time, of course, but Christ's return might cause men to recognize their sin and obliterate it."

"What in Hell are you talking about, Luís? Has the Scotch warped your brain?" Aaron looked at Luís and felt shock—something told him that his good friend was serious.

Luís remained quiet for a moment. He toyed with his glass, wondering if he should go on. "Perhaps you're right, Aaron. We should probably call it a night." Luís had known that the initial impact of his words might cause Aaron to question his sanity. "I have sprung this on you in the wrong place, at the wrong moment; but our Holy Father needs you. I need you. The world needs you. Please think about it. Please think about the last decades, the last centuries." Luís was now unable to stop. "Think about Jews everywhere and about the tyranny and persecution inflicted on them directly and on the Christian world that has supported them again and again." Luís's look intensified, as he sensed a glimmer of possibility in Aaron's expression. "At the highest levels of government, all attempts at peace have failed. Good and great men and countless millions have died trying to bring peace, trying to fight a ruthless enemy with unanswered prayer and hollow offerings. How will it ever change, Aaron, unless we apply our God-given talents to change it?" Luís struggled to keep his voice level.

The gravity of Luís' words disturbed Aaron. Remembering his Jewish history, he easily recalled instances during and after World War II when Christianity's support of Jews had been less than solid.

Now though, riveted by Luís' suggestion, Aaron looked into his friend's face.

"But how? Your brother . . . your faith  Where? When, Luís?" Aaron trailed off. His face contorted in uncertainty and lingering disbelief at the conversation.

"Let's get some sleep, Aaron.

Tomorrow I will tell you everything. If I can persuade you, we will embark on an unparalleled journey together, which with God's help will be for the good of Western civilization."

The following morning Aaron, seated at the breakfast table with Luís and looking haggard, simply nodded to Luís's questioning face. After further discussion Aaron realized that Luís was not alone in this remarkable idea but had the full confidence of the Vatican, and that a child, a remarkable child was already being prepared. He smiled wonderingly and said, "We Jews in Israel, and everywhere, have been blamed for centuries for killing Jesus Christ." Luís felt concern that these words presaged rejection.

But Aaron lightly pounded the table and said, "Damn it, Luís, if we help you bring him back, maybe we can finally let bygones be bygones?"

Luís took a deep breath and smiled, and when they stood up to leave, the two warriors embraced in a solidarity that both knew was impossible to articulate further.

Luís came back to the moment in Saint Peter's, back to the ceremony that would give him and others membership in the Equestrian Knights of the Church of the Holy Sepulchre. Cardinals Hernandez, DeAngeles, and Arias and Father Jonathan Kennedy assisted at the altar. Turning briefly, Luís saw General Aaron Yakowitz in one of the pews with other members of the Gutiérrez family. He looked ahead and felt great joy.

The presence of his close ally and the sight of his beloved brother conferring this honor upon him was the highest endorsement he could hope for. All doubt left Luís as he thrilled at the ceremony unfolding before him and at the great promise of the future.

The acclamation of the mass jolted Luís back to the present. He heard Juan Carlos repeat the familiar words . . . the words that had driven him since the funeral mass for his family—"Christ has died, Christ has risen, Christ will come again."

# General Aaron Yakowitz – A Jew's Return
### Israel – 2015

General Aaron David Yakowitz spent only a few hours contemplating his options. Further agonizing would be useless and contrary to his decisive military background. Besides, it would lead to the same decision no matter how long Aaron battled against what he had gradually realized was his leaning toward conversion. The long road down which he had marched became doubly evident to Aaron, as he waved farewell to Luís from the hotel room and climbed into a cab to return to Ben Gurion Airport. Mulling over Luís's words, Aaron thought of the Catholic acclamation he had heard when attending mass with his mother in New York, again with Luís in Colombia, and later in Rome.

*What if we could bring Him back?* Aaron recalled how he had initially felt dumbstruck, before the possibilities began to fill his brain. *Christ will come again.* Aaron previously scoffed at the words, clinging to his ancestral and instinctive Jewish dismissal of the mysteries of Christianity. *Hell, we Jews don't believe he's come yet!*

Despite emotional farewells to classmates and a youthful love affair, leaving New York years ago had been easy for him. Early on, Aaron understood that he was being prepared for greater deeds, that his homeland needed him in its endless battle for survival. But now he was witnessing Christianity's struggle.

Resorting to his usual sharp humor, Aaron tried to diffuse Luís's anguish. "What if His Holiness called once more for the crusaders? You could lead them, Luís. You'd look more than righteous in some sort of traditional robe and headgear. Well, maybe not," Aaron joked, "I think you'd better stick to jets and bombers. You'd probably fall off a horse."

Luís playfully jabbed at his friend and replied, "I know you enjoy sparring with me, Aaron, and how I wish it were a joking matter," he said and smiled thinly. "Last month, we uncovered yet another plot to bomb the Vatican. This time the library was targeted. And the FBI in America has kept close tabs on a budding group of Jihadists in Baltimore that threaten the Washington basilica, the Shrine of the Immaculate Conception."

Aaron grimaced. "Jesus, Luís. I wasn't aware of that threat, although in these terrible times, anything could happen. I'm sorry."

"You know, Aaron, even if we could raise an army for Christ once again, though that seems less and less likely as apathy and willingness to give in seems pervasive, where do we find a palpable enemy to fight? He's everywhere and nowhere. A formal combative plan is probably useless. No, our campaign must be waged by Christ himself, or at least somebody who is perceived to be Christ."

"I remember my father's reaction to my announcement to pursue a military career," Aaron responded. "He clasped his hands, kissed his fist, and then threw his arms around me in pride. He wasn't fit for battle and had found satisfaction in fundraising for Israel. Still, he always regretted not being at the tip of the spear defending his nation, so through me, he was given a second chance. He did everything possible to encourage and accelerate my military career."

With his father's influence, young Aaron had been readily accepted at the NATO officer school in Germany and was later a member of the core committee looking into strengthening the "Mediterranean dialogue" with North African and Middle Eastern countries. Aaron continuously grappled with the futility and yet the ever-present requirement of a military approach to support Israel's existence. He ached for peace, even as he participated in the active and brutal defense of his country. Remarkably courageous, Aaron enjoyed his subordinates' unquestioning respect, as well as rapid promotion.

But something was missing. Something had always been missing, until now.

Having studied Judaism under several prominent rabbis, and at one point having considered joining a Hasidic community in Israel, Aaron ostensibly ignored urgings of his Catholic mother to relent in his avid pursuit of his Israeli heritage. A tall blond, former model, gifted with beauty and cleverness, his mother had entered the world of advertising and rose to an executive level. While there, she met and fell hopelessly in love with Aaron's father when he came to her agency for help with his fundraising. Despite her hours of prayer in Saint Patrick's Cathedral on Fifth Avenue, battling temptations of the flesh, their attraction for each other won out. The product of their union, Aaron, grew up in a house where all aspirations were encouraged. At the same time, it was a house with conflicting gods.

"You know, Aaron," his mother would tell him, "it is an easy leap, if you embrace the ideology that eases the entry of Jews into the Catholic Church. It is simply the continuation and fulfillment of Judaism after the coming of Jesus, the Jewish Messiah."

Until his discussion and agreements with Luís, Aaron had fought his mother's arguments that "with the arrival of the infant, Jesus, on earth, born to a simple Jewish girl, Israel in fact had become the basilica of the Catholic Church. Can't you recognize the possibility, if not the probabilities, that Jews, by rejecting Christ, also reject Moses? Where does that leave them?" Aaron had no answer but now was helped in his decision by confronting the *Second Coming* in his mind. He had always been fearful of such a possibility and its implications that the world would end at that time. Since the Jews were still waiting for the *true Messiah*, who would bring peace, the objective of *The Return*— creating the illusion of a heavenly visit—allowed Aaron to fantasize about the outcome. Little else had produced any optimism in his mind, and he found himself sympathizing with Luís and with his brother, Pope Damasus, in their desperate attempt to halt the threat to civilization and consequent destruction of human life.

Did he truly believe in it? He still had doubts, but he knew some hypocrisy was needed to pull off such a deed. For the most part, Aaron worked quietly, as the project's technical aspects were developed. He was also confronted with concocting a plausible story to convince his superiors in the Israeli government.

"With lucrative concessions, new defense systems, and secret cooperation from the Central Intelligence Agency, along with US aid to assist the Colombian Armed Forces, the Colombians are a natural to work with." Aaron presented this several times. "I am sure you are aware that the brother of the current Pope, Juan Carlos Gutiérrez, is General Luís Gutiérrez, head of the Colombian Defense forces. General Gutiérrez is battling not only an intense historic insurgency but now may have weakened it, as he witnesses the papacy grappling with the continuing loss of much of the Christian world. As the varying sects are harassed and persecuted, it is unlikely that many of the escapees will become Jews." Aaron had spoken with his Prime Minister, as both explored the benefits that would accrue to Israel. "Colombia's strengthened military over the last decades is encouraging, but like us, their attempts at peace are often dashed, as their enemies take advantage of any cease fire or amnesty."

The two officials sipped coffee at an outdoor café outside the city. The Prime Minister, occupied with the ever-present threat of being voted out of office, was receptive to ideas that would enable him to hold onto power. The advantages to working with Colombia were evident. For Aaron Yakowitz, they were also convenient. As Commander of the Israeli Military, Aaron spoke of his professional relationship with General Gutiérrez and was able to make it appear that it was his Prime Minister's idea to pursue a papal meeting with Palestinians.

With Aaron on board, the years were filled with challenges. With each milestone, Aaron Yakowitz was more convinced that the plan would triumph in the future. The ultimate proof was in his first meeting with Christian, the extraordinary young man who would defeat a world of hatred without firing a single shot.

# Luís – Winning the Battle of Doubt
### The Pope's Apartment - April 2012

The support of Aaron Yakowitz was incredibly fulfilling. Luís returned to Rome with new hope to again face those inside the Vatican. Their acceptance of *The Return* was essential, and Luís now felt new confidence. Leaning forward in his customary chair in the Pope's apartment, he gazed at the still-skeptical faces of those gathered. Without their concurrence, the project would die, its undisclosed possibility for success or failure never to be known. For these secret gatherings, the participants automatically gravitated to the seats occupied during their first meeting. No one wanted to appear over-attentive to protocol, and the seating had become accepted.

The Pope, Juan Carlos, and his brother, Luís, had held more than a year of wrenching discussions before approaching the others. Luís often accompanied Juan Carlos in travels to influential areas of the world—sometimes in secret—sometimes as part of official visits. As attacks on the Church escalated, greater security was required for the diminishing papal audiences in less enthusiastic nations of a frightened world. In some countries, the threat was so palpable that requests for cancellation of his visit along with formal apologies were now received by an alarmed Vatican.

In the meantime, Luís conducted military and state visits to carry out his own responsibilities, as well as those on behalf of his brother, the Pope. Rapidly, they recognized a distressing mosaic of a harsh world, spiritually adrift. While Juan Carlos struggled to keep the Church afloat, Luís met with military leaders, all of whom had the same fear of a Europe's rapidly turning Muslim. Massive numbers of people resorted to their only option to avoid the turbulence shaking the old continent to its roots. They fled.

The number leaving the Netherlands and Germany had far surpassed prior emigration totals. The Muslim population in Europe soared. At 50 million in 2006, Muslims in Europe rapidly approached 100 million, and by the projected time of *The Return*, Luís learned that over a third of contemporary European children would be born to Muslim families. Already, Mohammed was the most popular name for newborn boys in Brussels, Amsterdam, Rotterdam, and other major European cities. The national pride that had clearly nourished and identified so many for centuries withered, while now, under the pretext of anti-war demonstrations, mobs increasingly flouted authority. Patriotism was undermined in schools, eliminating the study of western civilization's achievements and replacing it with a new level of mockery for what was left of patriotic ardor. Luís and Juan Carlos witnessed the decline and paralysis of nations, once defenders of civilized thought but now unable to resurrect the values that had made them great.

The Conference of Bishops in America, although aware of this crisis, quarreled with one another and struggled with schismatic groups ostensibly bent on the liberal push for women priests, homosexual marriage, and an end to priestly celibacy, all leading to an end of traditional papal authority. The Conference had sadly concluded that non-religious people now tended to forgo having children. So many perceived enjoying freedom as *not including children*, children so necessary to carry on Western civilization and the spread of peace.

The heavy burden upon his new office caused Juan Carlos to frequently seek out Luís. "I was always a child of peace, a man of peace, not a warrior like you, my brother. I have preached peace, and with you at my side, my safety was certain. I was shielded. I felt only the single dimension of the joy of peace, without having the need and, perhaps, the *satisfaction* of fighting for my precious freedom." Juan Carlos looked up at one of his own paintings of a peaceful shepherd with a flock of lambs on the wall. He turned and placed his hand on his brother's shoulder. "I know this changed for me after the murders of our family.

At the time, I felt my duty was to guide the rest of you through the agony of grief. You, Luís, were crushed almost beyond recognition, but gradually you achieved a re-birth. From that you were gifted with your presentiment of *The Return*. I am frightened, but I now share that vision and pray for the validity of my belief. I *must believe* that your concept is an inspired gift, a gift to me. That it is indeed God's will."

Stunned, Luís sensed the parting of a dark curtain. Many, even in the Vatican and throughout Christianity, felt the secularists' lack of desire to fight for religious freedom, since God—and hence an afterlife—played no role in their existence. Luís felt triumphant.

Having arrived at this benchmark in the quest for salvation, the plan for *The Return* took shape. Luís progressed in his struggle to preserve his God and identified those to be included. An initial dozen was pared down to six. Each met alone with His Holiness. Each had left those meetings in shock, disbelief, and anger, but had finally come to the unarguable realization of the need to restore faith; that this daring event could be the solution to a renaissance of souls.

"Jesus Christ must come out of the sky, gentlemen," Luís said, once everyone was seated. "That image is deep in the minds of millions." His logic was jarring and reminded them of early feelings that these preposterous conversations could *not* be serious. Luís observed the fidgeting discomfort and knew he needed to plunge ahead. His Holiness sat leaning forward with his hands in a prayerful position and his eyes closed.

All were present—Juan Carlos Gutiérrez, His Holiness, Damasus III; Cardinal Diego Hernandez; Cardinal Alfonso Romano; Cardinal Salvador DeAngeles; Cardinal Teodoro Arias; and Father Jonathan Kennedy.

The Instigator—or so Luís seemed to the others at moments of doubt—this instigator who had challenged their sensibilities and their sense of right and wrong, their unquestioning aristocratic existence, this Lieutenant General Luís Gutiérrez— dominating in his crisp uniform—sat before them. Luís wanted desperately to find words to erase the lingering doubt on their faces. Gazing at his audience, his beloved brother, His Holiness, could feel Luís's silent message. He whispered a prayer of hope.

Although their private struggles and initial suspicions had lessened with each meeting, shattered consciences still reeled from their tacit approval of the unthinkable. All required reinforcement—individual and collective assurances that would absolve them of their thoughts of treachery—those thoughts still in their minds. As plans unfolded, doubt returned, along with an almost comforting feeling that the project would never really occur. The lure of the seemingly impossible, the enticement of pulling off a manufactured miracle to counteract the fear of a world losing Christ was undeniable. *Could it succeed in helping the wobbling Catholic faith recoup its pre-eminent place among world religions?* They all repeatedly asked themselves this question. Unanswered prayers questioning the predominance of evil absorbed the Catholic clergy. The leadership ached to return spiritual solace to the world.

The small group had kept their attention fixed on Luís. They contemplated the return of Jesus—not in a modern manner—but as they and all the faithful before them, had imagined it—a return from heaven above.

"Look, let us consider a few things." Luís, elbows on his knees in an unintentionally prayerful pose, held his palms together with the edge of his forefingers tapping against his mouth. He had thought out his approach—it was now no longer debatable—the project was at least in motion and the how was to be explored. He had agonized too long over the growing absence of God in humankind's inhuman behavior. He plunged ahead.

"Historically, mankind has deified natural forces—the wind, the sun, the earth— all of it. Wonder is part of the human response to the world, so having *our Jesus* come back in a flash of light or on a pillow of clouds may not be the stuff of the diehard cynic, but it is the prayer of a world looking for hope—a world, gentlemen, where only very few do not worry about where their next meal will come from." He waited briefly for this unsubstantiated but believable statistic to sink in, as he imagined planet Earth with millions of unemployed, sick, and starving. He shuddered at the reality of a God who to date, hadn't provided for the multitudes of the world's poor.

He continued softly, "I know you all remember Descartes." Luís nodded at them questioningly. "Descartes had no time for sheer wonder. He thought *wonder* trapped man in a primitive state of mind. He actually thought *wonder* was beneath him. Yet, he did admit that it was natural for us to admire things *above us* far more than under us—or even at our level. Why is that natural? Look at the artwork. Look at the poetry. Much of it displays God's home as in the clouds. Michelangelo depicted God's creation of man through a connective touch on the ceiling of the Sistine Chapel. Why didn't he place it on the floor? Art depicts God hurling thunderbolts and rain and fire out of the sky." Luís spread his hands and gestured in amazement. "Small children, in their earliest depictions of God on paper, never draw Him coming out of the ground, do they? So what if we've proved that clouds, winds, lightning, even rainbows, are mere physical events. The poor find comfort and awe in these events. The romantic finds reasons for the actions of the beloved in these events. Even intellectuals still stare at the heavens and find cause to marvel."

Luís was galloping on, but he held his audience. They looked at him, and each recalled his own childhood, when innocence allowed boyish wonder. Juan Carlos pondered his brother's unpretentious sermonizing, found himself entertaining a first flicker of possibility—a possibility of healing the shambles of the world's societal and spiritual health—even to a small degree. Luís detected it and continued.

"Silver linings, the pot of gold, and the glorious rays at sunrise? We know where and why it's happening, the sun coming up just there over the horizon; but still, we stare at it in hope, even as we stare at it in fear that it may not happen tomorrow. We stare at it in wonder and wish—Oh God, how we wish—we understood it."

They were silent. They wanted him to go on. They did not want to comment or utter a response—not yet. Luís sensed agreement in their silence and felt growing assurance, as his listeners remained in private thought.

"*Mi querido hermano*, my beloved brother, my Holy Father." Luís stared at his brother. "Despite all your meditations, your studies, your prayers, your writings, I know you cannot tell us you don't have the same mental image of the return of Christ. I have seen the simple drawings you did as a child, and I have seen the magnificent paintings you have done throughout your life. I know that your image is no different than mine and probably no different than millions of others. We must turn this image into a reality. If our God, our Lord, our Holy Spirit wants us to love and spread his love, let us call him to return in a way that grasps the attention of all mankind." Luís' voice became gentle.

"Your paintings, Juan. Why do you paint them?

Are they not messages of your own  hope?" Luís asked.

Juan Carlos looked at his older brother. He felt the bond of blood, of love, and fleetingly felt he was in the presence of a stranger. He knew his brother knew him. The Pope strayed to thoughts of their childhood.

Juan Carlos and Luís Antonio had been raised by a *niñera*, a simple Colombian nanny known as Graciela, who loved them and cared for them during their childhood.

Graciela filled them with stories of Jesus. She described the birth of Christ, and told them of his crucifixion and resurrection. Her tales were simple. She showed Luís and Juan Carlos pictures in Catholic readers designed for young consumption. Juan Carlos, even as a toddler, could sit in Graciela's lap for hours or lie next to her in his bed, while she read and showed him the glories of God in the illustrated books. He would fall asleep and awaken still full of curiosity and contentment that formed his life and his future journey as a servant of God.

Over the years, Graciela took the young brothers to religious shows put on by schools and theatrical groups; shows that reinforced the doctrines of Catholicism, and to any movies she could locate with an acceptable religious theme. In time, Juan Carlos looked forward more to the comforting sessions with Graciela than watching soccer matches or the now popular US football. Juan Carlos demonstrated a healthy participation in everything Luís did, but as a child, he clearly heard his first calling from God.

One Easter morning, when Juan Carlos was six, Graciela tucked a coloring book and crayons into the enormous basket that his mother had filled with sweets and toys. Juan Carlos gave almost all the candy to Luís, who believed he had tricked his little brother by calling his attention to a page in the coloring book while he snatched another sweet piece from Juan Carlos' basket. Pointing to a smiling Jesus standing on a cloud waiting to be colored, Juan Carlos paid little heed to Luís's thieving; he felt drawn to the page, compelled to fill in the lines, to make the drawing alive and complete. Talent was evident, and Juan Carlos' work soon evoked a devotion that seemed to speak from his sketch books and canvases. Sports were soon replaced with art and painting classes. His paintings grew popular and drew admiration from his family and his peers. Later as Pope, Juan Carlos continued to paint, spending his few hours of leisure working at easels placed in a small room near his bed. Drawing pads lay about with sketches of natural and religious subjects. Luís came to believe that somehow God pushed the pencils and mixed the paints for Juan Carlos. His depictions of the risen Christ were masterful examples of religious realism. He gave many away, unconcerned with their artistic or monetary value. The Pope's imagination was hardly restricted to artistic talent. Although he was exposed to the stories of apparitions and other miraculous appearances—through mostly frightening tales from Graciela—he developed a curiosity for while in secondary school. Later Juan Carlos studied the of Fatima, Lourdes, Guadeloupe, Medjigore, and numerous lesser-known appearances of Mary. One appearance that intrigued him was in Cartago near the Iruzu volcano in Costa Rica, where the Virgin appeared at the Church of the Angels in the 17th Century. He was taken there as a child by a Mother who took pleasure in educating her sons and their younger sister through travel. Twelve-year-old Juan Carlos and the more mature Luís, then 15, considered it a memorable event. The miracle had resulted in thousands of reported cures by the faithful, who commemorated their good fortune with gold or silver replicas of the cured body parts and presented them to the church. Over time the inundated church installed long glass cases around the perimeter of the nave, each containing hundreds upon hundreds of silver and gold hands, arms, legs, heads, eyes, fingers, and feet. To Juan Carlos, it was a dazzling exhibition of confirmed miracles.

Luís, then first in his class in business and economics, put the motivation of the faithful aside. He could not stop trying to calculate the value of so much precious metal. While his mother and brother reflected upon the deeper meaning, Luís, who appeared to be praying, was actually counting cases and trying to tally the weight of gold and silver and translate it into dollars and pesos.

But even Luís abandoned his calculations when they witnessed a young pregnant peasant woman carrying a child who coughed incessantly. The woman, obviously poor, wore a simple cotton shift. She was moving slowly from the rear of the church down the marble floor of the center aisle to the altar on her knees. The sight caused tears of compassion in Juan Carlos. He felt her faith in a cure for her child, and he experienced the strength of her effort within his own being.

For Luís, the plight of the woman was touching, but as usual, he could not help but notice her bulging belly. An image of her making love sprung into his mind. He struggled with it, and as she passed their pew, he turned his thoughts to the possibility of her child's cure. *If the child were cured, if it happened, she would be obligated to repay the Virgin with a donation of gold or silver lungs. How would she purchase the gold or silver?* He got up, found his way to the sacristy, and located a young deacon folding altar cloths. He asked him to come to the door to view the altar aisle. When he pointed out the woman carrying the child, he placed a sizeable amount of cash in the deacon's hand and instructed him to give it to her.

As the years passed, Luís was drawn to the Church more by a curiosity about how his faith worked rather than a devotion to it. He thought about the Church's use of its power over the masses, advocating obedience and tranquility—not just vague expressions and words of hope. Years later, after the murders of his sister and brother-in-law, Luís had crumbled. Until their funeral mass, and his personal epiphany, Luís spent the days railing at God and denying His existence.

Juan Carlos had never ceased comforting Luís and tried to wear down his razor- sharp grief, prying at the shell surrounding him. They spent hours discussing family, their country, life's meaning, and the scourge of terror and violent death upon the world. Through the haze of sadness, Luís slowly healed. During this time, he never stopped talking to Juan Carlos about his dream and his visions and potential plans for a returned Christ. At first dismissing his brother's ramblings, Juan Carlos, in time, recognized the determination, and as he watched

Latin America and Rome wallow in the surrounding morass of a godless Europe, he gradually accepted the plan's shocking appeal.

"One day, Juan Carlos, you will ascend to the papacy," Luís often predicted. "When you do, my beloved brother, we will take our courage forward."

Juan Carlos looked at his brother and thought, *Instaurare Omnia In Christo— Everything for Christ.* He repeated the phrase daily, as momentum gathered for his rise within the priestly hierarchy.

Juan Carlos came out of his reverie, back to the reality of the group now in his apartment. He had talked with each of them regarding Luís's role. He knew that his brother held no ambition within the Church but fervently wanted to see its salvation. Now armed with the assurance of assistance from General Aaron Yakowitz, Luís wanted only to preside over the technical planning and execution. They ultimately knew the need for trust and agreed on Luís's lead role. They knew that as a military leader he would not meddle in the assigned tasks.

After outlining next steps, Luís left the meeting to make arrangements for further planning with Aaron Yakowitz.

# THE UNDENIABLE SPIRIT OF EROS
## April 2015

"Shall I tell you of my latest conquest, Cardinal? Isn't that the real reason you're here, to get a fix, a vicarious dose of titillation for your poor starving libido?" Countess Serina Cristina Caputo de la Guardia whispered to Diego Cardinal Hernandez, as he escorted her to the dining room in her Rome apartment. A striking and rigorously maintained woman of an age the Cardinal knew but never revealed, Serina led a carefully selected group of invitees to the long table where her staff waited to serve dinner.

Serina reveled in her title and her name, acquired from her wealthy Colombian background. She was at ease with the title of Countess, given to her by her deceased Italian husband, Count Alessandro Caputo. He had donated large sums to the Catholic Church and other worthy endeavors, some covering perhaps dubious business transactions but all maintaining his aristocratic family's prominence in Italy. His marriage to Serina gave her not only the title of Countess, but it also bestowed upon her an exceptional amount of money and properties scattered throughout Europe and the United States.

Serina Cristina Caputo de la Guardia. In adhering to old custom, the Countess used her complete name—first and middle, followed by her married name, Caputo and her Colombian family surname, *De la Guardia*. Historically, as populations expanded, the detailed name system declined, but in earlier times, the system better allowed one to know who was who in societies where a common surname was normal.

Guests, often from the Vatican, never turned down an invitation from Serina Caputo. The clerics were always intrigued at her brashness, even though it may not have been a healthy pastime for the soul. Her suggestive and controversial comments were designed as mild seduction, an amusing pastime  for Serina, whose life felt at once complete with money and accomplishments yet empty and painful, as the comfort and fulfillment of her love for Cardinal Diego Hernandez remained forbidden. She grappled with her denied desire versus her deep and sustained feelings for the Cardinal. Both emotions were stimulating. Both kept her motivated. At each meeting, Serina noticed any new gray in Diego's dark polished hair and any hint of a line in his face. She was angered by time's authority over lives. Yet the almost imperceptible change in the feel of his hands, which she took into her own in greeting at each meeting, reflected greater wisdom and caused within her an even greater desire and sense of urgency.

Serina strove continuously to overcome her doubts about the world around her. She had given up an earlier active political and diplomatic life, relinquishing the responsibilities for the world's failures and successes to a younger generation. She no longer held an abiding confidence in the abilities of current world leadership. She viewed the divisiveness among nations with disappointment. Often her personal hope grew shallow. For years, money had seemed the answer, as she pursued her ideals to promote a better world with her wealth. She had given a lot of money away in her life, but soon Cardinal Hernandez would persuade this doubting, idealistic woman to part with an enormous sum for an unknown but extraordinary cause.

Enjoying the conversational cut and thrust, Serina always took pleasure in maneuvering her guests to socially taboo subjects—politics, war, and religion. This evening, over another exquisitely prepared meal, it was celibacy.

"Since you and your predecessors have argued for centuries over the rules of celibacy," Serina teased her guests, "I doubt, gentlemen, that any thought of indiscretion on my part could shock your exemplary morals."

"As you most certainly recall, Countess," countered the always-amusing Cardinal Salvador DeAngeles, "the last debate over celibacy took place in November of 1563, and the suggestion that the Catholic Church should modify and mitigate its rules of celibacy was rejected."

"That must have been a most uplifting meeting, please pardon the pun," Serina commented slyly, covering her ignorance of the ancient meeting.

Cardinal DeAngeles acknowledged her mild vulgarity and subtle pandering with a thin patient smile. "The Fathers even considered clerical marriage. We see cases of it in the world today, but the prohibition still holds."

"I wonder who the head lobbyist was for that council," Serina interjected. "Maybe he was just having a bad day?"

Salvador allowed himself a chuckle. "Oh, my dear Countess, they realized the difficulties," he nodded, "and included wording to the effect that 'God would not deny the gift of chastity to those who duly ask for it nor allow us to be tempted beyond our strength.' They rejected the thesis that the marital state should be considered better than that of celibacy. The Council even voted to found seminaries to prepare candidates for the celibate life." The Cardinal looked at Serina, hoping for some crumb of approval. "By this time, that meant only unmarried men would be ordained. Since a notable shortage of priests was worrisome, one Father Desiderius Martino broached the possibility of ordaining married men, provided their wives gave consent. They and their husbands would have to live in continence." The Cardinal looked at Serina, knowing he had invited a deriding retort. "I'm sure you can guess that the measure was not deemed realistic."

"I would think not, Cardinal," Serina said, lifting her glass. "I would also suggest that Desiderius Martino may have been sadly typical of many priests who attempt sexual counseling yet haven't an iota of experience to draw from. Realistic? That sounds alarmingly ignorant." She smiled with such an endearing look that men had to decide and re-decide if she were coming on to them or simply joking. "The rapidly declining number of priests today seems a glaring indication to this archaic rule of celibacy. I don't grasp its benefits."

"Well, Countess, we are probably ignorant and maybe naïve, but I think the faithful appreciate the known deportment of a good celibate priest. If the issue is too burdensome, Vatican II provided a tiny chink in the armor, and later, in 1979, John Paul addressed it in a letter to all priests."

"And?" Serina asked, trying not to appear impatient.

"And basically the message remains the same, but in rare cases, a dispensation will be contemplated."

"And so, ladies and gentlemen," Serina replied, proposing a toast while storing the prospect of a dispensation in the back of her mind, "here's to the usual obfuscation from our beloved Church. *Viva la dispensacion.*"

Serina raised her glass. She was wearing a simple long black knit dress. Elegant as always, and understated, her black hair was coiled into a neat bun at the nape of her neck—in the style of a *flamenco* dancer—which held advantages. She could arrange it quickly, without the help of a mirror if necessary, and it accentuated the best features of her face—large dark eyes set into strong cheekbones, a small nose and full mouth. Her hairstyle avoided hours in salons.

Her aristocratic look also allowed her to appear to be seated on the conservative side of acceptable conversation, while she lobbed nearly unacceptable verbal darts at her guests. She enjoyed their uneasiness, and the clerics all enjoyed her disingenuous flirtation.

"A married celibate priest would seem to be pushing temptation a bit far, my dear Cardinal DeAngeles. Doesn't the cleric's brain register physical desire? Wouldn't the wives of such men need to be shipped off to some far away asylum?"

With Cardinal Hernandez present, Countess Caputo battled her own devil and suppressed her fear of sin by exercising her wit. Deeply in love with Cardinal Diego Hernandez, that fear kept her from going too far. Rejection was unacceptable. It was a loathsome state. He indeed presented a challenge, and she knew well his practiced discipline against temptation.

The strong attraction between Serina and Diego was held in check by several obstacles. Despite feeling an odd gratitude that the purely physical was not one of them, it did not matter much in light of the social and emotional taboos. Diego was a devoted priest. Although he was used to the attention his striking looks invited, he maintained control. But in the presence of Serina Caputo, control became a greater effort. He looked forward to each encounter—the repartee during dinners, the suggestive comments whispered at charitable events and official luncheons and receptions, when she would manage to seat herself across from him, next to him, or as near as possible, without feeding the extensive Vatican network of gossip.

Diego's vow of chastity had overlooked few infractions over the decades. But now he found himself facing a daunting assignment. He needed Serina's money to support *The Return*, and he knew any alienation could prove disastrous. Nevertheless, Diego felt her intense desire and fought the urge to reciprocate.

As Vatican Secretariat of State, Cardinal Hernandez seemed far too physically attractive to hold such a position. In public, women found his extraordinary looks distracting. His Holiness, having known Diego since childhood, was oblivious of Diego's physical attributes, or he simply ignored them. Diego was an extremely valuable asset to Juan Carlos, and he frequently relied on Cardinal Hernandez' advice and intercession on his behalf.

*Doña Serina*, as the Countess enjoyed being called, loved her teasing sessions with the clergy, but the most satisfying episodes were with Diego. Sparring helped to satisfy her feelings, and it allowed a little relief from the sexual tension. With the passing years, Serina occasionally felt a mild tug toward eternity. *So be it*, she decided. *These eyes and this mind and body will feast upon this earth and all that's in it. Through this great Church, I will work for the common good. My love for this servant of God must be God-given. How could He not approve?*

Serina always tried to rein in her emotions, but flirtation with Diego was irresistible. Mildly tempting with reminders of how frequently she received the Sacrament of Penance, Serina poured out details of escapades with lovers. Most were made up, and the Cardinal suspected this. Still, he would fake shock. Then Serina would merely shrug her shoulders and coyly press on.

"God endowed me with an appetite for men," she would lament, feigning despair. It was more than a bit of exaggeration, but Serina's charm made her mischievously fascinating. "It's your vocation, your 'calling,' your reason for living, to keep me in a state of grace," she'd say, taunting Diego.

With her head thrown back in laughter, men felt the space about *"Doña Serina"* light up. They were grateful for her presence. She glowed, giving joy to those around her. It was a gift to others, a generosity of self, which she never for a moment considered might be found worthy by God in eternal judgment.

Serina's invitations were always well received. The envious had dubbed invitations to her dinner parties "The Vatican Vitals." Despite her mischief, she received few regrets, and when her handwritten invitations on heavy cream stock arrived, they were given prompt replies. With exotic beauty, her brains and money, Serina's personal charity raised millions throughout Europe. It provided a great providence for varying Catholic charities and causes. A genius at seating arrangements and stimulating conversations that tested the faith of her Vatican guests, she made sure her parties were flawless. Conversations ran deep with wit, at times masking religious controversy.

Cardinal Hernandez, eager to get off the subject of priestly celibacy, commented upon the on-going war and corruption in his home country, Colombia. "The corruption remains a tragedy," Diego said, "It has worn away the country's ability to exemplify itself as a responsible and credible nation."

"Ah, but don't you still have the reasonable system of allowing your two political parties to essentially take turns in power? That seemed like good political balance," a Bolivian cleric schooled in politics interjected. "In Bolivia we can't seem to find suitable candidates who can last very long. It's hard to understand why more people won't step up to serve. Perhaps it's too much coca leaf chewing or the squalor of the tin mines, but upheavals in labor seem too much of a burden for young politicians to counter with satisfactory solutions. We only attract a few." Realizing his words were unflattering to his nation, he added, "Of course, I'm not there often and should refrain from judgment."

Serina looked over her wine at Diego. She wanted to turn the conversation away from Latin America and said to Diego, "My dear Cardinal, it's obvious you would single out our country, but how can you look at Israel and not say that religion, far more than a bunch of rebels, prevents the embodiment of a nation? How many more centuries will it take before the Middle East settles it divisions?" she asked. Serina placed a manicured finger firmly on the table. "The dire need is for peace that a brand new God might offer. Maybe a geographical shift from this hallowed ground claimed by too many religions?" Serina moved her hand and curled her fingers around the stem of her glass, circling it slowly on the white lace tablecloth. She leaned forward and continued, "Israel buckles under the weight of religious jealousy. As it is now, and always has been, the country of *The Chosen People* will never feel relief from the pain and death of religious conflict."

Diego was used to Countess Caputo's baiting him. "So the hope and instruction and discipline provided by Catholicism should be swept aside as though it is non- existent? What would that do to Judgment Day?" he replied.

"Ah ha!" Serina exclaimed. "If Judgment Day, as we envision it, ever happens," she looked at each guest and smiled, "it ought to be a real spectacle of *mis*judgment. It might indeed be the proof of a cruel, callous God, who holds disdain toward us for the battles we fight. We endlessly compete for His favor, but He decides who is right and who is wrong, despite our best intentions. How can there be other than an arbitrary disposal of souls." Her eyes returned to Cardinal Hernandez for his reaction.

As always, Cardinal Diego Hernandez ached for her in silence. He sometimes thought of Serina as his beguiling personal devil and wondered what judgment awaited such a woman—a woman who tormented and yet fascinated him. Were her efforts to tempt him evil in nature? Or were her conversational sparring matches good for him, in that she maintained his awareness of women, their beauty and struggle, and that she continuously challenged his mind in the defense of his faith?

Diego constantly offered her absolution in his mind, forgiving her of all sin and wondering if these sins were actually *hers* or *his*. Her charity to the Church had been enormous. *Did she count on her contributions to buy her way out of Hell?* Diego thought to himself. *What Hell, you arrogant, hypocritical fake? I'm just as guilty.*

"Surely, dear Cardinal," she said, picking up their conversation, "you know the American political machine is capable of inciting riots with the promise that Israel will be better cared for, get more money, more war toys? Suppose we could convince them that we wanted to shift the focus of Christianity to a new geography? After all, we've been trying to make Rome the true home of Catholicism for centuries. How many popes have gone to Israel? Not many."

Diego knew she was correct. Despite her ambivalence regarding her faith, those who knew Serina were impressed at how well-informed she kept herself. Her opinions were accurate, if not original, regarding strained relations between Rome and Israel. Non- Roman control over sacred spots and events in the Holy Land seemed like Vatican forfeitures. Strong influences and the demands of numerous faiths had caused Rome to bypass claim on the very essentials of the Christian religion.

"Why," continued Serina, "did the wealthiest religion on earth allow a mosque- like structure to be built over the traditional spot of Christ's ascension into heaven? Why is this tiny structure, with its cobwebs and broken windows, owned by Muslims collecting shekels for their candles? Certainly not to keep the peace in Israel. Peace remains a seemingly impossible goal."

"Perhaps to simply not add to destructiveness," the Bolivian Cardinal replied, "despite the irony of the 1996 rage by the Muslims over the Jewish tunnel beneath their mosque in Jerusalem. Granted, it's odd that the site of the Ascension could not be liberated during the Crusades. We now simply accept Muslim control over this holy place. For visiting Christian pilgrims, the Holy Land isn't very inviting today. Muslims who used to escort busloads to the site of the Ascension of Jesus Christ are even afraid. Now, very few risk some fanatic of their own faith blowing them up."

"Well," Serina said to the entire table, "you must agree that any such shift from within the Church might help divert the Israeli-Arab tensions. The Crusades aside, the Arabs never had a great history of argument with the west. Trade carried on for centuries. It was primarily the rise of Mohammedism which created the expansion we all fear. Is the Church we all love pushing back? Not that I can see. We merely try and avoid confrontation. It strikes me as a copout. Where is the leadership and integrity?"

The guests deferred to Cardinal Hernandez for a response.

"It's complex, and our arguing won't solve it, dear Countess. Please tell us the progress of your latest charitable endeavors. Didn't I understand you to be chairing yet another major function for the Catholic hospital?" He looked at her with such directness that she knew it was the end of the round. Serina respected his unspoken order and smiled at her guests, launching into a description of an upcoming charity dinner. Having thought out the details earlier, Serina noted committees and the roles of each person present that she counted on for assistance.

As guests departed, Serina quietly asked Diego to stay. She wanted to talk. It was mostly wine talk she realized, but it allowed Serina to rid herself of new invasions of religious doubt. She loved the Roman Catholic Church and ached for the faith she viewed in others. The faith, drilled in her from childhood, had escaped her after the tragedy of losing her husband, Dante. Surrounding herself with the best minds the Church had to offer, Serina hoped for the osmotic effect that would entice her soul.

Serina sat on her antique loveseat in front of a stone fireplace. She stared in envy at the rapturous expressions on the faces of Jesus, Mary, and Joseph portrayed in the enormous reproduction of Pompeo Batoni's *Holy Family*. Exquisite silk damask wall coverings in her apartment were tastefully covered with fine art, a good deal of it religious. The paintings offered Serina enriched satisfaction and peace with herself and her often elusive religion.

Serina frequently visited the priceless original of *Holy Family* hung in Rome's Capitoline Museum. There she would resist the urge to reach out to pull on the edge of Mary's sleeve, where it was caught— seemingly on purpose—under the small band of cloth around her wrist. It was impossibly beautiful and almost irritating. The disarray in the garment was obviously intentional, and she marveled at Batoni's ability to draw attention to Mary's hand, which gently cupped the right foot of the Infant. The fabric of the sleeve, shawl, blanket and swaddling, all in wrinkled disruption, were so perfectly rendered that

Serina had invited a well-known tailor to identify their weave, which he did handily.

In the painting, the Infant's face reflects agonizing love and foretells in expressive clarity of the anguish to come. Mary's face is serene but hints of distant events, and Joseph, with his weathered cheek resting against powerful hands, gazes on in love and contentment, seemingly oblivious to future harm. Serina felt her soul touched by its beauty. She ached for the peace of Christ, rather than the doubt that racked her soul.

As Diego poured brandy and turned from the sideboard with crystal snifters, he was about to compliment her on another successful party, but he hesitated and followed her gaze to the magnificent painting.

"It's not only the feelings of the painting, is it? It's an instant jealousy toward the artist. We are spellbound by the ability of one individual to touch our core without words, and we feel envy and almost hostility toward God for not granting each of us equal talent—the ability to express so exquisitely in paint, emotions about which we can only utter inadequate prose," Diego said. He smiled at her as he handed her the snifter. "It's quite exasperating. I find myself annoyed at our Creator's contempt for assigning us our meager talents."

Diego looked at the painting and then at Serina. "But since it does convey thoughts and ideas for which *we cannot find words*, He has really done us a favor." It was Diego's way of playing Serina's game. She knew this, and cherished their relationship.

Serina looked away from the painting, discerning the double meaning in Diego's words while digesting the suggestion of God's slight, but she was unable to leave the last word with him.

"Hmmmm," she said, exaggerating. "There you go again. We cannot blame God.

After all, He's a consequence of mankind's absorption with mercantilism, if you think about it. He's been merchandised in every conceivable manner."

Diego shook his head in mock exasperation and lifted the brandy to his lips, smiling at her.

"So the  great artists—Shakespeare, Mozart, Michelangelo—do they too merchandise God?"

"I suppose they do, but they do more than merchandise, they build love," Serina said. She lifted her brandy snifter and recited, *"The quality of mercy is not strain'd. It droppeth as the gentle rain from heaven upon the place beneath. It is twice blest: It blesseth him that gives and him that takes."*

"Portia in the courtroom of 'The Merchant of Venice,'" Diego was pensive.

"Yes, the great artists truly validate God," Serina said, her eyes misted, "How I envy them."

Having grown up among Colombia's wealthy, with loving parents, and attended by a doting nursemaid, Serina meandered through a happy childhood. In a country often uncivilized, she enjoyed all that a civilized world showered upon its wealthy young. As she matured, she versed herself in literature. She enjoyed reading and writing to her parents, and with an appreciation for composers, painters, and sculptors, she developed into an accomplished artist. She maintained a disposition and affection toward friends that harbored no rivalry. In a gradual progression, through perfect orchestration, Serina grew into a classical beauty with charm and wit.

While attending the private Colegio Gran Bretanal in Bogotá, Serina's social life expanded, and she experienced the first stirrings of desire and love for the dark enticements of Diego Hernandez. They met at an extravagant *Fiesta de Quinceanos*, the traditional 15th birthday party for young girls. A serious and quiet young man, Diego was captivated by the raven haired Serina de la Guardia. Their mutual enjoyment of the parties of Bogotá's ruling class ended before any pairing that might later be regretted, when Serina left Colombia for Wellesley College near Boston. Although her college experience diminished her adolescent feelings for Diego Hernandez, she later learned of his entry into the priesthood and followed the clerical careers of both Diego and Juan Carlos.

After graduation, Serina spent a few weeks with her roommate on the idyllic north shore of Long Island, walking the still, cool beaches, exploring the fashionable shops opening for the season, and attending graduation parties with friends. By early July she was ready to join her parents for her graduation gift, passage on the Queen Mary II from New York to London. Serina looked forward to being with her parents and spending tranquil days at sea, a respite after a string of Long Island parties. On the boat she met Alessandro Caputo.

Alessandro had watched Serina come aboard. Ordering a drink at one of the bars near the embarkation ramp, he watched Serina step on the gangplank, and was struck by her beauty and cool presence. He later told her over and over again of his first feelings. Taking care to grace their first meeting with social correctness, Alessandro managed to overhear her cabin number and arranged for an introduction at a dinner with the ship's captain.

Serina reacted to Alessandro's magnetism immediately, and their days on board were filled with intimate dinners, long conversations, dancing, and exploring each other's lives, while enjoying lectures and concerts and shows. By the time they reached Southampton, she had fallen in love with the dashing glamour and charm of Alessandro Caputo, and she never wanted him out of her sight. Equipped with wealth and the rank of Count, which he rarely used, Alessandro invited Serina to visit him in Rome, and afterwards they traveled to Bogotá, where her family, impressed with their daughter's choice, approved his request to marry Serina. They were wed in the cathedral in Bogotá. A newly ordained Father Diego Hernandez assisted at the nuptials.

Diego had tried to feel happiness for Serina, but his entire being was sick with disappointment and lingering desire. Lying awake in his room after the wedding, Diego prayed that God might free him from his heavy heart. Serina, having noticed him from under her bridal veil, consigned the image of the erect, handsome Diego in his priestly vestments to an empty spot in her heart, where she could allow it to dwell forever and call it forth as she wished.

Using Rome as a base for his worldwide ventures, Alessandro and Serina traveled extensively. Serina became an asset to Alessandro's empire. A quick learner, she was soon successful at negotiating real estate and financial transactions for Alessandro and quickly gained his complete confidence. Often finding themselves in different countries, they would arrange to meet at remote locations, to reconnect with one another in privacy.

Returning from one of the few trips on which she did not join him, Alessandro's small plane crashed off the coast of Barcelona en route home to Italy. Serina was interrupted during a business meeting and informed of the horrible news. Search efforts continued for ten days with no results. Sometime later a fisherman found Alessandro's leather jacket caught in the net with his catch. The tailor where Serina had purchased the jacket had stitched his name inside, and it eventually made its way back to her.

Serina's courage held. Even though mired in denial and the cruel recurring stages of grief, she carried on day-to-day business but shunned outside activities. When she was able to function, she summoned Alessandro's lawyers. They were ready, and Serina sat quietly as they described her staggering wealth. She was aware of her holdings and slowly forced herself to reconnect with the financial empire she and Alessandro had amassed. As Italy's wealthiest widow, she soon realized that being the steward of Alessandro's success was important work, and this fact offered comfort and the best path to memorialize her husband.

Serina found herself in her apartment, post dinner party, with a Cardinal of the Catholic Church. Rising out of her brief melancholy, she looked again at the intriguing painting, focusing on Mary.

"Ah Mary," she said, mildly vexed that she would never own the original. "Let's talk about the Virgin Mary. We believe she's been on the 'talk shows,' so to speak. Lots of people claim to have seen her, but most of us are just not quite sure. We poor Latinos are perhaps a bit more convinced of the whole story, don't you think?" she asked, in genuine sincerity.

Cardinal Hernandez nodded slightly, knowing he was being baited once again. In the back of his mind he filed "poor Latinos" away as something to think about later.

"We all want someone like Mary in our lives to unlock the hardness lurking in our heart," she continued.

"I've no doubt of the tenderness of your heart, Serina. Even though you try to place a hard shell over it at times, I can usually get through," he teased.

She ignored his little joke. "I wonder how many people out there have no one from whom they can recall a memory of kind words, a sweet touch, moments of oneness—no matter how brief. We are not totally sure of Mary's status, or even of her virtue. After all, the Church has not been exactly forthright in any discussion of siblings of Jesus, while other Christian faiths talk of it freely. I rather like the idea. It allows me to identify in some small way with the woman who was otherwise almost inhumanly inviolate. I mean, Diego, how can you aspire to be like someone who, we are to assume, had no sexual desire? What would happen to human procreation if we were all like that? No, no, I do not see that Mary as someone with whom I could be even remotely associated, no sexual embrace, no warmth, or desire." Serina looked at Diego intently. "She's hardly human," she finished.

The Cardinal was no longer uncomfortable with Serina's outbursts about the sexual behavior of the anointed. He had finally conceded that he enjoyed her frankness, as it provided him a reprieve to review his own fantasies and confront his own misgivings. "Think of her sacrifice, her strength," Diego said, as he considered Serina's words, summoning up his own images. He realized that so much of Catholicism was just that—images—illustrated books, paintings everywhere, statues in churches and museums, posters in school. *How many Catholics actually studied their faith beyond the annual appearance of Old and New Testament readings and a New Testament Gospel?* he thought, knowing that most relied on the simple homilies of their pastors for their education. *Being spoon fed their faith on Sunday mornings was convenient, and their own religious illiteracy rarely occurred to them.*

Serina confided to Diego that she could not rationally conform to the unrealistic dogma of a Church that believed a woman's body was an unsavory place for a man to dwell.

"It is hypocrisy," she lamented. "Procreation is essential and encouraged for gestation, but then, after exiting this safe and nourishing place, it takes on an evil implication. The trip out is often a rough one for a mother and certainly for an innocent child. It is a harsh beginning to an even harsher life. But let us be honest, the initial voyage is hardly unpleasant. You should try it," she teased him. "Why, my dear Cardinal Diego, should our sexual longings be considered evil?" she asked with exasperation. "Certainly, it's no good for children to indulge in random procreation, but responsible adults beyond childbearing need the physical closeness between a man and a woman more than ever." She gestured with a left and right wave and then continued, looking at him intently. "The Church often turns sex into a vaguely repulsive athletic event. How sad. The act is healthy and beautiful, and all of us need to touch each other with our minds and bodies. Tell me something, Diego, would you find it so repugnant if Christ physically loved? What does 'true God and true man' signify if we will not recognize that Jesus was a man in all respects and exhibited a manly nature?"

They looked at each other, while contemplating these ideas, and then once again retreated to a safer place in their minds—their desire in check, no harm done.

"Just shy of 'sufficient reflection' and still a safe distance from 'full consent.' I guess we can overlook the grievous matter part and consider ourselves quite pure, don't you think?" Serina asked, purposefully wide-eyed, as she cited the conditions the Catholic Church deemed necessary for mortal sin to occur.

Diego Hernandez had thought to initiate a conversation about the The Return this evening. But now he hesitated. His first thoughts were to utilize the mellow mood created by the wine as a time to introduce the concept. He did not wish to risk an abrupt adverse reaction, or worse, Serina's treating her first intake of preliminary and vague information as absurdity. Her mood at this moment was sentimental, romantic, and clearly not without the usual dusting of criticism of the very faith she longed for.

Closing her eyes with her head against the couch, Diego watched her as they listened to the finale of the "Hallelujah" Chorus from Handel's *Messiah*. Christmas was approaching, and Diego knew Serina was recalling the peaceful holy season they both remembered from childhood in Colombia. He looked at the painting once again and deeply enjoyed the inspired emotion of art and music created over the centuries.

He felt something else, an inexplicable release from some of the convictions that had defined his life. *Probably the brandy,* he thought. Cardinal Hernandez was aware that submission to the concept of *The Return* had given new meaning to the phrase *Playing God,* but now it did not disturb him so. Having been schooled in the diplomacy required for his position as Vatican Secretariat of State, Diego knew of the subtle attempts to undermine Juan Carlos' papacy. He felt protective toward the gentle Pope, his friend and confessor, but until His Holiness agreed to *The Return,* Diego had worried that Juan Carlos remained in denial over the gains by fanatics committed to the destruction of the Church and people too weak to resist it. A week or so after his own epiphany, and in thinking through the prospects the project represented, Diego's aversion had lessened markedly. For days, he had fluctuated between the certainty of God's rejection of them all and his favor for their inventive defense of Christ. He had thought of this peaceful attempt to bring about hope versus the massive casualties brought about by war. Diego regarded his Pope as the consummate servant of God. Although he thought he knew him well, he realized the agonizing decision Juan Carlos endured and the magnificent persuasive ability of Luís. With the hurdle of the Pope's acceptance now behind them, Diego and Jonathan Kennedy had climbed the same soaring wall of doubt but ultimately accepted the plan. Cardinal Hernandez recalled the lure of Rasputin and thought of the anti-Christ hypothesis. *Was any attempt outside the law to save the Church agreeable in the eyes of God?* He tried to honestly face the possible cynicism of historical judgment and looked within himself for the shame that would force him to pull away. He wondered if he were quite mad—if they were all quite mad. But by the time the sessions with Luís ended, Diego had relinquished any sense of ungodliness and welcomed the challenges ahead.

On this night with Serina, Diego Hernandez faced additional burdens. Along with the temptation she represented, he needed to plant seeds of deception. *Not tonight,* he thought. As the music ended, Diego felt the need to provide added catechistic encouragement to Serina. He accepted that as part of his engaging freely in the questionable ethics of the *The Return,* he needed to remain in God's service as a priest.

"You know, my dear Serina," Diego said, smiling gently, "this nagging misgiving of yours regarding God's validity is dashed when you listen to the music of Christmas. I'll grant you that God made mistakes in his creations. It's perplexing that a *snake* was allowed to influence Eve." Diego smiled at his reference to the fundamental Genesis.

"Why didn't he simply forgive her? He didn't, but He did give us artists—artists at whose abilities we marvel and whose works can bring us to heights of emotion. Imagine the thousands of choirs in this world performing, the artists painting, and the authors writing for millions who are renewed in faith at this season."

Staring at Diego, Serina knew he was right and loved him more for his concern over her doubts. Sensing the swirl in her mind, Diego added, "So, even if we invoke the theory of some human programming by a higher intelligence, did they mean for such programming to manifest itself in glorious acclamations of God and Jesus Christ?"

Smiling slightly, Serina looked at Diego's face and felt his love for God fill her being. She tried to hold her feelings in check. "I'll think about that and let you know," Serina answered.

Walking over to the bar, Diego put his empty glass down.

"Serina," he spoke casually, "the sacred halls call, and tomorrow I shall be all things holy to many that trust me with their secrets. How can I possibly absorb all of your and their sins without some sleep?"

Rising from the couch and walking over to the Cardinal, Serina placed her arms around his back and laid her head against his shoulder, suddenly tearful. He could not help but react and held her tightly against him, feeling the outline of her body next to his.

"Perhaps one day, Diego, we'll escape the prison of your doubts and submit to the joys and comfort of a loving God who gave us such gifts. Someday perhaps this small space still between us will vanish. In our thoughts, we are one already. I can feel that. In the meantime, you continue your mission of goodness—that's who you are, despite my continued attempts at an evil embrace." She looked up at him. "It's the price you pay for your admirable hope of achieving some holiness for me." She stood back and held his hands in front of her. "I'll keep praying shamelessly that it all falls apart before my ache for you for abandons me."

The Cardinal laughed with her, and in his mind he confirmed that the timing was not right to begin a dialogue in which he would ask Serina to give many of her millions. This bout with temptation would already cause a restless night. "Please advise me if God answers, Serina," he said softly, "and thank you for yet another unforgettable evening. I'll be in touch in a few days."

Diego had left Serina's flat and returned to the Vatican in deep thought. He thought about the increasing danger to his vows and wondered at the cost of priestly disobedience.

# SERINA
## April 2015

Serina stood at the balcony of her flat in Portofino, her favorite retreat overlooking the Ligurian Sea. It was flanked by the many peaks surrounding the area and terraced with colorful gardens perched precariously, one over another, on the slopes. She had flown from Rome to Milan a few mornings after her dinner party for Vatican guests and the late conversation with Cardinal Hernandez. She had thought a good deal about their relationship, and although knowing she was courting danger, she longed to see him. She had picked up her tiny Fiat Cinquicento and driven leisurely to the flat, after spending a night in the city. The drive to the coast from Milan had been most enjoyable, and she arrived in time to pour a glass of good Chianti and watch the sunset over the beautiful sea before her. After shopping the day before in Milan, she had met with her banker to ensure that her vast investments continued to be prudent and productive. Even with periodic turmoil in world markets, Serina's financial picture remained healthy.

Work, as commonly perceived, was not part of Serina's life. For her, work was the study of the right investments, and often against her banker's advice, she would pour hefty sums into the world's international markets, sometimes into a single equity. The banker, outwardly conservative as bankers are supposed to be, was smitten with Serina. Although fascinated with her adventurous transactions in the financial wilderness, they frequently alarmed him in light of his obligation to the centuries-old bank, as well as to her. But Serina's intuition rarely failed, and the more her net worth increased, the more the banker's fascination with her grew, both professionally and with her sensuality. Serina enjoyed their working relationship and tried to share his professional enthusiasm for her financial success, but she was unable to separate it from her discomfort at his personal passion for her. In any event, sexual satisfaction was never part of the equation. Serina valued his investment advice but nothing more.

The drive down from Milan to the villa was uneventful. Looking out over the blue expanse of the sea, she relished its mental balm. Its lure, though, represented a colossal sham—one experienced a sense of peace, but peace was a misnomer, which disguised the dangerous blue swells that hurled themselves with a savage strength against the barriers of sand and rocks.

After Dante died, Serina felt compelled to multiply her inheritance and immersed herself in careful study of world markets—an avocation about which, though diligent, she feigned a blasé attitude. With timing and luck, success had blessed her efforts. Temporary setbacks were barely acknowledged.

By the time she was fifty, Serina had amassed a huge fortune, which shamelessly doubled itself. Yet she came to the rapid realization within hours of the first millions earned that, on its own, success did nothing to restore happiness. Pragmatic, Serina accepted that fact, and without expectation, she flourished in her new role as an investor. The large haunting void of loneliness, an ugly escort, forced her to seek companionship. Being unable to lose herself in reading or financial studies other than for brief periods, Serina corresponded with family and friends. Even then, she would often put down her pen, turn off her computer, and telephone anywhere in the world to talk and make plans. She needed the presence and touch of humankind to alleviate the lingering sadness. Without it, loneliness would thread its way through her body, like a saturated string of thick wool—soggy, unpleasant, and weighty.

Even in her flat in Rome, the physical closeness to Cardinal Diego Hernandez became an unbearable frustration. Together at social gatherings, where she was able to flirt and tease him outwardly, her pleasure was still short-lived. Diego's social presence alone could not fill the emptiness, but its power caused her to neglect the very suitable and ardent attentions of other suitors. Diego enhanced Serina's gaiety and expanded her great desire to give of herself. She longed to surrender to the alleged sin.

Serina held an unopened envelope from General Luís Gutiérrez. Luís had ended their relationship soon after Juan Carlos, his beloved and holy brother, ascended to the papacy. She had avoided Luís, since his attempts at reconciliation some years after the death of Dante. His obsession with her was unknown to Serina, who after feeling bruised and slighted, threw herself further into the financial world. As wealth accumulated, the void in her life expanded. Her unyielding casing did crack occasionally, and the longing for peace would surface. Still, anger plagued her as she trifled with several men, upset a few marriages, and cast aside any acceptable prospects.

Diego's reentrance into her life had been chance. The extraordinary future of Serina's salvation presented itself in Juan Carlo's election to the papacy and his immediate selection of his close friend and confidant, Cardinal Diego Hernandez, as Vatican Secretariat of State. During a stay in Rome planned by Serina, to focus on social and Vatican connections and charities, she saw Diego at a fund-raising dinner. As they talked, her loneliness lifted. They could not revisit their childhood parting just yet, so they avoided it, danced around those events in Bogotá long ago, and absorbed the renewed attraction. Although Serina recognized a new prison in the aura of the holy city and in the re-entry of Diego into her life, she lacked the power to hold back. At repeated official encounters, the familiar pull could not be denied.

Serina leased a large flat near Vatican City. Surrounded by the majesty and beauty of the icons of the Catholic Church, she began an earnest study of the Catholic faith and fell in love with it, as she assiduously applied herself, turning over pebbles of doubt, and confronting the clergy on every detail. Her deep affection for the Church and for Cardinal Hernandez presented new frustrations. Often tempted to plunge into acts that would result in danger to her soul, she struggled with desire, placating her conscience by giving huge sums of money to the Vatican. Her motives, she well knew, were complicated, but the Church was quite pleased to accept her donations. Faced with her own hypocrisy and her belief in God's colossal foul-up, Serina thought to herself, *Why were things so amiss on this tiny planet that it required a Messiah in the first place? Why are we allowed to be so good at failure? To harm each other? Is punishing us for an endless litany of sins the realamusement in being God?*

She gazed again at the spectacular view, as she turned the envelope over between her fingers. She had delayed opening it and had speculated about its contents, as it rested on the front seat of her car like an unwanted passenger. Finally, she walked to her desk, located her letter opener, and quickly slit the envelope open.

Inside the envelope, which was printed with her name only, was another with a name and return address:

General Luís Gutiérrez, Comandante Comandancia de los Fuerzas Armadas de Colombia Bogotá, Colombia The inside letter read as follows:

My dear Serina, I have learned of your residency in Rome, and hope that we may soon meet.

Although it has been many years, I am hoping to renew our friendship. I again express my sorrow and apologize for any pain I caused you"

At the bottom in a postscript was an appeal that she review an enclosed proposal. It was a plan to assist His Holiness in a major effort to rebuild the Catholic faith. The document was poorly typed, and the proposed undertaking vague. Obviously, Luís himself had generated it. What was also clear was the implication of an enormous sum that would be necessary to carry out "... a long-term project," a project that must remain highly confidential. Luís alluded that knowledge of the plan would be limited to a select group.

For a few moments, Serina again stared out to sea. She sensed risk and disliked the suggested approach. As with many proposals presented to Serina, this mysterious request was unappealing, and she blocked it from her mind, as she put the sheets through her shredder. Recalling her dinner party several evenings earlier and her conversation with Diego afterward, Serina now felt a strong sensation that something had been withheld. Although conversation had been filled with the usual banter that characterized their "safe" flirtation, Serina experienced uneasiness and wondered if Luís's letter and Diego's reticence were connected somehow.

In her later writing, Nina Shelky had speculated: *Despite the lack of supporting evidence, if the return of Jesus was a fraud, funding such a plot would have required a huge sum by a magnanimous collaborator. Who would have been so motivated?* She jotted notes down quickly as the frenzy of news coverage over the event on the tiny island in Panamá continued. Nina had no answers and was swept along by the miraculous happening.

# Father Jonathan Kennedy – A Lamb of God
## April 2016

Prior to Father Kennedy's race across Saint Peter's altar on the morning of *The Return*, his misgivings regarding the project had been with him night and day. At the sight of the slumped Pontiff, however, everything in his mind vanished, as he asked the Creator to will his friend and mentor to live. Looking down upon Juan Carlo's ashen face, Father Kennedy knew death had won, and he crumpled with dizziness at the Pope's feet and saw the past decades slide across his mind.

Jonathan Kennedy, only fourteen when he learned about his father's identity as a CIA operative in Bogotá, Colombia, had been educated early on about the agency's security methods. His father's job required a cover. As a child, an unknowing Jonathan was happy and proud to have a Dad who owned and operated a cargo airline providing courier services to Colombian cities.

The company also flew supplies to remote Colombian churches, as well as to various military bases. The business provided ample exposure to illegal operations throughout the country, and so the intelligence value was considerable. Partners in his father's airline venture were members of the Gutiérrez family. They were well aware of the intelligence connection and sought to cooperate, and in the process, benefit financially as well.

Attending Catholic school and mass at churches in Bogotá and other places with his parents, Jonathan developed an early devotion to Catholicism. When he was ten, he found himself acting out mass, writing short homilies that impressed his teachers, and participating in school activities that focused on religious themes. Taller than most of his classmates, with a studious appearance, he had an athletic physique that was repeatedly proven on the courts and fields of his schools.

Jonathan often traveled with his father on short flights to cities outside of Bogotá and witnessed the differing approaches of the Church and the military of Colombia's social and political milieu. Recognizing his willingness to accept challenge, the young Jonathan paid attention to all of life, awaiting its invitation.

God's pull became undeniable when, accompanying his father on a trip to Santa Marta on Colombia's Caribbean coast, Jonathan was included at lunch, where he met Father Juan Carlos Gutiérrez and his brother, Colonel Luís Antonio Gutiérrez. Always a polite and courteous child, Jonathan did not need to be told to demonstrate respect and deference to the ranked brothers, and he listened attentively to the adult conversation.

"Don't you feel confined here?" Father Gutiérrez asked during lunch. "I'm sorry you are forced to hear all the complaints, the bragging, and the enormous lies my brother tells," he joked, nodding toward Luís. "You would probably be happier out on the soccer fields."

"Oh no, Father," Jonathan replied. "I feel very happy to accompany my father, and I know I am lucky and privileged to be with you and Colonel Gutiérrez"

"Ah ha! A diplomat like your Dad," countered Luís. "It is a pleasure to have you with us, despite what my 'Godly' brother says about me."

There was much laughter that afternoon, and Jonathan recognized the love between the Gutiérrez brothers. He was thrilled to feel the camaraderie his father experienced with these men and became absorbed in the priestly travels of Juan Carlos and the romantic tales of battle and conflicts Luís told. Jonathan observed that the colonel displayed an overpowering charisma, which even mesmerized his brother, the priest. By day's end, however, Jonathan's young mind felt increasingly drawn to the gentle and devoted man of God, Father Juan Carlos.

Enjoying team sports, Jonathan became physically fit by taking rigorous hikes throughout the countryside. He not only learned the geography of Colombia but during his growing maturity, faced conflicting challenges for his life. At first he worried that his inclinations might disappoint his parents, but as he progressed and evaluated his circumstances and opportunities, God's whisper to Jonathan Kennedy grew louder.

In a letter to Father Gutiérrez, thanking him for his generosity and kindness, Jonathan dared to reveal his aspirations and asked for the priest's prayers on his behalf. Meeting Juan Carlos again at social occasions, Father Gutiérrez leaned across the table during one family dinner, speaking quietly to Jonathan and said, "If that voice in your head is as compelling as I think it is, we must meet and discuss your future. You have much to consider. Can you come by next week?"

As God's summons persisted, Jonathan felt all the more certain and with great joy, accepted Juan Carlos' invitation. As Father Gutiérrez came to appreciate the depth of religious commitment in young Jonathan, he mentored him and grew to love him like the son he would never have. Over the next few years, Juan Carlos gained the title of Monsignor and assumed greater duties. He continued to tutor Jonathan on the historical and mystical aspects of his religion and sent him to others within the Colombian curia to learn about the Latin American Catholic Church.

During his studies, Jonathan also encountered Father Diego Hernandez, the Monsignor's closest colleague. They all met once a week, engaging in long discussions on the political world in general and the specifics of Colombia's historical turmoil. Other days, Diego Hernandez played tennis or chess or simply tossed around a baseball with Jonathan. Juan Carlos and Diego both recognized his potential, but Diego Hernandez saw more in Jonathan Kennedy—some of himself.

As a priest, Diego kept his distance from women as much as he could but never fooled himself about his feelings for Serina de la Guardia, whose presence was a temptation and whose departure tortured his dreams. Recognizing Jonathan's physical good looks and athletic prowess, Diego warned him about the pitfalls and enticements he would face in the future as a priest. Celibacy, he told Jonathan, was often a tough test, and it was difficult to make it to the grave without a slip from grace somewhere along the arduous trip to eternity.

With his dedication and the support and influence he enjoyed, Jonathan was admitted to the seminary at Catholic University in Washington, DC, and prepared himself for his future. At a farewell dinner, on his last evening before flying to the United States, Monsignor Gutiérrez, recently promoted "Brigadier General" Gutiérrez, and Father Diego Hernandez joined in the gathering to launch their protégé on his journey. The Kennedy family, initially reluctant to lose their son to God, had grown in their pride over his devotion. The Kennedy's and the Gutiérrez's became closer yet, in their friendship and love for each other's families. But despite their happiness, none of them could know what lay ahead.

Jonathan was an exemplary student, and his natural curiosity provided an appreciation for all that was Washington DC. He volunteered frequently at mass in the sacristy at the National Shrine. He coached soccer teams made up of inner city youth and participated in numerous events at the John Paul II Center on the Catholic University campus. Professors and superiors delighted at the young seminarian's progress and reported the good news to Monsignor Juan Carlos Gutiérrez in Colombia, as requested.

"I think your boy is ready," Bishop Juan Carlos Gutiérrez was told by Jonathan's superior. "He's finished up five years in our accelerated program and you can be most proud of him."

The final test, whether or not a seminarian has a vocation to the priesthood, is the call of the Bishop, and Juan Carlos believed God's timing was fortunate. "With your kind permission, I'd like to personally call Jonathan to the Sacrament of Holy Orders." The university agreed and in light of the joy felt over the Bishop's confidence in him, taking the vows of celibacy and obedience were, for Jonathan, added gifts.

"I would like to arrange for you to have your ordination in Bogotá. You will need field experience, of course, but after a few years, I want you to serve at the Archdiocese as my assistant. Would you consider that, Jonathan?" Juan Carlos asked. Neither of them knew then of the journey they would take on behalf of their loving God.

"I need you here," said Juan Carlos, smiling broadly as he embraced Jonathan at the Kennedy home in Bogotá after Jonathan's graduation and final farewells at Catholic University.

Jonathan felt exalted and smiled broadly at Bishop Juan Carlos. He ached for his ordination, to begin God's work, and his association with the Bishop.

"I would be honored, and I am humbled by your confidence, Your Excellency," Jonathan replied.

"Don't be too humble," General Luís Gutiérrez joked, placing his hand on Jonathan's shoulder and handing him a glass of champagne, "I am sure my brother will work you like a slave."

Jonathan's admission into the priesthood, when it took place, was a dazzling affair. Prior to his entry into Holy Orders, however, Bishop Gutiérrez advised him to spend six months in the mountains of Colombia. "Humbleness is critical to this profession, Jonathan. The time away will be a severe test, but I know its value, and I urge you to make this sacrifice," he said.

Although Jonathan was downhearted at the delay of the formal start of his ministry, he soo realized that Bishop Gutiérrez was right. The simple peasant faith that he encountered on barren hilltops among the poorest of Colombia, although often  discouraging, expanded Jonathan's sanctity and devotion.

Meanwhile, his parents, waiting to witness their son's ordination, ordered robes for him from Rome and were anticipating seeing him drink the blood of Christ from the chalice made for him from the finest silversmith in Bogotá. While Jonathan was engaged in his journey in the Colombian countryside, Bishop Gutiérrez was again raised in position, assuming the role of Archbishop and head of the vast Colombian Church.

Jonathan's ordination rites took place across from the Archbishop's palace in Bogotá's great cathedral, La Catedral Primada, which has stood for almost 600 years on the site where the first mass was celebrated after the founding of the city. Jonathan, having visited

Juan Carlos and Diego Hernandez there as an adolescent, was moved as he looked at the monumental Baroque façade and passed through the bronze door leading to the main entrance. It was in the hush of the ancient chapel that Jonathan's lifelong dream of the priesthood was realized.

During the mass and ceremony, Archbishop Juan Carlos Gutiérrez sat upon an ornate chair and gazed at his protégé, as Jonathan was called to stand before the altar. Juan Carlos' liturgical headdress, the miter, enhanced the Bishop's physical and ecclesiastical stature. He looked magnificent. As he rose for prayer, he removed the miter with its streamers, as was customary.

Bishop Gutiérrez reasoned with the audience that the young seminarian had been deemed prepared by his superiors for ordination, based on his grace, compassion, generosity and commitment to the service of others but then noted that "none of us truly deserves what Jonathan is going to receive in a few moments." Juan Carlos explained that priests are charged with the remarkable duties of consecrating the bread and wine into the body and blood of Christ, forgiving sins, initiating infants and adults into the faith, and preparing others "to see the Lord in their final moments." The bishop underscored, "The Priesthood is a remarkable, often unbearable responsibility."

When Juan Carlos Gutiérrez, Bishop of Colombia, destined to become The Most Holy Father, Pope Damasus III, asked the eager young seminarian in front of him, "Do you promise your obedience to me and to my successors?" neither child of God had any notion in their heart of their future world and the cause they would commit themselves to in the name of God.

As the litany of saints echoed in song throughout the cathedral, Jonathan moved to the marble floor, lying prostrate near the foot of the altar before rising to a kneeling position. Father Diego Hernandez and the other assembled clergymen walked single-file before him. Placing their hands on his head, each offered a silent prayer.

Visibly moved by the sight, Bishop Gutiérrez recited the Prayer of Ordination.

Diego vested Jonathan with a stole and the loose sleeveless chasuble. Reflectingafterward on the ordination ceremony, Jonathan told his mother that for him, the vesting was the most moving moment. "When the slight weight of the presbyteral stole was placed on my shoulders, I felt the Holy Spirit enfolding me," he said wondrously.

"Mother, I am now a priest of Jesus Christ." He embraced her in happiness. The agony would come later.

The conflict caused by Colombia's violence was never allowed to come between the Bishop, Juan Carlos, who continuously searched for peaceful reconciliation, and the General, Luís Antonio, whose duty it was to root out the insurgencies.

Violence was unavoidable but dialogue was urged and prayer encouraged throughout Colombian society. Despite repeatedly torn hopes, the brothers held fast to their love and respect for one another.

As a young priest, Jonathan was privy to the intricacies of the highest office of Catholicism in Colombia—the Primatial See, the Archdiocese of Bogotá.

He came to understand the frustrations and disappointments facing Catholicism and the nation.

Jonathan knew that, as Archbishop, Juan Carlos was charged with the spiritual responsibility of leadership in the lives of all Colombians.

After more than three years of missionary work in the poverty-wracked villages of the Colombian countryside, Jonathan pleaded to be moved to the Archdiocese in Bogotá to assist his Bishop. His field experience resonated in his résumé, reflecting an understanding of the people and the nuances of language within the Indian dialects. Jonathan could negotiate with rebel factions and regional issues. He was trusted, an important factor in his shepherding of the faith.

Colombian insurgents, though fascinated by the young *gringo* priest so favored bytheir Archbishop, remained wary. They appreciated Father Kennedy's care of their souls but mostly his potential usefulness to their cause. In counseling of rural priests caught up in the popular "Liberation Theology" movement that permeated much of Central and South America during the 1980s, it was easy to sympathize with their simple logic. They embraced the "fresh air" attitude of Vatican II as justification to oppose governments that ignored the plight of the poor.

"We demand that our poor be granted something here and now," argued priests. "Father Kennedy, are we not of the same mind to help our poor? They should not be forced nor expected to believe solely on the promise of paradise to come."

"Your intentions are noble, I'm sure, but you bring Rome's disapproval as you're asking papal approval of that which promotes a rebellion. Surely, you can see that your actions cause an adverse government reaction. When you exacerbate this fear by allowing the far left to exploit you, the only result will be a papal command to cease and desist." Jonathan looked into the dismayed faces. "Would you ask that our Holy Father sanction the actions of rogue priests advocating lawlessness and violence in their demands for land? It is a long road, but prayer and productivity will bring results. I will pray with you. I will do my utmost to promote your needs and the needs of your flocks." Jonathan knew he did little to placate the frustrations and the loathing of inequality by well-intentioned rural priests. Anti-government acts in the name of Jesus Christ, often resulting in pointless deaths, were an added burden to the Archdiocese's soul-saving missions in many parts of the world.

The Vatican, and Bishop Gutiérrez, relied on men like Father Kennedy to help quell clerical mutiny endangering the Church. While Liberation Theology priests felt holy justification, felt a sense of *Christ, the Liberator*, for their actions, leftist factions delighted in sympathetic priests facilitating their efforts. Father Kennedy mourned the carnage by coun ering right wing groups. In some countries, churches were attacked and rebellious priests were murdered in the bloody struggle for justice.

As unrest persisted, Jonathan was called upon as a mediator between governments and religious factions. He became toughened and skilled and discounted accolades received for his success as a crusader for the people and as a guarantor for his Church.

Seeing Hell in lives bereft of grace or hope, he tried to forge his teaching into a simple message—What would a world without God look like? Did he ever get through? It seemed never-ending.

Bishop Gutiérrez continued to be favored by the Church leadership. His work throughout Latin America, along with an influential family, propelled his rise through Church bureaucracy to the top, where the Vatican hierarchy dwelt. Jonathan watched in admiration, and no one was surprised when Archbishop Juan Carlos Gutiérrez was chosen to receive the scarlet. He was to be named Cardinal, *a Prince of the Church.*

"We are going to Rome to get Bishop Gutiérrez a new hat and cloak," Luís excitedly told the families with his usual humor. "Everybody will go!"

The delegation to Rome was sizeable, including most of the Gutiérrez family, Diego Hernandez, and Father Jonathan Kennedy, who felt privileged to witness the ceremony in Saint Peter's when the vivid garments of a Cardinal, a prince of the Church, were placed on this man he so loved.

*Juan Carlos "Cardinal" Gutiérrez,* Jonathan repeated the title to himself. He felt added happiness in his choice to become a priest.

"Choosing you as Cardinal, Juan Carlos," Luís conjectured later at the reception, "might be called a tactic in our over-arching Vatican strategy—part of the role that politics play here. I'm guessing that it's the hope of your superiors that by placing a Colombian in a high Vatican position, some greater influence might be exerted upon us *Latinos.* Luís, knowing this step for his brother was the penultimate move before the certainty of Juan Carlos' papacy, rejoiced as the last obstacles to *The Return* vanished.

*Amidst the chaos of drugs, kidnappings, and insurgent incursions, was it possible,* wondered Jonathan, *that Colombian pride in a native son would bring new recognition for the Latin American Church and stem the tide of its diminishing authority?*

"Let us toast my brother's success." Luís said, smiling, and quipped, "Let's hope it adds to my own."

Soon after his appointment, the new Cardinal Gutiérrez again summoned Father Kennedy to Rome. "I am so very happy to see you, Jonathan." The two men embraced in the small art studio, where the Cardinal wore a simple robe with a grey apron bearing spots and smears of runaway oil paint.

Juan Carlos had resumed his painting and had set up a studio in a corner of his apartment. The familiar odor of oils and turpentine confronted Jonathan as he walked in. It always made him slightly lightheaded, but the Cardinal's work was exceptional, and the odors of his artistic endeavor were endurable. Jonathan soon forgot any discomfort.

Juan Carlos had spent time researching the history of artistic renderings of Jesus Christ. Colombia had a large collection of images, but in Rome Juan Carlos was able to study the widely-varying likenesses formed in the minds of hundreds of master artisans throughout the millennia, including the earliest drawings created by candlelight in the catacombs beneath Rome.

While painting, Juan Carlos felt compelled to translate the imagery in his mind to canvas. Many reflected the life of a younger Jesus. Others captured the joy of the resurrection. Whenever the Cardinal visited a museum or gallery, works of the agony of Christ's crucifixion affected him deeply, and some canvases excruciatingly depicted the dreadfulness of crucifixion. Such depictions caused Juan Carlos painful speculation, as well as artistic intimidation. He knew early on that he did not possess the ability to bring to life that depth of anguish. He wondered why this was and often reflected upon his aversion for any display of man's cruelty to man. *Did it make him weak?* he wondered.

The horror of violent death he had often witnessed in Colombia had created a longing in Juan Carlos for the comfort of peace and beauty. He tried with prayer to push aside the memory of the murders of his family members years ago in Cartagena. His pain was usually held in check, but he had to deal with the repetitive pleas from Luís to gain the courage to go forward with the concept of a return of Christ. Cardinal Gutiérrez could feel the tiny fissures in his resistance to Luís's insistence on the plan. From his new perspective in Rome, Juan Carlos witnessed the large arena of useless killing and death—from the millions of unborn infants and the disposal of female babies in China and India to the sadistic torture and murder of thousands in the Middle East, Africa, and elsewhere. Since the first decade of the 21st Century and the murders and expulsions of Christian organizations caught up in the Iraq War and elsewhere, the intentional destruction of Christ-based faiths had spread.

Luís had told Juan Carlos, "All the cruelty in the world cannot be a shield or an excuse for our historical iniquities. Until we create a miracle *producing peace*, the mindless killing and human retaliation will continue."

Cardinal Gutiérrez now looked thoughtfully at Jonathan. "I needed you in Bogotá, and now, dear Father Kennedy, I need you even more here in Rome. But my selfish desires can't interfere with the needs of this great establishment, and so it must wait. I would like you to go back to America, to Georgetown University, to lend your experience to *The Colombia Project*, a study of Catholicism in Latin America. We are losing, Jonathan. Sometimes I feel this modern-day holocaust resembles the historic losses in the world of art and literature." Cardinal Gutiérrez regarded his current canvas. "Such enormous quantities of art disappeared during the Byzantine Iconoclasm," the Cardinal recalled. "It vanished in the attempt to destroy all religious images used in worship. Gratefully, the unrecoverable destruction did forge a later rebirth of Christian art," Juan Carlos said, scanning his canvases around the small room. "For centuries, influential artists painted portraits and sculpted monumental images of Jesus Christ. It was a renaissance, an immeasurable influence on society, culture, and humankind's perceptions of God. I often try to absorb too much from quiet moments in front of Michelangelo's *Pietà* in Saint Peter's. I'm overcome by the rock-carved churches of Cappadocia in the desert badlands of Turkey.

They represent such a loss of human souls, the loss of humanity itself. It's deeply troubling, Jonathan." The Cardinal covered his moment of sadness, which he was now quite used to doing.

"But for now," Juan Carlos said, brightening up, "I want to treat you to an evening in Rome and learn about what's happening at home. We will discuss the details of this project a little later."

As events unfolded in the world, Juan Carlos expanded his realm within Città Vatican. Colleagues called upon him to discuss the distressing state of the Roman Catholic Church in decay and increasingly relied upon his thoughtful opinions.

Father Kennedy returned to Washington DC and kept the Cardinal advised of the alarming decline in the faithful across the Atlantic, even as he wished he could keep the dismal results of his research and inquiries to himself.

During his advanced degree studies and assignment to the Colombia Project at Georgetown University, Jonathan was invited to the CIA headquarters at Langley to meet some of his father's colleagues. They were highly impressed and saw within Jonathan qualities of excellence and depth in his early priesthood experiences in Colombia. They could prove invaluable—they meshed with the agency's information source requirements—and so they courted him. Jonathan, however, resisted.

He promised cooperation. With the Cardinal's permission, he would share reports when possible, but he remained focused on Catholic history in the hemisphere, now with an emphasis on drugs and terror. Although content living in DC and accumulating knowledge of its inscrutable ways, he longed for the mountains and jungles of Colombia and a closer working relationship with Cardinal Gutiérrez. He could not yet know that his place in eternity would rest on an effort so overwhelming, so strikingly sinful, and so magnificent that it might be the answer to a world in dire need of spiritual healing.

On a crisp fall morning, Jonathan felt the colder breezes sweeping down the Potomac River, as he stepped out of the Watergate apartment complex in Washington. In late October, chilly mornings projected the winter to come, but now it was Indian summer. The air would grow warm as the sun climbed.

Washington, now resplendent in its gold and red leaves, offered exquisite unhurried sunsets. Mid-afternoon sunlight lit up the treetops, burnished in copper and gold highlights. A few trees held on to their green, reluctant to relinquish the summer foliage, resisting the call to go into winter hibernation. Jonathan mused over the schedule of the Almighty.

Catching the shuttle to Dulles Airport, he held the envelope displaying the Papal Seal.

The seal did not cause him concern. Since his ascendancy to the papal throne, Jonathan had received considerable correspondence from Pope Juan Carlos. The document with its familiar wax seal, set by Cardinal Diego Hernandez, simply requested his presence in Rome for discussions, a summons he had received several times over the past years.

Arriving at Dulles, Father Kennedy got out of the cab, collected his bag, and made his way into the terminal. He bought a paper and scanned the typical headlines citing daily terrorist attacks, murders in the nation's capital, natural disasters in the world, political rhetoric, and finger pointing. He bought coffee and a sandwich and sat down at a small table in the waiting area. Before boarding, he located the men's room, where in the privacy of a booth, he tore the letter and envelope into small pieces and deposited the contents in a variety of receptacles along the way to his gate. No pressing reason with such insignificant contents, it was just habit.

Recently, Father Kennedy had noticed his reports were not so thoroughly scrutinized. Notes and comments on his findings lessened. He sensed a change in His Holiness's demeanor, and during recent phone conversations, the Pope seemed distracted and agitated. *Sometimes*, Jonathan thought, *I sense fear in the Holy Father's voice.* As he waited for his flight he wondered, *Is this summons to Rome connected to that fear? Is he displeased with my work? Does he want me elsewhere?* Jonathan's premonition was right, but he could not then know how this visit was going to change his life forever.

# Jonathan's Cross
### The Vatican –April 2016

Father Jonathan Kennedy, the young protégé of His Holiness, Pope Damasus III, took a cab from the airport and was once again in the Pope's studio where his dizziness and nausea was not caused by the usual odor of turpentine and oil but in the shocking words coming from his friend, his superior, the Pope.

Even with the initial embrace and pleasantries, Jonathan felt uneasy and noted stiffness in Juan Carlos' demeanor. After years of friendship and service, Jonathan was alert to the Pope's moods. "Is something wrong, your Holiness?"

Always grateful for the young priest's sensitivity to his moods, Juan Carlos resisted the difficult moment ahead. Despite choosing his words very carefully, he knew there was no way to buffer Jonathan's reaction.

For a few moments, Juan Carlos busied himself rearranging the paintings spread about the room in their various stages of completion. Then, taking a deep breath, he asked Jonathan to sit down, and he too sat down and faced his young brother in Christ.

"Father Kennedy, you have been a source of great pride during my brief papacy and before. I sometimes feel you as an extension of myself, and I thank you. We all thank you for your tireless efforts on behalf of this great Church," he said, then hesitated briefly before continuing. "Dearest friend, you are a true servant to *this* servant of God. I know that what I am about to say will greatly trouble you, and at the same time, I need your loyalty more than ever."

Jonathan's concern grew, but he remained quiet.

"This Church is in grave danger. Over the last few years, we have suffered attacks throughout much of the world. We have been subjected to extortion, kidnappings, and the violent death of our clergy and laymen. We have tried to deal with these incidents quietly but have come to realize that our world support is sadly diminishing. We must fight back with other means." Juan Carlos took a deep breath. "Jonathan, I have studied the Crusades and have often questioned their legitimacy. Three centuries of Christian attacks to remove Muslims from the Holy Land. Three centuries. And now, many descendants of those Crusaders are angry Muslims that abhor both Christians and Jews. We can disavow their cruelty and stubbornness, but we can no longer ignore the radical change that is so rapidly spreading. We rail against it, but nothing changes," Juan Carlos said, shaken and pale, the brush in his hands trembling. "At what point do we accept that, and when do we grasp that those of *our* faith must create the change to overcome the raging evil?"

Jonathan tried to formulate an answer, but when he spoke, the Pope held up his hand and pressed his fingers to his lips. "Jonathan, a very small group of us have made a decision. *I* have made a decision," he said, hesitated and then added, "We are going to embark on a mission to bring Christ back to Earth, back to mankind."

The mission of *The Return* was laid out quickly to the young cleric, whose face grew pale as Juan Carlos spoke. Father Kennedy's disbelief was accompanied by the almost unspeakably daring plan. He hesitated and searched for words. His mind felt numb, as he scanned the sacred paintings around the room. He looked at his pontiff with a mix of fear and sadness. "Your Holiness, all I can think of is to ask if there is now doubt in the full meaning of the resurrection, denial for the words and actions that have always defined our Church and our very being. No matter how desperate our situation, surely we can't take such matters of faith into our own hands," Jonathan said.

Jonathan, still in disbelief, was agitated and shaking. A thin layer of sweat formed on his face, and his eyes filled with tears. "You are everything to me. Why do you shatter me? I feel as though I'm breaking into pieces, that Hell has engulfed me. Why, why are you even suggesting this?" he said, pleading with his hands clenched in front of him. "There must be another solution," he cried.

"We have searched for such a solution, Jonathan," Juan Carlos said quietly, "The agony and misgivings you are feeling are not strange to the rest of us.

*The rest of us?* Jonathan was barely able to take in the information.

"We experience it daily. I struggle with it at this moment, as I look at your shocked and bewildered face." Juan Carlos took a small palate knife from a jar of liquid, wiping it on a nearby piece of cloth. He continued, "The Church cannot rest until the world hears the Word. Do you suppose that if we ever achieved perfection in the eyes of the Lord, there would no longer be any need for all this?" He looked around the studio wired for music, with speakers facing the walls, safe from prying ears. He looked at the easel, where yet another painting of the risen Christ was in progress. "Recall that the only time the Church is mentioned in the Gospels is when Jesus renames Simon to Peter, saying, 'you are the rock, and on this rock I will build my church.' Is this what he meant?" The Pope's eyes pleaded for an answer, as he waved his hands to gesture at the grandeur of the Vatican. He had scraped a dab of burnt sienna paint onto the palate knife for a shadow on the canvas. "What Christ never had during those last agonizing moments was the hope of himself. As a true man, he had to go through the horror of crucifixion. We go to death with faith in Him. His humanness was at its pinnacle when he cried out in despair," the Pope said.

Juan Carlos looked into the face on the canvas in front of him. He had incorporated Pontius Pilate into the painting, gazing at the risen Christ with an expression of despair and guilt and hope, a hope that even he might obtain eternal salvation. "Sometimes I think of Pilate as a kind of fall guy. Like Judas," Juan Carlos said, smiling thinly, "He believed Christ was basically innocent, but he went along to mollify the political opposition. He saw his duty as reducing the threat to Roman rule and safeguarding the route of commerce to and from Rome. Christ's own followers interpreted a threat to the status quo and treated Him like a common rabble-rouser. For the good of Judaism, the local power structure agreed Christ was a disruption to Jerusalem, especially during Passover."

The Pope retrieved the small rag moist with turpentine and again cleaned the knife before returning it to the jar. "Did Christ dwell in Pilate? Did he leave a bit of himself within Pilate when he left earth? Did Pilate hate Christ? Hate, that elusive revulsion that winds through us, held like a kite string by Satan. Hate keeps us in opposition to each other, when we should be together in this world."

Juan Carlos saw Jonathan's pain and, for a moment, was silent. He knew that he had rambled. As Father Kennedy, drained of color, searched for words, Juan Carlos knew he had heard them all before, so he was prepared for what Jonathan would say next. "My dear son," Juan Carlos said tenderly, "as Pontiff, I can no longer ignore the evil assaulting our world. I know this is beyond difficult for you, and there are many days when I feel as though I am walking in the dark, that God has let go of my hand. But Jonathan, I ask how long can we sit in this ivory tower, watching this Church fall to ruin?"

His Holiness looked at his painting, imagining additional strokes of color in the background. "You know, Jonathan, every pope is judged by how he interacted with events, by what was happening in the world during his papacy. At the turn of the 20th Century, Pius X was loath to accept modernity, even issued an encyclical to instructors of the faith to banish teaching of technical progress. He so wanted to retain the simplicity of God's teachings and the faith of the Eucharist. He was naïve, perhaps, but he might have seen something of the wickedness to come," the Pope said. Juan Carlos looked thoughtful. "His successor, Benedict XV, was reluctantly ushered into the papacy in a world swirling with the winds of war in 1914," he continued. "That war and the catastrophic flu that killed thousands held the world's attention far more than a conservative and introverted pope. He was a small man physically, dedicated to the papacy, but unassuming and relatively unknown. Pope Benedict XVI, in contrast, was as John Paul II before him, instantly known around the world and plunged into a world filled with terrorism, a terrorism combined with a global environment in which man could access all data in existence from a small device in his pocket. In this postmodern world, we struggle to sustain the existence of peace and reason. We seem bereft of reason these days, Father Kennedy. But we are responding, finally. Perhaps our plan will fail, but Christ risked everything to save us. Does he not expect more from us than to cocoon ourselves in these ornate trappings? Does he not deserve our best efforts to keep him alive in the hearts of men? 'Take matters such as this into our own hands,' you say. Who else's hands shall we entrust to save this great Church? How shall this papacy be defined by future generations?"

Fighting off his own despair, Juan Carlos clutched the rag, as he looked at Jonathan and wondered if he was about to send his young protégé to ruin. Breathing deeply, the Pope continued, "This papacy of ours will not mark the demise of the universal Church, not if I can help it. We must act now to save Christ's heritage and demonstrate that we *are* in his image and likeness."

Jonathan finally spoke. "Your Holiness," he said in pleading tone, "you are suggesting a new theology, one that changes the return of Jesus from its storied place in God's design. It negates the disclosure of its revealed meaning. How can such an act bring us to God?" He suddenly felt very tired. He wished he was that young boy back in Bogotá, feeling the pull of an afternoon nap. His beloved Pope's apparent questioning of the will of God struck Jonathan like sharp blows of gibberish.

"As you know, we are well informed, and we have tried to favorably influence world issues in a way constructive to the Church," the Pope said quietly. "In the past few years, threats have dramatically increased. Attacks on all Christianity are rampant. I'm sure you read of it daily in Washington, and here we sit helplessly, as widespread devastation is carried out against established Catholic and Christian sects. Many are violent and murderous, but even more are the pervasive non-violent acts against us. You have seen that, too, in the United States."

Jonathan nodded, knowing that he and many within the US clergy attacked by the liberal left and the American Civil Liberties Union continued to soft pedal the encroachment, as their heads were being pushed into the sand.

"*We* cannot engage in armed defense, and the will of the world's secular governments is pathetically weak," the Pope said. "We can no longer raise an army of crusaders to penetrate the corners of the world and remove this threat. The world of the terrorists is counting on just that inability. However, we can perhaps serve God and begin, with a small clean slate, a new salvation of the universal Church by repeating the drama of Christ. It will be a grand endeavor. It will take years, and I don't know how much time we have. Hopefully, long enough. We may not be successful, Jonathan, and we may be damned forever, but Our Lord and Savior has not visibly reacted to our plight. We are soft—a religion of toleration. Sadly, this quality opens us to attempts of brutal overthrow. Our prayers are seemingly insufficient." The Pope smiled sadly. "It may be we are seeing the start of the biblical prophecy— approaching the fiery end of time. I want to believe that we still possess the capability to do our Lord's bidding and reignite faith. In Luke's gospel, when defectors left Jesus, Jesus asked the twelve 'Do you also want to leave?' Peter answered him, 'Master, to whom shall we go?'" Juan Carlos looked at Jonathan, "Where shall we go? We must believe that this is our calling, Jonathan. If it is not, then what is?"

Father Kennedy's mind was tumbling. He wished for a hopeful world in which prayers would be answered. He had often held intense discussions of the threats to the Church's existence. But younger priests had little authority and knew their obligations. They had been taught that fractious actions further diluted and weakened an already battered faith. So, in all but a few cases, they did nothing.

"Your Holiness, what does it mean if we are successful?" Jonathan asked. He felt the smallest change in his mind, an implied concurrence by using the word "we." He felt no desire to argue but could not yet make sense of the conversation. "Does it not suggest that the Church is a fraud and is going to engage in perpetuating this fraud?"

"A good point, Jonathan, and one that has troubled me. I hope not. I have no absolute answer for you, of course. I know we can continue to hope and pray that our faith will prevail, even as we observe its daily erosion throughout the world. But what will be the result? It is one of the great mysteries that prayer is not always answered—in fact, it seems to go mostly unanswered," he said. "Still, prayer comforts individuals who accept that their bad behavior precludes any answer from God. Prayer comforts those facing death. Those left behind experience soul searching at their inability to make it otherwise. Are we to assume that because we bear witness to a lagging faith, we should not act when all hope is gone? We are witnessing a loss of the Christian message itself—

the confident collective hope for the imminent salvation of the entire world."

Feeling his defeat, Jonathan asked, despairingly, "Holy Father, the paradox of the Eucharist, our belief that Christ is on the altar, but still, He remains the one yet to come. So this return to be carried out is to give the impression of a," he searched for a word, "a, visit?" He knew there was no answer. "How much time do we have?"

"Maybe twenty years, if we move now," Juan Carlos answered.

"Twenty years?" Jonathan calculated that he would be in his late forties when the mission took place and felt a fleeting reprieve. *Maybe it will never happen*, he thought.

"There is much to accomplish, Jonathan, and you will have enormous responsibility if you are willing," the Pope said. Juan Carlos placed his hand over Jonathan's. With his own tears blinding him, he lowered his head. "Please meditate. If you will go forward with me, tell me as soon as you can."

Juan Carlos stood up and embraced Jonathan. Then he stood back, his handsome face wet with tears of gratitude and sadness. He managed a small smile. "Go now. I know you need to think, and I know your inquiries will be extensive. When you leave this room, you will swim in confusion. My battle with this decision is over. You need to confront your own. This project needs you. I daresay it cannot go forward without you," he said.

Jonathan nodded somberly, and as he turned and walked to the door, he looked back at Juan Carlos scrutinizing his oily Pilate. "There is nothing for me to meditate upon, Holy Father. I love you, and I must trust you." Jonathan, despite his heart's breaking into small pieces, heard himself saying, "I will do whatever you ask, and may God help us."

Juan Carlos looked up one more time at the stricken face. *No more,* he thought, *no more from me.* "You will soon understand your role, Jonathan," he said. From his position at the easel, the Pope blessed this young man chosen to carry out the most critical aspects of *The Return,* choosing the new hope for the future.

Jonathan closed the inner door to the studio and passed through the outer door, gulping for fresh air.

# Papal Affirmation
**April 2014**

"You have scattered my sheep and driven them away. I myself will gather the remnant of my flock and bring them back to their meadow. I will appoint shepherds for them and none shall be missing, says the Lord." —The Prophet, Jeremiah 23:1-6

After his election, Juan Carlos plunged into the task of understanding the intricacies of the Vatican power structure and became increasingly grateful for the vast capability of the organization now available to him. Providing an array of expert assistants at his disposal, it assured him that the administrative requirements of the Church would be carried out correctly.

Despite being surrounded by people waiting only to do his bidding and the very few others in his confidence, His Holiness felt alone. The Church, being both human and divine, was to be the temple of the hopes and aspirations and the pleasure of humankind, even as it was the torment of papal continuation. Connecting problems of heaven and earth caused Juan Carlos to feel frustrated and ineffective in directing men of earthly weakness on how to strive for the principles of heaven. Assailed by politics, wealth, illness, doubt, and now war and death, the existence of Christianity, and the goals of its followers, were threatened. *The Return* required absolute secrecy. Juan Carlos forced himself to key in on the daily effort of keeping the Church intact, while, at the same time, became fascinated by the technical requirements and psychological challenge that lay ahead. By necessity, he was excluded from direct participation. He realized that although it had been his choice to go forward, he would have to entrust others to carry it through. He remained informed but hidden from any of those outside the Vatican who were required to be part of the planning. The project would take years, and he wished he could devote far more time to it, but the work and duties of a pope needed continuity. Juan Carlos relied on Luís to plan the details. Secrecy became second nature.

The agony of his decision caused Pope Damasus to question his uncontested power, given to him through Canon Law. Searching for the definitive argument that would supersede the teachings that Christ would return at the conclusion of earthly existence—the end of time— for the Last Judgment, Juan Carlos sought answers in the Vatican Library. An easier source, the 1977 work "Eschatology, Death and Eternal Life," written by Joseph Ratzinger, the German Pope Benedict XVI, offered Pope Juan Carlos some optimism. *Is Christianity so steeped in making the past its favorite moment in time that it has deprived itself of the future?* Juan Carlos wondered. *Are grace and salvation finished, and have we only judgment and punishment ahead?* Failure, Juan Carlos realized, would generate total and utter contempt from the world and create the unthinkable image of a fraudulent religion. He had continuously railed at God, and then petitioned Him for the answers, the support in halting the decline of the Catholic Church throughout the world. Indeed, much of Christianity had already succumbed to divisiveness. *I will continue to beseech Him*, he thought, *but not even the uncovering of fraud will matter if this Church is allowed to fall to ruin. We are engaging in anastounding gamble.*

The Pope was vigilant to the presence of Satan. He pictured the demon standing by confidently witnessing Juan Carlos' self-delusion—patiently waiting for his soul to find its way to him. His Holiness could hear the devil's raspy voice, while this puny servant of Christ struggled on, alone with his doubts. At moments Juan Carlos sensed evil permeating the project but then forced himself to believe that this undertaking would not be permitted without God's desiring it to happen. *Thy Kingdom Come—a supplication by early Christians, who prayed fervently for the end of the world and a sweeping new reality, one which would bring with it salvation and peace and deliver them from evil. If introducing Christ's promises as a false hope for an imminent escape from their plight and their poverty was wrong—and yet God allowed it—was then God not a weak second behind Satan when it came to deciding the fate of humanity?* Juan Carlos thought. He loathed this never-ending mental gaming and so endured God's inaction.

Only a few were trusted. At his peer level was his brother, Luís, and his oldest friend and closest confident, Cardinal Diego Hernandez. As Juan Carlos was invested as a new Cardinal in the grand ceremony in the Sistine Chapel, Diego Hernandez had remained a bishop in Colombia. But the two were in daily communication. After being chosen Pope, Juan Carlos' first call was to Diego to request his handling of the major portion of international communications for the papal inauguration. Soon after the installation, His Holiness bestowed the purple of Cardinal upon Diego Hernandez and summoned him to Rome.

As seminarians in Bogotá, Juan Carlos and Diego teamed on theological projects and became lifelong friends and spiritual colleagues. As Juan Carlos's most trusted colleague, Diego's association to the hierarchy of the Colombian Church provided a smooth transition for successors in the Bogotá Archdiocese. His Holiness tasked Cardinal Diego with choosing his own successor to lead the enormous Colombian flock. Finding the best man he could in an increasingly threatening environment, Diego departed his country with some reluctance to transition to the position of Vatican Secretariat of State.

Blessed with diplomatic prowess, Cardinal Hernandez was a man of impressive bearing. Diego was tall and handsome and athletic. Upon seeing him in person or in photos or on television, Latin American women blessed themselves, holding their unholy thoughts in check. Other women lamented the waste of manhood and privately speculated on his vigor.

With *The Return* now firm in his heart, Juan Carlos held meetings with select members of The Pontifical Academy of Sciences, with Cardinal Hernandez usually at his side. Filled with prestigious scientists from various nations, these members of the curia were held in great esteem within the world scientific community. *The Academy has an inside track to God,* His Holiness thought, as he listened to briefings on challenges to faith presented by scientific advances—evolution, human cloning, the mysteries of the heavens, and the quest for the bioethical well-being of an intelligent world society. Holy, yet with insatiable curiosities, the academy's members had an ability to adopt unblemished and fresh approaches to a variety of investigations. There was no judgment of one to another.

Despite a fascination with science, particularly evolution, Juan Carlos remained true to Saint Augustine's 5th Century emphasis on the poetic language of Genesis. Sympathizing with the interpretations of Fundamentalist Protestants, who held Genesis to be scientifically accurate and historically true, he wished he could accept such a simplistic stance. He gently argued to convince some of the accepted Catholic belief— that in each human emergence, God is involved in the creation of a new soul. Whether or not a physical force later created a human is unimportant. What is important is that our God, at some point in the evolution of the species, decided to "breathe" a soul into the body—a soul in His own likeness, he'd tell people. Despite a world drowning in hatred and horror, Juan Carlos frequently called on this simple truth in his sermons.

Juan Carlos listened to every word from this tiny group of trusted men directly involved in *The Return*. He became encouraged by their dedication. He enjoyed moral relief and moments of what felt like divine guidance in the transforming power of the project. Struggling with evil, ever present, Juan Carlos could only pray for an end to the continuous cruel slaughter of humans. The possibilities for a shining future kept Juan Carlos, a man of God, moving forward.

In discussions, the small group had reasoned that bringing Jesus back to a remote island would be far more credible to a cynical and Godless populace than a miraculous appearance in one of the world's great holy shrines. They accepted that despite the monumental undertaking and cost of *The Return*, its initial effects would not immediately be recognized; but if God granted them success, the Church and the world would in time reap rewards. "We will," commented His Holiness using the biblical phrasing, "bring him back into the presence of the least of us."

With a formal starting date selected, the Pope performed a familiar ritual the day before. Juan Carlos washed his hands in the presence of the key participants—Cardinal Diego Hernandez, General

Luís Antonio Gutiérrez, and Father Jonathan Kennedy. Although the old guard Cardinals—Adolfo Romano, Salvador DeAngeles and "Teddy" Arias—were present, the main tasks would fall to younger men. Like Pilate condemning an innocent man in order to satisfy the political demand of the masses, the Pope prayed for the safety, for the innocence of them all, and for forgiveness.

The Vicar of Christ, Pope Damasus III, the holder of the keys to the Kingdom, watched the clear water drip from his clenched hands.

"I wash away our guilt and our worry. I love you," he said to their solemn faces. "I love that you are willing to shoulder this burden. I love that you are willing to take on a task that we may not live to see completed. I love you for your protection of me over this span of time. Though weakened, our Church will prevail. We can no longer evade the responsibility of dealing with the destructive and suffocating presence of evil. We have come far in the decision to take action against the danger found in empty souls, Godless souls. We will remain full of hope and spirituality, and we will augment God's gifts in a peaceful mission to attack iniquity and injustice. Dear Lord, guide us."

Throughout the project, Juan Carlos often retreated to his studio and painted. His works were now well-appreciated by the rich of the world. The poor of Colombia, only able to buy inexpensive reproductions of his earlier works, tacked posters on worn walls in places of honor in their humble homes. The paintings reflected the simple faith of Juan Carlos' childhood, leaning to fundamentalist depictions of the life of Jesus. Later canvases gradually revealed the Pope's deep contemplation of the crucifixion and resurrection. He balked at selling his originals but in time relented. Numerous works captured large sums, which Juan Carlos directed be used for inexpensive reproductions of his works for the masses.

In time, His Holiness painted the image of Christ he envisioned as the one to come again. It took years and seemed guided by a hand other than his own. In the final year before the project's implementation, some of the Pope's paintings had taken on an abstract quality, embodying Juan Carlos's prayers for the resurrection of his beloved Church and the salvation of all mankind. Others—those that closely resembled Christian, whom the Pope never met—took on a magical life of their own. A short time before his death, Juan Carlos quietly shipped several—one to his brother, Luís, one to Father Jonathan Kennedy, and one to Diego Hernandez. Others made their way to the open market, where prices soared after the Pope's death on the altar. Years later, there was speculation on the amazing similarities in Juan Carlos' portrayals of the Jesus described by the islanders who saw Christian descend on the island. It became grand fodder for the media. Juan Carlos had not anticipated his hour and had been artistically drawn to the verbal descriptions of Christian provided to him by Diego and Jonathan. Even with the corroboration by some of the islanders of the uncanny likeness, no concrete connection was ever made, and the unplanned publicity allowed Pope Juan Carlos Gutiérrez a greater participation in *The Return's* success from beyond the grave.

# Justification for Jonathan
## April 2014

Father Jonathan Kennedy sat on a threadbare purple velvet divan in Cardinal Salvador DeAngeles' office. He imagined nervous penitents sitting here, picking at the armrest fabric over the decades, and found his own fingernails tracing the torn patterns.

Cardinal DeAngeles, among other duties, headed up the office of The Sacred Apostolic Penitentiary, a high ministry of justice headquartered in a separate building on Via della Conciliazione, which leads into Saint Peter's Square. It serves as the Vatican's tribunal of penance for the gravest sins. His friends affectionately referred to Cardinal DeAngeles' quarters as "the papal penitentiary" and nicknamed him Sinbad. DeAngeles' credibility depended upon an inviolable shroud of secrecy. This aspect was not to create mystery but to offer security to the sinner. That culture of concealment, already well- established, would be vital to *The Return*.

Unlike Jonathan, who wrestled with his conscience after his initial astonishment at the Pope's plan, the Cardinal found himself captivated by the concept. He knew Juan Carlos had a vivid imagination but this was the gravest sin ever concocted.

Salvador DeAngeles was a scholar of souls, having peered into many of them. Some he saw as crucibles full of molten sin, and he always felt grateful when the forces of good plumbed the bottom of the crucible and his penitent left his ministry cleansed. In his time, Salvador DeAngeles had seen a rare few like Juan Carlos, whose souls held a purity that shined, even through this unimaginable plan.

After months of research and contemplation, the Cardinal had made peace with his own doubts. He recognized breathtaking potential and was now behind the gamble for good. Cardinal DeAngeles—like Diego Hernandez, Teodoro Arias, and Cardinal Adolfo Romano—had been drawn into the miracle they were on the verge of creating. *We're capable of this.*

The Cardinal wished for a moment to be back at the small rose garden on the veranda of his apartment. As he studied his pink and red blossoms, the Cardinal considered them a far greater proof of God's existence than much of scripture. The roses had it all—beauty, fragrance, delicacy, color, and intricacy. Their thorns seemed the tagline for a God who managed to place a warning in front of anything that seemed perfect.

But at this moment, staring at the young grieved face of Father Kennedy, full of suspicion, he was experiencing uncertainty for the hundredth time. He knew his task was to coax Jonathan to come on board, to convince him that the good outweighed the evil, that sin could well be absent in this effort, and that this small coterie were the new Crusaders, guided by a divine hand. They were crusaders of Peace and Hope, without any intention of slaughtering thousands to reach their objective.

Cardinal DeAngeles realized that his persuasive gifts would require divine assistance, and he had worked to prepare himself. A young and capable man was required for the extraordinary tasks ahead. Knowing that Jonathan Kennedy was up to it physically, the Cardinal now had to probe the intellect and find the trigger in Jonathan's mind to cause him to commit. Cardinal DeAngeles recalled walking out to his veranda to his favorite thorny rose bush, hosting large blood-red buds, awaiting their moments of glory as well as graceful deaths; a far more pleasant task than what lay ahead of him.

DeAngeles expected Jonathan's. For his part, Jonathan remained mired in despair, resulting from his meetings with His Holiness. DeAngeles realized the need for patience, but at the same time, the Church could no longer waste time. Despite his agreement to the plan, Father Jonathan Kennedy felt like an angry beast clawed at him. He felt physically nauseous. Jonathan had been attracted to the Holy Orders because of his devotion to God and his admiration for then-priest,

Father Juan Carlos Gutiérrez. Now, worry caused deep creases in his pale, young face.

Cardinal DeAngeles acknowledged the young priest's discomfort with a sympathetic look but a confident demeanor. "There, there, my friend, my dear boy," he said, his usually gruff voice softening. "Do not be too distressed. You're going through classic phases of suffering—doubt, fear, distrust, disbelief and probably flashbacks of your entire life." Cardinal DeAngeles leaned forward and looked into the young priest's face, as he had done so often in admonishment of others' careless attitudes toward their sins. Words and timing were critical. Metaphors, always part of his strategy, Cardinal DeAngeles turned to old teachings.

"Why does man suffer, Jonathan? Do we perceive that God strictly wants yes men? Or should we be exercising some of our infinite ability to do the right thing, as we see it, on His behalf? No Jewish, Muslim, or Christian effort to date has succeeded in creating a peaceful world. Would you agree with that?" The Cardinal, not looking for an answer, continued. "We believe that man inherently knows good from evil. Why then can we not find a suitable implementation of good, a common ground? Doesn't God want us to have peace on earth? Should we, in the seat of Peter, sit back and allow evil to eat away at all we hold to be decent and civilized? Maybe we're testing God's faith in us." Cardinal DeAngeles shrugged his shoulders in a questioning gesture. "There's not a nice coherent and philosophical text to go by. Remember Job's arguments with God."

Jonathan, of course, knew the tale, but also knew that Cardinal DeAngeles would continue with the story of the prophet who dared to question.

"God," Cardinal De Angeles said, in a manner that suggested personal friendship, "was annoyed by Job's arrogance. When Job questioned God about man's suffering, God told him to consider not the suffering but instead the wonders of the world. Job was never given a straight answer," Cardinal DeAngeles said, "and neither have we. The story reminds us that our puny intellects are not equipped to deal with the imponderables. Oh, we can speculate, and we can know ourselves to be at the apex of the animal kingdom, but we really have little choice in our beliefs. We've accepted—bought into—the direct revelations given to the prophets as being 'the Word of God.'" The Cardinal paused. "Why there has not been much in the way of prophets recently is anybody's guess," he said, with a small smile. "Maybe God has said all he's going to say. Or perhaps we aren't listening. Maybe we're just mired in the past. Sort of like that song, 'Is that all there is?'" The Cardinal smiled again at his efforts at a little humor. It was lost on Jonathan, who remained in quiet misery.

Salvador DeAngeles' voice pushed on, saying, "What we'd really like is a barter arrangement. Rather like, 'If I believe in and endorse You, what do I get for it? What positive good is there for me?'" He leaned back in a squeaky office chair, throwing his arms up in the air.

Father Kennedy mentally acknowledged the Cardinal's point and briefly moved to his own experiences as a novice in poor Colombian towns, where impoverished inhabitants exhibited blank stares when he tried to respond to their doubts with mere words. Jonathan knew he lost many souls along the road to salvation. *What indeed do we receive here on earth for our adherence to our faith? What does anybody get? A sense of comfort at moments, a sense of miracles at moments, a sense of all's right with the world at moments. But not enough moments,* he thought. Jonathan concentrated on the doubts of life, doubts that plagued him and most of humanity.

As a boy and frequently exposed to Colombia's political condition, Jonathan had listened to confidential discussions his CIA father held with officials regarding Colombia's endemic violence. The FARC, one group of armed communist insurgents in Colombia, were part of *La Violencia* that caused tens of thousands of deaths in the mid- 20th century. In its aftermath, armed groups traveled to remote parts of the country, with internal borders between areas. The resulting exclusion of large sectors from Colombian political life fueled creation of insurrectionists in the 1960s and 70s. Jonathan studied many of these groups funded by the Soviet Union and Communist China. By the end of the 1980s, most were gone or had been absorbed. The FARC and the National Liberation Army (*Ejercito Liberacion Nacional*— ELN) endured, fueled by the immense narcotics trade after Soviet and Chinese funding dried up. To pay for the protection of their fields of marijuana and coca leaves, they had perfected the profitable but despicable business of kidnapping.

Despite fears for his safety, Jonathan's parents allowed him, as a twelve-year-old, to volunteer for the rescue efforts during massive mudslides in Armero in the mid-1980s. Jonathan worked alongside the faithful and the outlaws. He became dedicated to his fellow man through that experience. *What did it all mean now?* he wondered, as he sat dejectedly, loathing Cardinal DeAngeles' impossible words.

"Do you recall 'The Ranters,' who came up with the subversive doctrine of the holiness of sin?" Cardinal DeAngeles asked. Jonathan's attention returned, as the cardinal bracketed his hands about the word. "In the 1600s, a fellow named Jacob Bauthumely preached and wrote that sin was not an action but a condition, a falling short of our divine nature, and that divinity existed in every creation. The worship of localized gods was not idolatry but common sense—a guarantee for the rain and the crops." Cardinal DeAngeles leaned forward. "Let's face it, Jonathan, our divine nature is an elusive state, and for the most part, guilt and fear of eternity is what puts us on the 'right' path. It's what the critics call 'control of the masses.'"

Jonathan thought about leading his tiny flocks in the construction of small churches in remote villages in Colombia. *Did he control the masses? He supposed hedid!*

"We are often not honest," the Cardinal said. "We dread Judgment Day. Despite rhetoric about a loving Father, we do not envision that moment as a party where a gracious host ushers us into paradise. Hardly. God mostly seems to be a heartless and sadistic being. The Israelites, believing that any direct meeting with God would surely be fearful and unpleasant, sought constant reassurance from Moses. Moses related that God would send generational prophets for the task of confronting the Almighty and to bear the shock of godly collisions. That's what we all want—a spokesperson," Cardinal DeAngeles said, slapping his palms on his desk. "I think not so much for our sinful state but to cushion God's downright disappointment that we didn't accomplish as much as we could have for Him."

Father Kennedy noted a lessening of the grip in his stomach, felt himself shoving at the doubt and confusion. He even felt a jab of amused sympathy, thinking of mankind's common condition of misery at the moment of judgment.

Prior to this meeting, Jonathan had immersed himself in canon law, referring over and over to Book III, "The Teaching Function of the Church." He recalled Canon 750 and the difficult Paragraph 1, stating, "A person must believe with divine and Catholic faith all those things contained in the word of God, written or handed on." Canon 750 spoke of "the one deposit of faith entrusted to the Church, and proposed as divinely revealed."

Jonathan knew these words bound Catholics to their faith. He thought about *The Return* and its blasphemous implications as defined by the Catholic Church—"an obstinate denial or doubt after the reception of baptism of some truth." *How does this plan fit?* he wondered. He considered "The Chronology of Revelation," a detailing of the final judgment of God. Jonathan knew Revelations was loaded with symbolism, metaphors, and frightening imagery. The interpretations were numerous.

*Christ will come again—maybe?* Jonathan wondered. *Christ will come again to judge the living and the dead . . . but this return has nothing to do with that!*

Needing a break, Jonathan attempted to lighten up in hopes that it would be just that—a light and frivolous debate, an exchange of words with few real consequences. Still, in his head there was an image of an individual returned to earth, one who appeared to be Jesus Christ. *Could it result in a holy event?*

"Do you think when Judgment Day arrives, our Church leaders, our world leaders will be able to negotiate for us, Cardinal?" Jonathan asked. "Will there be any opportunity to negotiate? Suppose everybody gets three minutes. How long would that take?"

Cardinal DeAngeles frowned at Jonathan but loved him and knew his jesting was an evasive tactic, a way to break the tension. The planners knew that there were few priests Father Kennedy's age more dedicated to the Holy Father. Nonetheless, he admonished him.

"Careful, my boy. Remember, the seeds of the centrality of the covenant were provided by Moses. He too wanted to know 'what's in it for us?' We believe that he convinced Yahweh to choose the Israelites as his beloved people above all others. It was at that moment," he poked at the air, "Jewish stubbornness and detachment were born." He chuckled, "We all have some criticism of the Jews for their belief that they are the chosen people. That we regard that as arrogant bunk reveals our hypocritical nature." Cardinal DeAngeles smiled mirthlessly, "But then again, two-facedness almost seems unavoidable. When we try—and we certainly go through gyrations of trying—to integrate with our Jewish brethren, we remain at odds over the fact that the *Jews killed our Lord.* We certainly don't forgive them, but as to the notion of the 'holiness of sin,' we believe that by killing him, our faith was born in the resurrection." Cardinal DeAngeles shrugged, and with his fleshy palms open and up, he asked, "How would our faith have unfolded without Judas and the Jews? Talk about the 'chosen ones,' our *all-knowing God* had to have pre-selected Judas to do the deed. So was he at fault? Or does Judas end up being more blessed for his enormous role in the development of Christianity? The holiness of sin to be sure!"

Aware that these mysteries had been debated for centuries, Jonathan said nothing. "Good God!" Cardinal DeAngeles almost shouted, as he went on. "Aren't we all blameworthy? Holy wars endlessly scar our defense of monotheism. Instead of seeing God as a symbol to challenge our prejudice, we insist on using Him as an endorsement of egotistical scorn. We insist that God support us in what we are—mortal killing machines."

By now Cardinal DeAngeles had raised his ponderous body off the chair and was on his feet. "Since the Reformists introduced death and destruction *in* the name of God, we've developed a greater fear of God, and we now give the endless cycles of murder a religious rationale. We depend on the profession of faith in Deuteronomy for kicking aside all other deities." DeAngeles pretended to write in the air. "From this point in history—no multiple Gods! The same was adopted by the Jews and so spawned the rampage. We say the whole world believes in the same God—bunk. When radical Islamists piloting planes into buildings prayed to Allah and Christian passengers in those planes pleaded with God for salvation, were they talking to the same God? Who won?"

Jonathan managed to find his voice. "I guess man hasn't changed much, has he, Cardinal? He has a tough time separating miracles from magic. Some miracles of the gospels cause one to wonder if a special effects master had a hand in it—like the early apocryphal gospels that really embellish events. In the Gnostic gospel of Thomas, little Jesus was able to make birds from clay and knock playmates dead with just a word. In Peter's gospel, Jesus, over ten feet tall, is resurrected in full view of the guards and disciples, complete with giant angels."

"Yes, one can see how those didn't make the cut," the Cardinal said, nodding, pleased that Jonathan was at least participating. He removed his glasses and pressed his thumb and forefinger into the corners of his eyes. "Ah, yes, Jonathan, that stuff answers any need for the spectacular but fails in filling the void in our hearts, doesn't it? What is the truth? What prevents the truth from getting through? We struggle with this—and the shouting never allows the truth to be heard." The Cardinal paused, searching for the right words. "Father Kennedy, we believe it is our destiny to at least attempt to restore some order through a new focus on Christ. In this world of mayhem, we could do far worse, and we need to engage all our energy and our intellects to the goal of spreading the faith by bringing him back.

Jonathan again felt shock at DeAngeles' words. *What would it take to appeal to the Cardinal's sense of monumental sin?* "What of our Judgment Day? Even if we succeed, how can we ever be forgiven?" Jonathan asked. Repeating his earlier unanswered question to Juan Carlos, he asked, "How can we reconcile an imposter with a genuine returned Christ."

The Cardinal smiled sympathetically. "Father Kennedy, forgiveness is all around us. Perhaps I'm at an age when, having not contributed much to undo this state of utter chaos, I reach out for a chance to join in the greatest act imaginable. As for judgment, I might rely on the doctrine of *Epikeia*—'according to the spirit and not the letter,'" the Cardinal said.

Father Kennedy reached back into his seminary days. He knew the hypothesis had been put forward that the traditional doctrine of *epikeia* might provide a moral solution for divorced and remarried faithful—that Catholic moral theology had given ample room to *epikeia*. "I'm not sure how *epikeia* fits here," Jonathan said, preparing for the Cardinal's next discourse.

"Aristotle, Saint Albert the Great, Saint Thomas Aquinas, and many 20th Century scholars have offered explanations. They left no doubt that *epikeia* was seen, in the strict sense, as a moral virtue—a quality belonging to one's moral formation, a principle that some decisions are not only good, but very good, even excellent. For Aristotle, 'the equitable is the just' or even the perfection and completion of justice and other virtues. The original context is from actions governed by the laws of the Greek *polis*. Scholastics added forms of behavior governed by canon law or perfectible human laws. Both Aristotle and Saint Thomas saw this as a kind of guidance, 'a directing of a defective law because of its universality.' They wrote that a well-formed person knows what is commanded or forbidden and knows why. So, if the law is expressed in universal terms, something *could* occur that does not fall under the universal norm. The virtuous, understanding person realizes, in this case, that literal observance of the law might lead to an action that harms."

"Like what?" Jonathan asked.

"When the human lawgiver *overlooks* some circumstance because he was speaking in general, it becomes necessary to consider *as prescribed* what the lawgiver would say or include if he were present—if he'd known the case in question. *Epikeia* is not invoked out of kindness and has nothing to do with tolerance. If a case requires it, it becomes the rule that must be followed—a kind of higher rule for humans," the Cardinal said. "We must apply *epikeia* as a higher rule, an appeal to a higher level of moral principle for an exceptional case." He picked up a small paperweight in the form of Adam and Eve sitting on his desk and turned it in his hands. "Let's look at a very exceptional example, Jonathan. What would be the situation if, after a war, only one man and his sister were left on planet Earth—or a man, his sterile wife and another fertile woman?" Cardinal DeAngeles allowed the question to hang in the air. "Sexual intercourse would have to take place in order to continue the human race." He looked for Jonathan's reaction. "But such an act would be different from the natural law we know today as incest and adultery."

"Forgive me, Cardinal, but there would be no way for these few to know that the rest of the planet was wiped out. Shouldn't they first search for other life?" Jonathan asked.

Cardinal DeAngeles brushed aside Jonathan's question.

"Some hold that an act such as this—an act forbidden by a negative natural principle—can never become morally permissible." Cardinal DeAngeles looked down at his desk in thought. "I think we all know what is intrinsically evil. But objections arise. We can't avoid that human actions create physical results—the negative moral norms like adultery and murder. We've known that these have exceptions. Are there no actions by those whose intention in relation to reason might hold a legitimate defense, an exception to the fifth commandment? We know exceptions exist for war and personal defense. The same logic could apply to the rather silly thesis that the holiness of marital relations is an exception to the norm of 'do not fornicate.'"

Jonathan interrupted, saying, "I thought, Cardinal DeAngeles, that the Ten Commandments are more or less etched in the human heart. It seems that the need for written law is because of the confusion of the *unwritten* in souls trying to justify their, or somebody else's, sin. We believe our divine mandates are binding—precious rules of life for every human creature. Violation, with consent of the will, if the matter is grave, is considered a grievous offense against God." Feeling his brain on overload, Father Kennedy asked, "So, Cardinal DeAngeles, should good be based on law, not law based on good?"

"Perhaps," replied Cardinal DeAngeles. "The ethical framework that led to the concept of *epikeia* is different. Virtues are overall goals of absolute and universal validity. They make sense. They are good and desired by mankind. To go back to our example, virtuous habits—having sex only with your lawful spouse and creating new life—is an action that achieves God's plan. This is good. Outside of marriage this same action is bad, unless we are forced by events outside our control to take that bad action and turn it to good by achieving a new goal of good—a new virtuous habit. *Epikeia* is necessary because—regardless of what the letter of the law says—justice and ethical virtues must allow exceptions."

"But, Father, it doesn't mean, nor has it ever meant, that because of exception, it's okay to allow a little injustice, a little lust," interrupted Jonathan.

Cardinal DeAngeles continued firmly but kindly, "Canonical law strives to ensure the common good. We call upon both the natural and the divine law to avoid adulterous unions. This ensures the credibility of the marriage sacrament and exercises the Church's duty to safeguard the ecclesial and public reality, such as Christian marriage.

"Upheavals and lenient divorce laws now prevail. They prevail in countries with long Christian traditions regarding the indissolubility of marriage. The common good of the faithful demands a more attentive Church, a firm striving to maintain this value. We shouldn't give in to the pressure of a non-Christian culture. It affects the faithful and becomes the reason for the sad situations everyone laments. A Christian marriage is vital to the common good of humanity. Should we 'write off' our Christian culture—dismiss it? Our popes need to hold fast to tradition, Jonathan. Otherwise the Church is no longer the Church, and its complete dissolution would surely follow in a tragic dismantling.

"Okay, so we come to the point," DeAngeles' face turned more serious. "Trusting in divine guidance, His Holiness Juan Carlos has made a decision of great magnitude. It will, dear God, be for the common good. If we're discovered, if we're found out, it will generate a multitude of legal issues, which may take centuries to unravel. It will open new debates over good and evil, but we must have faith that good will prevail. And that's assuming we're ever found out." DeAngeles allowed himself a tiny mirthless smirk before continuing.

"Most people have never heard of *epikeia*, Jonathan, and yet they exercise it in the privacy of their own conscience. In fact, at one time or another, don't we all?"

Cardinal DeAngeles looked at Jonathan somberly. "We are very close to the death of our Church as we know it. You have seen statistics, and I can show you others. So, we have concluded that we have *a very grand exception*, for which this action is justified. Our actions must be viewed as divinely directed, drawing their legitimacy from the viewpoint of epikeia." Cardinal DeAngeles sat down again, exhausted by his own arguments.

Father Kennedy looked at Cardinal DeAngeles with a mix of respect and confusion. *This old Cardinal,* he thought, *is almost three times older than I am. He has history and experience. He could call it quits, yet he keeps going.*

Sitting down, Salvador DeAngeles emitted a slight groan of age, and he said wistfully, "Future lawgivers might deal with whether or not our individual and collective actions are contrary to the common good of the faithful and whether or not we have imposed an unbearable burden upon the earth."

Father Kennedy felt lightness in his heart, as he bent slightly toward commitment.

He looked at his superior and asked, "Even if we change the tide of despair with a successful outcome, will we be absolved, Your Eminence?"

Looking up to an imaginary heavenly judge and knowing that rightly or wrongly he had achieved Father Jonathan Kennedy's acceptance, His Eminence took a breath and offered silent thanks. "Will we be absolved? Will we be absolved if we turn one soul back to Christ? I don't know Jonathan. There are moments I think *epikeia* is merely an excuse—an escape—but it has become the formal rationale for going through with this monumental event. 'Necessity makes licit what is illicit,' to quote Pope Gregory IX. And, dear God, may it please You." Cardinal DeAngeles clasped his hands and shook them in supplication heavenward.

The Cardinal's triumph was brief as the tough assignments required immediate disclosure. "Now, Jonathan, to your tasks. They are formidable to say the least. Cardinal Hernandez has outlined a plan, and, in the hopes that you would be convinced, he will join us."

Cardinal DeAngeles was always on schedule, and Diego made sure to arrive at DeAngeles' door at the appointed time. He recognized acceptance in Jonathan's face and felt that odd mix of relief and disappointment. It was tempting to sympathize further, but he avoided it.

The three of them sat down and exchanged looks. After Cardinal DeAngeles finished a prayer of petition, he looked to Diego to begin.

"Here in the Vatican, nothing will be written down. We will brief one another at times set in simple code. You will be in direct contact with me. If I am removed for any reason, your next in command will be Cardinal DeAngeles, then General Gutiérrez, and finally, His Holiness."

Jonathan wondered what would happen should *he* be removed from the scene, but he remained quiet.

"You must locate and recruit those with the technical know-how to carry out the mission. This won't be easy, but success will depend on an almost miraculous combination of people within our ranks. Doubts will intrude frequently. When they do, reflect on the wholeness of this small motivated group, some of whom you will not be aware. Roles are clearly defined, and although we'll face setbacks, I marvel at the lack of any immediate obstacles.

"Are you with me so far, Jonathan?" Diego asked. Jonathan nodded, and Diego continued, "The technical talent will, hopefully, come from one Dr. Desmond Dennison, the American scientist. He's known as 'Denny,' and you will need to become familiar with him, see him in action at one of the Advanced Science Conventions. He is always a featured speaker in his field. We will monitor Dr. Dennison's progress in certain areas over the next year or so. He lives in Georgetown, and at the right time, you will arrange to meet with him in Washington. You will be impressed. The question is—when the time comes, will he?"

Cardinal Hernandez pressed on, as Jonathan fought to concentrate. "Your family connections to the US Intelligence Czar and the Central Intelligence Agency are highly important, as their cooperation will lead to our Jewish brethren's participation, the Cardinal said. "General Gutiérrez will convince those in the Jewish community who need to know. Their participation will mean a greater push in their own quest for peace. The Jews are holy, but they are also pragmatic. If helping us to bring 'Christ' back to earth means even a slight distraction for Christianity to another location, they may perceive that they have one less problem to contend with in their plight against Arab hostility." Diego smiled, "It may take time, but perhaps a bit of the peace of Christ will enter all their hearts. A successful outcome could give pause that would encourage peace. We simply don't know."

Cardinal Hernandez placed his hand on Jonathan's shoulder. "But, dear Father Kennedy, your priority and *greatest challenge* will be to find the infant who will grow up to be our Christ. We would like you to go back to Washington to tie up any loose ends and then, as soon as possible, to begin this search. We will officially assign you to the implementation of your Colombian research in Bogotá. Unofficially, you will seek out the child, arrange his early care, and in time develop and implement a training schedule that will arm our Jesus with nothing less than Herculean strength, inviolable faith, and unprecedented knowledge. He'll need to possess an abundance of all virtues, and his way will be tough, as he faces doubts and temptations. A life after the mission will need to be fabricated for him." Diego ignored Jonathan's brow, furrowed in disbelief. "Moreover, that life will need to be pious and probably secluded. Since the actual mission won't take place for another two decades, there's a good chance that most of us won't be here to witness it. If I'm not here physically but my faith and forgiveness serve me, I'll have a front row seat in a good section," he said, smiling.

Diego wished he could stop and relate it all in much less haste. "Forgive my rush, Jonathan. I know this is difficult, but there is really no other way. We couldn't feed this to you gradually. Despite concerns and obstacles that we haven't considered, for now try not to think; we can discuss any issues once you formulate your own plan. Those who follow us in this great religion may learn of us and judge us, or they may not learn of us and yet enjoy a world of greater spirituality. If suspicion arises, they may create a cover- up, or, as with many alleged miracles, they may ignore the event." He cocked his head quizzically, "That remains to be seen."

Cardinal DeAngeles turned his eyes from Diego, looked at Jonathan, and nodded briskly. "Part of me wishes I were you. But that is not the case," he spoke somewhat wistfully. "And if you have no further questions of me, I am very tired, Gentlemen. Please excuse me, I need a nap."

Cardinal DeAngeles waited for the two men to exit. He returned to his apartment, went out to his balcony and examined his rose bushes for insects which might harm them. With small clippers he kept in his robe pocket, he trimmed away a few dead leaves, pressed his nose into some blossoms, and walked to his bed, with the scent of beauty filling him.

# Jonathan and the Countess at the Vatican Museum
## April 2016

Despite realizing that a discussion on religion required more than a little diplomacy, Serina relished the opportunity to test the responses of those within her circle of clerical acquaintances.

Since childhood religious doubt had haunted Serina. The charity, devotions, adherence to Catholic law, and ritualistic demands often annoyed her and resulted in spiritual ambivalence. Some days a burning passion for Christ and the need to heal would carry her into the confessional, where she would drop to her knees in fervent prayer. Remorse and regret would flood her, and, with guilt purged, she would emerge drained but cleansed. A temporary peace would ensue. As the days passed, however, so did the veneer of spotlessness. Her psyche reminded Serina that the foundations of her faith had never been truly secured. Misgiving would assault Serina, appearing like a mischievous ghoul perched on a mystical shelf grinning at her. She had given up trying to rid herself of her uncertainties, as days of rejection of God battled with those of deep devotion. Serina chalked some of this up to erratic hormones and the devil-filled siren that would take over. She indulged in a cross-examination of priests, trying to trick them on one or another uncertainty. With charm and intelligence, she would lure, mesmerize, and then, verbally pounce upon the unsuspecting ones.

Fascinated by her probing questions and flip retorts, priests would search their stores of dogma and faith to satisfy her. Occasionally, they would hit the mark and perceive understanding and satisfaction in her face—a tilt of the head, a slight lift of the eyebrow, and a widening of Serina's extraordinary eyes. They would leave more content than before; they believed they had fulfilled their vocation and saved a soul.

More often, however, the Countess's face would lack expression. Her eyes would hone in on the face of the hopeless messenger of God, as he attempted to explain the unexplainable—the Almighty's motive for any number of cruel situations suffered by man. Serina's stare often reduced her lector to feeling the fool, and many encounters ended in angry frustration. Most of them, nevertheless, realized the value of her insights, and more than one implored God, "spit in my ears and touch my tongue so that I too can hear and speak" in searching for a response to Countess Caputo.

During the week of Father Jonathan Kennedy's visit, Serina sponsored a benefit for the Vatican museums. Rome's wealthiest patrons strolled through the museum's rooms, marveling at the art unhindered by the usual crowds.

Father Kennedy was ordered to attend by Diego. His concern for Jonathan was valid, as Jonathan experienced despairing distress and spent several afternoons in his small room in denial, mulling over the logic, the outlandish plans, and the swooning sense of disaster for which he might be responsible. Luís and Diego had expected this reaction but needed to get the young priest past his anguish and alternated spending time with him. They had finally coaxed him to attend the museum event.

Cardinal Hernandez escorted Jonathan into the museum. Upon meeting the young priest, Serina had felt an immediate curiosity about him, perhaps because of his youth in a sea of mostly older clerics. He was clearly uncomfortable, and after a brief handshake in the receiving line, she noticed him off by himself, feigning attention to various paintings and sculptures. She sought further information from the nosey, gossipy, but often useful Italian Bishop, Vito Carpenello.

Carpenello choreographed official visits and had access to dossiers of those entering the closed society of Vatican regulars, as well as those hanging about the fringes. Carpenello wore several hats. One was liaison for events. Another was titular head for the numerous organizations dedicated to Catholic principles, known as the Conference of International Catholic Organization—the OIC. His unspoken role was that of the Vatican *yenta*.

With a theatrical flair for public relations, Bishop Carpenello used his tried and true lines on museum audiences—"The collections of the Vatican Museums represent the Church's immense contribution to humanity's cultural heritage. More importantly," he would say, "the works manifest the inspiration of the gospels for contemporary artists and for their viewers, who see a reflection of Divine beauty—a Divine beauty, which Saint Augustine described as 'ever ancient and ever new.'" It was beautifully presented and, without fail, impressed the wealthy patrons.

Weeks ago, Cardinal Carpenello had spoken with Serina. "International Catholic organizations bear witness to the actions of God in the world," he told her. "Countess, you know we are a world continuously in a state of formation, brought about through difficulties and immeasurable grief. The Word of God never abandons the world, but it unfortunately does not pay the maintenance on our magnificent museums. So, will you loan us your gracious name for this event?"

Serina listened politely and knowingly. She was more than willing to sponsor the event and was amused when during the evening, Bishop Carpenello publicly described her as one of "the first fruits to exceed the promise of its blossoms."

*Oh, dear God, what drivel*, Serina thought to herself, as she graciously nodded to him in appreciation.

Always pleased at the Countess's attention, he responded to her inquiry, "Young Father Jonathan Kennedy is here in Rome from Washington on a special assignment at the pleasure of His Holiness."

"Really? You must tell me all about it, your Eminence," Serina commented. She emphasized "Eminence," while smiling up at him engagingly. Serina's generosity to the Holy See allowed her total admission within Church social circles, and she played the Cardinal expertly, dangling her own tidbits of information and then smoothly changing the subject. She held his attention with her charm, and he gathered information whenever possible to feed to her. It was immediately obvious, however, that Carpenello did not know why Father Kennedy was in Rome and had no other useful information to share. Carpenello, once relieved of whatever gossip he had, became deadly boring. Without dropping so much as a crumb of scandalous intelligence herself, Serina thanked the bishop for giving her a few moments of his valuable time, before breezily excusing herself. He watched her walk away, determined to revisit the rumor mill and create an excuse to again seek her out.

Serina approached the young priest herself to determine whether his acquaintance was worth pursuing. She observed him, as he peered into one of the museum's glass cases, contemplating a small marble statue. The simple little figure paled against the general magnificence of the room. His face was solemn, his features hard, as he tried to reconcile the incongruity of the vast fortunes within these walls to the terrible poverty rampant in many nations of the world.

"My dear Father, are you all right? I can certainly understand your wish to flee this crowd, but you rather look like one of Daniel's monsters," Serina commented, with a feigned look of alarm. You don't think all this is a bit over the top, do you?" she asked, tossing her head back toward the crowd lined up at a lavish buffet table.

"I'm not sure what I think, Madam," Jonathan replied stiffly, clearly unhappy to be there.

"Well then, why are you here with that serious face? Are you one of those Vatican spies? If you are, be careful—remember the big trouble with the apocalyptic prophets," she admonished jokingly, hoping to draw him out.

Jonathan looked at the stunning woman in front of him. He was at once fascinated, yet taken aback by her brazenness. He sensed the need to steel his defenses and smiled at her, as he replied awkwardly, "Perhaps not."

"Well, you must instill within your flock a sense of the imminence of the Second Coming. You must have us believe it is in another hour or two, tomorrow, next week, within a month—soon, soon."

She drew closer to his face and said, "After all, you can't very well tell the voters that this or that promise will occur sometime in the next five hundred to thousand or ten thousand years and hope to win."

In light of his conversation with Juan Carlos, Jonathan felt some alarm, wondering, *Does she know of the plan?* Recovering his poise, he asked, now smiling, "Do I look so ferocious? Perhaps I need a lesson in salesmanship or one of those self-help books," He attempted to tamp down his frustration at this woman's uncanny intrusion into his secret world.

Serina ignored his question. "I mean, what good would that do for the average Joe, the everyday worshipper looking for his rapture?" she asked, teasing him. "He too wants to see the bad guys shot down by the horrific weapons of a vengeful God!"

Jonathan, having difficulty with the quick-moving conversation, tried to show good manners in the presence of this beautiful woman, but he was becoming irritated by Serina's flippant manner and finally said, "I'm not certain where your authority comes from, Madam, but I must say, it's a complex view. My name is Jonathan Kennedy. May I ask yours, so that I might connect a name with all this wisdom?" Jonathan exhibited a tight-lipped smile, remaining aloof but hoping not to appear impolite.

Serina raised her brow at his impertinence, knowing full well that she was bordering on rudeness, but as usual, she enjoyed the upper hand. She continued in the same vein. "I'm surprised you don't know who I am, since I paid for this soirée and those bubbles you're sipping, and I would be pleased if you would at least *appear* as though you're having a good time," Serina said, smiling at Jonathan. "If you're campaigning for Bishop, Father Kennedy, I would try and wear a more cherubic face. Hell may well be more tolerable than that look you're wearing." Serina thought she might yet elicit a hint as to the purpose of his visit to Rome.

"What look?" Jonathan said, now completely nonplussed.

"Actually, I can't blame you. Look around. Most artists' depictions would indicate that God has little time to love any of us, that he spends all his time thinking up fiendish eternal tortures.

When Father Kennedy arrived in Rome, he had hardly been prepared for the likes of the Countess. From his knowledge of Colombia, he knew who Serina Caputo de la Guardia was, of course, but the wistful Bishop Carpenello, who spoke with a vague unidentified yearning, had only provided a short briefing about Serina's crucial role in the Vatican's secular concerns.

Cardinal Hernandez stood some distance away, watching Serina's exchange with Jonathan. He always enjoyed observing her performance, when she seemed fully under the direction of a glib Satan. Although tempted to come to Jonathan's aid, he knew from experience that the religious sparring had an educational benefit for less-experienced priests. He knew it would further sharpen Jonathan's response to any query, a talent he would need very soon. Being grilled and taunted by a beautiful older woman was a multi- level test. Diego watched as Serina's magnetism clouded the young priest's intellect. *Yes,* he thought, *It is an excellent lesson,* even as he felt deceitful and realized that neither Kennedy nor the countess was aware of the other's complicity in *The Return.*

Serina tried a more direct tack. "What brings you to Rome, Father? The hard left hasn't totally driven the Church out of Washington yet, has it?" she asked. Extending her hand, she added warmly, "By the way, I'm Serina Caputo"

Father Kennedy was taken back. "Of course, I apologize, Countess. I should have recognized you. Too much on my mind, I guess. It is a pleasure to meet you." Jonathan added, "I am aware of the loss of your husband some years back. May I offer my very late condolences?"

"Thank you, Father. It has been quite a few years now, and my life is fulfilling, for the most part. I trust yours is as well, as whatever it is on your mind is beyond my hostess skills to dispel, Father. I'm a little disappointed." Serina said, coyly.

"Well, as you can see, they haven't made me Bishop yet, Countess, he said. Jonathan felt a shred of normalcy replace his deep depression. Chatting over champagne about mundane subjects and the charisma of the Countess were providing some relief. "I'm visiting Rome to consult on the Church in Latin America. My studies at Georgetown University indicate some worrisome reductions in Catholic populations. We are hoping that His Holiness may choose to visit one or more nations before too long," Jonathan said, lying.

Serina accepted this explanation, although her intuition told her that there was more to be learned. *Perhaps later from a different source*, she thought. Smoothly transforming back to the gracious hostess, she excused herself, after introducing Father Kennedy to other guests who had joined their conversation. A few moments later, she noticed that Jonathan had also excused himself after a brief exchange and left.

Cardinal Diego Hernandez, having watched the interaction as he mingled with other attendees, moved toward a large canvas at one end of the room, with the goal of intersecting Serina's path. She moved close to him and feigned interest in the same painting. He smelled her presence, a mix of perfume and something else that was exclusively hers. Serina cast her eyes sideways at Diego's handsome profile and whispered to him, "I pray that God forgives me for loving you as much as He does. It's disheartening," she said, briefly edging closer to him. "He doesn't seem to grasp the concept of 'sharing,' does He?" she asked.

Diego felt the usual struggle with his feelings. He wanted to stay, but he remained concerned for Jonathan Kennedy's state of mind. When Serina extended her empty flute toward Diego and suggested another glass of champagne, Diego changed his mind and decided that Jonathan might well need some time alone and walked with Serina to the bar.

Diego was unaware that Serina's brief exchange with the young priest had worked some magic. Father Jonathan Kennedy had returned to his room feeling less depressed. For a while, he lay awake in his bed. Without even realizing it, a plan had begun to formulate in his mind, and he gradually fell asleep in the midst of creating, editing, and prioritizing a rough to-do list.

# PART SIX – DOUBT AND FULL CONSENT

# The Child, Christian
## Colombia - March 2015

Dwellers of the coastal cities along Colombia's Caribbean shores measure distance in something other than miles and often comment, "We've never been there— it's far away." This was the reply to Father Kennedy's inquiry on directions to a series of small mountain towns.

Father Jonathan Kennedy marveled at the blessings enjoyed by the cities of Santa Marta, Cartagena, and Barranquilla. The towns had received riches from ancient volcanoes—great fertile lands that produced flowers, coffee, and an abundance of marijuana and coca plants. *Were these latter an unknown blessing?* Jonathan often wondered, while contemplating the moral dilemma of this God-given plant felt by many to offer medicinal promise and yet abused to the point of self-destruction. The magical plants had fueled a war unto itself and fractured the country into ragged-edged pieces.

Santa Marta is situated at the mouth of the Río Manzaneres, on the Gulf of Santa Marta, 46 miles northeast of Barranquilla. Geographically, the religious diocese of Santa Marta covers an area of over 20,000 square miles. In the mountain area east of the coast, less than 50 priests labored to serve the mostly poor population of 100,000, scattered throughout the region in small villages. Transportation was difficult and so administering the sacraments and saying mass were infrequent events.

Hoping to draw no undue curiosity, Father Kennedy had acted the part of a foreign tourist looking into family histories and environmental purities. He wore khaki pants, an open-collared, inexpensive front-button sports shirt under a light windbreaker, and tan buck shoes with laces and thick socks.

Father Kennedy had come to find an infant. He had only his innate faith in God to assist him in locating a child—a child to be loved and nurtured, while trained in languages, drilled in doctrine, and immersed in biblical history and world religions—a superior child, imbued with a consummate love of God, who would grow into a superb young man, capable of enduring hardship and isolation. All this and more would be necessary for him to carry out the greatest deception of all time, personifying Jesus Christ returned to earth. Jonathan felt dizzy thinking about it.

After their last meeting with General Gutiérrez and Cardinal Hernandez, Cardinal DeAngeles called Jonathan to discuss his travel. After a year of planning, they were ready to go forward with this critical task, the choice of the human being to become the new promise of God.

They discussed selection of the child for months. They were, after all, an unlikely group to seek an infant—men of the cloth, for whom fatherhood was a natural wish, but a taboo that sometimes caused their vows of celibacy to fall heavily on their shoulders. This aspect of the project was looked on with immense anticipation. Although the islanders' well-being and future roles were critical considerations, selecting the infant who would grow and develop into the manufactured redeemer caused all of them to shudder at such a challenge. Then the promising words of one or another on the greatness of this endeavor would convince them again. They concluded that discipleship demanded more than bearing witness, more than lecturing and coaxing from pulpits, more than missionary treks into ungodly lands, more than the shocking amount of martyrdom at the hands of radical hatred, and, certainly, more than fund raising for ever-greater edifices to the glory of God. They would take an infant and infuse him with all that was good, holy and Christ-like—with knowledge, virtue, and excellence. They would somehow forge in him an ability to speak the unspeakable—the stroke of the artist, the notes of the composer, and the crux of being. The planners now avoided any negativity, and as they would get caught up in enthusiasm over a future of goodness, they would thrill at the prospects.

Father Kennedy, wishing he weren't alone in his weakness, felt like an unwilling accomplice in an astounding hoax. He was part of a conspiracy, a plot to trick mankind into sanctification. Had he abandoned the law of God, or was he participating in its new glorification? It was useless to attempt its description. Language was simply inadequate.

Jonathan mused about the roots of faith. *When God gave Moses the Commandments, was it simply to restrain the excesses of wicked men? Were they wicked? And does this scheme I am abetting break a commandment? Are we all nuts? Can we manifest the celebrated Holy Spirit in every man? It's mostly words. Love your neighbor, "do unto others," words and cathedrals, lavish robes and ceremonies—these were the accessories of good men of God. Good men now daring to satisfy their yearning for God,* he thought.

Jonathan recalled his instructions from that last meeting.

"You must locate a male infant who will fit the requirements," Cardinal DeAngeles said. He had said this to Jonathan carefully and slowly, as though he himself didn't believe the words coming out of his mouth. At the end of their meeting Salvador DeAngeles and Diego Hernandez looked hard at Father Kennedy, waiting for his reaction.

Back then, Jonathan viewed both men with fear, trying to make sense of the jumble in his brain, trying to push failure out of his reasoning. *They're asking too much of me,* he thought. On that afternoon through Cardinal DeAngeles' window, Father Kennedy could hear birds singing and hear the light rustle of leaves. When he acquiesced to His Holiness earlier, Jonathan had been still unaware of his role. *But this was an impossible request. Who do they think I am?* He wondered helplessly.

Cardinals DeAngeles and Hernandez had deliberated over methods for finding the child. Jonathan, caught up in the brainstorming, and finding his strength, pretty much devised the plan to be followed. The Cardinals, grateful for his full participation, nodded their approval and felt relief. Several days later, Father Jonathan Kennedy was packed and on his way to the Colombian coastal city of Barranquilla.

A colorful blend of humanity had settled the tiny villages on and near the coast of Colombia from Santa Marta south to Cartagena.

For many, life had changed very gradually over the centuries. Catholicism had blended with pagan rituals, which, like other forerunners of the great religions, deified an assortment of Gods who ruled their weather, their crops, and the continuance of their numbers. Nevertheless, the Spanish influence from earlier centuries elevated Catholicism as the primary influence.

The coastal people were handsome, a result of a contribution of genes to the indigenous inhabitants, first by Spaniards and then an assortment of pirates and explorers.

Changes in physical attributes emerged in subsequent generations through early rivalries between Spain and England in and around the troubled the ports of Colombia's coastline.

English pirates frequently attacked and looted these towns, as they pirated the richly laden ships crossing the Caribbean. Liaisons with women, already exotic blends of Indian and Spanish, contributed to new traits, which in time added to already beautiful physical features.

From his previous work and visits to the area, Father Kennedy vividly recalled these people. They were of above average height and had a range of eye and skin colors—byproducts of both the lust of pirates, unmindful of the ruination of young girls, as well as mutually agreeable liaisons of genuine affection and caring. In the final analysis, it didn't matter—the resulting descendants were most pleasing. Added to their basic physical attributes was a diet of fruits and vegetables augmented with fish and meat, creating strong agile bodies. Jonathan recognized their splendid characteristics, especially as his research led him near their coastal area. From this human pool, he would seek a child. The inhabitants, living an existence removed from the areas of marijuana and coca growth, planted their fields and fished. For the most part, the outside world did not concern them.

Jonathan walked through one of the small villages and contemplated his next move, which was abruptly and thankfully made for him. A well-built young man in his twenties eyed the young priest from the doorway of a small crudely-built house. He took an interest in Jonathan as a distraction to his otherwise dull existence. He was not a thief and had no intent of harm, only a craving for a break from the mundane.

Trying to sound as respectful as possible, he called out, "Do you need help?" in Spanish.

Father Kennedy, happy for the social contact that this human represented, responded by saying, *"Ay si, Senor. Claro que si, por favor. Muchas gracias."* (Ah yes, absolutely, please. Thank you.)

Jonathan Kennedy had no trouble understanding and copying the local guttural accent. He had traveled enough throughout Colombia to have learned the nuances and dialects of the country. Despite often well-founded suspicions regarding those from outside their world, common courtesies usually paid off.

"Who are you?" asked the young man, surprised by the stranger's command of the language.

"I am Juan," Jonathan answered, "and you?"

Sensing Jonathan's quiet authority, he said, "I am Ernesto Gomez, but most call me Tito."

"Mucho gusto, Ernesto. May I call you Tito? I'm pleased to meet you in this place, which is strange to me. Where do you live? In this house?"

His curiosity growing and ever-mindful of a possible payoff, Tito examined Jonathan Kennedy. He sensed opportunity. "No, this is the house of my friend. I live in the country—over the small mountain," Tito gestured toward the distant hill with his head, his lips pursed, "not too long a distance from here."

"Will you take me there?" Father Kennedy asked, generally understanding the location.

*"Si, como no, Señor. Pero, porque?"* (Yes, of course, but why?)

Jonathan responded, "To find those who wish to have their confessions heard. I am a priest, you see." Jonathan showed Tito a small card, which identified him as Father Juan Gomez from the main archdiocese in Bogotá.

Tito was somewhat deflated at this turn of events, and his hopes of a windfall collapsed. Sensing his dismay, Jonathan said "I could use your help and would pay you for your services. The Church is concerned for sinners who have had little opportunity to bring their pain nd suffering to the attention of a priest. I can stay a while and offer the sacraments of marriage and baptism as well. Would there be a place where I could lodge for a few days?" Tito beamed at the mention of payment and nodded enthusiastically.

With his forged identity but genuine priestly credentials, Jonathan was welcomed at a small town and began his short ministry. He said mass and heard confessions, events that most villagers had never experienced and viewed with attitudes ranging from distrust to the wondrous impact of a newly-spotless soul. Jonathan had always been moved by the mystery of confession. Rich or poor, a small dirty spot for some was an ugly spreading stain for others.

Jonathan studied the small population. They were an attractive and bright people, some with infants and toddlers, but none fit the exacting conditions he sought. His determination to do no harm in completing his task ruled out the children he saw, surrounded by loving extended families. *How could I justify taking one of these children?* he thought. As the days passed, Jonathan felt lonely and discouraged, as he struggled with the recurring mental pain caused him by the overall plan.

Late one afternoon, looking up from his priestly office, after the daily prayers and psalms required of all priests, he had watched the sun inch down toward the top of the next mountain. As the rays of light from the disappearing sun flooded through the small window, there was a soft knock at the door of the two rooms provided to him by the local leader, the *cacique*. The small stone building, attached to the *cacique's* office, was infrequently used as a church.

When Father Kennedy answered the door, he felt a sudden rush at the sight before him. There stood an exquisite young woman with a girl of perhaps twelve standing next to her. Both had a long tumble of brown hair and wide green eyes in honey-beige faces. Father Kennedy could instantly see the rich history of this great country—the beauty of the native mixed with the English, the French, the Portuguese, some German, and, of course, the Spanish—all of it in these two beautiful creatures, here because of an insatiable appetite for gold and rich land. Father Kennedy's appointment with destiny had arrived.

*"Buenos tardes, Padre,"* whispered the older of the two visitors. Her nervousness was only surpassed by the younger girl's trembling. She held the back of her hand to her mouth, her head down, and Jonathan could detect the tears in her frightened eyes.

*"Bienvenidos, Senoritas,"* he replied, assuming a single status for them both. "How can I help you?" he asked.

The older girl stammered and revealed that they were sisters from a neighboring village where they had heard about the priest's visit.

Jonathan tried to acquire more information, but both girls were crying and visibly suffering. He felt the rush again and an even stronger certainty that his journey's purpose was before him.

*"Por favor, no tengas miedo,"* Jonathan said, as he tried to calm their fright. He beckoned them inside and left the door open.

"She is with child!" the older girl finally cried. Jonathan caught his breath. Both girls took this as a remonstrance, and knelt before him. Trying to collect his thoughts, Jonathan gently encouraged them not to be afraid and to come in and sit down in the rickety chairs by a wooden table. He felt his heart race with fear and joy.

"When will she give light?" Jonathan asked quietly, using the local phrase pertaining to an impending birth, *"Cuando vas dar la luz?"*

*"No se exactamente, Padre, yo creo en cuatro o cinco meses."* (I don't know exactly, I think in four or five months.)

Father Kennedy noted her slight belly and calculated the time. He cautiously continued. *"Y el padre?"* Who is he? Where is he? Does he want this child?"

These questions caused more tears and appeals for forgiveness. "She is innocent, Padre. He took advantage of her innocence and now he has disappeared. He doesn't even know. Will she be forgiven? What can we do? Please help us."

"Where did he go?" Jonathan asked.

"We don't know, we think to Santa Marta. He works on the piers for the coffee shipping," she replied.

"Tell me his name and why was he in your village?" Jonathan asked, with some command.

The older girl hesitated but under Jonathan's serious gaze blurted out a name, Ramirez, and spoke of a village festival that had attracted some of the workers on a few days leave.

Father Kennedy asked the older sister to describe Ramirez, and when he heard the description, his heart pounded. Looking at this exquisite child and hearing the physical description of the unwitting father, he concealed his anticipation. He questioned them further and learned they had told no one else. He instructed them to keep the secret for now and to return in two days. Jonathan soothingly promised to pray for them and to help them.

After the sisters left, Jonathan sought out Tito, who located an old truck. They drove to Santa Marta, where Jonathan left Tito, arranging to meet him later. Using another forged document identifying him as an official from the *Presidencia* seeking statistical information on coffee shipments, he was escorted by a burly dockhand to an area where containers of large burlap bags, flush with fragrant Colombian coffee beans, awaited loading aboard ships. The aroma of roasted beans emanating from already closed and loaded containers was undeniable, as it mixed with the smells of salty air, sweat and oil, and aged hawsers straining to keep ships fastened to their moorings.

Jonathan had feigned an official but friendly manner, as he conversed with dock workers and asked questions. He pretended to know one Ramirez and asked if he were in the area. With such a common name, his attention was directed to several men. Shaking his head from side to side, another young man was pointed out to him, and Jonathan knew he had found who he was looking for.

He asked Ramirez about the weight of the bags, how the beans were roasted, and what he knew of the growing areas and the destinations of so much coffee. The young man was polite and offered brief answers. Jonathan noticed the hint of gold in his brown hair and the tanned smooth skin in a face not unlike the two young women. His eyes had an almost topaz hue. He wore a small gold cross on a leather cord around his neck. Jonathan asked him if he attended church. He brightened. "I am sinful and find it hard to resist the temptations that come the way of a dock worker. I try to repent. I really want to be a man of God," he answered sincerely.

*And so you may well be*, thought Jonathan, determining through further conversation that Ramirez had been at the mountain village festival. He did not bring up the seduction of the young girl. He asked Ramirez a few more questions, thanked him, and left. On the trip back with Tito, Jonathan's preoccupation was all encompassing, as he pretended to listen to the young man's stories.

Two days later, the sisters had returned to the makeshift church and appeared more relaxed at the prospect of a favorable outcome from the young priest. They had placed their fate in his hands and with some of the fear erased from their faces, they were more beautiful than he had remembered.

Turning to the oldest, he chose his words carefully, saying, "Your sister is very young to raise a child. The child would only continue the cycle of illegitimacy in your village. And your sister's reputation is at stake, as is that of your family." The elder sister nodded fearfully.

"As you are aware, abortion is out of the question. But I think I can help with a suitable adoption. Both looked at Jonathan, with mixed expressions of relief and loss. They were quiet, and he discerned the sadness in their eyes. In the final analysis, however, it was a simple and logical solution. Jonathan felt certain of success, even as he wondered about the sex of this unborn child and contemplated his next step. He realized that the young girl was almost four months into the pregnancy. He proposed that both attend a school in Bogotá, where they would be safe and cared for. The windfall for the girls was explained to the parents as a diocesan project arranged by the Bishop to help train Colombian girls as nurses and teachers. They would be home again, Jonathan assured the skeptical father, within six months.

Satisfying the family members, Jonathan took the young sisters to a small convent near the city of Santa Marta, where the Sisters of Charity had established a hospital and school in 1883.

The Mother Superior was a stern looking woman, who bore little resemblance to the nuns of yesteryear. Holding enormous respect and affection for the Gutiérrez family and well-acquainted with the young

Father Kennedy, she did not question his requests or instructions. Happily, she was also a midwife.

Christian was born five months later in a small clean room in the convent. Arrangements had been relatively simple and direct. His young mother had been carefully monitored, schooled, and cared for prior to her delivery. Jonathan spoke favorably to her of adoptive parents in Bogotá, waiting to give this infant a loving home.

Despite some misgivings, the nun acceded to Jonathan's request for a cover story that would allow the young girl to return home free to start her life over. Shortly after the delivery, the nun quietly stood by, holding the young girl's hand, as Jonathan gently told her that complications had developed and that her child had been born dead. She did not understand and wept, but her weeping was short-lived, and her youth allowed acceptance and a rapid recovery. Within a week, the sisters were returned to their village with their certificates of learning and money earned. They engaged in teaching their young peers the simple crafts learned through the kindness of the Church. Both would go on to live satisfying lives as wives and mothers and later as teachers in Barranquilla. Their faith in God never faltered.

A generation later, they would learn of the miracle of the return of Christ on an island in neighboring Panamá.

# Encountering Denny Dennison
## The Conference - San Francisco - May 2020

Seven years after Christian's birth, Father Kennedy attended the annual convention of the finest scientific minds in San Francisco. He had prepared as much as possible for the critical new chapter that would lead to *The Return*. This phase would require that he convince an atheist, a great scientific mind, to abandon his life's agenda and conduct all his scientific work and effort on behalf of a Vatican vision. Although even the thought of success seemed ludicrous, Jonathan often recalled his doubts in the hills of Colombia. They had been washed away, and he prayed for a similar outcome to the challenge ahead.

Jonathan arrived at the auditorium in enough time to find a seat in the rear of the large room. The crowed was awaiting the presentation by Dr. Desmond "Denny" Dennison, the colorful world-renowned expert in a variety of scientific fields. His presentation would focus on climatic change. Jonathan had arrived late from Washington's Dulles Airport, and with no time to go to his room to change, he appeared in his priestly garb but had a story ready for the curious.

In addition to the thousands of scientists gathered for the conference were journalist stringers and others looking for a "Twilight Zone" story to titillate the imaginations of readers. Nina Shelky was among them. Her assignment was not serious.

She was at the conference as a sort of fling, an advance reward prior to a long and dull assignment ahead covering the Italian elections in Europe. Nina did not look forward to the heavy security she would encounter in the land of the now not-so-popular Vatican. Sociologists had observed a post-Christian Europe for some time, noting the slow change to an Islamic sphere. For now, Nina put it out of her mind. Covering the weighty scientific issues seemed a welcome diversion. Collecting and reading copies of the lectures, although technically complex, she believed she could do a credible piece, even without any deep understanding of some aspects.

Although many sessions of the meeting were tedious with theoretical presentations that would interest only a few, others were fascinating. With her love of the oceans and her longing to return to Contadora, she looked forward to the forum on "Ocean Uses for Forced Climatic Change." Presentations by Denny Dennison were always fascinating.

Waiting in a back row for his presentation on Geo-engineering, she had noted in the program the deliberate modification of the climate to counteract undesirable changes. Nina looked over the synopsis of Dennison's lecture. Then, scanning the crowd, she noticed a priest sitting a few rows from her. Her journalistic curiosity peaked. She wondered the reason for his presence at such a symposium. He had a strong profile and a very appealing appearance. It caused Nina to continue glancing at him, reliving the schoolgirl amusement of staring at good-looking priests. Most of her Catholic friends in high school had admitted to crushes on priests at one time or another.

Her thoughts were interrupted by the unannounced and somewhat noisy appearance of the speaker. Well-known, robust, a physically large man with a heavy shock of gunmetal gray hair featuring streaks of silver, Dr. Dennison arrived at the podium smiling, waving, and shouting comments to colleagues in the audience. He was utterly compelling in both delivery and appearance. Joking about climate changes, which had already occurred and which were presumably the fault of mankind, Denny enjoyed the commotion he created, and rather than stifle the audience's enthusiasm, he simply began speaking. The crowd settled down quickly.

"We're back ladies and gentlemen. Back to wail and berate the entire world's irresponsible citizens and ourselves for further despoiling the planet. I suffer my usual ambivalence over placing blame, but we need to continuously address this area, and with many studies underway, we are." Denny Dennison said. He spoke in a deep, pleasing voice, which added to his enormous presence. "However, don't believe everything you hear. We need to weed out the quacks in the quest to solve the riddles and puzzles of our blue planet. Our target forever, it seems, remains the global warming that climatologists expect to result from the still-increasing levels of carbon dioxide in earth's atmosphere. Indications are that our temperature will continue rising over the next forty years or so. If we believe this, can we put the brakes on humanity's irresponsible contributions? If so, temperatures should level off for future generations. Even so, we may be in for some nasty dog days of summer in future times, and possibly, new shorelines. That nice tune, 'April Showers,' may have to be retired, or at least undergo a re-write of the lyrics." Denny was serious about climate change but knew it was politically sensitive, and he wanted no part of politics. "The canonical response to abating the Greenhouse Effect is to cut the amount of $CO_2$ produced by burning fewer fossil fuels. Scientists are becoming less reluctant to discuss this with the gyrating oil prices since the turn of the century. I suspect a closing of the ranks among oil giants will preclude any real serious discussion of burning fewer fossil fuels until fossils fuels themselves face extinction. It is doubtful anyone will put the oil companies out of business until the puddle of black muck dries up. Science notwithstanding, the prospect of such an eventuality should get our collective fannies moving." Denny smiled affably, as he looked out over the packed auditorium.

"Peculiar as it might seem, a concern to mend the climate, fixing it as it were," he said, "could reduce man's efforts to avoid harming it. In other words," Denny continued, ready for a semblance of a punch line, "if we were able to quit worrying, complacency regarding the climate could set in and render it vulnerable to new irresponsible behavior" His audience smiled. "As for me ladies and gentlemen, I still drive a big car. I need a cure for us 'gasaholics,' as well as a cure for my girth." Denny laughed along with his audience.

Sipping from a nearby water glass, Denny continued, "Ladies and gentlemen, I am hardly a wizard with a crystal ball, and I'm not sure the sky is falling. Still, we can do some pretty neat stuff, if the situation gets nasty. To improve the $CO_2$ situation, we could pump it from power stations into the ocean depths, where the gas eventually ends up anyway by way of the atmosphere. It could be sucked out of the atmosphere by growing new forests or fostering photosynthesizing plankton in the sea. Effects could be counteracted—mirrors in space or dust high in the atmosphere could block out some sunlight. Greenhouse gases would still trap heat, but less would get into the atmosphere in the first place. Simple, hmmm?"

Nina felt the delivery going over her head but noted the rapt attention of the young priest. *Was he a science junkie?* Nina wondered.

Denny continued. "Another effort involves ocean fertilization with iron. Parts of the oceans contain lots of basic nutrients but little life. Lack of iron is the culprit and has kept life from these waters. So adding iron might have an impressive effect. Plankton could then multiply to eat up nutrients and, in doing so, they would suck up CO2. As the plankton die off, they would fall to the ocean floor and we could well be relieved of CO2 as a climatic concern. Plankton only needs a little iron—one iron atom for 10,000 carbon atoms—so not much metal would be required." Denny paused and shrugged, "However, there's always a catch. Even though just a few oil tankers full of iron filings could fertilize the seas around Antarctica, the trick is spreading the iron evenly. In one test, small plankton-like plants increased, but little planktonic animals living slightly lower glommed on, and Geo-engineering became lunch for them. After just three days, the iron clustered into lumps and sank out of reach, not a happy ending at all. It was back to the drawing board."

Denny shook his massive head in disappointment, but then his expression brightened. "Perhaps we need to skip relying on the cooperation of living things. A simpler and more predictable thin layer of dust is easy to put into the stratosphere by battleship guns pointing straight up. This could successfully shield the earth from the sun. Recall in 1991 the eruption of Mount Pinatubo threw twenty million tons of muck into the stratosphere. That pall around the world, only recently settled, appeared to have cooled the surface as computer models predicted. Fine dust every few years would maintain a shield reflecting away about one percent of incoming sunlight, reducing intensity by a few watts per square meter. Of course, such a shield would need constant replenishment, but that's got an upside—it suggests that it is easy to remove if necessary. Plus," he raised his forefingers, and with a broad smile went on, "this would visibly dim the sky and might be aesthetically pleasing, enhancing sunsets for example. That could possibly be accomplished with additives to airline exhausts. Granted, my friends," Denny continued, "side effects confound us all. Everyone in this field has limitations. Even without biology to complicate things, chemistry and physics offer enough complexity to confuse any budding engineer. The bottom line here is that our well-loved and desirable clear skies *are* more subject to greenhouse warming than cloudy skies. So uniform cooling by a stratospheric shield would be a return to Eden. It would lower temperatures but not limit changes in regional climates. That however, might upset weather patterns. I realize that most of this is not new. Still, we have a tendency to blah, blah, blah in this world. And although I am here to urge additional scientific action, I need to make it clear that I don't subscribe to the dictates of growing modern environmentalism. At this stage, we are still unsure if humankind is the culprit in climatic change. Some groups, believing they are talking in scientific terms, often seem to assume a religious fervor in environmental preaching. Unlike science, the truth of religion is mainly one's faith, and the environmental zealots need to take care that impostors are not dictating that faith. Let me get a bit more technical " Denny launched into a detailed discussion using charts and formulas that befuddled Nina. She quietly exited for a break and returned to hear the scientist's closing lines.

When Denny finished, some attendees gathered in the rear, where coffee and refreshments were set on a long buffet table. Nina managed to become part of a small group around Dr. Dennison and found herself next to the young priest.

"Actually," Denny was saying, "I heard a moral approach recently in Washington during conversation about this. A guest there suggested that perhaps humanity deserves to suffer for despoiling the planet. This fellow commented that escaping suffering might be morally wrong even if practical. The party had a collection of professors and students, and it was apparent that some feel changing the environment is wrong in and of itself, rather than being wrong only if it brings about harm."

"Wow," Nina said, speaking up. "It is refreshing, Doctor, that ideas we sometimes consider pompous and above moral thinking may not be so absurd after all. Hearing this from you is inspirational."

"Thank you, young lady," Denny said, smiling at Nina. "However, I don't want you thinking your confession is required or . . ." Denny gestured toward his neck, glancing mischievously at Jonathan's priestly collar, ". . . that you've committed a mortal sin if you throw the empty Coke can in with the trash."

Nina laughed and turned to introduce herself to Jonathan Kennedy standing nearby. Continuing the light conversation, she asked, teasing, "So, Father, do you think there's still hope that science and religion can co-exist?"

While Jonathan hesitated, Denny added, "I guess, Father, that we should take into consideration that it might be immoral or unwise for a single superpower to darken the skies, without regard for religious consideration, but it is possible." He looked beyond him, lost in his own thought. "It is possible," he said again slowly to no one in particular.

"Watching this crowd," Nina kidded, "it's obvious that scientists will always need further research. It's good, I suppose, to understand the benefits and disadvantages of even hypothetical global warming. Does nature take her own course, or do we take nature's course for her?"

Jonathan finally spoke. "Maybe it's a bit like tinkering with the creation of the gods themselves. Back in the days of the first New Years Eve celebration, partygoers recited an annual poem with the impossible name of 'The Enuma Elish,'" he said. "The what?" Nina asked, chuckling.

"'The Enuma Elish.' It was recited to celebrate the victory of the gods over chaos in the world."

"Ah, that it would be so simple. Forgive me, Father," interjected Denny, "but in these days of war and divisiveness, it's hard to imagine anyone's God exercising victory over chaos."

"Perhaps. But in one of Isaac Newton's letters to the Dean of Saint Paul's, Newton suggested that God, although supremely intelligent, was primarily a mechanic."

"An interesting premise," said the affable Denny, now slightly uneasy at his inability to recall such letters, a probable result of little or no interest in religion. Nina, though vaguely annoyed at her own deficiency of religious history, enjoyed the repartee.

"Newton wrote in one letter," Jonathan continued, "'Gravity may put ye planets into motion, but without ye divine power, it could never put them into such a circulating motion as they have about ye sun.'" Jonathan feigned the accent. "I'm impressed that Newton knew back then that if the earth revolved at only one hundred miles per hour instead of a thousand, night would be ten times longer. The world would grow too cold to sustain life, and with the heat created by the longer days, all vegetation would shrivel."

Denny continued to smile. He remained quiet but interested in the priest's comments, religious based, but not so foreign to his own thinking.

"So?" Nina said, looking at Jonathan inquiringly, "Are you saying that God sat around tossing planets out to space and then pondered which one would get life?"

"No, but the earth's spin is just one of God's demonstrations that has forced man to seek and understand him."

"Who let you in here?" asked Denny laughing. "Actually, that kind of thinking requires unfaltering faith, something lacking but often envied in my line of work." He put his glass down and said, "Now, if you lovely people will please excuse me, I have a meeting to attend." He walked to the exit, turning back once to look at Jonathan Kennedy.

Nina awakened the next morning in her hotel room. Although her dreams were nonsensical, they included the usual cast—Marcos, the island, and something— someone—else. Father Jonathan Kennedy. She reached for her journal on the bedside table and removed the pen clipped to the cover. She lay back to make sense of her confused thoughts. *Why was a Catholic priest attending a scientific conference? What was he really doing here?* Her curiosity intensified. During his brief appearance at the reception the previous evening, Nina had studied Father Kennedy from across the room, before engaging him once again in conversation. He had explained his love for science, particularly rockets, and joked about his possible future need for a ride to heaven.

She noted his keen observation of Dr. Dennison. What was his agenda? She wrote the question down and laid the open journal on the bed as she got up.

Father Jonathan Kennedy had left late the previous evening on the "red eye" to return to Washington. The interest in him by the young journalist, Nina Shelky, crossed his mind, but occupied with thoughts of Denny, he soon forgot it. He would never know that Nina wrote the decisive article about Contadora Island. And neither knew then that they would both be present in Saint Peter's on the morning of *The Return*.

Jonathan's mind stayed on Dr. Desmond Dennison. He had researched the Doctor's career and now felt confident of his capabilities and his potential. Jonathan believed, along with his colleagues, that they had located the right man to take on the technical aspects of *The Return*. Jonathan began to think of a plan to approach him.

# FUNDING FOR THE LOVE OF GOD AND OF HIS SERVANTS
**April 2016**

Diego had agonized over the task ahead. He had telephoned Serina a few days after their evening in Rome. She had not answered, so he called her Ligurian apartment on the coast. When she heard his voice, Serina felt the usual schoolgirl shiver and wondered if all women felt this reaction to their beloved's voice.

"I need to discuss an important matter with you, a financial matter. Could you come to Milan and meet me on the piazza in front of the Duomo tomorrow about noon. I'll get an early flight. I'll be feeding the pigeons when you arrive. But even if you're late, I'll take you to a quiet lunch somewhere where we can talk," he said, joking. I plan to fly back to Rome tomorrow evening. Can you make it?" he asked. He listened to her soft breathing, as she mentally rearranged her schedule to be with him.

"Of course," she replied, already visualizing her wardrobe and anticipating the joy his company would again bring to her. She brushed aside the little voice in her head, repeating the same old warnings. *The conversation had the feel of a date,* Serina thought, smiling at the romantic notion. Although she assumed Diego needed additional fund- raising help, it seemed curious that he sounded so urgent.

"I received a letter from Luís, Diego," Serina said. "He referred to a financial matter and attached a brief and vague proposal. Do you know anything about it? Are yours and his one and the same?" Serina waited for Diego's reply. Instantly angered at Luís's pre-empting, but understanding his eagerness, Diego recalled discussing Serina's possible willingness with Luís but had been adamant in insisting that he handle the matter. He hoped that the disconcerting presence of the sexual tension between them might at least soften her resistance to considering the huge sum he needed. Diego experienced discomfort and guilt but knew he had to find adequate words to approach Serina with the request. He knew he needed all his wisdom and diplomacy for the right words at the right moment. Physical feelings for Serina greatly obscured this undertaking. After discussions with Cardinal Teddy Arias, Diego had been stunned by the Cardinal's calculations of projected costs. He realized his failure would spell failure for the entire project. This weighed heavily on him, as he continued the conversation.

"Diego?" Serina said. She questioned his hesitancy.

"I'm sorry, Countess. There have been conversations over several projects, and I think Luís and I just crossed signals. I look very much forward to seeing you in Milano tomorrow."

After they hung up, Diego telephoned Luís. "Luís, we cannot disagree. I am fully aware of the importance of Countess Caputo's cooperation. You must leave that aspect to me. The subject is beyond delicate, but in our efforts, we need to remain as one. We have our separate tasks, and we each must adhere to them. God knows, we are a far cry from any holy trinity, Luís, but we must strive for that unity at all times. If we do not coordinate, we will be just one more bureaucratic nightmare. Our continual reassessment of the tasks and intimate communication must be without a hint of confusion. It endangers our mission."

Luís, chagrined at his intrusion, begged Diego's forgiveness. Luís knew his own motives were clouded by his attraction to Serina Caputo, and as a military leader, he knew full well the disastrous results of deviating from a given plan.

"I apologize, Your Eminence. I look forward to your progress and hope to see you in a few days. Go with God, Diego."

Diego hung up, removed his clerical clothing, and changed into light wool slacks, a sweater and sports jacket and hailed a cab outside his Rome apartment. Feeling brief seconds of recklessness as he envisioned the striking Colombian Countess, Diego allowed himself a moment of anticipation, even as the tremendous importance of the meeting and the weightiness of priestly vows disallowed such a pleasurable indulgence.

Diego was anxious, as his plane descended into Milan airport. He tried to focus on the vast garden vistas of the plains, divided into small lots by rows of mulberry and poplar trees. From the air, the scenery evoked images of ancient neighborhoods, separated by now barely visible walls built to keep the peace in long ago times.

*Now,* Diego thought, *centuries later, are the root causes of human conflict still the same as in ancient days? Are our current ways of solving conflict under God the best ways?* He felt depressed at his inability to come up with a positive answer. *Today's terrorism includes release from any inhibitions to kill, released from a belief in the* sanctity of life. The intentional and indiscriminate killing of innocents has so damaged *not only our Church but all of God's earth. The centuries-old understanding of "church providing sanctuary" was all but gone. We must get it back.*

Diego released his seat belt as thoughts of Serina came to mind. *Dear God, can I ask this woman to share in this awesome undertaking to restore the sanctuary? The risk is great, but then, so are the potential gains. We recognize the value of each human life.*

*The Church—our guarantor of life—should that be my theme to Serina?*

Serina exited the glass doors from the enclosed mall to the piazza in front of Milano's elaborate Duomo. As she walked across the plaza's wide expanse, her heart quickened when she caught sight of Diego on the opposite side, leaning against the kiosk, intently reading from a journal. In civilian dress, he was immensely attractive, and it was even more difficult for her to hold on to thoughts of purity.

"What's so intriguing there," she said, wagging her gloved finger at the journal, "that you're not obviously anticipating my arrival?" she teased, recalling similar repartee during their school days in Colombia before Serina's marriage to Italian royalty. "I spent the morning carefully selecting this outfit. I thought I'd surpassed even the finest clerical robes in there," Serina said, tossing her head toward the magnificent cathedral. Dressed in a fitted gold wool jacket with elaborate buttons over a white silk shirt and black pants, she stood in front of Diego with her gloved hand on her hip. In this city of great fashion, Serina was never outdone. But beyond her appearance was the person, mind and body, and for now, joyous with the sight of this man.

Diego had looked up from the article he was perusing and smiled at the woman in front of him. She indeed was magical. He closed the magazine. He had learned enough for now from the impassioned article he had been reading while waiting. It talked of an idyllic and distant dot in the ocean off the Pacific coast of Panamá. At that moment it had all fallen into place—*The Return* would occur on the tiny island so lovingly described.

"You look most elegant, Countess, "Diego had complimented with a wry smile, taking in her flawless appearance and momentarily forgetting his mission and the island.

The coincidence occurred to him that the resolution of his two major taskings might be found in the magazine in his hand and in the vision in front of him. Diego wished he could tell Serina about this island, but for now, it had to wait. He leaned in to politely kiss her on both cheeks and detected her faint perfume layered upon the somewhat mysterious fragrance that was hers alone. For Serina, drinking in the brief scent of Diego's breath seemed to purify the air around her. It held sweetness, an indescribable pungency that was intoxicating. *What to do about those confounding vows?* She smiled inwardly at her sinful thoughts.

In a relationship overshadowed by the necessity of sexual suppression, a disagreeable condition that always left them frustrated, Serina had almost given up trying to conceal her longing for the Cardinal. She had tried to adhere to society's rules of acceptable behavior, but she never fooled Cardinal Hernandez, who battled with his own desires. They maintained the charade and usually guarded the curtain that hung between them. Today, Serina ignored the crowd in the piazza, as she put her arm through Diego's, and they strolled slowly to the Carlton Hotel Baglioni on the Via della Spiga near the Duomo and the celebrated Teatro La Scala. For a few brief seconds, as she looked up into his face, she felt that damnable curtain disappear, but the small suspension of time was soon interrupted by the din of voices and city sounds around them.

Arriving at the restaurant, Diego had asked for a quiet table away from others and ordered a carafe of wine. They spoke lightly of their surroundings. After the waiter placed the wine and glasses down, Diego told him that he would signal him when they were ready to order. Serina waited expectantly for Diego to explain the reason for this meeting. Any reason would do, but she suspected that there was something of grave importance on his mind.

With an air of studied restraint, belied by the manner in which he drained his wine glass and poured another, Diego began. He plunged into an elaborate and convoluted story that Serina was having trouble following. She recognized his nervousness, and although perplexed, made an effort to lighten the mood. "What's wrong, Diego. Did you bet on the wrong horse, or at long last, do you finally have some sordid indiscretion to confess to me?" she asked.

Serina knew Diego better than he had realized, and she sensed that the so-called humanitarian project Diego had concocted was a deliberate cover-up—an obvious attempt to deceive her. She regarded Diego with confusion and found herself staring into one eye and then the other, trying to see deep inside him.

Diego did his best to ignore her prying looks and prattled on, intent upon not meeting Serina's searching gaze. Then his eyes met Serina's, and horrified he realized she had not believed him from the first sentence. A feeling of panic rose in him, and he wondered how she could possibly have divined his disingenuousness so quickly. Where was the feeling of elation he had had just a short while ago, when he had been sure success was at hand. Now, he imagined the project crumbling.

Serina was staring down at her hands, examining each perfectly-manicured finger, and feeling a wellspring of pain, both his and hers, settling itself in the pit of her stomach. Diego, too, was in despair and felt wretched. *How could he have been so foolish, so dishonest?* he thought. "I'm so very, very sorry, Serina. I have botched this very badly."

"Well, Diego," Serina said, her eyes glistening, "if some crazy extremists were to arrest me for being a Christian, do you think there would be sufficient evidence to convict me? You want me to give you millions of dollars and not ask why? Is this the cost of my sometimes uncertain devotion?" She looked azsss pt him disappointedly, trying to diffuse the tears pooling in her eyes and hoping to relieve the pounding in her head. What she had heard made no sense. Recovering, Serina had tried to inject some humor. "Hmmm, Judas only required 30 pieces of silver. There's inflation for you." It didn't work. Tears of disappointment and confusion tumbled on to her cheeks, as she felt pointing stabs in her heart. "I'm not worth much, Diego, if you have to lie to me."

Diego struggled to find the right words. "Forgive me, *my beloved Serina*. I have bungled this badly," he spoke, unaware of his endearment. Furious at himself for his clumsiness and distraught at the pain he saw in Serina's face, he heard her stifled sob and saw the rivulets of tears fall over her cheeks. He paused and then blurted out, "I want you to give me a huge sum of money, with no strings attached. And even though it sounds preposterous, I want you to somehow feel assured that the funds are for a cause of unimaginable consequence—a last-ditch attempt for world reconciliation. But you must understand that the less you know the better. It tears me apart to keep this secret from you, but I beg you nonetheless for your trust and your confidence."

Diego's simplicity and belated honesty pierced Serina's misery. His use of the word "beloved" had been swirling crazily about her mind, confusing her even more. She was not even sure if Diego realized he had said it.

Serina sat quietly, dabbed at her eyes, and struggled to regain control. She picked up her wine glass and looked at its deep crimson contents. Within moments, she regained her composure. "I know you well enough to know you're not going to buy the Taj Mahal or the White House. Besides, I'd find out. I have sources," she said. Serina smiled sadly and looked at this man she loved and saw in him the embodiment of everything that was good in the world and important to her yet impossible to possess.

A moment passed as Diego stared into his own wine glass, unsure of his next words.

Serina did some mental calculations and well knew that despite Diego's outrageous request, she would remain more than financially comfortable. "So how do you want it, my dearest Cardinal Hernandez, in small bills?" Serina asked quietly, filling the void, and smiling softly at her own humor.

Diego loved her more than ever at that moment for her trust in him. She seemed almost saintly to him in her forgiveness, in her giving, in her extraordinary faith, and confidence in him. Even though Diego had believed she would give him whatever he wanted, he was stunned. Overcome with emotion, his tears spilled and ran down his face. He was afraid to speak. He loved this woman more than he loved God. His struggle with chastity evaporated. He reached for her hand across the table and held it to his lips. She felt the wetness of his tears on her fingers and remained quiet. She had never seen Diego cry.

"I want something more, Serina. I want to come home with you now, my precious Serina," Diego whispered.

All doubt lifted from Serina. The money, the unknown project, her invasion into the chosen life of this man, none of it mattered at this moment. She hoped God sat between them and recognized the undeniable needs of his beautiful creations. But if He didn't, right now it no longer mattered. A feeling of lightness came over her, as she knew that they were of a single purpose. Diego laid a bill on the table and muttered a hasty apology to the waiter. They left the restaurant and hailed a cab. Serina gave the driver directions and held Diego's hand tightly between them.

When they arrived at her flat, Serina turned the key and opened the door. Facing Diego, she trembled, holding his gaze, as she questioned him one more time without words. Diego slowly reached up and pulled the ornate gold pins from Serina's hair. He was astonished at the beauty of the sight of the cascading mane that now fell across her shoulders.

Serina and Diego had been tardy in their arrival at such an exquisite state, like polite guests holding back from a lavish buffet. Giving in to the joy of the release of physical captivity offered wholeness and righteousness; a delivering of a precious gift in a surge of bliss.

Any remaining shred of doubt was torn away to reveal long-denied perfection. Two were one in body. Souls touched and merged—God's perfect creatures feeling what He felt, acting as He had planned. They became one, fed by an intensity of giving, and Serina felt at last that God was on her side. Diego drowned in the joy of being within this woman he loved. He heard her muffled rising moan urging him on, and he cried out in ecstasy, as he knew he had finally experienced God's most beautiful gift.

"There is no disguise which can for long conceal love where it exists or simulate it where it does not."—Francois Duc de La Rochefoucauld Nina Shelky jotted the quote down, adding it to her notes, as she recalled locking eyes ever-so-briefly with Countess Caputo at Saint Peter's the morning of the Pope's untimely death. *Despite the anguish of the moment, I couldn't miss the look of loving possession and alarmed compassion by the Countess toward the highly attractive Cardinal racing toward the falling pontiff. After noting a similar gaze when the Cardinal processed in at the beginning of the momentous mass, I recognized the intimate connection. I will store the impression away for now, but I  remember her graceful hands pressed to her face and the grief-stricken eyes in the slow motion uproar and fear among the congregation.*

# A Young Eagle Prepares to Soar
**June 2015**

Israeli Air Force Lieutenant Avi Noam had shifted some of his heavy load and tried to focus on the desert landscape views, while he trudged up the steep crooked trail with his unit. Although he and his comrades faced a grueling physical undertaking in searing heat wearing full battle gear, the young soldiers held up, as their months of physical training paid off. The march to Masada hadn't been so bad. More than that, their pride of achievement had overcome all else.

Masada, towering 430 meters above the Dead Sea, is a boat-shaped, craggy mountain. Upon it, one of the great epics in history was played out. It is a symbol for men who cherish freedom and the centerpiece of an annual ceremony in which recruits of the Israel Defense Forces shout their defiant cry and swear the oath of allegiance on its summit, saying, "Masada shall never fall again!"

The Israeli Defense Forces use this classic episode as an example of the courage and dedication that they are looking for in their military. Avi remembered the riveting attention to his instructors as they told the story of the zealots of Masada, and he reflected on it now. That story, like many, had been reinforced repeatedly, and now, before the ceremony, standing on the precipice of the fortress palace and looking down and out over the Dead Sea, Avi felt his young soul expand with pride and determination.

The Jewish Zealots had taken over Masada from the Romans in 70 AD. The mountaintop fortress was a triumph for King Herod, whose celebrity status as the creator of numerous architectural wonders in the 1st Century had eroded through history until his name invoked little more than the story of the cruel horror of the massacre of the innocents at the time of Christ's birth. Children throughout the world learned to dread Herod's name, after learning of him as part of the Christmas story of Christ's birth. Few know the full story of King Herod's extraordinary accomplishments in engineering and construction.

"Masada shall never fall again!" the recruits shouted repeatedly in unison, as the fine desert sand collected on their boots. Rifles would have to be disassembled, cleaned, and reassembled. Even then, commanding officers would probably insist on repeated cleanings. But to the young soldiers, the invasive sand and fine dust conveyed the ancient message of courage. The rocky structures remaining at the old fortress and the tales of events that took place there are etched into Israeli memories.

Air Force 2nd Lieutenant Avi Noam had grown up in these hills, overlooking the Mediterranean Sea near the beaches of Caesarea. His father had served before him as a tank commander, and his grandfather, who had arrived so young at the Promised Land, saw combat in five wars in less than four decades. Still active at fifty-five, Avi's grandfather ultimately became a casualty of the 1982 Operation Peace for Galilee, killed while crossing the northern border into Lebanon to eliminate Palestinian Liberation Organization strongholds.

Avinoam, as he was called, pulling his first and last name together, loved the tragic legacy of the zealots of Masada but was always deeply saddened at the story's end. He felt as one with the remaining 960 brave resistant Jews, who had defended the fortress from the Romans for three years, before committing collective suicide. They had killed their wives and children first and then died free, rather than become slaves to the Romans. He felt their pain deeply and shuddered within at the thought of "suicide," a forbidden final act for Jews.

Now, centuries later, Avi stood on the mountain with his friend, Yosef. They stood in their dusty uniforms with their bibles and their M-16s, reinforcing their fierce loyalty to the defense of Israel. The Zahal, Israel's Unified Defense Forces, imbued young inductees in all branches of service with inspiration from past military feats. Their training included a wide range of subjects, including language, history, civics, and the art of war. They absorbed legends of their ancestors and felt memory reaching back through the generations. They revered their nation's past and vowed to defend it always.

Avi had seen photos of Israeli soldiers on the morning of June 7, 1967, after they had defeated the combined forces of Egypt, Syria, and Jordan. In one photo at the Western Wall, Israel's holiest shrine, a group of then-young soldiers gazed at the very same wall in awe. It had been cut off from them for eighteen years by trenches, barbed wire, and battlement. Now Avi ached for that same glory, and at this moment of their arrival at Masada, he felt its first twinges.

The young soldiers studied the development of Israel's harsh landscape, made fertile so long ago. The greatest challenge had been to bring water where none existed. Herod's ingenious solutions to that absence remain monuments to man's abilities. At several locations, but most startlingly at Caesarea and at his mountain retreat in Masada, Herod had designed and constructed a sophisticated water system that created large pools on a rock high above the Dead Sea. Additionally, he built a complex of over two dozen storerooms, which held food and supplies. These amazing achievements, resulting from the need for a defense system, were admired by the young soldiers, as they surveyed the views in front and behind them.

The ceremony marking this trek to Masada would begin shortly. In the remaining moments before their formation, Avi had contemplated the uniqueness of his homeland.

It was far greater than its allocated 21,000 square kilometers. He had seen his country from the air, flying her length and breadth in mere moments in Kafir fighter jets during his pilot training. The diversity of Israel's landscapes gave Avi a sensation of vastness.

Mountain and desert and forest were within a few miles of each other, and to this young pilot, it seemed like a universe. It did indeed mimic a universe, a microcosm of three continents at the crossroads of Asia, Africa, and Europe.

As a young recruit learning his military history, Avi became enamored of the courage of Israel Shohat, who in the early 1900s founded the Hashomer, the first Jewish armed force in modern Palestine. He strived to be like them—marksmen, horsemen, and fierce protectors of early Jewish settlements. Avi also had a passion to soar high above his land and root out the enemy like a hawk on the wing. Avi had always wanted to fly.

It would be some time before he traveled from this land. At that point in his young career, he couldn't have imagined that one day he would play the role of God's messenger and deliver a brave young redeemer to an insignificant island in the Pacific Ocean. The hopes of much of the world, his own included, would ride on that deliverance.

Avinoam had had several comrades-in-arms within his group. One, Yosef, had lost high school friends in a PLO raid on a small van full of classmates. Yosef had missed the afternoon bu that day and suffered horrific recurring visions of his classmates' limbs flung along the roadside next to the charred remains of the bus he had tried to chase down just seconds before. Through a blinding screaming rage, Yosef had raced to the scene of horror and stumbled upon the torso of his closest friend. In shock and fearfulness, he gently removed a ring he recognized from the bloody hand still attached to a nearby arm.

Yosef's family and classmates, members of the Lubavitch faith, mourned together. His friend's parents, grateful for the ring, eventually had wanted to know the details of the incident. "What did his face look like when you found him, Yosef?" the mother pleaded. Yosef had lied and told her that her son's twisted face with its expression of realization and pain had been peaceful and unaware. The Lubavitch Jews' emphasis on their love for fellow Jews, along with faith in a Jewish leader as the presumptive Messiah, had their own bond within an already bonding religion. As Yosef struggled to heal, he found consolation in his Lubavitch faith, despite criticism of the sect by orthodox rabbis. He trusted the Lubavitch teachings that the Messiah would come after tragedies and bring an age without hate and horror. Yosef needed his faith, but once enlisted in the military, he kept his feelings low-key in the presence of more orthodox members. He suffered alone.

The Masada march was long and healing for Yosef, but irrepressible hatred still swirled in his mind, as he fought the vision of his murdered childhood friends. It was deep, too deep to be stomped out by boots in the hot sand.

Avi had found Yosef late one afternoon, sitting against the wall behind their base barracks, sobbing in yet another bout of grief.

Uncomfortable at first with what seemed Yosef's weakness, Avi also saw sorrow too strong to bear and urged him to talk. Yosef hesitated but then felt trust, looking into the blue eyes in Avi's dust-covered face. Choking out his agony in small stilted bits, Yosef gave up any attempts at composure, letting the rage and anger spill out. Avi waited.

Listening to Yosef's story, he fought off his own fury, searching for the empathy to deal with his comrade's agony. Then unexpectedly, a familiar feeling entered Avi. It seemed ingrained from long ago, a gift of calm, of words, and understanding. He remained quiet as he looked out across the landscape that was Israel and waited. When Yosef's racking sobs diminished, Avi asked him, "So would you prefer this to be erased from your memory, Yosef?"

With his face contorted and tear-stained, Yosef looked at Avinoam in confusion and disbelief. *What an asshole,* he thought to himself. He shouted angrily, "Of course. Better, I would prefer it to have never happened. What, are you stupid?"

"Possibly," Avi said. He remained calm. "But think about not remembering, Yosef. Not to remember the face of evil makes us incapable of knowing the evil we're capable of. Without the memory of the iniquity done to your classmates, how can you possibly recount the stories of their lives? Lives that are now extraordinary. Do you really want them to have simply disappeared?"

Yosef had stared at Avi with angry bewilderment but felt a small understanding in the ruins of his mind. "No," he stammered and looked down at the sand.

"Knowing in detail lets you tell the story of their lives, not for vengeance but for the sake of justice. We are here, Yosef, to learn how to mete out justice. Your friends now depend on your memory and the memory of their families to tell the narrative of their lives. To do your sacred duty, Yosef, take up your past, take it to a life that gives it new meaning." Avi felt on the verge of tears himself. Yosef looked away and nodded quietly. After a few minutes, when he looked up at Avi, his eyes were clear. "Thank you, friend. I think you have saved my life."

The two young soldiers stood up, walked back to their quarters, and soon became inseparable. With Avi's encouragement, Yosef recovered. He told his family and friends and his waiting fiancée, who marveled at his newfound courage and purpose and loved him even more deeply. Throughout his career, Yosef told new recruits his story and tried to instill within them an added measure of personal strength.

From his basic training and now this experience at Masada, Avi had developed his gift for deep compassion and empathy, a trait that would serve him in leadership roles to come. The men under Avi's command regarded him so highly they would follow him to the stars to earn their commander's respect.

On this day on top of the mountain, Avi had put his arm around the shoulder of his friend, Yosef. They looked out over the wilderness that was Israel and knew their land was worth fighting for. They turned and joined the formation for the ceremony.

Some years later while on leave, Avi had wandered into the old city of Jerusalem, lured by its labyrinth of narrow stone lanes. Inhabited continuously for well over 4,000 years, Jerusalem's massive 16th Century walls hold a singular global distinction. Among a tangle of buildings crammed into seemingly impossible spaces, old and holy shrines of diverse faiths exist. There is little evidence of any planning to the jumble of structures,  rather they reflect repeated conquests by successive tribes of varying religious allegiances and subjugation of the losing tribes, which managed to retain their faith, a faith for which they were often willing to die.

Despite the architectural mayhem, once airborne, the aerial view reveals distinct divisions within the city. As a pilot, Avi had flown over Jerusalem numerous times. Much like the very soul of Israel, individual religions inside the old walled section border each other like pieces of a puzzle but cannot combine into a whole. Avi never forgot this view and his reaction to it. He imagined God's disappointment in His promised land that was so bitterly divided. Years later, at the private meeting during which the startling details of the mission of *The Return* were disclosed to him by General Aaron Yakowitz, Avi had remained seated in the small office alone. He thought about the ancient denials and acceptances of God. In his prayers to the God of Jews and Christians alike, Avinoam wondered if there might yet be a chance for a peaceful renewal and if he would now finally be able to contribute to it.

# THE ANATOMY OF SIN
## Rome 2030

For years now, since the project's funds had been put in place, Cardinal Diego Hernandez had had meetings with Cardinal Teddy Arias, who counseled Diego on negotiating the money trail. He assumed the role of banker as he received and then doled out Countess Serina Caputo's funds via an array of secret accounts. Although the mission was never far from mind, Diego experienced a dilemma of contradictions. Now, with his vow of celibacy broken, Diego had waited for the unspeakable guilt he expected. It didn't come. He felt only happiness with Serina. Cardinal Arias, unaware of Diego's relationship, was able to arrange a series of transfers that allowed direct withdrawals from Serina's accounts, thus removing Diego from ties to accounts. Not treating his disobedience lightly, the offense of his broken vows seemed less burdensome to Diego than the shameful secrecy required for the disbursement of Serina's money.

For her part, Serina never questioned Diego, trusting that he would reveal the purpose of her investment when the time was right. Since that day in Milano, she felt only joy in their unrestrained love and intimacy. Serina was well aware of her complicity in her affair with Diego, but even as they shared the responsibility, the guilt remained absent. Diego now experienced so many new and loving sensations, so long suppressed prior to the breach of commandments and vows. He knew he had never been happier. Basking in this sublime state, he took care that his responsibilities to his holy office were fulfilled. In addition to routine duties, the enormity of the challenges he faced would never go away and arose frequently to torment him.

In Diego's travels throughout the holy city of Rome, he managed to meditate at a variety of the overabundance of churches available. *This servant of God,* he thought, *is losing the humility that has been his centerpiece, his life, and the firm foundation that has bound him to his most holy vows. Where did that humility go? What was the source of the love he felt? Was the ecstasy a gift from God? Was Serina his reward for years of living his life in God's grace as his good and faithful servant? Or was she a temptress sent by the devil, seeking to test his fidelity to his solemn vows? Were that the case, what a prize he would be for Satan! On the other hand, maybe, just maybe, the devil could be using him to deceive her for a few pieces of silver. Was he no better than Judas? Could he give himself up so completely? Did his mission to obtain financing to save western civilization condone destruction of his own journey through life? Was he compromising Serina's quest for her own eternal salvation?*

Diego searched for a rationale, a justification for his behavior, while trying to preserve his anointed place at the foot of God.

Awakening on mornings next to Serina with their bodies touching, he knew he was not alone. Others had confronted the ancient dilemma, the fundamental burden— *defining* sin. Such a definition had confounded all but the most sheltered clergy for centuries. *Through the ages,* Diego reflected, *the definition of sin has not remained constant, even in the holiest of places. War has erupted many times over its varying definitions.* As his love for Serina persisted, Diego felt a relaxation of the burden which had consumed him, a burden which Diego did not ask for, but one he joyously accepted as human love grew deeper.

# THE COSMOS CLUB IN NORTHWEST WASHINGTON DC
**May 2016**

Brilliant pink and white azaleas, blossoming along the street in front of the Cosmos Club, not only proclaimed the arrival of spring but also spread splattering bursts of needed color against the old dun-colored mansion.

The historic club, founded in 1878 as a place for the "advancement of its members in science, literature, and art, and their mutual improvement by social intercourse," was long a social headquarters for Washington's intellectual elite. Inside, the air was heavy with knowledge, and the embracing walls were covered with photos of brilliant scientists. The collective minds represented in these images had split the atom, taken man into space, cured disease, settled wars, written Pulitzer Prize-winning books, and probed the universe. Knowledge crept along the aged thick rugs and wafted up the staircases to a library, filled with solutions to much of humanity's plight. New ideas continuously passed through the doorways, often unaware of their human impact, and were examined over the white tablecloths in the main-level Garden Dining Room.

The Garden Room had one oversized table for two alongside the curved window at the far end of the rectangular room. Through the window was the West Garden, where a large sculpted lion guarded the active Garden Committee's creations. The lion looked bored, as though his job of protecting plants and flowers was quite beneath him. The opposite end of the room opened to a hallway, beyond which a dark horseshoe bar smelled of polished wood and good scotch.

Father Jonathan Kennedy was at the Cosmos Club for lunch with Dr. Denny Dennison, and at that moment, his mind was struggling in an effort to accommodate his surroundings. Jonathan realized his difficulty was not the magnificent old club—after all, he had seen the sights of Rome and the Vatican—or the erudite conversation to which he was, thus far, mostly listening, but that of the sheer presence of the famed scientist across the table. Desmond Dennison III, PhD— "Denny" to his friends and colleagues—was at times tough to follow. But Jonathan was captivated. Denny had seemed large in the cavernous hall at the San Francisco scientific conference a year ago, but in this smaller setting, he seemed to fill the room. The two martinis and half-bottle of cold Chardonnay he had consumed over lunch seemed only to further warm his cheerful mood. Jonathan knew of the drinking from his sources and was alert for behavior that might cause doubts about Dr. Dennison's abilities. But, daily imbibing by the scientific genius manifested itself in just a few broken capillaries in cheeks that occupied a fleshy handsome face.

Alcohol seemed to oil his mental wheels, and Denny enjoyed not only his own brilliance but was amused at watching Father Kennedy cringe at his recitations of man's frenzied attempts to wreck the planet. The young priest's concern had gradually been overcome by Denny's entertaining solutions to some of nature's less desirable conditions, some of which Jonathan recalled from the conference. Denny verbally saved planet earth from eventual extinction some eight million years away and felt rewarded by Jonathan's audible sigh of relief.

This affable display of Denny's knowledge had simply been window dressing, an effort to delay the soul-searching questions he expected from this man of the cloth. Denny assumed the young priest was well aware that for him science pretty much ruled out the existence of a deity, and he was slightly uncomfortable at his own nervousness. He knew that this was no casual lunch.

Denny was perfectly groomed, in a well-tailored and expensive dark pinstripe suit. Jonathan guessed the neck size of the custom shirt to be somewhere in the twenty- two-inch range. Thick graying hair was neatly combed back, but here and there unruly chunks escaped total confinement, and curled ends rested on his collar. His hands were huge, with long strong fingers that he wrapped around the wide brim of an over-sized martini glass. There was a natural grace in his movement, when he signaled the attentive waiter for the inevitable refill, a natural sophistication that obviated criticism and made drinking seem acceptable and even desirable. Everything he did was to excess—drink, eat, charm, and seduce. But Denny's impeccable manners made his excesses excusable. He was loved, and those closest to him were infected with what one colleague dubbed "Des-mania." Denny liked the characterization.

Sought out by colleagues and invited to the best parties in and out of the scientific community—the "in" for his brilliance and the "out" for his showmanship—Denny provided all a host needed. Although it was joked that he required a seat and a half of table space, women adored his flirtatious humor. Despite endless rumors of brief affairs with ladies of all ages and marital obligations, his discretion belied the validity of gossip. Marriage had passed him by after the collapse of one serious love, and although profound, his sense of loss was short-lived, and he recovered in the arms of the young, the old, and the sympathetic. Variety was exhilarating, and Denny came to realize that a serious relationship would upset his career. He appreciated women and had a rare capacity for bringing forth the "inner woman" from even the most sophisticated female.

Denny had negotiated the table in the window over time. It was now considered his. In the club's bar, he had appropriated a position on the left side, where he would repeatedly test his theory that more was gleaned from slippery less-inhibited tongues than from cautious pompous duffers upon golf courses, but he was unable to gain exclusivity in the often crowded bar. Denny was never suited to the golf course, and despite a passion for fixing the earth's atmosphere, he disliked fresh air. He also disliked more than one lunch companion, preferring one-on-one intimacy.

The club offered him an arena—an audience of onlookers, who often pretended to be minding their own business but who were wishing they could eavesdrop on Dr. Dennison's conversations.

Practiced diction and just enough space kept his fans out of earshot and allowed him to conjecture unheard through most areas of possible human accomplishment.

Denny realized he was gifted, and although sensitive to God, he practiced no religion. Was his gift the work of a supreme being? He felt little need to dwell upon this age-old question; he knew that its scientific basis was scanty and saw no reason to worship that "being." He liked the philosophers John Locke and Saint Augustine—they both concluded that it was wise to believe in God, since if right, there was everything to gain, and, if wrong, there was nothing to lose. Such wisdom Denny admired, and he actually believed more than Locke and Saint Augustine allowed—that his own qualities of mind could only have been crafted by a deity, and one having a sense of vast wit and humor. So, by that one tentative rationale, he liked God, or at least tolerated him.

Earlier, Father Jonathan Kennedy had driven up New Hampshire Avenue, crossed over Massachusetts Avenue, and passed the Cosmos Club's impressive frontage. Knowing Dr. Dennison's reputation, Jonathan had decided to wear his collar and black jacket. He wanted to display his own authenticity and integrity and assumed that Dr. Dennison had already considered any inquiries from friends or colleagues in the club. After parking in the far-too-small lot, a doorman ushered Jonathan into the reception area. Immediately seeing the club's description of itself—"An extension of the world and a haven from it," Jonathan felt mildly intimidated. His mind was flooded with the problem of how to ask Dr. Dennison to "please figure out a way to discharge a human being from an aircraft and have him gently float to earth in the manner of a celestial being."

Obtaining the lunch invitation had been surprisingly easy. Father Kennedy had whetted the Doctor's appetite in a telephone conversation. "I need to discuss a sensitive matter of grave urgency," Jonathan said, hoping that he didn't sound eccentric. He added to his Vatican credentials by reminding Denny that he had attended the scientific conference in San Francisco the previous year. "I attended," Jonathan said, "not as part of the delegation of the Vatican Office of

Science but at the personal request of His Holiness, Pope Damasus III."

"The *Third*, you say?" Denny feigned the exaggeration to get the upper hand, and Father Kennedy realized his impolite blunder. Holding the belief that all scientists were atheistic or at least agnostic, Jonathan had felt compelled to clarify Juan Carlos' official name.

But Denny was curious. He recalled the priest's presence at the conference and retained a hazy recognition when he heard the voice at the other end of the line. Realizing that the young priest had poked in to a closed portion of his mind, Dr. Denny Dennison agreed to the luncheon.

Now, over the well-chilled chardonnay on a perfectly set table, Denny sensed he was about to embark on a remarkable, possibly fearful, conversation. But despite his strong desire to know, he continued to divert his luncheon guest with scientific tidbits. He noted his own nervousness and felt perspiration through his wool suit but found himself unable to stop talking. He delayed getting to the point by rehashing the highlights of his speech to the five thousand scientists attending the San Francisco meeting. He looked for any reaction in Father Kennedy that might give him some hint of what was to come.

They had spoken about "the causes of crime," "from whence came man," "the dire predictive urge of global warming fanatics," "forced climatic changes," and other subjects. Jonathan was interested but reserved as he mused over possible reactions by this notable scientist to the request to be made. He had been startled when he heard Denny speak about "the recent oddity of the appearance of weird fauna and flora and the mysterious occurrence of reduced gravity noted on some small islands off the Pacific coast of Panamá." Denny's radar had at last picked up the vibes broadcast from Father Kennedy. He glanced down at his wine so as not to acknowledge any mental reception and continued.

"Well, Father, I'm not certain what issue holds your interest specifically, but as you recall from the conference, I am all for deliberate modification of the climate but only if needed." Denny made some sort of gesture that brought the waiter over, and as he did so, he looked at Jonathan and asked, "Is that what interests you, Father?" Then he hesitated. "Wait a minute, let's order."

Jonathan, not wanting to violate protocol, told Denny he would have whatever Denny ordered. He worried that it would be a large lunch and was grateful that Denny had ordered soup and a spinach salad.

When the waiter departed, Jonathan acknowledged the subject matter and commented on his reading some of Denny's theories in various publications. Still fearful of the outcome, Jonathan too held back.

In his preliminary search for the answer to the riddle of the island's periodic lack of gravitational pull, Father Kennedy had read about greenhouse effects in Geo- engineering publications. He lifted his own wine glass, as he watched Denny down his second glass from a newly uncorked bottle.

Denny grinned at Jonathan, saying, "Perhaps you like that idea of a stratospheric shield allowing a return to Eden. If we could just get the people back to an Eden mentality, huh, Father? Realize of course, that might put us both out of jobs."

Jonathan laughed along with Denny. "What about world public opinion?" Jonathan was now more relaxed but knew his time was coming. Soon the waiter cleared the table and put down a dish of ice cream for each of them, along with a small pot of coffee. He did not interrupt Dr. Dennison. The bill would go on Denny's tab, and the waiter knew he would be generously tipped later. He left silently and went home. His shift was over.

"I guess it would take quite a sales job, Father." Denny took large spoonfuls of ice cream and poured coffee for them both. He added cream and several teaspoons of sugar to the large mug. "Everyone in this field is fearful of public opinion. To my mind, it is the inevitable by-product of 'political correctness,' a social state that should delight us but in truth, only further divides us. Still we always need to proceed with caution. The complexities are bewildering to any engineer. As for me, I ache for such a challenge. Of course, in your line of work, there's the God angle." Denny now stared into Jonathan's face. "A lot is possible, Father, but it sometimes takes great courage to go forward." Denny had then become quiet.

Father Kennedy had realized that he must act. The moment had arrived, and as he gathered his thoughts, he had an odd premonition that Dr. Dennison had guessed what Jonathan was going to ask of him. "Doctor, I've read a little about anti-gravity fields. Can they or something that mimics them exist? Could any phenomena or manipulation of gravity be strong enough to allow a slow, controlled descent of a human being? If assistive devices were still required, could they be disguised or hidden?" Jonathan realized his question was rambling, incoherent, and precipitously revealing. He stopped talking.

Denny looked at Father Kennedy directly and was about to expand on the failures of the old Gravity Research Foundation, but he hesitated. He knew the moment for the young priest was at hand and that he should reply with a reasonably professorial answer. He was, however, taken aback, as he regarded the seriousness in the young priest's face.

"Why, Father?" asked Denny in amazement. "My God, why in the world would you want to do that?"

The dining room was now empty. A few staff members went about their tasks, but all tables, save Denny's, were now set for the evening meal. The two men were left alone. Jonathan had rehearsed the actual wording of his argument and presented it to Denny as concisely as possible. As Jonathan spoke, Denny looked at his remaining wine but left it on the table. He sat in disbelief and felt his throat constrict. As Jonathan watched him grow pale and become silent, he became apprehensive and anxious about Denny's reaction.

"Dr. Dennison, can I get you anything? Have I made you ill? I am so sorry to have troubled you with this." He knew an apology was not appropriate. He had to press on, but first he needed an answer. "We believe that you are the only one capable. Will you help us?"

Denny had temporarily blocked Father Kennedy from his mind and had briefly moved into a world separated from his surroundings. Recalling sessions when brainstorming allowed theories to be tossed out by fellow scientists, Denny remembered the angst of some over exposing themselves to potential ridicule in the public forum.

Sometimes embarrassed by their own absurdity, the sessions provided a freedom for scientists to express outlandish concepts. Ideas could be kicked around like an old football. No one's feelings were ever hurt. These scientists had much to give and time was precious. The current moment, however, was completely different.

Denny heard Father Kennedy calling his name from across the table. Part of him was exhilarated beyond speech, as he could already envision the descending Christ. He felt that everything he had ever done was for this moment, as he mentally calculated the glaring obstacles in pulling off such an achievement. Recovering, he had looked at Jonathan and nodded almost imperceptibly, almost unknowingly. Denny gazed at the relieved priest and recalled the concept of sin for the first time since childhood.

"I need to tell you a good deal more, Doctor." Jonathan could almost feel the brainpower at work in the massive head of this accomplished man. Denny still had not spoken, but Father Kennedy felt the energy between them.

Reaching for his wine, Denny held it up and briefly stared at it and then at Jonathan. A broad smile covered his large impressive face, and with his glass lifted, he invited Jonathan to a toast. Jonathan enthusiastically joined in, and with a resounding clink of their glasses, they drank deeply.

"God be with us," Denny said, surprised at his own prayer.

"Amen," Jonathan replied.

Jonathan stood up to leave, instinctively knowing it was better to allow Dr. Denny Dennison time alone.

"Thank you, Doctor, for lunch and for your."

"Insanity?" laughed Denny. Father Kennedy laughed in reply.

They had arranged for their next meeting, and Jonathan walked out of the Cosmos Club into the spring afternoon feeling exhilarated.

For good or for evil, Denny Dennison needed to ponder the predicament of bringing Christ back to earth. He knew that the anti-gravity approach was probably not a viable option. He hailed a cab outside the club and rode home to his apartment. Alone with the emotions of the afternoon, he found himself weeping. He wept because in all his swaggering multifaceted endeavors to save the planet, he had ignored God. He wept for joy because God had seemingly not ignored him.

For good or for evil, Jonathan Kennedy had confronted his second task. The result of his first effort was the child, Christian, now almost 9 and immersed in a broad and deep curriculum, preparing for the future. Today was the beginning of the profound relationship that Denny Dennison would develop with a most unlikely group, which would soon include Christian. Years of secret maneuvers and the selective education for the perfect development of the child were one thing. Perfect development of the brilliant, yet egotistical Denny Dennison was quite another. Jonathan wondered at what point he would be able to introduce Dr. Dennison to Christian. He believed that a mutual dependency would engender a protective love and an admirable respect between them.

# Developing a Miracle Maker
**May 2016**

Dr. Denny Dennison was a wealthy man. He had played the Washington funding game for more years than he cared to remember and was well aware of the financial power of the scare tactic. Feeling somewhat ashamed at moments, Denny knew that the high fees he commanded were often the direct result of cagey lobbying. Universities, non-profits, and others enjoyed large grants by sometimes manipulating the findings of scientists within the arenas of climate, global warming, and the vast heavens. The public was vulnerable and gullible and could be easily frightened with doomsday predictions born of their own bad behavior. By avoiding alarming predictions, based upon incomplete data, Denny moved through the scientific world with integrity, diplomacy, and charm. Although possessing capabilities more far reaching than he generally revealed, Denny had, until now, chosen the more learned persona he had created for himself.

Standing at the desk in the Cosmos Club's well-endowed library, Denny took the Bible the club librarian handed him. He took in the rich dark wood walls and bookcases, the ornate stone fireplace, and the elaborately molded ceiling. He walked across the rich carpets toward the chairs by the windows. Still standing, he turned to Genesis and began reading. Soon dismayed at what seemed God's lack of fair play, Denny found himself drawing on innocent childhood images of Genesis as a strict truth. Even for those who were mainstream fundamentalists, he wondered how anyone could love the God who meted out an incredibly cruel punishment to Adam and Eve.

Denny had not so much as glanced at a Bible since childhood and had forgotten most of it. Even the librarian was taken aback when he asked her for it. Denny hadn't planned to involve his mind in Genesis, but he settled down in his usual comfortable leather chair from where he could see copies of his own books on the shelves near the entrance. Within a few moments of reading, an angry Denny concluded that Adam and Eve were guiltless kids who had no concept of a heritage, no parents, and not a single example to go by. Not having a clue about the difference between right and wrong, they were shoved out on their own. Aware that such thoughts pushed him into the fundamentalist category, he stopped and looked out the window. *Good God,* he smiled to himself. *I'm actually acknowledging the existence of Adam and Eve. This is highly unbecoming of a Cosmologist, an engineer of the skies, a master in the study of the totality of all things. Still, what were you thinking, God?*

Although raised in a Catholic environment, Denny had lost his way somewhere between venial and mortal sin. As a youngster, he had attended catechism classes in rural Italy, where he lived with his expatriate parents. He remembered the nuns teaching about all eternity. These weren't easy words for an 8-year-old. Denny could grasp that all eternity was probably a long time. But when told that "it never ends," the words took on a more ominous implication. Sin became a never-ending matter. The interpretation of "stealing," another issue that contributed to the collapse of his immature faith, was presented thusly: "A theft less than $5.00," the young and pretty nun explained with total sincerity, "that's a venial sin. But over $5.00? That's a Mortal sin. You can't get into heaven if you die with a Mortal sin on your soul," she cautioned.

That was bleak news indeed, and Denny had taken it seriously. In a later class he raised his hand. "If you steal $4.99, is that still a venial sin?" Denny's intellect was forming early, and he followed on. "My mother said that bread and milk cost more this week than last week." Denny's mother had no part in his query, but he knew that using her as an accomplice might carry more weight. He genuinely wanted the answer. "If someone stole bread last week that cost under $5.00, and this week it costs over $5.00 dollars, does that make a venial sin now a mortal one?"

Denny knew his teacher would have difficulty with her reply, and he felt a little shame at his desperate need for answers that would appeal to his intellect but would be at her expense.

Although her hands and her face were the only body parts visible beneath her drab gray habit, the young nun was still attractive with her smooth skin and long fingers. She had learned to expect such questions from the innocently naïve, as well as the occasional wise guy. Her unblemished face, framed in the tight white headpiece, took on an authoritative seriousness. She looked at young Denny and replied, "I know your conscience gives you a simple and direct response to right and wrong. Still, if that doesn't serve you, you will need to discuss your particular dilemma with Father during your next confession." Then, hoping to deflect the point, she had addressed the entire class, "I encourage all of you to take advantage of the sacrament of Penance through frequent confession." Inwardly the young nun hoped her reply sounded humble and that her vagueness demonstrated deference and respect to her superiors. She didn't like the sense she had of her own inadequacy in trumping Denny's logic, and she felt a regrettable lack of fair play in directing the boy to address his questions to a priest in a confessional environment.

Denny instinctively knew there was no answer. He never bothered asking the priest. But inside he regretted having what he had then perceived as the upper hand. He liked the nun and admired her devotion to enlightening juvenile minds, which usually arrived fairly empty at the door of her catechism class. So he had raised his hand again, and she reluctantly acknowledged him.

"I'm sorry, Sister. I meant no disrespect. You are right about our consciences; we should all listen to them more carefully," he said. She blushed at her sudden fondness for Denny. It signaled the development of his great charm.

From then on, Dr. Denny Dennison had sought answers to everything, unfazed by any discomfort he might cause to his responders. He sought out the Achilles heel, the weak link, and the toughest challenges to his intellect. He was unbeatable in the one-two punch arena. Nevertheless, despite an ability to point out error, he was a practical man when it came to flaunting his intellect. With consistent good nature and humor, Denny always dispelled embarrassment to colleagues, and all loved him.

After his lunch with Father Jonathan Kennedy, Denny felt deeply challenged intellectually and spiritually. The initial urge to joke away the young priest's absurd request had disappeared, and he wondered if after all these years of paying little attention, God was now testing him. Despite reading the works of numerous commentators, some of which he deemed written with religious authority, he still felt their insights were only just that—the thoughts trying to come within reach of the truth. However, they had presented no proof.

*What am I?* Denny wondered childishly. *Am I a good man ready to pursue something horribly wrong or a bad person about to do something very good?* He pondered the good versus evil struggle. Over the millennium, the human condition had changed, but human beings always questioned justice and injustice. *Have we made any progress?* Denny felt resigned. *Right or wrong, for good or for evil, I am going to go through with this.* Even as he contemplated his potential damnation by God, he began to mentally plan the quest ahead. *How could it be done?*

Returning to the club the following evening, Denny sat at the small popular horseshoe-shaped bar on the club's main level. He was sipping his second vodka martini, waiting for his guest, a respected lawyer, well-known scholar and biblical expert, Dr. Kelly Masterson. Denny wanted to reacquaint himself with God, a subject he had forgotten during his years of solving earth's atmospheric mysteries.

Dr. Masterson was a typically disheveled professor. Denny noted a few spots on his old tweed blazer, as he slipped on to the bar stool next to him and further loosened his already askew tie. The two greeted each other warmly. They rarely indulged in much small talk, and Kelly Masterson, knowing something was on Denny's mind, offered the obligatory comments and inquiries, while Denny ordered another drink for himself and one for Masterson.

"Let's talk about religion," Denny said in his direct manner. "What do you think about Genesis, my friend?" Denny chewed on an olive, pulling it off a plastic toothpick. He was grateful that the bar was mostly empty. Just one couple, engrossed in each other, sat on the far side.

"Religion, Denny? Are you feeling ill?" Kelly Masterson asked jokingly. "I have no idea what's on your mind, but I do love talking about Genesis," he said. "And I venture to say, I will enjoy such conversation with you, since I'm confident I know a Hell of a lot more about it than you do," he added, chuckling. Dr. Masterson realized immediately, however, that Denny sought more than his quips.

"In my humble opinion, the best dissertation on Genesis, is by Alan Dershowitz, the ingenious legal practitioner and scholar; and with due deference to him, I'll draw on it," said Masterson. "Dershowitz' point was that the great thing about Genesis is that it makes all ages question God," he began. "Of course, you have to believe in God in the first place," he looked at Denny questioningly. Denny, aware of the irreverent image he projected and his reputation for dismissing the unscientific, knew he was considered an atheist by his friends and colleagues.

"But I do. I really do." Denny nodded rapidly. "I've just been wondering how anybody could avoid questioning the terrible deal Adam and Eve got from God. They were punished for disobeying God's commandment—not to eat from the 'Tree of the Knowledge of Good and Evil.' Why, if before eating off that tree they had no concept about good and evil, should they be punished for it?" Denny expressed his bewilderment with his arms bent and his large hands outstretched. Why do we even give kids the book of Genesis? The characters in the book cheat. They lie, they steal, and they murder and get away with it."

"Genesis is a moral teacher," Professor Kelly said quietly. "Look Denny, I don't know where you're going with this, but I need to assume you read this as a child, and for some reason, it's now bursting out of your consciousness. Did some woman get to you?" Kelly gave him a somewhat accusing look. Denny did not reply but merely waved off the idea.

"Anyway," Masterson continued, "all this is written metaphorically, because when you think about it, the underlying meanings are so profound, they are better told in a simple story form. Genesis is like that. In the end, it simply tells us about eternal issues of right and wrong. It tries to address human origins. Of course, the parables in the Bible need some explanation, but carrying through to the lessons learned from the lives of Jesus and Mohammed, the teachings are clear. Who can object to Christ's 'Sermon on the Mount,' or Jesus' answer to the crowd about to stone the adulteress, or with the story of the Good Samaritan? The same is true with the Torah. And the Koran. It's the life of Mohammed—himself a great moral character."

"Well, at least in this country we're beyond stoning our naughty girls," Denny grinned. "They are stoned for feeling the same desires as the boys for God's sake. It's tough to grasp that many fanatics go to war for not only territory but the privilege of sex and spoils. Then they kill off the feminine objective of their battle, stone them, just because the vanquished feel the same lust as the victor."

"Hey, if we could pattern our behavior after Jesus or Mohammed," Masterson said with feigned righteousness, "we'd consider ourselves morally 'just' persons. Mohammed presumably enjoyed sex. Jesus presumably did not. How do we evaluate the difference? Should we? It's seemingly crazy, but is it just? What behaviors lead us to justice?

"In the Jewish Bible, Denny, we're shown flawed heroes, good people who sometimes do bad deeds. Ecclesiastes tells us that no righteous person does only good and never sins. Human failing begins at the beginning. Even the God of Genesis is imperfect. He's not invincible and, it seems, not always good. He apologizes in a promise not to flood the world again. Abraham lectures Him about unfairness. Job gave God hell. The Jewish Bible actually teaches fairness with its stories of injustice and imperfection. Perhaps they exaggerate to make their point."

Kelly Masterson had paused and signaled the bartender for another round. Denny knew he should refuse another martini but loved the simplicity and logic of the conversation and didn't want to be distracted. He promised himself to drink the next one slowly.

"I'm betting you love Genesis, Denny." Masterson sipped his drink. "It provides the kind of challenge you react to—to think, to disagree. It goes far beyond any accomplishments to date of our high-tech kids, or adults who are still kids, because it provokes questions. It encourages conversation with the ages and with our concept of the heavenly unknown. Justice is implied in Abraham's attempted murder of both his sons. Justice is in God's genocide against Noah's contemporaries—those guys didn't make it on to the ark—and Lot's neighbors."

Denny had to think to recall the ancient stories. Listening to Kelly Masterson, he realized that as a child, he had taken biblical narratives at face value.

"You know, Professor," Denny admitted, "I don't think I did much in elementary school but mostly take this stuff for granted. At Catholic mass we learned these stories from Old Testament readings, but that was pretty much only once a week. What fires you up so?"

"The same thing that fires you, Denny. We're not that different. You want answers. I want answers. I believe some of what you find in the scientific world will help me, and maybe I can help you here tonight with whatever it is you're seeking." Masterson, also a curious man, hoped that his gentle prodding and the mind-easing effects of the martinis would cause Denny to confide in him.

It wasn't happening, so Masterson went on. "I keep digging at these questions. The tales simply cannot stand on their own. Studying the Old Testament, especially Genesis, can drown one in a quagmire. If you're a critic, you are doomed to struggle with it all. At the same time, Adam and Eve's downfall was pushing the envelope too far, and I believe that's the lesson." Professor Masterson smiled at Denny. "You'll like that Maimonides, the legendary Jewish teacher, was convinced that Torah study was so demanding that husbands occupied in this work should be obliged to only have sex with their wives once a week. The studies were too draining." He chuckled, "The working rich guys on the other hand, were supposed to have sex with their wives every night— poor devils—and regular working stiffs twice a week. Is that it, Denny? You're thinking of switching professions, and you're researching the benefits of the job?"

Knowing Denny's reputation with women, he had enjoyed the look on his friend's face. They both laughed.

Denny then said as he smirked. "I don't agree that biblical learning should interfere with your sex life, dear Professor, but you too are caught up in the ambiguities of this stuff. I guess you have to question and you have to get annoyed. Otherwise, like me, you'd be confounded in your work and left empty. Both of us have to find answers."

"Bingo!" smiled Kelly Masterson.

Denny had stared at the liquid in front of him. He felt a certain peace in this conversation and knew he had ignored religion for so long because of his inability to face his own doubts.

Masterson toyed with the napkin under his drink. "I enjoy the Torah. It challenges me to reinterpret, and I get a little smug about that. I apologize for being a lawyer too," he laughed, "but I first thought about justice when I was a kid and read Genesis. I couldn't simply accept God's decision to destroy innocent babies in a flood and later in the fire and brimstone of Sodom and Gomorrah. How could we admire Abraham for his agreeing to surrender his son by killing him? Where did Cain get a wife if Adam and Eve had no daughter? The questions have been asked for generations. The answer, or answers, only strengthen faith in the divine origin of the Bible or the Torah and in the goodness of God and His prophets. Sure, some require a leap of faith. But then you think there's no doubt left." Professor Masterson shrugged and said, "Huh? Even with no doubt left, I continue to ask. So do you, Denny. If you have one answer to changing the planet's climate, you create for yourself a whole new litany of questions. Am I right?"

"Of course," Denny conceded, "but my answers don't change eternity or where I might spend it. Or if it even exists. Yours seem to do that. I envy that, my friend, and I envy your faith," Denny said, draining his glass and berating himself slightly as he munched on the olives at the bottom of his glass.

Professor Masterson had looked at Denny sympathetically. The bartender looked at them questioningly, but by then, Denny knew further imbibing would cloud his capacity to remember this conversation. He suggested dinner.

As they sat down at Denny's table, the waiter brought wine goblets. Kelly Masterson continued, "Remember that in Genesis God makes a deal, a covenant with humans. The people believed they had a contract. They had a deal which, they thought, also obligated God. He was supposed to justify what He commanded, at least some of the time. This stuff had a powerful effect on my young mind and made me view the world in a skeptical and questioning manner. So, I guess, it was the Bible that really caused me to pursue law and to find out what 'justice' is all about. Genesis taught me that faith is a process, not a static mindset. I find this comforting when everything I believe goes to hell. Faith must be earned, perhaps even by God. When I was a kid, I used to test that old God relationship. You know, I'd invent my own conditions, like, 'Okay, God, I'll be faithful, if You do this or that for me.' As it is, there's hardly any wiggle room, if you take every word of scripture literally. God said it. I believe it. Case closed."

They finally ordered rare steaks and salads, and Denny sat intrigued. The martinis had done their job and actually sharpened his mind. He was transported back to parts of his childhood and youth. He felt a twinge of renewed acceptance.

"What about guys like me?" Denny asked. "The atheists, agnostics, and those who have rarely opened a Bible? I rather think of the Bible as great literature, like Shakespeare or Homer."

"Well yes, Denny, it is great literature, *the greatest*," Masterson said. "It's a holy book, the Word of God we're taught, the guide to our behavior. We are supposed to act on it, not merely ponder its insights. No one was ever burned at the stake for misinterpreting 'Macbeth.' But, even if you buy bible teachings hook, line and sinker, who wrote it? A Jew, a Christian, a Muslim? We judge the divinity versus the humanity of the authors. We simply don't know. But instead of scoffing at Muslims for their belief in a paradise with lots of virgins if they martyr themselves, it would no doubt be wiser to join this dialogue among generations, as Pope Benedict tried to do. Interpretations change in the ever-unfolding excitement of modern knowledge. No religious position is loyally served if it can't consider some strange unearthed theory, which may well turn out to be factual. New truths allow us to better understand the truth of Torah and help us debate the Bible. Free inquiry, isn't that what we're looking at? The big deal in this is trying to claim being right about one or another religious volume. You simply can't claim any religious or other authority as final. Discussion must continue. Proving or disproving the divine origin of the Bible or the superiority of any religion is ridiculous. After thousands of years, nobody's been able to do it." Professor Masterson was on a roll, having never had the opportunity to lecture Denny on religion. He was enjoying himself. "So don't we continue to question God? Don't we want the writings to be truth? We want all the answers to be absolute proof that God is good. Well, it's no sin to feel doubt. After all, the human capability for doubt is endowed. We question everything. The sin is to act haphazardly on these doubts."

"What do you mean, 'act haphazardly?'" asked a suddenly alarmed Denny.

"Well Denny, my boy," Masterson raised his shoulders in mock admonishment, "do you think in any religion that rigorous theological purity is more important than simply obeying the commandments? Do you think that stealing and killing and committing adultery can be justified by doubt?" Masterson noted the slight look of shame on Denny's face and continued softly, "There's always the question of who wrote the Bible, who wrote the gospels? This has been a long debate by academics and by housewives at mass. Why one passage made it into the texts and others didn't. Who decided? Was the Jewish Bible written by God and given to the Jewish people at Sinai as a single document? How about the discrepancies? In one, Moses describes his own death. Places and peoples are mentioned that didn't exist until well after the Torah was supposed to have been given at Sinai. So nobody knows."

Denny, noting the professor's agitation simply commented, "Kind of tough to buystories of injustice that are supposed to teach us about justice?" Now drinking soda water with lime, perplexing the club waiters used to Denny's ample consumption of bottles of expensive wine, Denny said, "It must have been one hell of an editing job."

"Yes," said Masterson, calming down, "but it doesn't make any difference. It's still *The Book,* the sacred writings. They don't require a literal fundamentalist approach. Intelligence is the basis of these writings. I mean, obviously, the Torah was not given to ignoramuses. Pope John Paul II made a similar point—fundamentalism does put undue stress upon the inerrancy of certain details in the biblical texts. I mean, everybody makes mistakes. Fundamentalism tends to adopt very slim points of view. This narrow view blocks dialogue for a broader way of seeing the relationship between culture and faith. Of course, Denny, without fundamentalists, it's probable that the symbolic or figurative adherents might not have come forth."

Totally confused, Denny asked, "Well, where the hell does that leave us?"

"I have no idea at the moment, Dr. Dennison. I think my mind is muddled by the spirits and the wine. I daresay this conversation and this evening have been extraordinarily stimulating and downright fun. However, right now I couldn't interpret my own name." Professor Masterson had laughed at his own feeble humor, and Denny wasn't sure his friend believed his own religious meanderings. Sensing Denny's uncertainty, Professor Masterson, without humor said soberly, "Tradition is comfortable, but it can't serve as the end-all for interpretations. We can't be too concerned about the beliefs of those who have gone before us, just because they got their ideas in there first. That would prevent our own interpretations."

Masterson rose smiling. "I don't know what you're after, dear man, but you should investigate it completely. Otherwise, you squander a part of the reason you were created. The vast wisdom you have was bestowed on you from above. Don't forget that."

Denny, wishing to avoid any further inquisitiveness from the now tipsy professor looked directly at Masterson. "Hey, Professor, don't take me too seriously. I'm just a mad scientist who gets the heebie-jeebies once in a while over possibly ending up in Hell. I enjoyed this, and you have provided me with a good dose of post-Sunday-school learning. Thanks for your usual good company and your insights. Those kids are all lucky to have you."

At this final flattery to Professor Masterson, they said their goodbyes, and Denny, realizing that he was more than a little drunk, decided to stay at the club. With his frequent attendance and heavy spending, the accommodating staff kept a small overnight bag for him. He was a bit unsteady getting the old fashioned key to work properly but made it into the small comfortable room. Once down on the bed, Denny fell asleep immediately. In the morning, he had the concierge check on the time of mass at Saint Mathews Cathedral on M Street. As a child, he had attended JFK's funeral mass there with his parents. At this point in time, it was the only Catholic Church he knew of.

# The Final Gathering of Holy Planners
### April 2034

It was shortly after lunch. Juan Carlos had finished a papal audience earlier and was dining alone in his apartment. He, as well as the attendant nuns and kitchen staff, had noticed a decrease in his appetite over the past weeks. All concerned blamed it on the stresses of the world upon the Pope and a resulting lack of sleep. As the mission date grew closer, Juan Carlos had found sleep was almost impossible.

Sitting in his favorite chair, a dark leather recliner sent by a Knights of Columbus group from upstate New York, the Pope took pleasure in knowing that the chair had been donated by a countryman. The Grand Knight, a Colombian-born lawyer had acquired a fortune defending the Hispanic population in the US and convinced fellow Knights that the Holy Father never enjoyed such rich trappings in Bogotá, Colombia.

Despite a light lunch, His Holiness felt lethargic. *Sloth*, he berated himself; but these days he gave into it. The chair was an escape, *perhaps the lap of the devil,* Juan Carlos thought. Italians in the leather business criticized the chair, until convinced that the leather hides had come from their factories. Juan Carlos mentally thanked the good Knights once again for their diplomatic acuity.

Rubbing his eyes from fatigue, Juan Carlos awaited those few who were tied with their souls to the mission of *The Return*. This would be their last gathering prior to the journey leading them to heaven or

Hell. Private misgivings had been dealt with as much as possible. Each fought his fear, his weakness, and his desire to cave in. *There was still time. Was there still time?* he wondered.

The few would include Diego Cardinal Hernandez, Father Jonathan Kennedy, both protégés, and the Pope's beloved brother, General Luís Antonio Gutiérrez, the mastermind of the mission.

Three others, part of the original group, would be absent— Salvador Cardinal DeAngeles, Prefect of the Congregation for the Doctrine of the Faith; Adolfo Cardinal Romano, Juan arlo's personal aide, and Teodoro Cardinal "Teddy" Arias, head of Vatican Finances. They had shared in the initial almost-innocent fantasy that had become a reality. Feeling like children who had slipped on a steep hill and could not regain their footing, they had also felt headiness and a sanctifying purpose for their existence.

Cardinals DeAngeles and Arias were now dead.

Salvador DeAngeles had known his time had come. One rainy morning several years before *The Return* took place, he had sensed the presence of death in his study. He felt no fear, but despite years of rationalizing the righteousness of the project, he worried for the souls of his colleagues and perhaps more so for Christian, whom he had never met.

Without aving said mass publicly for some time, Cardinal DeAngeles recited, by heart, his office of daily prayer. Having no family left, he remained in his Vatican apartment, graciously insisted upon by Juan Carlos. The others brought news of progress to him and always petitioned him to hear their confessions. Despite his own duplicity in *The Return,* he hoped his absolutions would be valid. On his final morning, after finishing breakfast served by an attendant, he had managed to get out to the balcony to his rose bushes and had cut several stems for the vase, ready with fresh water, on his desk. As he placed the first long stem in the water, a large thorn pierced his forefinger and spurted blood. Sitting down, Cardinal DeAngeles was surprised at a sudden loss of feeling in his hand. He knew what was coming and said a final prayer. In a few seconds, he had slumped over on his desk.

Years earlier, Cardinal Teddy Arias had set up a brilliant array of financial accounts. During the last phase of the project, the bulk of the money was channeled to General Aaron Yakowitz, who doled it out to Denny Dennison's operations and, as agreed upon, had made donations to the Israeli Defense Forces. More was drawn by Cardinal Hernandez and Father Kennedy as needed. When Cardinal Arias was confident that all finances for the project were safely administered away from the Vatican financial realm, he had retired to a valley in Panamá known simply as El Valle. Knowing of Contadora Island, he had made one trip to see where *The Return* would take place, and he wondered about the future of the small island, *Will it be blessed or scorned?* Diego Hernandez had visited the aging brilliant financier periodically and learned of Cardinal Arias' peaceful death ten years prior to the mission with sadness and appreciation.

Cardinal Adolfo Romano, now ninety, had long retired to his small farm in Tuscany and gradually assailed by Alzheimer's, had little remaining memory of his Vatican career.

Luís's gifted tongue and persuasive logic had, so long ago, broken the resistance of them all. Each participant had been thoroughly analyzed, and ultimately, Luís's choices were men of good minds, who understood the danger as well as the overpowering need to save their Church. It was a giant gamble.

Juan Carlos Gutiérrez had fought the need to remove himself from any blame in the event of failure. But the Church's survival required the Pope to restrict himself from direct participation, and, isolated on the fringes of progress, Juan Carlo's painting continued to be his solace.

His selection as the first Latin American Pope, twenty-five years earlier, had been a bold move. Now Pope Damasus III pondered his papacy and the act planned to give renewal to the Catholic Church. Before his pontificate, doubt had persisted regarding a Third World pope. The Italians and other Europeans had initially balked, but the latter were so weakened in faith that they welcomed help from another quarter. Additionally, they rationalized, blame for the downtrodden Church could be shifted to this second-tier pope, if necessary.

The Americans remained neutral but harbored a similar hope that the geographic shift at the Vatican might inject greater resolve by all Christians to help the Church survive. The United States was unlikely to produce a pope, but within a polarized world, it was hoped that a binding force from the Western Hemisphere would contribute to worldwide calm and unification. With a natural empathy between the poor of Latin American nations and those on the African continent, the thought of a Latin American pope had been appealing.

New generations of Americans had resulted from millions of Hispanics who flooded across the Mexican border. The Cuban population in Miami was joined by others from Latin America to establish a new society. Of those who found a way to America, most worked hard and generated a river of money, which flowed into their home nations. In a world in danger, America adjusted to its changing ethnic and cultural mix but not without conflict. As in all of history, it was an achievement to please a sizeable percentage of any electorate, and a Latin American pope brought great satisfaction to all minorities.

In selecting the name Damasus, Juan Carlos honored the past. Both Damasus I and Damasus II had endured exile and fought for their papacies in the mid-4th and mid- 11th Centuries. They had inspired Juan Carlos. He admired the *Damasi Confession Fidei* (The Damasus Confession of Faith), written in 377 AD and considered the earliest precursor of the Credo of the modern mass—'I believe in one God ' Both Damasus popes had worked toward Church rejuvenation, a goal to which Juan Carlos had prayed his own papacy would contribute. He had wondered what Damasus the First and Second might think if they knew what was about to take place a thousand years later on a troubled globe, a globe they were never aware of.

Juan Carlos despised his helplessness in the decline of the Church throughout the world. He felt himself a pawn, a convenience within political and economic worlds, particularly in Latin America. He felt he had arrived as the Vicar of Christ, The Holy Father, Pope, and The Holy See, not in a donkey cart from the poverty of Colombia but almost because of it. Thrust into an increasingly God-hating world, acts of humility and prayer to counter the arrogance and pride that he might one day actually *achieve* the  throne of Peter were unneeded. He was wealthy, respected, loved, and talented—and void of self-importance. But these attributes had meant little, as Juan Carlos struggled against the inevitability of encroaching evil.

Several gentle knocks at the door of his study brought the Pope to the moment at hand. He lingered a little while longer. Confession and penance had not brought the peace he yearned for, and despite the self-evident sinfulness of their actions, he gave in to the euphoria of imagining, over and over, the actual moment of *the return of Christ. Well, not Christ, of course,* Juan Carlos continued to remind himself, *but this young man whomight bring the renewed love of Christ. Would it come perhaps, after all? Even if I do notlive to see it?* Juan Carlos thought. He felt anxiety tighten around his heart.

Juan Carlos called to the visitors to enter. As they did, Diego checked the security, the devices that would cancel out attempts to listen in. Juan Carlos watched Diego and was reminded of human weakness. *Am I, the Vicar of Christ, and these before me, traitorous to God? Or do we engage the freewill God gave us to act for His greater glory?* In the agony of decision, Pope Damasus thought deeply about the unquestionable and uncontested power given to him through canon law and divine succession. He realized that failure of *The Return* would mean total collapse and the unthinkable image of a religion of fraud.

"Prayer is quite splendid," Juan Carlos said, recalling one of Luís's earlier arguments. "But we're always praying during or after the tragedy, during the war, after the death, after the great forces of nature have obliterated large chunks of humanity and changed our landscapes." He had questioned the group, "Do we expect our God to endorse prayer alone and expect it to appease his expectations of us? Our cruelty to one another is well known. No animal exhibits such diabolical possession. How did it get in us? God had to have allowed that. How do we purge ourselves of it? God demands that we achieve that for Him. Christ was the instrument that brought the world out of darkness so long ago. Let us try again."

The agonizing deliberations were years ago, and today, as the final day approached, the world condition needs Christ's word more than ever. *Had I tried harder, had I not had The Return to fall back on, would it have been any different?*

Everything was in place. It was indeed, as was so often said, *in God's hands.*

"I love you," he said to their solemn faces. "I love that you are willing to shoulder this burden. I love that you were willing to take on a task that we still may not live to see to completion. We have come far to challenge the devil in his quest for the world, to do peaceful battle against the frightening danger of empty souls. Souls absent of God. This project has taken your lives—or at least a good part of them. We gather here for the last time, full of hope that the use of our gifts in this peaceful mission to attack iniquity and injustice will succeed.

Luís had envisioned a peaceful world but understood its chances were slim. Jonathan Kennedy thought only of those now in preparation in Israel. Diego struggled with his vision of the future, as Serina filled his mind.

"Dear God, forgive us," they heard the Pope whisper.

# PART SEVEN – PEACE ON EARTH

# At Work In the Field of the Lord – Christian on the Island
## April 2035

On Contadora Island, his flight mission a memory, Christian instructs the islanders day after day under the tropical sun around their modest homes. He speaks to the men on the beach as they prepare to fish and to the women as they wash. He speaks to the islanders as they tend their plots of corn, yucca, and their plantain, banana and lemon trees. Papayas, watermelons, and cantaloupes, brought from the mainland years ago, provide seeds, which grow rapidly in the sandy ground. They require little attention.

Christian teaches but is also the student, watching the small shoots of growth that emerge so quickly from the internal secret of the wet black seeds of the papaya and watermelon and the pale clusters of life in the cavity of the cantaloupes. Fat elongated fruit quickly appears on the papaya trees' stalks directly beneath wide protective leaves. Christian uses the process that so exemplifies the glory of life itself in his teaching. He is struck by the gift of creation, as the women cut chunks of ripened fruit and douse the flesh with juice from lemons picked moments before. Allowing themselves moments of relaxation between chores, they lounge in hammocks, listening to Christian and sharing in the dripping treat, appreciating their natural gifts.

Christian watches them closely and in tutoring them about salvation, his daily awareness of their innocence grows. He has been on the island for almost three weeks and the persistent reminders of his own inadequacy prick at his mind. He looks at their smooth olive skin, their sturdy firm bodies, and their thick dark hair surrounding their soft facial features. *How perfect they are,* he thinks. No longer did Christian feel the "I-it" mentality, a some what debasing manner of looking at this precious collection of humanity as a single manipulative object. He is drawn into a rhythmic daily harmony and has learned a profound sense of "I-Thou," the recognition of the worth of each individual.

For their evening meal the islanders sit at wooden tables with benches, made by the men who, Christian has come to realize, have a natural understanding of the generous and holy "give and take" of a limited society. *Can they take this and their belief in me to the Hells outside this world of theirs?*

It is early afternoon and the sun causes the islanders to seek shady areas. Fishermen are back from their morning run. They pack up their catch to put on the plane for the afternoon flight to the restaurants in Panamá City. Despite this daily ritual, no one informs the pilots of the presence of Christian. For their own consumption, part of the catch is kept aside. The corvinas are filleted, the snappers are gutted and stuffed with garlic and onions and breadcrumbs. Shrimp and lobsters are put into boiling pots of salty water. Fish heads and tails will be later used for soup and for bait for the following day.

Wet laundry hangs on lines between trees to dry in the bright sunlight. The simple dwellings are tidy, and the children are clean from playing in the ocean and rinsing under the natural shower of fresh water from the small stream on the island's south side. Their numbers gather to enjoy the main midday meal of rice and fish, fried plantains, and beans. Christian breathes in the fragrance of just-cooked rice, waiting in the ever-present pots atop primitive stoves. Rice, basic to the islanders' diet, is prepared in a traditional manner, as grains are washed and strained, and still wet, tossed into hot oil. With brief frying, the rice loses its faint transparency and turns chalk white. Salt and water are added, and the mixture is boiled down to a bubbly thickness before the pot is covered and the heat reduced. As other foods are prepared, the rice absorbs the water in a process that prevents the grains from sticking, except for the thin flavorful crust coveted for its crunchy texture at the bottom of the rough-hewn iron pots. Leftover rice goes into a *sancocho*, a thick stew of meat or chicken with yami, a potato-like vegetable that thickens the broth. Onions and garlic, and corn, and yucca are added, as well as salt and fresh cilantro. Christian savors the food and watches the preparation with the anticipation of a growing appetite. The women are skillful, utilizing methods handed down through generations.

"Have you eaten enough, my Lord?" After generous meals, the islanders retire to woven hammocks and chairs for *siesta*.

"Ah yes," replies Christian. "And you give me far more than food alone. As messengers of God, you will all bear a heavy burden, but you must get through to the deepest parts of so many hearts now empty of our heavenly Father."

"But how?" They ask him repeatedly, as he studies their capabilities and convinces them gradually to overcome their anxieties.

The heavy midday meal is functional, practical, and historical. The food-induced traditional nap allows bodily rest during the hottest hours and eating their main meal mid- day avoids spoilage in the tropical heat. To prevent raiding insects and animals, meat and fish are prepared early. Christian's pupils will take in his lessons with greater attention after naps.

As evening falls, the island people require only a small supper. When plates and utensils are cleared away and cleaned with care and when the men have made their plan for the following dawn, they gather again, some drinking the native sugar-based liquor, *Seco,* while others sip tea. Christian teaches into the night, sometimes on the beach under the brilliance of a million stars. The children play nearby or lean against him or sit at his feet and are removed gently as sleep overtakes them. Marcocito displays rapt attention and is always reluctant to go to bed. Only the reminder of his date for dawn fishing with Mario convinces him. Knowing then he can relive the moments of Christian's descent, Marcocito departs and lies in his hammock before sleep. His young brain retraces the events of Christian's arrival and of his rising awareness of the world around him and his future in it.

Watching their rapt faces, full of trust and curiosity, Christian thinks, *I am in paradise already.* Gazing upward, he tells them, "This is the classroom of God," wishing he could remain there forever.

Christian's approach to the islanders is uncomplicated. As Christ before him, he uses simple parables and repeats ancient instruction and ageless wisdom. Although the reasoning for their being chosen is unclear, the islanders gradually push aside any sense of inferiority, an inferiority imposed upon them over the centuries. As faith and confidence grow, they become anxious to tell their own amazing story. For now they remain patient and reinforce Christian's calm with one another. Men's voices are less harsh. Remaining indignation from last year's political arguments is forgotten. Domestic disagreements all but disappear, and the islanders exhibit concern for each other. They have been captivated by their Savior.

As they grasp the "miracle" of Christian, they slowly understand that for a reason, they were chosen. A final judgment day frightens them all, and Christian, thinking about the wall of the Sistine Chapel, winces at his own memory of Michelangelo's depiction of the end of the world. He tells them that the fate of souls will not be known until the end of time, a time not to occur just yet. He knows they understand these basics, and as he overcomes their fear, their trust troubles him. Christian's own anxieties grow as he is increasingly unable to ignore the fact of his deception.

Although doubt for the new apostles lessens as Christian assures them that his visit's purpose is to act on behalf of the Father and to restore faith, their questions become pointed. "Isn't my end of time when I die?" asks Gordo, who now seeks God daily, as he goes about his work. He often finds Him in the simple miracles of the abundant life around him and knows that Christian is responsible for this new belief in his sense of salvation.

"The mystery of the end of life on this earth is as it should be. God, our Father, will determine the fates of all, and so you must speak of his power to others and trust his will as you live good lives in this tiny paradise.

"What shall we tell people about you?"

"Fill yourselves with happiness and wonder at the fact of my presence here. Tell others to love and forgive, so that all might enjoy the kingdom to come." Christian feels uneasiness in his vague answers. Still, frustration over one's eternal soul is a presence that hounds rich and poor alike. Christian, always striving to ease the uncertainties over his descent onto their island, wants the peace of the Holy Spirit to nestle within him as joy, not as the growing anxiety he now experiences.

"It is simple," Christian says, "very simple. You believe in me, and then you believe in one another. If you accomplish that, you take that simple message to the world."

"To the world? How can we do that? Why will they believe us?" They ask again.

"Because of what you have seen, because of this," Christian says softly, opening his hands in a gesture toward them all and then pointing to himself. "I cannot stay with you long, but after I leave, you must reveal this story of us. You will be inspired to do so, but understand that you will not be believed. For what you have seen, you will not be believed," he repeats, "at least not for a while. Do not be afraid. After I leave you, never be afraid to teach others what my being here has revealed to you."

They tell no one, but question Christian incessantly to clarify his message in their minds, to have the greatest understanding possible of what lay ahead. *Why did he come here to this little island? How did he get here? Where did he come from? Would he go with them to the entire world? How big is the world?*

Christian, knowing the mission has been contrived by learned men, knows also that in the chaos of the world, they all lack full understanding of the simple nature of these new apostles and that an overwhelming task lays ahead in the effort to pierce the soul of a godless, technology-driven world.

"You see, you—all of you—and this world, were *created,* but God was not created. He has always existed, and you are chosen because you represent unity. You are like the trinity—several in one. You will present yourselves to the world in this manner. This island is a church, your church. You are one—bound to this church—and now, bound to me, you will enter those having no unity and only bound unto themselves. They lack faith, tell themselves that the universe—the stars and the earth—all this," Christian stretches his arms to the skies, "was born of nothing and will come to nothing.

"You ask me how I got here. How did *you* get here? How did you learn to fish, to harvest, to love and care for each other? How perfect you are for God's task."

"But are you really Jesus?" Marisol asks, without any discomfort but only the polite innocence of her age.

"I don't know," he replies, uncomfortable with the truth of himself, "but it doesn't matter. My words are pure. The divine is within me, as it is now in you. We are an extension of God."

*Am I getting through? Will it work?* Christian feels shame, as he looks into the faces of this cluster of humanity, whose awe for him never wavers. He silently begs for inspiration and longs for the future he sees in their eyes. Will he see success from some far away vantage, some yet-to-be determined future for himself after this is over? He pleads for success, for a better world, for the saving of his own soul.

# RAISING CHRISTIAN
## 2016 -2035

Within Vatican City, there exist hundreds of buildings and palaces and thousands of rooms and offices. Over the centuries many who inhabited the tiny kingdom expended, for political advantage, enormous energy to find out the deeds and words of others. Willing and unwilling subordinates were tapped by superiors to become spies. They plied information from colleagues, lesser staff members, and even from custodial workers. Some of the latter had been at the Vatican for decades and enjoyed an occasional opportunity for gain or for celebrity status when a document, a pill bottle, or other evidence might be located in the routine task of tidying up Vatican apartments.

If one hoped to remain at the core of power, it was usually thought necessary to become part of a coalition, a coalition with a leader who might one day achieve the papacy. If a career path did not lead to the pope's inner circle, it was best to move on or at least try another path. For these reasons and others, it was determined that the child, Christian, would not be housed and schooled within the Vatican walls. The possibility of disclosure of his purpose was too risky.

Father Jonathan Kennedy was valued by those who had planned *The Return*. Fluent in more than a few languages, experienced, and exposed to all social and economic levels, Father Kennedy obtained results, working with even the most unpredictable personalities. He also held credentials. He was from a reputable and highly- connected family, respected in the United States and throughout Latin America. Although Jonathan suffered privately over *The Return*, he was committed. His family and their friends simply accepted his absences and infrequent visits. His loyalty was beyond question, and once Dr. Denny Dennison was safely away from Washington in a secure laboratory housed in Israel, most of Jonathan's time and energy had been dedicated to the child, located far away from the Vatican.

Father Kennedy had resisted dwelling on Christian's future, as he walked in and out of the child's life. But he drew close to fatherhood in actuality, if not biologically. Each time he visited Christian during the infant and then toddler stages, Jonathan found himself in the vortex of parental concern. He became totally engaged with a little boy he had rapidly grown to love.

Diego Hernandez saw the subtle change in Jonathan, and both knew that strategies for elaborate covers were needed for the years ahead. Avoiding discussions of their own deaths, they were nevertheless aware that the remaining group at the hour of *The Return* would be minimal. For now, everyone involved participated in the areas relative to their expertise—everyone but His Holiness Juan Carlos, who was briefed, but shielded. All experienced fulfillment and hope without remorse and felt confident that they would face their own eternities under God's grace.

Father Kennedy and Cardinal Hernandez had carefully selected tutors for Christian. In the beginning, the selection simply required faithful and trusted servants to provide the warmth and secure climate for the childish happiness necessary for a little boy. Elderly and kind, the early caregivers were led to believe that Christian was an abandoned baby, an *Esposito,* as orphans were named, perhaps born to a domestic in the employ of a member within the Colombian Church. They were easily persuaded to work for the holiest future for this child. They may have wondered but never voiced curiosity as to why he had not been formally adopted. They believed in and trusted their superiors.

As an infant, Juan Carlos agreed with Luís to place Christian in the care of their own beloved *niñera* from Bogotá, Graciella. Honored and thrilled to be needed again in her later years and to be entrusted with such a task, the venerable Graciella was provided with a young assistant to do the physical and housekeeping tasks.

Graciella had started preparation several weeks ahead of Christian's birth. After his birth, they resided together in her small comfortable apartment, where she lovingly devoted herself to the tiny infant, who, because he came to her from holy men, she decided to call Christian. She reported the baby's progress through simple handwritten letters sent to Luís at his family home and forwarded to his office by family members. No one questioned the personal envelopes from Graciella.

Luís and Jonathan made visits to monitor the small child and, without the benefit of experience, soon understood his needs and capabilities at different ages. Looking into Christian's cherubic face, they were confronted with the joy of semi-fatherhood, tempered by their guilt and fear for his future.

As Graciella raised Christian, she taught him the simple stories that Juan Carlos and Luís had so loved in their childhood. As a toddler, Christian was carefully integrated with other children and was instructed daily in a firm but simplified version of the Ten Commandments. Christian went through his paces with only minor difficulties. He was a bright and inquisitive child. Physically he was the perfect image. Having large green eyes, a medium complexion, and a head of soft dark brown curls, Christian appeared angelic.

To avoid inviting a lasting connection to their entrancing little student, instructors were hired for only short terms. Graciella had been forewarned of that intention early on, and although she longed for him when he was taken from her, she acquiesced, knowing that she was getting on in age and that Christian's growing requirements were more than she could offer. The separation, though gradual, was wrenching. Subsequent caregivers were careful to exercise patience, once they knew their services would be only temporary.

Christian's teachers and companions spoke a variety of languages. He grew up fluent in several tongues and dialects. Over time, there were scholars and linguists, physical trainers, and philosophers. Some teachers were psychologists, some were funny, others serious and tough, and some were lenient and always generous.

There had never been a guarantee, but by the grace of God, Christian grew into a healthy, intelligent, cooperative, and personable young man. Through strict athletic training, not only did he acquire a splendid athletic physique, but it was evident that his appearance, as hoped, would develop into a composite of the Jesus Christ created over the centuries by so many masterpieces.

Photographs of Christian were kept to a minimum and never transmitted electronically. They were produced using old technology—a Polaroid camera—and the accompanying film material was destroyed. Still, Luís, Jonathan, and Diego knew it would have been unthinkable to deprive the small group of devoted men of the opportunity to share in the changing images of Christian. They coveted the single photo taken twice a year, passing it among them, and hating to finally destroy it. Christian's facial features and coloring seemed faultless, and although the images were all too infrequent, they were beyond what had been envisioned and always brought renewed hope and joy. Each successive photo helped lessen their lingering doubts. Perhaps God was with them after all.

As for His Holiness, the Pope, the photos caused him great wonder. He committed them to memory, and without realizing it, his canvases portraying Christ bore a striking resemblance to Christian. Juan Carlos' strokes on canvas were unpremeditated and seemed to flow from a Godly hand.

Father Kennedy and Cardinal Hernandez carefully monitored Christian's progress. It was reassuring that those whom the young boy encountered were deeply imbued with a love of God. The planners discussed and carefully calculated the time, the moment when they would tell him of the mission ahead. The deed would fall to Jonathan Kennedy who understood that, at some point, Christian would confront the devil's introduction of doubt. He had to be fortified and ready.

At different ages of understanding and study, Christian was disguised and exposed to atheistic lectures and anti-Christian rallies. These outings were risky, but they tested and strengthened Christian's mind, as well as his devotion. He developed an ability to deflect the tempting, often logical reasons for a shallow denial of all he had been taught. After subjecting Christian and his Catholic teachings to general ridicule, he was probed and interrogated to determine any damage to his faith. As he progressed, Christian handled the defense of his teachings with calm and logical rebuttals.

Christian's unswerving faith and his growing readiness to understand the mission ahead were gratifying. As time went on and he matured, Jonathan broached the subject of Christian's sexuality with Luís and Diego. As he turned thirteen, it became obvious they needed to adapt to Christian's imminent maturity. These were difficult discussions since, for the few involved, it exposed their own weaknesses. Would he understand and agree to celibacy? Should masturbation be suggested as an acceptable behavior, even a desirable one? Should they consider pairing him with a woman? A young woman, an older woman? What would be the outcome of such actions in relation to their own moral authority? Would anything less than insistence on celibacy cause them to undermine their own principles? Would they lose Christian if they insisted on celibacy? Would he be honest with them?

During these days, Diego Hernandez prayed, as he so often did, on the mystery of human sexuality. He awakened one spring morning a few months before Christian's fourteenth birthday and felt overcome with the renewed beauty of spring. His own vows broken, Diego experienced the glory of the profound sexuality of earth now taking place. He had fought with himself over his denial of sin and argued with his confessor, Cardinal Salvador DeAngeles.

"How can the intricacies of new life manifest themselves in a display so magnificent without a loving, creative, and certainly approving God? Should we, like so many primitive cultures, *not find great joy* in the drama of the world reproducing itself, of the primal desire of wanting to bond, male to female?" he argued.

Cardinal DeAngeles nodded sadly, increasingly sympathetic to the observations of this fallen priest. "I pray for you Diego, but I cannot give you absolution, even though I recognize your happiness and the added ability it may bring to your tasks as we move forward. Within celibacy, all of us who adhere, presumably good men, surrender that wondrous portion of our human existence—our ability to physically love and to bear children. Never stop talking to God, Diego. You may perhaps hear his forgiveness, and if you do, act accordingly."

Diego and the others could only marvel at the progress Christian exhibited. Finding it exceedingly difficult to forego credit for his achievements, they tried to hide their pride and feel only gratitude and increasing satisfaction for Christian's Christ-like conduct and bearing.

For Christian, the journey to his destiny would not be without the complications of m oral law. Humans, endowed by the Creator with morality, faced the natural urge to propagate themselves. Christian was only slightly prepared when faced with what he had been taught was a great negative temptation.

When he turned sixteen, Jonathan formally introduced Christian to the mission. They had hiked and hunted during a three-day retreat at a quiet mountain cottage in the Andes belonging to Diego. Jonathan tried to anticipate the negative reactions, the shock that he would see in Christian, but there was none. Christian listened without surprise and only asked for some time alone. He left Father Kennedy in the doorway of the small house and walked to the nearby hills. For Jonathan the wait was long, and the longer he waited, the more the dark shadow of doubt swept over his landscape. *Would Christian walk out of their lives? What would he say to the others?*

Frightened and soon near panic, an increasingly distressed Jonathan had remained in the doorway, paralyzed. Feeling weak and sick as the sun changed position overhead, he wondered what judgment would await such a stupendous waste of life and faith for him and for the others. He thought about the early plans for Christian's curriculum and remembered Cardinal DeAngeles' teasing him about his extensive planning of Christian's education.

The Cardinal had told him the tale of Francois Rabelais' "Gargantua," in which the father had demanded of his son, Pantagruel, a great undertaking. DeAngeles had taken a well-worn text from a shelf and begun to read from it, "'I intend and insist that you learn all languages perfectly, first of all Greek; then Latin, then Hebrew, then Arabic and Chaldee. I wish you to form your style of Greek on the model of Plato, and of Latin on the style of Cicero. Let there be no history you have not at your fingers' ends, and study thoroughly cosmography and geography . . . .'" Jonathan listened as Cardinal DeAngeles read more of the requirement set forth for the young man. "'You should also have a perfect knowledge of the works of nature, so that there is no sea, river, or smallest stream you do not know for what fish it is noted, whence it proceeds and wither it directs its course; all fowls of the air, all shrubs and trees. Most carefully pursue the Talmudists and Cabalists, and be sure by frequent anatomies to gain a perfect knowledge of that other world called the microcosm, which is man.'" Cardinal DeAngeles had paused, smiled at Jonathan, and continued, "'Master these in your young days and let nothing be superficial ' Take this copy, Jonathan, it is an excellent teacher."

Jonathan had left the older Cardinal, reading the piece in its entirety. Later Jonathan committed it to memory and thought of it now as he waited. *We have only one chance, this one chance. Dear Christian, please don't abandon us*, he thought.

Then, he heard running and saw Christian jogging toward him smiling. Jonathan stood up and embraced him. Christian lifted Jonathan off the ground and swung him around. Putting him down again, he pulled away, nodding vigorously and laughing. "Yes, yes, yes. But, can we eat now? I'm starving."

After his seventeenth birthday, Christian was taken by Luís to the Israeli airbase, where he would meet Denny Dennison and undergo extensive training and grueling preparations for the final years before the mission. Apprehension was building among the Vatican conspirators. They fretted over whom this virile young man might meet, and their concern soon proved valid.

After arriving at the base, an instructor accompanied Christian to a briefing room for a preliminary look and orientation on the basic aircraft that would take Christian to Contadora Island. Not wanting to attract undue attention to Christian, Luís and Aaron Yakowitz prepared a cover story regarding a planned exchange of students.

Luís, mentally preoccupied with other concerns, had failed to ask for the identity of the briefer. As the young Israeli pilot came to the podium, Luís was struck by his blunder. One glance at Christian confirmed his reaction. Christian's upbringing had included women, but more recently for the majority of his formal classes, he had been tutored by men. Occasionally a younger married woman might be sought out for language or math. Credentials and background were thoroughly checked, and often Jonathan Kennedy or Cardinal Hernandez were present.

The young Israeli officer was tall and slender. Christian was visibly impressed by her appearance in her uniform khakis. Able to discern her figure through the loose fitting flight suit she wore, he didn't so much undress her visually but rather redressed her in gowns and fashions, as they appeared in magazines. Christian was startled and alarmed by the flushed feeling in his face and stirrings in his groin. Luís glanced at Christian, whose gaze was riveted on the young woman standing at the front of the room.

"Good morning, Sir," she addressed Luís, recognizing him as the senior officer present, indicated by the stars on his uniform. From her education in the militaries of the world, she recognized the rank of any member in uniform. To remind her, charts of the shoulder boards and arm insignias of the military forces of every country hung on the walls along the corridors leading to the briefing room, allowing her to pre-identify ranks. Although the highly-secure base didn't receive many foreign visitors, the colorful charts helped her to avoid error. "And *shalom* to all of you." She had dark hair, pulled back and collected within a black ribbon. Her smile revealed white teeth in a full mouth void of makeup. "I am Air Force Captain Alana Dyan, and I am very pleased to welcome you."

Christian was vaguely aware of her words.

"I will be giving you an orientation briefing this morning, followed by an unclassified intelligence briefing."

Christian heard Captain Alana Dyan's voice. It sounded honey-soaked, with a little rasp on the edge. She spoke in Spanish, and her slight accent captivated Christian. *What was it?* He was well-schooled in languages and understood it to be an accent, but had never heard anything so melodious and beautiful coming from a sensuous mouth so close in front of him. He never wanted it to stop.

Captain Dyan proceeded through the basic makeup of the IDF, the major headquarters of the various services, and some of the latest equipment. She asked for questions at the end of the first briefing and had a simple inquiry regarding manpower from a serious-faced Major, who felt it polite to question the young Captain. The rest of the students were too naïve and ignorant to react. Alana then proceeded to an intelligence briefing. She had done it many times but kept it fresh and current. The shifting situation in Israel was always edgy. Threats, bombings, kidnappings, snipers, and potential and real mortar attacks were ongoing. Alana gave some background.

"The Israeli air force has repeatedly demonstrated its ability to bring military power to bear at distant points and in unconventional operations. In 1976 its transport aircraft ferried troops to the Entebbe airport in Uganda to rescue passengers on a commercial airplane hijacked by Arab terrorists. In June 1981, F-16 fighter-bombers destroyed the Osiraq (Osiris-Iraq) nuclear research reactor near Baghdad, Iraq, flying at low levels over Saudi Arabian and Iraqi territory to evade radar detection. In 1985 Israeli F-15s refueled in flight and bombed the headquarters of the PLO near Tunis, Tunisia, at a distance of more than 2,000 kilometers from their bases." Her pride was obvious.

The cover of an exchange student, the charade of his being present, was known and accepted by Christian. He felt privileged to hear all this from this beautiful woman, and despite the illegitimacy of his presence, he could not take his eyes off Captain Dyan.

Luís felt some alarm, knowing that Christian's attraction to the young officer introduced an issue that had the potential to destroy years of work. In his heart, however, he empathized with the normal reactions of a young man. Luís could only gamble on the progression within Christian's mind that would determine the outcome.

After Captain Dyan's caution to her audience of the crucial need for Israel's constant vigilance, she announced the end of the briefing and once again asked if there were questions.

Now fearful of her disappearance, Christian blurted, "Can you tell me please, more about your country."

Alana glanced at the Lieutenant Colonel, who was the deputy in her office. He, in turn, looked at General Luís Gutiérrez, who nodded imperceptibly. Luís felt a boyhood amusement watching Christian's efforts to keep Captain Dyan in the room. He concealed his anxiousness.

"That's a comprehensive request," Alana smiled and said. "If you can remain awhile, I'll be happy to provide you with some maps and reading material. Would that be okay? If not, you can come by my office tomorrow."

In the mysterious world of human physical attraction, Luís Gutiérrez knew the inevitable was about to be tested. Having never abstained from sex, Luís had an atypical view of celibacy. He never mocked the choices of others. He consistently defended and sometimes even envied his brother, Juan Carlos,' choice of chastity. When in their late teens, Luís had bragged of his conquests and teasingly questioned his brother, Juan Carlos had placed his hand on Luís's shoulder and said, "I hope you will always treat the women who submit to you with great respect Luís. They are giving of themselves. I do not feel I deserve this from a woman, and I have fought the urge of desire. I think I'm stronger, and I embrace the challenge of celibacy. God has me totally. Perhaps He gave you the added dose of hormones," Juan Carlos added, grinning.

"But........."

"There is no but, Luís. It is what it is."

Luís simply nodded, embraced his brother, and spoke of it no more.

Now, he looked at Christian sitting in the classroom chair, willing Captain Dyan to stay longer. Luís recognized the physical pull exerted by the first unplanned stirrings of desire. The uninvited moment had arrived, and Luís had no weapon to fight it. His next steps, he knew, would be crucial.

"We will come by at ten hundred hours tomorrow," Luís said, looking at his watch. "Will that upset your schedule, Captain? Will that be okay for you?" he asked, turning his glance to Christian. Christian nodded, seeing the uncertainty in Luís's eyes.

"That will be fine, General," Alana replied respectfully. "I will look forward to your visit. Good afternoon." With that she turned and headed to the door.

"Thank you," Christian said, reluctant to see her depart. She turned at the door and smiled at him, detecting his innocence but feeling intuitively that the inner flame of the young student could be easily ignited.

The others departed, and Luís and Christian sat alone in the classroom. Luís looked out the window at the harsh Israeli wasteland beyond the base runways and then at Christian, whose face bore a worried expression. It was the most provocative moment of truth that Luís remembered, and he wished it had happened to Cardinal Hernandez or Father Kennedy, not to a womanizer like himself.

"There is a weakness in man, Christian, and it is meant to be. I have been privileged to witness it for you, as you have just seen it walk out through that door." Christian nodded, as he was incapable of lying to Luís. "In six months or so, you are to begin the most rigorous stage of your preparation for the mission. As I have told Father Kennedy and Dr. Dennison, I suspect it may prove to be *too* rigorous. Most of that will be up to you. Have you thought about this very much?"

Christian was thrown off momentarily, as he tried to decide which avenue of thought General Gutiérrez was taking. He sat quietly for a moment and then turned to Luís and looked at him thoughtfully. "I am afraid, of course. I am afraid for my own physical safety, and I am afraid for what I will miss in life, what I *am missing* in life. I am afraid for my soul. After the mission, I will need time to decide my future, as I will be free to carry out my life. I feel weakened in the presence of Captain Dyan. I'm attracted to her." Christian shook his head gently, "It is not my desire to worry you, any of you, but you might perhaps be more worried if I never exhibited any interest in females, don't you agree?" Christian smiled broadly at Luís Gutiérrez. Luís smiled back, nodding. He was suddenly no longer concerned.

When they met again, Alana had put several maps on the walls and had a folder of other information for Christian. She felt drawn to the young student, and it belied her usual self-control. Her attraction was not so much physical, although the perfect physical specimen in front of her desk was highly appealing. When Christian entered her office, she had felt a connection spiritually and fought back the desire to tell him. After a dutiful explanation of locations and missions, Alana invited Christian to lunch. Over soup and sandwiches in the base cafeteria, she responded to his questions about her family and her life.

"My father, Colonel Alan Dyan, flew fighter jets and was shot down shortly before my birth. He was still in the hospital when I was born." Captain Dyan was talking in the general direction of a photo in the small cafeteria. In the photo a pilot in his flight suit stood next to an aircraft. She smiled and said, "Despite an old superstition that says naming a child after a living relative is bad luck because the angel of death, an easily confused spirit, might take the baby by mistake when coming for the older relative, I was named Alana. My father died a few hours later. So, you see, I never knew him." Having no idea who his biological father was, Christian sympathized.

Curious over her feelings of comfort with Christian, Alana spoke at length about her childhood, her pilot training, the endless warring in the nation, and the missions she had flown. By the time, she left him to return to her duties, she realized she had learned very little about the young student.

Christian in the final analysis, exceeded the hopes of his superiors and mastered his carnal urges. Within the small group of men now fully engaged in the project, each looked into their own hearts and knew that often, they had not achieved the same success. They remained ewildered but immensely satisfied with what had been created in this extraordinary human being.

# ONWARD CHRISTIAN'S SOLDIER
## Contadora Island – April 2035

By the time April passes, the days of hot cloudless skies show hints of change. The swells of sweet water form daily in the Caribbean, as cyclonic low-pressure air picks up moisture from warm seas far away and rolls toward the Gulf of Mexico. Accompanied by thunder and brilliant lightening, heavy black clouds advance on to Panamá and begin to release their cargo on the Atlantic side of the isthmus. Traveling across the fifty-mile-wide strip and contributing untold gallons of fresh water to Panamá's Chagres River and to Lake Gatun, which supply the millions of gallons of fresh water required to get a single ship through the Panamá Canal, they quickly reach the Pacific and continue across the islands off the coast, fully emptying far out to sea.

By the end of May, rains will begin to fall again on the islands. October days will often boast two rainfalls, the first near noon and then again in the late afternoon. Since the rains are so predictable, and indeed, the thick dark clouds bloated with tepid water can be seen and heard from a distance, the islanders utilize the rumblings as a dependable signal to take cover and pull any forgotten laundry off the lines.

Never having known a father and suffering the reality that his very existence is the product of brief passion, Fulito grasps the need to be closer to Christian. A man with a past, Fulito was guilty of a host of petty thefts. He extracted money and gifts from unsuspecting tourists in the days of the island's grandeur. He duped young women, seduced them, and discarded them in many a dramatic vacation departure.

Now, although he regrets his actions and tries to understand this notion of salvation, Fulito is faced with new confusion. While he yearns to give himself over to the goodness that this Jesus, this Christ, this Lord offers, Fulito grapples with a devil that invades his dreams.

One early dawn, Fulito awakens slowly from sleep, possessed by a lingering image in which he is a man of importance. Still in his hammock, he listens to the emerging sounds of the early morning. As daylight appears, he gets up to start his chores, still dreaming of anticipated fame. The dream is hardly new, but in this case suggests that he is doing something with his newly-elevated position. Caught up in Christian's flattering definitions of them all, a new ego has surfaced, the self-importance at being one of the "chosen." Fulito can no longer endure the secrecy and, despite his unsavory past, he is unable to resist self-aggrandizement. He desperately needs to be someone again.

In his simple logic, Fulito has determined that no good will come from this event if the world remains unaware of Christian. The world for Fulito does not extend much beyond the string of tiny islands. Even the mainland—another world—has been limited to short visits and occasional television news programs. It is hardly a priority for Fulito, for whom fishing, its accompanying maintenance and worries, its abundance and scarcity, and its burden of responsibility for others, have kept him isolated and away from any quest for outside knowledge. Realization of his own ignorance has now overcome Fulito. If he is going to be an important messenger in spreading word of the coming of Jesus to his island, *his island*, Fulito needs more information.

That afternoon, Fulito approaches his Jesus hesitantly, uncertain of his questions or of Christian's reaction. But Christian's years of preparation have equipped him for almost any inquiry. Natural responses have been formulated somewhere deep inside. As Fulito questions, Christian listens attentively and understands his anxiety. Encouraged, Fulito becomes convinced by Christian's assurances that he *will* influence a worn-out world, bereft, in so many places, of hope.

Fulito questions Christian daily, seeking him out in the early hours, when he should have been tending his nets and his fishing. Fulito wants Christian to explain everything—how he got to the island, where exactly did he come from, and wherever that was, what did he do all day and night? What will he eat in eternity, where will he sleep? Fulito, believing he is only one of just a few to ever ask, looks at Christian with frustration and shouts, "Why are *you* here, and why are *we* all here?"

Despite Fulito's scanty education, he has been able to absorb Christian's teachings. Born to these islands and these waters, Fulito has fished the surrounding ocean since childhood. His uncanny instinct is second nature, and he is relied upon by Gordo and the rest to determine the daily direction and location for the most promising catch. Keenly observant and, although as terrified as the rest as he watched from his fishing boat while Jesus Christ came out of the sky, Fulito continuously mulls over shadowy memories of the descent. He scoured the area where he saw "Christ" go into the water, repeatedly diving and trying to find some evidence of the fall. How could the billowing garments have disappeared?

On many occasions, Christian has watched Fulito from the hillside. The intense questioning and burning curiosity of this man, set apart from the others by his striking blond hair, causes Christian to recognize that Fulito might well be the key to the intent of this undertaking. As he observes Fulito's doubt, he thinks about his lessons on the Gnostics, who perceived God as a "thought" that became an entity that brought wisdom and knowledge and truth. According to the Gnostics, God sent his son, Jesus Christ, to nurture the sparks of man to coax them into becoming divine beings. Christian, intrigued by such stories, wonders if the blond misfit on the beach holds sparks of divinity. *Is hethe loving betrayer, the Judas required as much now as in the Garden of Gethsemane?* Christian brushes aside his digression from Catholic dogma while exercising caution and patience, a patience that will hopefully propel Fulito into action.

Concentrating on Fulito's spiritual education as much as possible, Christian draws upon his years of study, converting large amounts of knowledge into simple messages. Unaware that passion for his own fame could generate the first sparks of righteousness and new faith in God, Fulito now becomes the primary focus of Christian's endeavors.

Mindful that he needs to teach the islanders in a way that permits the sustainability of mystery, Christian recognizes the dichotomy of his mission. He must capture the imaginations of the new apostles and implant a burning belief in himself— while still keeping himself a *mystery*. Will it be enough? Can he establish in Fulito, and the others for that matter, sufficient conviction to enable them to proselytize enough of the population and take a new message to the far corners of the world? Once they are caught up in the whirl of excitement initially kindled by Fulito's revelation, will the story of the presence of "Jesus" on the island be lasting and effective or will it die between the lines of a cynical press, never reaching the hearts of world-weary humanity? How many were lastingly touched by the miracles of Guadalupe, Fatima, Lourdes, and Medjigore? *This* massive undertaking needs to far surpass those and other visions of the Virgin Mary that lacked proof but which offered comfort and hope. In this age, the often dubious value of technology will spread the story of Christian, once fully revealed, in just hours.

Christian needs to move quickly. His thirty days on this staging area will soon be over. His scheduled pickup, an elaborate ruse planned long ago, is to be conducted by Colombian military frogmen during an exercise designed for the purpose. It has been timed precisely, with only minutes on either side.

Having often contemplated his future, ambivalence still plagues Christian, as he reflects on his options. With no definitive course, he knows the affection and devotion held for him by the planners in the Vatican do not mean a safe haven. How strange it seems that there will be no contact with any pope in Rome; knowledge of his effect on the world and on the behavior of the Holy Father will only come from public sources.

When Christian learned from Marcos of the death of Pope Juan Carlos on the very morning of his descent onto the island, he was stunned and frightened. He managed to gain control of himself and spoke to the islanders about the great reward granted to Pope Damasus for his service and his faith in his God. It was an unexpected event, but Christian used the fact of his presence among them as a means of comfort to the islanders and counseled them on the now even greater purpose of their work ahead.

Those Vatican personnel involved with *The Return* had already contemplated the dilemma presented by the question of Christian's future. Father Jonathan Kennedy had kept the future vague during their discussions, knowing that once his mission was completed, this extraordinary young man would need space and time to think in a secluded place. At the request of General Gutiérrez, Jonathan made early arrangements for Christian to reside temporarily at the small retreat in the mountains, where Jonathan first revealed the mission to Christian.

And so, the hoped and prayed-for deed; the outcome of this extravagant, well-intended and holy hoax; and the betrayal of the new *Jesus* was seeded in the mind of a *campesino* fisherman. With all the technology at their disposal, no one within the Vatican, no one with any connection to this adventure could have anticipated who would be the first to seriously think of revealing Christian's presence. The planners had truly relied on the transformative power of grace and entrusted the great mission ahead to a small mass of simple people living marginalized at the edge of humanity. That Fulito, through Christian, would succeed in taking the first tentative steps was beyond their knowledge. They had only their well-honed store of human psychology to enable them to calculate when and how this might occur. With their monstrous feat in motion, they could only pray for God's favor.

As God's creature, when Fulito's divine spark formulated a simple plan to tell of *The Return* and of its message, would God approve?

# CHRISTIAN AND MARCOCITO
## April 2035

Sitting among the island children, Christian is mindful of their idolization, rooted in great part in their memory of his mysterious descent. Those children who were present to witness the event possessed an extraordinary mental absorption. Unburdened with a more mature reaction of thought regarding the how and why, these children are able to summon up every detail. Within hours of Christian's arrival, they lost no time in describing the vision to others. Although secondhand versions could never match the images recalled by those who were present, an added tendency to some embellishment was irresistible and helped to assuage the disappointment of those not actually present.

But the children's love of Christian is sincere. They see him as the embodiment of good. In their innocence, they are full of grace and are in the enviable state of having perfect faith in God, through Christian's portrayal of Jesus Christ. Their trust is sometimes troubling, as Christian contemplates his departure from this idyllic setting.

Leaning against large rocks jutting out from the sand near where Christian had landed, the children are attentive to Christian's drawings made in the smooth wet sand with a staff that was cut for him by Marcos' machete. The machete, for centuries considered a symbol of power to the poor throughout much of the continent, is for the islanders no longer a weapon capable of penetrating deep into enemy flesh but an ancient tool used to clear the land, dismember meat and fish, slice papayas, cut banana stalks, hack branches for the cooking fire, or decapitate a snake and rendering it less poisonous without a head. Using his smaller knife, Mario carved the head of the staff into a fat pineapple, symbolizing friendship, and Christian carries it with him at all times.

No one has access to modern cameras or equipment, but the need to record the miracle of Christian's presence occurs to them. There are no photos of the descent, and even though Fulito and others have taken snapshots, Christian manages not to pose deliberately, and so the images do not display much detail. In these photos, Christian appears to be just one in a group, and his unspoken wish not to be photographed has been for the most part respected. He explains that the veneration of the event of his presence will be manifest in more subtle ways and in a different medium. "It will flow from *you*," Christian convinces them.

Marcos watches Mario's first attempts to capture Christian's likeness in wood. Able to carve most any figure from gnarled chunks of driftwood found washed up on the beach, Mario sees hidden figures within the dry and twisted branches. Marcos envies his father's eye for the graceful line a particular grain will produce, resulting in a finished piece using natural distortions in the wood.

Never having developed this skill, Marcos recollects his vain struggle to force his own babyish fingers to mimic his father's movements. Without Mario's talent, Marcos soon abandoned the effort, and Mario never pushed him. When it became evident that his son's passion was books, Mario encouraged him by locating reading material, always scarce on the island. In the past, he had asked hotel guests and visiting boaters for castoff books and papers, which resulted in an eclectic array of subjects. Pilots from the planes servicing the island also helped by delivering books to Marcos, and after time he easily read both Spanish and English.

Grateful for his son's education at American schools, Mario felt proud of Marcos' position, representing his islands in the national assembly. Mario allowed Marcos to find his own way, insisting only that his son learn the craft of weaving shrimp and lobster traps and, most important, the art of casting a fishing line with ease and precision. He proved to be a natural and loved mornings with his father prior to his career in politics. For some years there had been only the business of the assembly and little time left for such pleasures. Now, with

Christian's arrival, Marcos' priorities shifted to again indulge in the simple contentment of being with his father and his son, Marcocito.

Showing an exceptional talent for carving, Marcocito has become his grandfather's prize pupil. The timing is ideal, and Marcos feels satisfaction and amazement in his son's ability to emulate his grandfather. Mario, attentive to the detail in Christian's body and face, soon observes his grandson's smaller fingers imitating his work. Laboring to create his own memory of that morning in his crudely hacked pieces of wood, Marcocito displays a fierce determination to depict the images burned into his consciousness. Within a short time, as Marcocito's skills are honed, the child wants to discard earlier carvings, but Mario insists that he keep them, even though he cannot yet grasp the significance that his and Marcocito's creations will hold for the future. Wood- carved portraits of Christian from the world's logs and branches carried on calm and stormy seas to the island's beaches will be an unexpected bonus to the Vatican. The carvings, simple proof of the miraculous event, will be later replicated and reproduced in the millions.

With deep affection for this new Savior they call *Jesus,* and despite his lingering skepticism over the reality of it all, Marcos does everything he can for Christian to ensure his comfort and safety. He is uncertain of the future but keeps Christian's presence private.

The islanders, convinced Christian *is* Jesus Christ returned, also feel a need to protect him. Prior years of ostentatious tourism have steeled them against uncaring outsiders, knowing that they had often been ignored and perhaps cheated by foreigners. Excitement generated from planeloads of moneyed tourists wore off once they understood that their smaller bodies and nutty brown skin fit into this new world as only a temporary exotic attraction. The end came about abruptly with the entrance to power of a new and often abusive dictator in Panamá. In fear of the vise of a drug-trafficking nation, the swarms of tourists disappeared.

Initially disappointing, the feeling of loss was fleeting, and the adjustment by the islanders took less time than the forest growth. Most had developed natural protective cocoons to preserve their simple culture. The reversion back to traditional ways was the setting the planners of *The Return* had hoped for. Unaware of their future role, they did not understand the need to prepare to spread Christian's message. Even though their miraculous Christ had awakened their belief in equality among all people, they still felt inadequate and had not yet acquired the desire to take his message to the wider world. They made no demand to be acknowledged beyond the fact of their existence. Ever aware of their future on his behalf, Christian strives to prepare them.

Seated against a rock, Christian wears a native *montuna*, made for him by Marisol's mother. It consists of a simple unbleached cotton shirt and drawstring pants like those worn by the men of the region for generations. With the tradition of the shirt still used by native dance troupes in the city, and in the hinterlands, the skill of embroidering on the shirts, with their open collarless necks, has been passed down for generations. The colorful stitching can be highly detailed, and for Christian's, a primitive rendition of his arrival has been stitched across the back with a small cross over the area of the heart. It serves him perfectly and respectfully sets him apart from the other men, who now don T-shirts from a variety of sources. Christian finds the shirt and pants to be cool and comfortable. Other than a handed-down swimsuit, he wore the outfit constantly.

The children around Christian are usually clad in bathing trunks or shorts, along with the inevitable T-shirts. Many of them wear baseball caps, given to them in lieu of monetary tips by departing tourists. Cases of hats and T-shirts bearing the island's name and left behind at the hotel shop were eventually distributed to the islanders. They are the only practical items left, and over time, their meaning has faded from memory, along with the past.

Christian instills in his students the knowledge of the marvelous power of God, instructing them that the creation of the galaxies provided an additional spectacle for the senses of man on earth. He reinforces their own creation story and presence, telling them how privileged they are to see more of the celestial and heavenly bodies here in this remote setting than in crowded light-filled cities. He himself marvels at the sensation of being able to almost touch the heavens.

Usually sitting with Marcocito at his side, Marcos listens attentively, deeply appreciating Christian's words, fondly recalling blissful days and nights with Nina Shelky, under these same heavens over two decades ago.

As the high tide approaches and eventually covers the drawn circles and stars, Christian reminds them of God's prerogative in the fate of all. Day after day he teaches them, mesmerizing them, as he speaks convincingly of the existence of God. The innocence of their minds sometimes disturbs Christian. They become drunk with the love of God, and Christian fights his worry over his expectations of the islanders. *Are they up to it? How can they possibly be expected to change the world?*

On walks on hot and eroding roads, Christian marvels at the tenacity of the thriving palms and succulents able to bear the scorching sun. He asks Mario to dig up a cactus, so they see with new eyes the phenomenon of endurance, the gift of everlasting life. He creates parables, using the patience of the dry trees as the point of instruction on the promise of the kingdom to come. He had known of the transformation of the island's plant and animal life with the first rain. Seeing it, however, Christian's thrill at the life created by the sweet rain is contagious. New growth is rapid, and he is delighted to share the miracle with those who had long taken the phenomena for granted.

After one of the first intense afternoon rains, Christian reflects alone on one of the smaller beaches. His breaks from the group are more frequent, as he confronts a growing melancholy. At the bottom of a rocky cliff, Christian watches Marcocito select a large branch that has washed ashore. Marcocito sits down on the sand with his knife to address the challenge of the wood. He holds the piece at different angles, deciding on the location of the first cut. Christian joins him, and they sit together facing the sea.

"How do you choose the wood you carve?" Christian looks at Marcocito with deep affection, while the boy brushes sand from his new piece and in his mind, already pictures the likeness of Christian he sees in the wood.

"I find the driftwood on these beaches," he answers, searching Christian's face for new details to be cut into this latest work. "The rains wash logs and branches ashore, and they dry in the sun over the course of the winter, the 'dry season.' I often wonder where they come from." Carefully examining the piece after his first cut, Marcocito smiles at Christian.

"You take the dead and raise it up to a new life," Christian says, nodding toward the carving.

"Like you, Jesus?"

Christian feels a pang of shame. "Yes, and perhaps far more effectively, *miamigito*. As you grow, the spirit that is now inside of you will grow as well. You will make mistakes and change your mind many times. A great noisy flood of doubting words will assail you, and you will be challenged to defend what has happened here. Someday you will become a great leader; but in the meantime, you must stay strong, Marcocito."

"But, Jesus, I know so little, and I don't know how to say it. One day I will know, but for now, I can carve you." he looks at Christian and with a beaming smile, holds up the hard gray wood bearing the beginnings of his newest proof, his compelling need to record Christian's presence. His talent blooms with each new effort to recreate the amazing sight he witnessed above him on the jetty ledge just weeks ago.

Both Marcocito and Mario seem in competition to shape the finest images. Mario is energized by the work, but in his heart, wants Marcocito to excel. All the while, the creative whittling allows Mario to instruct Marcocito in finding the precise positions of the hands and feet in the lines and color of the wood, gracefully draping the folds of the billowing cloth they beheld during the first moments of Christian's fall to earth and providing accuracy in the details in the face. Both of them have started head carvings that will allow a larger surface for facial features. Marcocito's understanding of the wood's shape and textures is keen. He is able to see Christian in branches and logs and needs only to extract him.

"Why do you make so many carvings of me?"

Marcocito looks into Christian's face. "To show people that you were here." He returns to his work. "How long will you stay? I don't want you to go away. I have to prove to the world you are real, and I'm afraid. I'm afraid there will not be enough time for me to know what to do. Please tell me, how long will you stay here?"

Picking up a small chip from the beach, Christian is overcome with remorse at the deception he has perpetrated upon this paradise. The monumental trickery used to get him here suddenly overshadows the noble effort to overturn the horrors taking place elsewhere. For Christian, here and now, war and death and the moral decay of humanity seem worlds away.

He chooses his words haltingly, "Marcocito, I may not be who you believe me to be. I am growing fearful for all of us. I too am afraid," Christian blurts out, unthinkingly.

Stopping his work, the child looks up at Christian. "Afraid? Why would *you* be afraid?"

"I am afraid that we are asking too much of you. You are so few, and the world has such treachery." Christian is now weeping. "It is wrong to ask you to take on such a task, to ask you to solve the causes of centuries of conflict that *no one* has ever been able to solve."

Tears stream down Christian's face, as he visualizes the now-dead pope he never met. Visions of Denny Dennison, Jonathan Kennedy, and Luís race across his mind. The years of dedication, the gamble of Aaron Yakowitz, the courage of Avi Noam, and even the unwitting participation of Alana Dyan—all of these images painfully lurch through his mind, bumping and jostling for attention. Filled with loathing for his treachery, Christian closes his eyes and dread fills him.

"Don't worry, Jesus," says Marcocito, now becoming concerned at Christian's sadness. "We'll be alright. We'll just do our best."

"But I'm not......."

"Yes, you are," Marcocito says, with the matter-of-fact assurance of the very young. "Yes, you *are*." he says again, louder and more insistently.

Christian opens his eyes and looks into the child's face, seeing there a strange authority, wisdom and something else. He nods almost imperceptibly.

Marcocito holds the unfinished wood likeness out in front of him and then wraps it and his knife in a cloth at his side. He moves closer and puts his small arm over Christian's shoulder. Christian feels the hardness of the young strong muscles that work wood into his likeness. "Please now, tell me when you will go away. We need to be ready for that."

"Not much longer, but it will be long enough." Christian feels the calm pass through him, as he grasps the significance of this brief exchange. They look at each other with understanding and acceptance. "Marcocito, I feel the Holy Spirit at this moment. I believe you will become a great messenger to the world."

Neither of them could know then how precious Marcocito's carvings would become, but in these moments, gazing at his own face in the piece of wood, Christian feels his resolve returning.

They walk up the beach, Marcocito carefully holding his latest carving and leaving the whittled fragments behind. The incoming tide would claim them.

In the months after the revelation, Nina Shelky tried to make sense of the reported miracle. Remembering the past joy of the island, she felt she understood a godly decision to stage an attempt to spread new hope in this particular setting. Perhaps they were divinely directed after all. Nina reread her earlier composition and recalled her memories of the beaches of Contadora Island. As she wrote, a story began to take form but was frequently overtaken by her memories of Marcos.

Within weeks of the reported miracle on Contadora Island, Nina Shelky began to lose sleep in the impossible task of staying ahead of the volume of press coverage. Trying to make sense of the reports—the factual and the blatantly fabricated—her mind was never far from her own memories of the island. Nina felt she understood a godly decision to stage an attempt to spread new hope in this particular setting. Notwithstanding a pestering hunch of her own involvement, a hunch she continuously discarded as purely arrogant, Nina tried to surrender herself to the wondrous possibility of an absolute miracle. Even though she prayed that such speculation could be the truth and a new world might prevail, she could not help but formulate a variety of fictional possibilities. *Was such a descent divinely directed?* Nina reread her earlier notes that had resulted in her article of long ago. The phrases and descriptions revealed her passion, and certain passages made her blush as she recalled her memories of Marcos and the beaches of Contadora Island.

# Behold, the Angel of Death
## April 2035

Gordo sits on the bench in the stern of the boat, and, as he is prone to do, dozes while maintaining a light but sensitive grip on his pole. Neither a fish nor the pole has ever gotten away from him.

Lucas, used to voids in conversation, busies himself in anticipation of hooking another bonita. One large hook is already baited and thrown over the side to drop to a depth of about twelve feet. The remaining rope lays coiled in the bottom of the boat, with its end fastened to the stern by a large hook screw.

Fulito, nervously harboring the secret of his revelation of Christian to people in Panamá the day before, sits quietly on the center bench, thinking about his life and his future. Feeling dejected at the reaction of those he told, Fulito now suffers shame. The disappointment is impossible to express, as it would tip off his indiscretion. For now, he battles his remorse. Thoughts of his foolishness cause him to be silent.

Gordo and Lucas ignore him and lower their nets into the clear water. They have yet to hit a good school of fish and have drifted out a half-mile northwest of Mogaba Island, counting upon deeper water to save an otherwise unproductive day. Their hope is to catch the silvery corvina in their nets and, with sturdy poles and baited hooks, perhaps catch a grouper. Grouper can run into the hundreds of pounds, but Gordo and Lucas are hoping for twenty to twenty-five pounders. That would be good luck. It would give them enough for their restaurant shipment later in the day, and the remainder could be slowly roasted over their open fire pit and feed a good number of their small community. Using poles is also an opportunity to enjoy the sport of fishing, a luxury outside the day-to-day need to provide for their families.

Once the nets are in place and the poles set with hooks and chunks of Bonita, the men talk. When "shop talk" of boats and equipment is over, they speak of the miracle of Christian. They have taken him fishing several times, which always resulted in a good catch. While such bountiful harvests produced while he is aboard might not be considered miraculous, they associate his presence on their boats with success.

Over the past weeks, they have all broached subjects which they once would have hesitated to bring up. First, they consulted Mario or Marcos or Gordo about various religious teachings, seeking their approval to ask Christian. "*Por favor, Don Mario,*" Lucas would address the elder Mario formally, knowing the issue required reverence and a humble attitude if they were to be taken seriously. "Is it proper to ask Jesus how he was able to walk on the water?" Mario, terrified to be perceived as impertinent or rude but also curious for an answer, counseled them to not be afraid and to ask Christian directly.

When Lucas finally acquired the nerve, it was on the beach, as they got ready to depart for the afternoon. With a hearty lunch of meat, soup, and rice in his belly and a short nap to strengthen his resolve, Lucas found his voice.

Christian, having answered Fulito's ceaseless questions for many days and now expecting, and desiring, many more, looked at Lucas and said gently, "Lucas, you and the others are people of faith. You possess a natural and uncorrupted faith. When Christ was first here on earth, miracles were performed to nurture faith and hearten mankind, which knew no hope of salvation. As a man, the destiny of Jesus was not to remove himself from the suffering of the cross. It was to die for the forgiveness of all mankind and for the faith of new generations."

"Yes Lord, but . . ." Christian knows there will be many "buts," as like children, their curiosity and desire to understand are limitless. He had expected this and been drilled in hundreds of answers to a myriad of possible questions that might form in the minds and spring from the mouths of these ingenuous people.

"Yes, Lord, but aren't you yourself Jesus Christ?" blurts out Gordo. "You can do anything you want." Lucas nods nearby, grateful that Gordo is once again taking charge.

Christian turns to Gordo and lays his hand on the strong brown shoulder of the large gentle man. "No, Gordo, I was not sent here to *test* your faith. I believe you *have* that. Our Father above knows you do. I am here to reaffirm your faith and to ask you to treat my time here as instruction that you will pass on to the world."

"To the entire world, Lord?" Gordo's expression is of disbelief and confusion. "We are poor islanders and know little of the world. How are we to have any effect beyond these islands?"

Fulito broke in tentatively, "You can have the whole world as a kingdom." He imagines, as do many, images of Jesus wearing a crown and reigning over the earth. "Why did you pick this little island? Why," he asks, "did you pick us?"

Christian, knowing of Fulito's absence over the last two days, smiles at him. "Yes, the kingdom is vast. Nevertheless, it is not the world as you are thinking. My realm is the human heart." He puts his arm around Fulito's shoulder. "*You* are the human heart, and you have *already* affected the world."

Fulito looks at Christian in alarm. *He knows. He knows what I've done.* In his mind he begged God's forgiveness for his clumsy revelation on the mainland yesterday. Frightened, Fulito begins to stammer, "Oh, Lord, I "

"Hush, Fulito." Not knowing what action he may have taken, Christian decides to speak with Fulito alone later after the boats return. "As yet, no harm has been done," Christian continues softly. "When I leave here, I will live on in you, and you will spread the word of my coming. You will not be believed at first, but with all of you as a single voice, the world will come to believe little by little what has taken place here."

Lucas felt naked and helpless at the thought of Christian's departure but remained quiet.

"Leave us?" Fulito looks perplexed. He is shocked but relieved. He has been indiscrete concerning the miracle of Christ Jesus on his island, but perhaps it has not been a mistake after all. In truth, the few on the mainland whom Fulito had regaled with the tales of Christ returning from the heavens were more than skeptical.

Unaware that his reckless divulgence had been hoped for, that it was his purpose to initiate this first inept disclosure to humankind outside his small island world, Fulito still fears he has committed an unforgivable sin. Those to whom he told the outlandish story had tucked the wild tale away in their minds. Fulito had always been somewhat of a braggart, and they concluded that too much of their native liquor, *Seco*, had produced the story. For now they remain unaware of their future star value until the outside world's full attention is on Fulito's island. They too will be able to retell the story and be believed.

Lucas and Fulito follow Gordo to their boat with renewed purpose. They say nothing but push off the beach and prepare for their work. Each is lost in his own thoughts, as their boat moves across the warm blue water.

Christian's words of the coming end to his stay here on earth have caused Fulito to panic. *Leave us?* Fulito's mind keeps repeating the question. *Leave us? How can I be anybody without him? I have to tell him what I have done. I will tell him when we return this afternoon, or I will tell him tomorrow. I will tell him, and he will forgive me.*

As the three men walk to their boat and complete their preparations, Christian hears the small engine come to life and take them out to sea. He feels uneasy. The sensation is contradictory. Everything is in place, and the mission is coming to an end. He will soon be removed, *rescued,* from this beautiful and satisfying quest, this false and deceptive charade. He feels sick as he repeats, "Forgive me, God. Forgive me, God.

Forgive us all." The three men and their boat become a small speck in the distance.

Gordo, Fulito, and Lucas are far out to sea. Lost in thought, they pay little attention to their work or to the boat's inevitable creaks as it bobs in the calm waters. At sea they are hardly alone, but they are not prepared for what prowls nearby.

Two miles from their boat, a dark shadow knifes through the deep water. From above, an observer wouldsee a 20-foot brownish gray Tiger shark making her way toward a fishing boat of equal length. Like other members of her suborder, she is characterized by five-gill clefts, two dorsal fins, and one anal fin. Her fading mottled stripes indicate her maturity. She is one of an aggressive genus of sharks in the "requiem" group, a voracious hunter with a slender body and rounded snout—a sleek and hungry killer. Intrepid attacks on man, although infrequent, have generated her fearful reputation. Her presence in these Pacific waters of Central America is rare but the fossil record indicates that she has been fulfilling her predatory role in the world's oceans for eons. Unknown to the Contadora fishermen, her distance from them is rapidly lessening.

Having traveled for weeks after straying from the Australian reefs, she now circles warily in the currents off Mogaba Island. Unsuccessful in finding sufficient prey in her immediate surroundings, she has ventured closer to the islands, trying to appease her gnawing hunger.

She catches the scent of the bonita flesh on Gordo's line several hundred yards away and swims in its direction. With the scent stronger, she circles twice well beneath the boat. Then, wary of the shadow above her, she circles once more, while concentrating on her target. Bursting up at an angle, her jaw clamps over the chunk of meat and yanks, causing several yards of the heavy line to play out from the boat in a quick jerk. The line itself slides into a space between her rows of razor-sharp teeth. Before it lodges there, the hook at the end of the rope sinks into the soft roof of her mouth. Surprised and confused by the sharp pain, she thrashes through the water, trying to quell the excruciating throbbing in her mouth. The line slackens, and she circles back toward the boat. Reaching the surface, she briefly sees the small vessel and the men in it. Instinctively, she dives again, and in the effort to free herself, she instead further tightens the line, embedding the large hook deeper into the roof of her mouth. As it tears into her flesh, she becomes frantic.

Startled by the sudden watery cyclone surrounding them, Lucas watches in fear as the line uncoils and plays out. The end is tied to a ring implanted deeply into a three-inch thick block of wood. The block is fastened with six-inch nails bent back upon themselves, after having been hammered through the side of the boat. It is strong but has only been tested closer to shore.

Lucas sees the tautness of the line and feels the boat being dragged through the water, its bow dipping in and out of the surf and seawater flooding in with each erratic pull. As they catch sight of the huge gray body, they know what will happen. They have seen this before and know the futility of fighting such a monstrous foe.

Gordo scrambles for his knife and glances at Lucas, with a flash of reluctance at giving up their hook and their heavy line. Fulito, fearing death and an eternity in Hell, is unable to move. Losing the shark, despite the value of the fins and meat, now dismays them little. Their boat, their equipment, and their lives now drive their actions. The boat is yanked through the surf, as Gordo desperately hacks at the tight line and finally cuts through it.

The shark feels the release but no relief from the pain. Continuing to thrash wildly for several moments, her head breaks through the surface once again, causing additional panic to the boat's occupants. Her body arches spasmodically and hits the starboard side of the primitive hull with great force, threatening to capsize the small craft. The men cringe in fear at the terrible sight of their rope and hook lodged between row upon row of jagged teeth inside her gaping mouth. At last she sinks back into the sea, and the swirling water subsides into its usual gentle wavelets. Lucas tentatively pulls the line, now short and limp, back into the boat. The men remain tense for long moments, until certain that the enormous shark has departed. They begin the trip home. Lucas prepares another line but waits until they are closer to the island. Looking tentatively at Gordo, who nods his approval, Lucas throws the newly baited hook over the side. He monitors it as Fulito heads the small boat back toward Mogaba, and within a short time, Lucas pulls in a large grouper. His fear is forgotten.

With no memory of the boat or of her would-be executioners, the shark swims aimlessly for ho rs, the pain causing her to lose all sense of direction. Her heart rate has increased, but with fatigue, her pace slows. She plunges into deeper water and to the seabed. Resting on the soft sand, she tries repeatedly to swallow the sharp matter in her mouth. Slowly waving her dorsal fins, attempting to rest and reduce the adrenalin coursing through her body, she drifts to a rock formation and settles in under the overhang of a large flat rock. Her efforts are unsuccessful. The physical exertion necessary to force out the foreign object is torture and further irritates the deep and ripping puncture in the roof of her mouth.

With only a rudimentary brain, she has no concept of her fate. Crazed by the combination of pain and hunger and the taste of her own blood, she is reduced to primitive survival instincts. Gathering strength, she swims up closer to the surface and knifes her way blindly through the peaceful morning ocean toward the rock jetty close to shore. Her eyesight is keen, but the throbbing pain distracts and disorients her, and navigation is confounded.

As she races to escape her suffering, she dives again to the depths. Again drained of energy, she hovers close to the ocean floor. Abruptly, her brain registers the electric current of a beating heart and detects the presence of more blood. The direction becomes clear. She makes her way toward her destiny.

# APPOINTMENT WITH ETERNITY
## April 2035

Christian awakened before dawn. Lying in the hammock that has served as his bed for the past weeks, he feels the invigorating power of a new day. Although he begins to feel its strength flowing through him, he remains reluctant to transition from dreamy sleep to consciousness and resists the reality of waking. Daily rebirth quickly erases the images of dreams and forces physical movement—despite the mind's inner battle to hold on to a face, an occurrence, a different life.

Rising up out of his peaceful slumber, Christian senses the first hints of light. His fading dreams are replaced with sounds—the feathery melody of the air and the gentle creak of the tree trunk that supports his hammock. He listens to birds, insects, and small indeterminate noises in the nearby jungle. He has heard this many times here and while growing up, on outings to study nature and to learn the boundless mysteries of God's Earth.

But always in the background is his favorite sound—the ocean. As the breakers climb up the beach, their crashing, limitless energy transmits a sense of awe of the ever- present and powerful ocean. Even at a distance, Christian knows instantly that the tide is rising and is almost at its highest level. After weeks of listening, he recognizes the absence of the faintly melancholy echo of withdrawal that characterizes an ebbing tide. He has become, in this short period, able to identify the stages of the tide almost unconsciously. Although less audible at the center of the island, the faint whisper is always present.

Christian pictures the still uncovered portions of the beach, and in his mind, sees the water rising over the surface of the white sand. He imagines standing at the water's edge and gently sinking into the wet yielding sand, creating soft sucking pools that cover his feet. He has done it so many times.

Then the pleasant sounds and thoughts are replaced with the uneasiness experienced on the previous afternoon. *Oh God, what are these moments of apprehension?* He grips his stomach and tries to focus on prayer to rid himself of the unpleasant sensation.

The air is cool during these early morning hours, yet he feels perspiration within his arm pits and across his forehead. Damp hair clings to the back of his neck, and strands are pasted to his cheeks from the frequent twisting of his head during a restless night of Hellish dreams. In Christian's erratic sleep, Hell is the terrifying place he read of in Dante's "Divine Comedy," as in the mural on the rear wall of the Sistine Chapel. Christian conjures up Michelangelo's frightful, larger-than-life portrayal of "The Last Judgment."

Like many visitors to the Vatican Museums, Christian often hurried through the rooms and corridors during his education to hasten the climax, the arrival at the Sistine Chapel. In private visits he spent hours there, as experts tutored him on its art and its portrayal of the mages defining man's relationship with God. His instructors, the finest in Italy, were told nothing of the reasons behind Christian's detailed studies, and with so many students of varying ages, they soon forgot the young boy, who had demonstrated little enthusiasm for the lessons but had assimilated them with quiet ease.

Like so many rooms in Rome, not a corner of the chapel had escaped the artists' touch. Arching over it all was the magnificent ceiling and the magic of Michelangelo's brush. Michelangelo had disguised the sharp corners of the chapel creating the illusion of a gentle curve leading to the painted account of Creation.

Christian wondered at God's evident love for Michelangelo to have blessed him with his talent. The entire Chapel was a treasure to Christian, but his eyes invariably moved, were drawn to, "The Last Judgment" wall, with its intense Jesus officiating at the awful and decisive ceremony, his right arm held aloft in a moment of ruling, his eyes focused downward on an unknown soul. He is almost naked but stands on a long strip of swaddling which travels up behind his legs, over his lap, up his back and over his left shoulder.

Christian had grown to understand Michelangelo's choice of the ceiling for the story of Creation and the wall for Judgment Day. The contrast always startled him—a short existence after the miracle of life and then the frightening implications of eternity.

The Virgin Mary sits by Christ's right side, a demure yet non-judgmental expression on her downcast face. Her look of melancholy frames Christ's decisiveness, which was burned into Christian's young memory. He was afraid, for their facial expressions and their posture indicated to him that the soul being judged in the painting had been eternally damned. Mary could do nothing for him.

Now, in the final days of his mission, Christian sees himself as one of the crowd of souls surrounding Jesus, awaiting their eternal fate. He wonders how he will be judged. He wrestles with his obligation to those who sent him and tries not to imagine the potential consequences for him and for the Holy See if the truth were to be exposed. *Yet, no matter,* he cringes in thought, *Christ will know the truth!*

In tempering his fear, Christian's self loathing is lessened, reflecting that it is the greater glory of God that is intended. *Only good can possibly come from this.* He puts thoughts of sacrilege in a deep recess in his mind. Christian has been drilled in doctrine, and his whole being, body and soul, is infused with obedience to God and faith in his mercy. It cannot be otherwise.

Imagining himself as a lamb, a lamb he identifies with in so much of scripture, Christian recalls his agreement to be led and has a defined purpose to do good. He feels chosen, but the mental wrestling never stops, and he reluctantly acknowledges that no matter how noble his intentions, he is *pretending* to be Jesus Christ.

In the dark dawn, uneasiness about the future again wheedles its way in. He ponders the scheduled retrieval, an elaborate military operation, now only days away. Christian is to swim under the cover of darkness to a small beach on Mogaba Island and make his way to the far uninhabited side, where two Colombian frogmen will be waiting. They will dress him in a light wetsuit and use powered, hand-held engines to ferry him to a miniature four-man submarine waiting some two miles off the coast. The sub will in turn meet a Colombian U-boat that will take the men and the sub aboard and continue in secret and silence to their target location.

Other than Christian, the participants will be part of a joint military exercise, testing the defenses of the Colombian navy. As cover, they will pick up several Navy Seals from other islands over the period of a week. Christian will fake illness late in the exercise and be transferred to Bogotá, where Jonathan will intercept him. After several days of debriefing, he will travel to the small mountain retreat in Colombia, funded by Luís. There he will rest and have time to reflect on his future. At the request of Cardinal Hernandez and Luís, and after a suitable interval, he will be allowed his freedom—if he so wishes it. *Freedom*, thinks Christian. *What shall I do with freedom?*

General Aaron Yakowitz planned every detail of Christian's extraction with Luís Gutiérrez. Christian has rehearsed numerous times in varying conditions, calculating times and distances by the clear heavens full of guiding stars. He no longer wants to think about it and longs to have it behind him.

Reaching back and grasping the sides of his hammock with both hands, Christian swings his body to the side and raises his legs over the edge of the thick fabric. He lightly surveys the cement slab floor with his feet, seeking his rubber sandals. He is hungry and wishes it were later, so Marisol or Anna would be up to make breakfast. He would like to cut the mangos and papaya and banana and feels that the simple rite of a shared breakfast would help to quell his apprehension. He craves the fresh eggs, fried plantain, baked bread spread with guava jam, and thick sweet coffee that have been prepared for him each morning.

But knowing it is too early to disturb others, he decides to walk. He will make his way to one of the beaches to swim and pray and think. The exercise and meditation will make his breakfast more enjoyable when he returns, and his mind will be clear.

Christian folds the light blanket and stows it at the top of the hammock. His movements disturb a small lizard near the hammock's wall ring. It darts up the wall and disappears into an impossibly tiny crevice. Slipping his feet into his sandals, he makes his way down the trail to the northwest side of the island, fighting the pervasive foreboding accompanying him.

Walking to a mostly-deserted part of the island, Christian again feels perspiration bead up and trickle down his body, despite the cool dawn air. It isn't a steep climb, but a steady one, to the top of a flat plateau covered now with drying weeds and grass—a bluff with a commanding view of the ocean to the west and Mogaba Island close by. It is an advantageous location from which to watch the sun rise and to relive the preparations and the trepidation he felt on that first dawn almost a month ago.

Christian has frequently walked at dawn, and the others, although aware of many of his destinations, have grown to understand his need for privacy and have stopped following him. Besides, chores— the simple acts of rising, going fishing, kneading the bread dough for the morning meal, gathering laundry, and tidying up their sparse homes—demand their attention. They will eagerly attend sessions with their Lord later in the morning. They are now disciples and await instructions on how and when they will begin their own simple ministries to spread the word of this miracle.

From the cliff where Christian now stands, only a few areas provide a foothold leading down to a tiny white beach. It is inaccessible, except from the primitive path blazed over the years by adventurous hikers or from the ocean itself. Although pristine and exquisite, it is too difficult for most and so is rarely visited. The exertion of hiking up to the cliff and now confronting the climb down to the beach causes Christian to sweat more heavily. As he lowers himself over the side, still holding onto the top with its tough dry-season weeds, he lifts a hand to wipe the wetness from his eyes and brow. His foot falters on a small protrusion, and he begins to slip on the jagged rocks. Trying to regain a foothold and finding none, Christian grabs a bare branch growing from the stony cliff side. In the hot dryness, the brittle branch gives way. Along with dislodged rocks, Christian falls out of control. The rocks buffet his head, as his body scrapes unprotected along the stony points and lands on the hard surface ten feet below. His head hits the ancient boulders on the beach.

Briefly unconscious, Christian awakens to hear the comforting sound of the small breakers. Through blurred vision, he lies quietly on the rocky surface, watching the gentle surf some fifteen feet away. He knows that the now-exposed beach will be covered within a few hours. Disoriented but conscious, he reaches out to feel the comfort of the soft cool sand. Blood covers two of his fingers, and as he tries to sit up, he feels searing pain in his left leg and notices additional bleeding cuts along his abdomen. Blood trickles down his face into his eyes, and he reaches up to feel a painful lump at the top of his forehead.

He has lost a sandal during the fall, and the other one, although still against his foot, has torn. Christian removes it and tosses it onto the beach, near where the other one has fallen. He attempts to stand up, but the pain in his leg and dizziness overwhelm him. Sitting down again to allow his head to clear, Christian inspects his wounds. They don't seem serious, but he can see the swelling on his left ankle and feels the inflamed bulge on his head, which is now throbbing. Quietly trying to collect himself, Christian attempts to pray. His earlier worries are now accompanied by a growing sense of fear.

Carefully raising himself up on his hands and knees, Christian reaches back to the cliff wall and stands up slowly. Sand has mixed with blood in his wounds. He limps painfully to the ocean's edge and wades into the gentle breakers. He bends over to wash, watching each receding wave carry away the sand and blood from his hands and legs. Trying to assess his injuries and angry at himself for his clumsiness, he savors the cool healing saltwater on his wounds. He ignores the blood, now clouding the clear water with little explosions of crimson. Seeking greater relief, he swims further out and looks back toward the shore. Treading water and trying to gage the next closest beach he can swim to, he feels some relief from the pain. The comfort of the temperate ocean against his body allows Christian to forget for the moment the uncertainties of his mission.

Twenty yards off shore, Christian is startled, as something brushes feather-light against his leg. He glimpses a thick tan fishing line, like the one Gordo uses, bobbing and moving through the water. Unmindful that the loose line might be connected to something, it does not occur to Christian that he is in any danger. He looks around with curiosity and only then sees the black shadow lunging toward him. The shark has honed in on the scent of blood from a weakening prey and has raced to its location.

Without warning, a violent jerking motion pulls Christian under the water, brutally shaking him and pushing his body up through the surface. His lungs gulp for air, as he tries to prevent himself from going under again, slapping the plane of water with his palms. His body has registered the trauma but his mind has not yet caught up. It takes several seconds for his instincts to re-emerge, and he reaches down to investigate the sharp pain in his lower body. A movement at the periphery of his vision distracts him from his objective. He turns to see the shark release a bloody chunk from her mouth. Christian's left foot, hanging from his severed calf, is carried out of his reach by the current. A second of denial is followed by the horror of realization. Most of his leg is missing and Christian feels nausea and dread, as shock sets in and prevents full awareness of his body's systems and senses.

The shark returns to the larger mass, which is now almost unable to move on its own volition and is sinking downward in an eerily slow motion. A small part of Christian's brain recognizes that the shark is about to renew her attack, and he weakly flails his arms, desperate to fend off the new assault. Her jaws open and close around his neck and the back of his head. Christian's hair fans out in the water as she shakes her upper body back and forth, ripping open his skull. His vision dims as awareness fades. In his last seconds, Christian is filled with regret and feelings of failure. He thinks an apology to those who sent him here and to his beloved apostles. As remaining life dims, Christian wonders where his soul will reside on the other side of death. He silently mouths "Forgive me, Father."

The shark continues to charge and rip at the body, whose flesh and blood are her survival but whose soul has now departed. Circling and clamping her jaws down again and again on Christian's body, the large hook embeds deeper. Her own fate is sealed, as in delirium and crazed with pain, she pushes into deeper water. She is quickly met by the appearance of a half dozen of her own kind. Having caught the scent and tumult of combat from miles away, they swam rapidly from different directions to the bloody waters. Within the hour, Christian's earthly existence and that of the devouring shark are obliterated.

The tide, unaware of the drama that has taken place, rises to cover the small beach, and at its high point, repeatedly washes over the large rocks, cleansing them of Christian's blood. In keeping with its ageless rhythm, it recedes again over the following hours, leaving a scattering of shells and a pair of rubber sandals on the newly-washed surface.

# DARKNESS
## Colombia - May 2035

## News Release - Missing Frogman

BUENAVENTURA, *Colombia (AP) May 2035—According to a Navy spokesman* from Naval Headquarters in Bogotá, one of the Colombian Armada submarines has just completed joint training with several US and Israeli Navy ships during a brief deployment under the Advanced Diesel Electric Submarine Initiative (ADESI) off the coast of Colombia. The ADESI program, established in 2020 as part of an ongoing enterprise almost two decades ago, has engaged several South American navies with diesel submarines to conduct a series of exercises and international deployments. The *goal is to support fleet training exercises and tactical development events. This exercise was the first to test newly developed operational methods to combat drugs and terrorism. Colombia remains plagued with drug trafficking and subversive activities carried out by several long-standing insurgency groups.*

*Although details remain classified, it was reported that an unidentified Colombian frogman, who was to rendezvous underwater with other "seals" further north near the Panamanian coast, remains unaccounted for.*

General Luís Gutiérrez sat in a leather chair behind an expansive desk in one of his remote offices on a small military outpost near Buenaventura. In front of him an anguished Denn Dennison had difficulty remaining composed. He was unable to speak and his pain was evident, as unabashed tears filled his eyes and his hands clenched tightly on the polished wood surface of Luis's desk. General Aaron Yakowitz, unable to offer comfort as he pondered the ramifications of Christian's loss, stood behind Denny with one hand on the shaking shoulders of the man who had defied all odds in bringing about the *The Return*.

Cardinal Diego Hernandez and Father Jonathan Kennedy soon arrived from Bogotá, both in civilian clothes and wearing jackets against the chilly Colombian air. They nodded to the others and took seats provided. The men exchanged hopeful glances but soon realized there was no further news. They sat in silence, not knowing how to start conversation; a conversation that could only surmise defeat. They were unable to console one another, as the twenty years of effort and promise unraveled.

Central to their loss was Christian, his disappearance far more devastating than the mission's failure and all it meant for the world. With only scanty details, a sliver of hope occupied each man. Maybe he had never left the island. Perhaps he had become ill or an accident had prevented him from swimming or even walking. Whatever happened, Christian's fate was unknown and those in the room were beset with sadness and grief. None dared to speculate. No one could speak.

Earlier, Diego had telephoned the archdiocese in Bogotá and left a message for a return call. Coming to this place directly from the airport, he had not wished to arouse any suspicion but hoped to search out any additional information the clergy and staff there may have received; any shred of rumor or news that might provide some relief from the pain of the vacuum in which they found themselves.

While they waited, food and wine arrived, but their appetites were non-existent.

When Diego's phone finally rang, they all stared at him hopefully. The conversation was cordial and centered on upcoming conferences at which the Bishop hoped Cardinal Hernandez might be a guest speaker. Diego, deeply involved in his relationship with Serina and feeling uncomfortable posing as a moral authority for his colleagues, now wished to withdraw from official duties and made excuses about needing to check dates.

"Anything else happening, besides losing more of our congregation, Bishop?" Diego tried to keep his tone light and conversational but slightly admonishing.

"Only the wild rumors coming out of Panamá," the Bishop replied. Diego caught his breath and sat up rigidly. "I don't know too much yet, but the elected Assemblyman, Marcos . . . Wait a moment, I have it here." Diego could hear a paper rustling, as he stared at the floor. "Yes, here it is," the Bishop continued, "Marcos Rivera. He's from that group of small islands off the Pacific coast and has apparently gone to the Bishop in Panamá City. He's telling an elaborate story about a return of Christ on one of the islands. It's probably nothing but a prank, but I don't know. I was surprised that the bishop asked me to come to Panamá next week to sit in on some interviews with islanders who corroborate the claim."

The phone was put on a speaker cradle, and Luís looked at the changing expressions of each man in the room, as he felt tears fill his eyes. He cleared his throat and regained his composure. "Well, that should be interesting," said Diego, hiding his emotion.

"Yes, there are supposedly quite a few of them who witnessed this. If it was just one or two, I guess it would be written off as the usual fantasy. In this case, there are several dozen in addition to this island legislator, Rivera."

"Uh huh," Diego said tentatively. "Well, it is always of interest to delve into the minds of those whose hope drives such a notion. I need to get to Panamá next week myself. Perhaps I could sit in?"

"I don't see why not. I am certain our colleagues in Panamá would welcome your input once the statements are in. I don't know who will be doing the questioning, but I believe the plan is to keep it as quiet as possible for the time being."

"Is there any indication of who this "Jesus" is and where he is now?" Diego asked, trying to sound offhand and casual.

"No, and that's what has prompted the islanders' revelation. It's pretty farfetched. The story is that the young man . . . 'descended' onto their beach about a month ago. Then a week ago, he simply vanished, and that's about all I know."

Diego glanced at the others. On their faces was a mix of emotions. "I tell you what, I'll meet you in Panamá at the Intercontinental Hotel tomorrow. Can you make the arrangements?"

"Of course, Your Excellency. I'll get back to you with the details."

"Thank you." Diego hung up the phone and remained quiet.

# Return to Eden
## November 2036

Nina Shelky had continued to write. A syndicated journalist, she specialized in researching and writing in-depth articles on the trials and successes of Latin America.

When the stunning news of the story of Jesus Christ's supposed descent upon Contadora Island first appeared in the media, it was brought to Nina's attention by an old colleague who knew that she had visited the island many years previously. Nina read and re-read the small story, which had been given little space and less credibility. Soon however, the story took on a life of its own, and Nina was startled to note Marcos' name showing up in the coverage.

Nina was unaware that she had contributed to the creation of the Vatican's great venture—an event now viewed by millions as a miracle. She would never know of Cardinal Diego Hernandez' decision to select Contadora for *The Return* after reading her article, nor would she connect the intimacy in the fleeting look the Cardinal exchanged with the stunning countess in Saint Peter's at the mass only months ago. But she continued to live with an odd new companion—a quiet whisper in her brain, telling her that she held a small fragment of the puzzle of this mysterious event. This absurd speculation, bothersome and persistent, was impossible to cast aside. In time she embraced its possibilities in her narrative.

Mentally revisiting the mass at Saint Peter's in Rome, Nina repeatedly thought back to the tragic and shocking death of Pope Damasus on the altar. Her reaction to the confusion and commotion had been to crouch down among the chairs—an automatic response to the almost-daily treachery of religious terrorists. She remembered the frantic priest, Father Jonathan Kennedy, kneeling over the Pope, during the long sad moments when the Swiss guards ushered the shocked and weeping faithful out of the cathedral. The memory of her conversation with him and Dr. Dennison at the Scientific Conference in San Francisco years ago now further piqued her curiosity. It was odd indeed that the man of science, this reputed confirmed atheist, was at the mass that ended so tragically. Nina's disturbing memory included the look of uncontained grief on Dr. Dennison's face, as he too was pushed along in the mass exodus from Saint Peter's.

Nina sought the whereabouts of Father Jonathan Kennedy. Her efforts revealed only that Kennedy had abruptly left Rome and returned to Colombia shortly after the death of Pope Damasus. Informed that Father Kennedy was in seclusion, Nina accepted that she would probably be unable to contact him.

As the world reacted to the miracle of *The Return,* Nina allowed her vague conjectures to nest within the confines of her mind as she added to her notes. Compelled to write, she compiled every detail and, in time, her disjointed efforts developed into several stories. The mysterious and miraculous event that now gripped the imagination of the world all but consumed Nina. Relying on her own vivid recollections of the island, new narratives on various theories regarding what might have happened poured from her mind. However, other than a few articles about the island and its people, simple assignments from various editors for publication, Nina withheld her thoughts.

Feeling a powerful draw to the intriguing accounts, Nina avidly followed Marcos' still-limited accounts in the press. She knew coverage of his relationship with this returned "Jesus" was being sensationalized, as she perused the world's media in print and on the internet; but Nina knew that if Marcos were involved, there must be an underlying truth.

Deeply sympathetic to Marcos' forced entry into celebrity status, Nina nevertheless relished seeing him in televised reports. She taped every occurrence and afterward minutely studied his every facial expression, word, and gesture. He was still her Marcos, but also evident was something else—serenity shined through, a brightness in his face and a new breadth of being.

Long obsessed with the man and the island, the memories of Marcos once again took control on the pages of her journal. She thought about him so often, so deeply, that she had to write "to him," as though he were present, as though she could still look into his tanned face and dark eyes and speak to his heart.

Nina once again contacted Bernardo, her colleague in Rome. He was as excited as she about this strange turn of events but with typical Roman skepticism over miracles, not much had been reported in the Italian press.

"I promise to immediately feed you any additional coverage, if it becomes available," he said eagerly and then recalled the article about Contadora that she had sent him years ago. Unable to remember its final disposition, he reminded Nina of it and apologized for having lost track of its whereabouts. Bernardo, who had only scanned the article at the time, sought out the publisher to whom he had sent it but hit a dead end when he learned the publication was long out-of-print, its publisher now deceased.

"Don't worry about it, Bernardo," Nina replied, withholding the fact that she still had a copy. "It was hardly a prize-winner," she added, yet feeling the article's odd intrusion on her being. In addition to scant coverage in the local press, the Vatican had relegated inquiries about the incident to various lower-level Church officials assigned to collecting the myriad of information regarding apparitions and visions. They were also referred to the Bishop's office in Panamá.

In Panamá, despite doubt expressed by the Panamanian archbishop after the first account by Marcos and a hand-picked few, the bishop held several meetings on Contadora. He first met collectively with the thirty or so who claimed to have watched the descent and then with the others who had had personal contact with "Jesus." The witnesses all told the same stories but could only produce the laundered *montuna* shirt and pants they claimed "Jesus" wore and dozens of wood-carved images as proof. Detailed pages of depositions from each individual were carefully recorded, further confounding the inquisitors, who looked for flaws and inconsistencies and found none.

The scarcity of proof was frustrating to the interrogating clerics, but as word of the miracle leaked, they were forced to act. A conference of bishops was finally established by the Apostolic See, encompassing the bishops of Panamá, Colombia, and the other Andean nations and the countries of Central America, Mexico, and the United States. Within two years, the complicated processes promulgated by canon law had set in motion the actions to be taken relative to reported miracles, the possible construction of a basilica, and the establishment of an international shrine.

During the early phases of the media frenzy, Nina had battled restlessness within. Even in sleep, Nina's dreams were filled with the islands, Marcos, and the presence of God. Awakening one morning from her recurring dream of reuniting with Marcos on the island, Nina felt the intense sweetness of his physical touch. Wanting to hold on to the closeness forever, Nina was pushed into waking and without further doubt, to take on her uncertain destiny. She dialed the Ministry in Panamá City, where Marcos now presided over the large Department of the Interior.

"*Muy buenos dias.*" Her Spanish had improved with study over the years, and she maneuvered through the bureaucracy to finally reach one of Marcos' aides. She cordially identified herself and was told that *el ministro* would receive the message and, if he desired, would return her call.

Within a half hour she heard his voice, a voice which stopped time and set her heart pounding. Although years had passed, it seemed not so between them. Nina sensed the new dimension in Marcos, as he related, still consumed with amazement, the wonder of what had happened.

After several minutes, the conversation idled. Nina wondered if perhaps she had been foolish to have called him. Feeling uncomfortable, she tried to find a graceful exit to the call, when Marcos interrupted, "Nina, *mi preciosa* Nina," he began. "My life is incomplete without you. I need you. I need you so much. For months and months, I have been smothered with publicity and yet feel so alone. There is so much, Nina, that I wish to share with you. I need you, and I know that I want to spend the rest of this miraculous life with you. There is so much to be done—so much that we can do together."

Over the next half hour, while the joy in Nina's heart grew, Marcos struggled to describe the consequences of the island's newfound fame and the unfolding obligations for all of them. He told her of unsubstantiated rumors of a cathedral to be erected on the large island of El Rey, nearby to Contadora, to accommodate the clamoring mobs who ached to visit the site of the miracle. For now, Panamá coped with the expanding throngs of visitors.

With the excitement of the new possibilities taking place within their conversation, Nina responded, "Take me back to the island, Marcos. Take me back please. I must see it, and I must see you. Will you take me there?"

Marcos thrilled to Nina's words and eagerly agreed. As she hung up and joyfully prepared for her journey, Nina wondered why she had hesitated for so long. Happiness filled her and she wondered at a future of hope for so many.

The years apart seemed to have been erased, and Nina knew they would soon share the physical closeness long denied. Nina could feel a new miracle—a spiritual reawakening filled her, one she knew was spreading far beyond the shores of Contadora Island.

Landing at Tocumen Airport and walking toward customs, Nina saw the posters heralding the return of Christ on the walls. She then noticed the trio of men walking toward her. Marcos had told her to look for them. "*Bienvenidos*, Senorita Shelky," they greeted her warmly. Assured of their official capacity, Nina gave them her documents. With a gracious flourish, she was led through the airport crowd, past immigration and customs to a side door. They smiled with Latin charm, welcomed her once again with the customary *Bienvenidos a Panamá*, and gestured her through the open door. Marcos was waiting on the other side.

The moment felt as it had twenty-five years earlier. Nina had carried in her memory a vision of this man as he had been two decades ago. Now up close, she marveled at his appearance. As Marcos came to her, Nina again saw him walking toward her on a white beach on a tiny island in the Pacific Ocean.

She had not been sure she believed the entire story of *The Return*, but for now, she would not doubt it or question him. She turned her face up to him. "Marcos, Marcos," Nina whispered, smiling. "It's been so long, and so much has changed for both of us. What of this Christ?" She took his face into her hands, looked in his eyes as she had done so many times years before, and asked, "Has he taken all your love from me?"

"No, no, Nina," he answered, "nothing has changed inside my heart. Yes, much has happened, but the ache for you has never left me. I have so wanted this moment. I will tell you everything but now, let me hold you."

He embraced her and buried his face into her neck and hair, reveling in the never-forgotten scent of her. He held her to him and wept with joy.

The plane used by Marcos was familiar to the islanders. They looked up as it circled to the south and approached the runway. He, Mario, and Marcocito now lived in a hillside home above and to the left of the cove where "Jesus" had descended. None of them lived any longer on the small hillside directly above the beach called Playa Manta. The new location held a commanding view of the beach, as well as the complex of little homes and thatched *bohios* where the islanders had slept and cooked and eaten and listened to Christian's teachings. Marcocito, now twelve, secretly wondered if he might have seen anything different had he been in this location *behind* the descending figure that early dawn three years ago.

The road leading from the beach to the hilltop was now cordoned off from the public onslaught. People came by plane and by boat and tried to carry off a stone or even a little dirt from the path that Christian had used so often. A sizeable contingent of security personnel was already required to keep pilgrims along the designated paths. The elderly and sick were content to walk or sit on the beach at low tide and to pray and meditate near a large wooden cross that had been constructed on the now-protected rock jetty. Marcos longed for the island view as he had seen it that dawn. Now the small surrounding areas above the beach where Christian had walked was altered and would never be the same. Until his death several years after *The Return*,

Marcos' father, Mario, had worked diligently to return the island to a place of normalcy, but it was an impossible task.

Marcos also maintained a Panamá City apartment, and, even there, was pestered by the press. He was forced to deal with harsh critics. "Why," the President and his cabinet and his colleagues in the assembly demanded, "did you not go public earlier? Why did you keep *the presence of Jesus Christ* on his island a secret while *Christ was there?*"

Frustrated but remaining calm, Marcos asked each new interrogator, "What would you have had me do? Can you honestly tell me," Marcos countered, "that you would have given me or my constituents even a second thought, let alone an audience in these chambers, for such a tale?"

Marcos brooded over his future role and that of the islanders. Nina gently questioned his carrying out the seemingly impossible task of changing the religious mindset of millions. "I'm afraid for them, Nina." Marcos said. He frowned, thinking about the relentless pursuit of the islanders, now both legitimate and impersonated.

Working closely with the Archdiocese of Panamá, Marcos had validated all those personally associated with Christian. The verifiable witnesses present that dawn when the descent took place were barely twenty in number, although another dozen had come out of their meager homes and fearfully made their way down the road as Christian came ashore. Others had learned secondhand and had listened many times to the miraculous tale. They soon took it into their very being and so claimed to have been present. The islanders' relatives on the mainland took full advantage and co-opted some of the fame, thus sharing the work of spreading the word and fulfilling the planners' hopes.

After the disappearance of "Jesus," the revelation of his having arrived on the island "out of the sky" by Fulito and a few others whom the Church was unable to silence, was described again and again to hungry reporters, who often embellished the facts. The witnesses were endlessly interviewed and photographed from every angle.

As the madness continued, Marcocito the first to see Christ drop into their midst on that Holy Week dawn, and the other children were instructed by the Church to simply relate the truth about what they had seen. It was soon known that Marcocito had been the first to speak to the miraculous figure, and the handsome child, so well-spoken and intelligent, was sought out continuously.

The image of the brilliant figure of Jesus Christ gently gliding through the air, falling in a billow of white cloth to him—to him— never left Marcocito's memory; but over the years, he struggled with this image and the doubt exhibited by Christian during their final conversation. As Marcocito grew up, this small insistent thought took up residence in a corner of his mind. The good remained, and with the exception of Fulito, whose exploitation of his new fame added to the spread of faith, all the islanders endured the media blitz without sacrificing their humility.

World attention on the happening caused an amazing resurgence in the Catholic Church, an outcome that pleased the Vatican mightily, even though they played the role of devil's advocate and sought to discount the event.

A papal announcement was delayed for as long as possible.

# Epilogue

After Christian left earth—absence of any visible evidence to the contrary—most on the islanders chose to believe he had once again ascended.

Reporters and forensics specialists had initially swarmed to the island. Murder was suspected and then rejected. This "Jesus," this "Christ" had simply disappeared, as had all evidence of his presence. Footprints had been obliterated by tides and rain. His handmade shirt, the *montuna* bearing the cross, was now held by the archdiocese. Its loose draw string pants and open-necked top offered little in determining Christian's size, and all investigators had to rely upon were the descriptions given by the islanders. Utensils from the evening meal the night before had been washed and put away. Potential DNA evidence was gone. Fingerprints did not hold in the sand or on the bark of trees. Even the coarse hammock in which he slept had been routinely laundered the morning he disappeared. The rubber sandals given to Christian by Mario were also gone.

The FBI, CIA, and military intelligence groups sent agents to Contadora Island. So did Scotland Yard, the French Deuxième, and what remained of the fragmented Panamanian Department of National Investigation, known as DENI. Delegations and commissions from numerous countries and organizations searched the island thoroughly.

MOSSAD sought investigative instructions from the Israeli government, after a vague tip from military intelligence about the irregular flight schedules of one retired Israeli Air Force General Avi

Noam. They never received any feedback and cobbled together a few reports from shared intelligence available on computer networks.

Italy's intelligence coordinating agency, the CESIS, pulled together a meeting of both military and civilian agency directors. It was a time of what was described as "natural rotation in positions of delicate responsibility" within an ongoing broad overhaul of the country's intelligence services. The independent Vatican City service bristled at interference, but Italian cardinals secretly wished for any information suggesting Vatican complicity during reigns of non-Italian popes. In the bureaucratic skirmish for information, suspicion of withheld reports circulated but fizzled.

Church committees of all denominations visited—the great and populous and the struggling spin-offs, still uncertain of their doctrine and hoping to find it. Television evangelists crowded onto the islands, some with garish entourages and others in humble small apostle-like groups. Still splintered, factions of the modern evangelical movement were brought together to reexamine their agendas.

But there were others. Charlatans, quacks, and swindlers seized the opportunity to set themselves up in schemes of every type. The sand on Playa Manta, where "he" had appeared and walked, was gathered in bottles, buckets, and trucks, and marketed throughout the world. When the government finally cracked down and re-sanded the beach, sand and shells and stones were taken from other beaches throughout the islands. Ocean water in which he was said to have swum and fished with the others was bottled and sold. Coconut shells he had *reportedly* drunk from, plates he had eaten from, utensils,linens, clothes, sandals, and anything he had touched was fair game for exploitation. Cheap plastic souvenir replicas were marketed as a commemorative of the "Return of Christ."

Future faithful would come to the beach for baptism and to recreate an old practice of symbolically reenacting the death of Christ. They would submerge themselves in the water and feeling his life within them, rejoice in the glory of resurrection, as they broke through the gentle warm surface.

By the time the Vatican responded to this worldwide reverential interest, two years had passed. With the ceaseless jangle of propaganda, paparazzi, editorials, and film, the new pope eventually recognized the need for official involvement of the Church. He and those around him pondered his decision, as television's talking heads, congregations, researchers, and others questioned the legitimacy of the current pope. Was he still the head disciple, the authentic successor of Peter? If Jesus Christ had, in fact, returned, was there a need to redefine the ascendancy of the papacy? Canon law, that magnificent work of scholars, who over the millennia sought to chronicle the righteous laws to govern the holy Catholic Church, came under scrutiny. Ultimately, no revisions were made.

In Rome and around the globe, the Vatican felt awe, wonder, and some confusion at the rapid and spontaneous increase in the number of faithful in the Roman Catholic Church. Other Christian religions expanded as well, and new sects evolved.

The Acclamation of the Mass, "Christ has died, Christ is risen, Christ will come again," was debated throughout the entire Catholic community and its wording scrutinized by Vatican councils for possible change or deletion. But it remained in the mass, and with time it was recited with greater feeling and awareness by the congregants. As a nation, Israeli Jews made no attempt to discredit the event. Even highly orthodox Haredi communities in Israel, the United States and elsewhere, including the studious Misnagdim and Hasidic clans, mostly ignored the media blitz. They made no public comment and stuck with their uncompromising tenacity to the dictates of ancient law and customs.

Despite contempt for secular Jews and the spin-off Jewish sectarians, who either derided the story in private discussions or indulged in intellectual speculation about another prophet—long overdue they sometimes joked—Jewish conservatives remained circumspect. Others converted.

Greek Christians found the event in keeping with their early beliefs that the joy of the transfiguration of Christ on Mount Tabor was a far more important experience of God than the suffering of Calvary and Gethsemane. They indulged themselves in the story's joyous beginning and lamentable, but certainly ambiguous, conclusion.

Additionally, the early belief that God was better-described through the imaginations of artists was revalidated. Most of the original canvases painted by the late Pope Juan Carlos Gutiérrez hung in the Vatican museums, while massive quantities of reproductions were distributed throughout the world and sold along with replicas of Mario and Marcocito's carvings. The revenues generated funded the construction of the cathedral, Cristo el Rey (Christ the King), built on the island already bearing the same name, El Rey. New icons, canvases and sculptures appeared. God was everywhere. The American Civil Liberties Union lost credibility in their disdain of an almighty God, and the liberal press soon wearied of them, and their organization withered to inconsequence.

Within the war-torn Islamic nations, there was some approval. The event provided further affirmation of a basic Koranic teaching— that Christians made a big mistake in pushing the idea that only one man contained the whole incarnation of the divine. Muslims sought a new understanding and urged greater belief that God dwelt in all men. They finally worked to contain radical factions and encourage a belief in a holy world— one in which the planet and its creatures of God deserved their respect and care. "Reason," as a part of the human relationship with God and emphasized during the reign of Pope Benedict XVI during the onset of radical Muslim attacks throughout the world, was reinforced. The destructive, senseless death heaped upon innocent masses under the deceptive pretense of God's will lessened over time.

Hindus, always tolerant, remained tolerant and embraced the added dimensions of righteousness. Many other religions stayed the same.

Many people prayed that those few who had been chosen to have contact with him would somehow impart a touch of The Holy Spirit to their own souls. They prayed they might overcome the disappointments of human relations and that the essential yearning he had filled for the humble islanders would be filled for them as well.

Officially, Diego retired. He and Serina secluded themselves from the outside world. Delighted in their possession of each other, they lived in a variety of villas and seaside locations in Italy and Colombia.

Diego repeatedly confessed his broken vow of chastity and gradually earned some sympathy from trusted confessors. He had recognized fate that day in Milan years ago, when he sought to possess the female body and accepted the wondrous gift of sexual love. Diego and Serina floated in their magical matured state of being in love as the years passed. He listened for God's forgiveness.

Serina never argued for that portion of Diego that would always remain with God. Diego witnessed Catholic conversions in many sectors with satisfaction, and although forced to preserve the secrecy, retained his deep friendships with Vatican colleagues.

General Luís Gutiérrez retired to Israel. He and General Aaron Yakowitz formed a small defense-consulting firm, designed to train leaders of foreign militaries. Their close ties to intelligence services allowed them to periodically delve into the activities of certain zealous individuals, who were known to be successfully proselytizing the Catholic faith in various regions of the world. The two investigators sought out every news article and compiled reference books concerning the successes and failures of the growing numbers of new and humble disciples roaming the world.

Nina and Marcos remained in Panamá and frequently visited the island. Nina wrote a series of articles over the continuing phenomena on Contadora Island and eventually completed a book. Mario remained with them, lovingly tended by young Marcocito but unable to join the others in their pursuit of souls. He died one morning sitting unnoticed on a quiet beach near Playa Manta. Next to him was his fishing pole, a small knife, and his final carving of Christian.

Father Jonathan Kennedy, devastated by the loss of Christian, battled depression until the news of a strengthening Church and a gradual spread of peace in parts of a war- torn world finally brought him to a feeling of contentment, even triumph. Jonathan graciously declined a Vatican post, opting to become the pastor at a small church in Cartagena, Colombia. His congregations were devout locals and many tourists visiting the ancient city. He noted that numerous televised and written accounts gave credit to the miracle of Playa Manta in the Pearl Islands for a swelling number of participants and greater devotion by communicants.

Dr. Denny Dennison pondered and grieved the disappearance of Christian. Two years after the project finished, he died peacefully in his sleep, a devout Catholic. A massive funeral was held for him at Saint Mathew's Church in Washington DC. When some had questioned the whereabouts of the flamboyant playboy-scientist over the past few years, news articles speculated that Dr. Dennison's participation in top secret endeavors in astronomical and climatic change was responsible.

The new Pope, Juan Carlos' successor, pondered the indecisive conclusion; he was never able to verify the episode. The usual spies within the Vatican walls alluded to a mission carried out in great secrecy, but none had concrete information. The Pope fashioned a story, mostly of his own making, and spoke of it continuously to his cardinals as a means of atonement—a channel of confession for what he initially perceived as Satan's greatest triumph, the wolf in sheep's clothing. But how? He contemplated the possibility of Pope Damasus III's having been the Anti-Christ warned about in Corinthians. However, Gutiérrez was loved, and he was gone, and no one wanted to sully the beloved Pope's memory.

In the end, His Holiness had no one else to confess to about his continuing angst over the event. With time, he began to accept the view that perhaps someone *was* sent by God—a messenger, a visitor for whom, despite the possible mischief of men, divine approval was evident. Much of the divisiveness of the dogmatic religions seemed to diminish, and he wondered, *Was there a presence of God in every man that could truly acknowledge the abundance of God in another earthly being?*

Noting general improvement in global events, the Pope could not at first bring himself to attribute a nicer world to the miracle on Contadora Island. However, the initial distance of the Papacy from any connection to *The Return* gradually lessened; but the Pope took great care to avoid the presumption of assigning ownership of the good events to himself—*He shall come again to judge the living and the dead.*

"The Cross of Christ must not be emptied of its power,
because if the Cross of Christ is emptied of its power,
man no longer has roots, he no longer has prospects,
he is destroyed."
—Pope John Paul II, Good Friday, April 1, 1994

# The End

# POST SCRIPT

Nina met Marcos at the open French doors, as he came out onto the veranda of their home overlooking the beach. He had just arrived on the island from his Panamá City office.

"I've finished a book, darling, a novel. I wonder if you would take a look at the first few pages," she said.

Marcos embraced and kissed Nina, then pulling away said, "First, I would love a swim, a cold bottle of wine, a good dinner, and you. Would you mind if I looked at it in the morning?" Marcos replied.

Early the following morning, Marcos opened Nina's computer. With a cup of sweet coffee, he sat at a small table, looked at the sea, and pulled up "Book" from Nina's computer files and read the first line.

"The aging Colombian niñera named him Christian....."

# AUTHOR'S NOTE

The concept for *The Return* came to me shortly after moving to Washington DC from Panamá. When I left Panamá, the island of Contadora, where my family had owned a vacation home for a dozen years, was on the decline from its glory days in the 1970s and 80s.

For a few years, I thought about the outrageous plot but wrote nothing. It seemed profane and absurd. Continuously pestered by my thoughts, I created a brief outline and jotted down a few notes. Then, for another year or more, wrote nary a word. It still seemed profane and absurd.

When I climbed out of my "Catholic Guilt," I moved ahead, writing a few chapters and allowing myself the process of releasing onto paper some of the characters that were occupying a lot of space in my head.

Contadora Island and Panamá were easy for me to write about, as I lived in Panamá for many years and built a beach house on the island in the early 1970s. In the mid-90s, I traveled to Rome and to Israel, both Catholic Church-sponsored trips that contributed to my knowledge and encouraged further research. Those trips, and return trips to Panamá, were inspiring, and by 2005 I was well into the book, and the characters were becoming my friends.

My hesitation was my Catholic faith and how such a story might classify me as a heretic. Sometime later, I read about post- modernism. The article talked of the "modern world" beginning near the time of the discovery of the "new world" and post- modernity as somewhere in and around the advent of technology. It spoke of interpretation of ideas, mostly religious, and how science and discovery changed interpretations, actually diluting those ideas. Part of its conclusion was that we have "interpreted" ourselves into nothingness. In so many parts of America, the world, values are gone, and it is difficult to tell our children to take it easy on the materialism in their lives and to include church on football Sundays. I believe that nobody regrets receiving communion or feels bad when they leave church—any church.

The story will probably generate some raised eyebrows from the clergy, my family, and my Catholic friends. Oddly, it is Catholicism that inspired me.

The astounding effort to restore faith in the faithless backdrop of this story is no longer troublesome to me. As I researched information over the years and began to attend theological classes, I found myself reaching far deeper into my faith than I had planned. It has been an unsettling journey. I can't preach it to anyone, as no one can put God in a box and thrust Him upon others, but one can learn about Him forever.

I hope the book provides a good read and allows an opening up to what I believe most of us cherish and hold dear in our hearts.

As for Panamá, it has boomed since I started this book. Before the first grand development plans on Contadora Island took hold in the 1970s, I swam frequently at the beach where Christian descends. When the general decline in the late 1980s replaced the grandeur, I felt, and I guess "hoped," the island would again become almost dormant, as it does in my story. I have returned several times and have friends who maintain homes on Contadora. These friends have never lost their love of the island and continue to nurture it.

In 2008, the Pearl Islands are still sparsely developed. They may not be the pristine paradise I first found there in the late 1960s, but drastic change has been minimal. Now, with the real estate boom occurring throughout Panama in the early years of the new century, it is doubtful these "pearls" can remain that way much longer. Still, I'm hopeful there remains within people of vision a need to keep them as they are.

I'd like to thank my family and friends who supported this effort. Many gave me insight from the pulpits of Catholic churches, in classrooms, and from the pages of books and articles. My children probably questioned my sanity and wondered if I would ever finish, but they did think a story that pretends to *bring Christ back* had interest.

A former work colleague and friend, Melissa Bassford, patiently helped me by phone and email and made numerous visits to my side to help edit and instruct me in the daunting task of formatting.

I offer love and gratitude to my nephew, Bill Blank, a gifted editor, musician, and technical engineer, whose reading resulted in valuable comments and suggestions that so improved the story. My California producer friend, Michael Bremmer, offered insight and allowed me the fun and thought-provoking scenario of *The Return* as a possible movie. My college classmate, Marge Dwyer, offered practical advice and loving encouragement. My talented son-in-law, Paul Fontana provided the cover based on a haunting painting of Christ by a remarkable artist, Rafael Gallardo. Thank you all.

To my husband since 2002, John "JJ" McNally, who spent long hours reading, editing, and encouraging me from the first evening I met him—I love you.


Gail Dawson McNally
Alexandria, Virginia
February 2009

# About the Author

For twenty-five years, Gail Dawson McNally lived and worked in Panamá. With an extensive background in government intelligence work and in the private sector in sales and marketing in the United States and Latin America, she now resides with her husband in Alexandria, Virginia.